BLOOD ON THE MOON AND STAR

BEAR HASKELL, U.S. DEPUTY MARSHAL

BLOOD ON THE MOON AND STAR

A FRONTIER DUO

PETER BRANDVOLD

THORNDIKE PRESS
A part of Gale, a Cengage Company

Thorndike Press® Large Print Western.
The text of this Large Print edition is unabridged.
Other aspects of the book may vary from the original edition.
Set in 16 pt. Plantin.

LIBRARY OF CONGRESS CIP DATA ON FILE.
CATALOGUING IN PUBLICATION FOR THIS BOOK
IS AVAILABLE FROM THE LIBRARY OF CONGRESS.

ISBN-13: 978-1-4328-5228-3 (hardcover alk. paper)

Published in 2021 by arrangement with Peter Brandvold

Printed in Mexico
Print Number: 01   Print Year: 2021

TABLE OF CONTENTS

■ ■ ■ ■

SHOOT-OUT IN
JULESBURG

■ ■ ■ ■

CHAPTER 1

There was a slithering sound, like that which a snake makes crawling through sand . . .

Jamie Lockhart opened his eyes to see a shadow grow before him in the nearly impenetrable darkness of Hell Hole, as the dungeon was called at the Colorado Territorial Penitentiary in Trinidad.

The shadow stopped near where Lockhart slumped. A vertical white line appeared. As it did, a fetid smell, like that of something dead, assaulted Lockhart's nose. Hell Hole characteristically smelled like something dead — namely the numberless men who had died in Hell Hole's bowels, as Lockhart figured he himself was bound to do. But this smell was ripe enough to rival even those.

"Lockhart."

The voice was raspy and deep, like the roll of a distant drum. It was then Lockhart

9

realized this new death smell was not a death smell at all, but the smell of a man's breath. He recognized the voice.

"Mic?" Short for McGeehy. Oscar McGeehy. One of three of Hell Hole's "hounds," which was what the dungeon's guards were called.

The Three Hounds at the Gates of Hell.

Each fit the description, too, for they were large, animal-like men with heavy fists and shoulders and flat, dead eyes. Brutal men. Heartless and violent beyond words. They'd leave a dead man in the Hole for days, until he'd swollen up and stank like an overfilled privy in the hot desert sun, and then they'd come down and haul him out, laughing and cajoling the prisoners who'd had to live with the stench.

"Me, all right," McGeehy said in his thick Irish accent. "Mic."

"Christ, Mic," Lockhart said, shaking off the bonds of a shallow but welcome sleep. "What the hell did you eat for supper? Your breath would choke a dog off a gut wagon."

There was a dark flicker of movement, a rustling sound. Mic's huge fist slammed against Lockhart's right cheek. It was a sledgehammer blow, slamming Lockhart's head against the solid stone wall with a resolute smacking sound. Crimson flowers

10

opened behind Lockhart's squeezed-shut lids. For a few seconds, he felt as though every tooth in his mouth had been jarred loose by the vicious wallop.

Lockhart shook his head, fighting off the grabbing hands of unconsciousness.

"No-no," Mic said, blowing more of his foul air at Lockhart's face. "You ain't gonna pass out on me, Jamie boy. You got places to go. Men to see. Things to do."

There was a clinking sound as McGeehy plunged a tin cup into the water bucket beside Lockhart. The cup flashed in a flicker of ambient light as McGeehy hurled the water at Lockhart's face.

Lockhart yelped against the water's sudden assault, instantly chilling him, sucking his breath from his lungs. He got some of the water down his windpipe, and he choked on it, making strangling sounds in the Hole's stony silence.

"You fucker, Mic!" Lockhart wheezed. "Oh, you fucker!"

Mic chuckled.

As Lockhart continued to shed the bonds of semi-sleep, he heard the rattle of keys and the jingle of a chain. The slight tug on his left ankle told him McGeehy was unlocking the stout padlock holding a log chain fast to the shackle that gripped Lockhart's

11

ankle as tight as a clenched fist. The other end of the chain was attached to a stout iron eye embedded in the stone wall somewhere to Lockhart's left.

A voice said in the darkness to Lockhart's right, quietly echoing off the stone walls, "What in the hell you doin' over there, Mic? You turnin' Lockhart loose, are you? What time is it? Must be the middle of the night."

Hans Gunderson was the only other prisoner currently confined in the dungeon. Like Lockhart, he'd been asleep, slumped against the wall, before the guard had shown up.

Mic stopped what he'd been doing. In the darkness, Lockhart saw the big Irishman straighten, turn, and stride over toward Gunderson.

"What you doin', Mic?" Gunderson said, both suspicion and wariness threading his voice. "Pullin' Jamie out of the dungeon in the middle of the night . . . ?"

Mic's footsteps had stopped several feet to Lockhart's right. The guard's bulky shadow seemed to hover in the air over there. Lockhart heard the clink of a chain as Gunderson moved his leg, shifting his position against the wall.

"Shoulda stayed asleep, bucko."

"No, Mic — *no!*"

12

There was a muffled yelp. Then a scuffling sound, a strangling sound. Gunderson's chain clinked as it flopped along the floor. Finally, there came the grinding, cracking sound of Gunderson's neck breaking. A final grunt.

Silence.

A thud and final clink as Gunderson dropped to the cold stone floor.

Lockhart laughed. "How you gonna explain that, Mic?" He laughed again in delight at the thought of the trouble the guard would get into when the warden got wind of a prisoner suffering a broken neck under McGeehy's watch.

"I ain't." McGeehy knelt beside Lockhart once more, poking his key in the padlock. There was the sudden ease of tension as the chain fell away and clinked to the floor. McGeehy's fetid breath again pushed against Lockhart's face. "You see, bucko," he said, "it's your lucky night. We're gettin' outta here. Me an' you — see?"

"Me an' you?"

"Sure." McGeehy smiled. "Ain't that sweet?"

"I don't know," Lockhart said, trying to hide his surprise. "You ain't proposin' — are ya, Mic?"

McGeehy grunted as he slammed another

13

haymaker against Lockhart's cheek, rattling the prisoner's brains again.

"Goddamn, you're a brutal bastard!" Lockhart complained when he'd regained full consciousness once more. His ears rang from the blow.

"Now, you gonna keep makin' smart?" McGeehy said. "Or you wanna get outta here?"

"How you gonna do that, Mic?" No prisoner had successfully escaped Trinidad Pen in the past seven years. Only three had been fool enough to try in that time, and they'd been shredded with bullets from the guard towers before they'd even made it to the outside wall.

"You just keep your gums from flappin', an' follow ole Mic, and I'll show you. Okay? You understand what I'm sayin', boyo?"

"Sure, sure, Mic," Lockhart said. "Whatever you say, Mic."

He was more than skeptical. Why would McGeehy help him escape? Must be some trick. Lockhart was sure of it. But what did he have to lose?

He'd been in the dungeon for the past six days. Six days after a ten-day stint a little over a month ago for gouging out another prisoner's eye and shoving it down his throat. He moved only as far as the chain

14

would allow, eating only bread and water, hoping a rat would drown in his water bucket during the night so he could fortify himself with meat.

Dungeon dwellers who couldn't bring themselves to eat rat meat usually died in the dungeon.

McGeehy removed the shackle around Lockhart's right ankle. The prisoner cursed and gritted his teeth as the blood flowed freely into the pinched flesh. He could feel it burning like diamondback venom in his foot.

"Come on," Mic said and moved off into the darkness, in the direction of the ladder. His heavy, cork-soled boots clomped on the stones.

"Hold on, Mic!" Lockhart rasped. "My foot ain't had any blood in it for six days!"

"Stop pussy-footin' it or I'll leave you down here!"

Lockhart hurried after the big guard, limping, wincing as his bare feet ground pebbles and sharp bits of flaked stone, food scraps, and rat droppings. He could see maybe one or two feet in front of him. He almost ran into the wall up which the rope ladder climbed, and would have if he hadn't heard the creaking of the hemp as McGeehy climbed it, grunting quietly as his bulky, inky figure grew against the hole above, which was a four-by-four-foot square of weak amber light.

Lockhart watched the big man gain the hole, his heart thudding, hoping that this wasn't one of the sadistic guard's jokes. As soon as McGeehy was out of the hole and kneeling beside it, beckoning, Lockhart leaped at the rope ladder.

His right foot ached horribly as he climbed, the ladder buffeting around him. Several times his hands or his feet slipped from the raking hemp, and he nearly fell back to the dungeon floor.

His heart turned cold at the thought.

He'd given up on the idea of being released from the dungeon anytime soon, after he'd beaten a fellow prisoner senseless in the prison rock quarry — over what, he couldn't even remember. In prison society, any slight was reason enough. If you didn't respond to taunts or threats, those taunts or threats would just keep coming and grow in venom, and you might end up with more and more men against you. In prison society, only the strong survived. They survived by proving every minute of every hour of every day that they were stronger, more savage than the men around them, and not to be trifled with.

More often than not, it cost them time in Hell Hole, but it was better than the alternative. No, Lockhart had given up on the idea of being let out of Hell Hole soon, maybe not for another week or so. But now that that carrot had been placed before him, he found himself chasing it like the most desperate of hungry ponies.

When Lockhart was near the top of the hole, McGeehy reached down, grabbed his arm, and painfully jerked him up out of the hole. Lockhart rested there by the hole on his knees, breathing hard, grinding his teeth at the pain in his right foot, looking around.

They were in the Hell Hole entrance corridor lit by two guttering lanterns bracketed to the sandstone walls.

There was a small woodstove and an ancient, overstuffed parlor chair positioned in front of the stove, a seat for whatever guard was posted at the Hole at any given time. A small table stacked with old, brittle, water-stained newspapers and magazines stood beside the chair.

Beyond rose a flight of stone stairs, lit by two more guttering lamps, to a heavy iron door with a barred window. Lockhart studied the door. It was partway open. Odd. Lockhart had spent enough time in the Hole to know that door was always locked.

What was even odder was that one of the other two guards lay slumped at the bottom of the stairs. That was Bingo Dwyre, a lout from the streets of New York City. He lay with his head cocked back against the corridor's right wall, his neck bent at an odd angle, blood trickling down from one corner of his mustached mouth. His leather-billed, dark-blue hat lay overturned on the floor near his head.

"Your work, Mic?" Lockhart asked.

"Whose do you think?"

Lockhart curled his upper lip. "You do that for me?"

"Just for you, Jamie, me boy. Just for you!"

"You must think I'm mighty special."

Mic placed a big hand on Lockhart's left shoulder, grinning down at him, the guard's long eyes slanting devilishly beneath heavy, rust-red brows. His scraggly mustache of the same color rose with his lips. "Ten thousand dollars' worth of special, me boy. Come on!"

"Ten thousand dollars?"

Mic ran up the stairs, taking the steps two at a time.

Lockhart stared after him, incredulous. Then, not wanting to be left behind, he pushed himself to his feet and ran as fast as he could up the steps behind the big guard.

He followed Mic through the door and down the long, stone hall, barred windows on each side letting in the cool night air that brought to Lockhart's nose the smell of woodsmoke and the perfume of the Colorado desert and the pines of the southern Rockies.

It was intoxicating. Lockhart drew a deep breath as he ran, forgetting about the misery in his foot and ankle.

The corridor seemed to trail off into infinity. To each side were heavy barred doors marking the way to various cellblocks. McGeehy's large figure was a jostling shape ahead of Lockhart. Sometimes the big guard faded into the darkness altogether, and only his running footsteps told Lockhart he was still ahead of him.

They pushed through two more doors, both unlocked. Beyond the last door lay another dead guard — the impossibly fat George Stinson. McGeehy had unlocked the doors beyond Hell Hole. And he'd killed two guards. At least two guards. There might be more.

Lockhart didn't worry about it. All he could think about now was keeping up with the big guard lest he be left behind and returned to that stinking pit. A part of his mind still believed in the possibility that this was all a cruel joke being perpetrated by McGeehy for sport — you couldn't put it past ole Mic — but all Jamie Lockhart could think about was making it to the outside — to the vast, broad, open night filled with the perfume of the Colorado desert, and freedom . . .

Finally, they came to a last door. It, too, was open. Another guard lay dead just inside. As he stepped over the dead guard and pushed the door open enough that he could poke his head out for a look around the consumptives' exercise yard, McGeehy glanced back at Lockhart now breathlessly catching up to him.

"Here's what we're gonna do, boyo." The guard was also breathing hard, filling the air around them with his stinking breath. "We're gonna run across the yard here and climb the first wall. Keep to the right, near that tower right there — understand?"

Lockhart brushed his fist across his running nose and said, "Near the tower?" But there was a guard armed with a rifle in each tower.

"Don't worry about the tower. Just vault the first wall and get into the shadow of that tower as quick as you can. Follow me. I'll show you where a rope is hanging down the inside of the outside wall. We're gonna climb it, pull it up, drop it over the outside wall, and scurry down. Got it, boyo?"

"I got it, Mic — I got it!" Lockhart's blood sang in his ears, his heart racing at the prospect of freedom.

McGeehy looked around once more, carefully, and then he bolted forward, crouching low at the waist. Lockhart followed him, barely keeping up, and gained the inside wall, near the tower that stood just beyond it, on the inside corner of the outside wall.

Lockhart hurled his big body over the six-foot-high wall, and managed to scramble up the wall, as well. Clumsy from pain and weakness, from being chained up for six days and nourished by only bread, water, and the occasional rat, he tumbled down the other side to land with a grunt in the dirt.

"*Shhhh!*" McGeehy admonished, crouching over Lockhart. "You tryin' to wake the bloody dead, ya bloody fool? For the love of all the saints in Christ's heaven!"

Lockhart scrambled to one knee and looked at the brick guard tower facing him on his right, in the northeast corner of the outside wall. He could see only darkness there beneath the tower's peaked roof, but there must be a guard in there, armed with a Sharps rifle. The guard had to have heard

Lockhart and McGeehy running, and Lockhart's fall.

Why hadn't they been perforated by bullets?

Because the guard in the tower had thrown in with McGeehy, Lockhart told himself, and he smiled as he ran behind the big guard toward the outside wall. The rope was there — hanging down the inside of the wall, right where McGeehy had said it would be.

An elaborate plan. One that had been sketched out well in advance. McGeehy had been paid ten thousand dollars to squirrel Jamie Lockhart out of Trinidad Pen.

Why?

Never mind. He'd likely find out soon.

They climbed the rope. It was easy. Lockhart had no trouble. Freedom beckoned. His foot felt fine. He could feel his hands bleeding from the hemp's rough rake, but there was no pain. All his brain registered of that climb was the perfume of the desert in his lungs, and the hammering, aching prospect of freedom after wasting away for the past ten years in the pen.

McGeehy dropped to the ground at the base of the outside wall. The light of a sickle moon shone in his eyes when he looked up at Lockhart dropping down behind him.

Lockhart released the rope, hit the dirt, and rolled.

"What now, Mic?" he whispered in the darkness, the open night enshrouding him, nearly taking the breath from his lungs. *There was the moon, rising over those spindly trees by the river's cut. My god, the moon appeared close enough to reach out and grab in his fist . . .*

"We cross the river, boyo," McGeehy said. "Don't worry — it's dry. There's a break on the other side, near a big cottonwood. If all's gone accordin' to plan, two horses will be waiting for us there. Their saddlebags will have a change of clothes in 'em for both of us. Come on, boyo — we're almost home!"

"Hold on, Mic."

"What is it?" McGeehy glanced behind him.

Lockhart had found a fist-sized stone. He lunged forward with a savage grunt and rammed the rock against the dead center of McGeehy's forehead.

The guard dropped like ten tons of hard freight.

When he was down and groaning, blinking, trying to shake off the assault, Lockhart beat his skull to a bloody pulp, trying to stifle his own laughter.

"There you go, Mic," he said, wheezing. "That's for everything."

He dropped the rock and removed the man's socks and boots. He donned the socks and boots. They were too big for him, but Lockhart didn't care. He grabbed the guard's revolver from his holster, blew the dead man a kiss, and ran for the dry riverbed and freedom.

And revenge.

CHAPTER 2

"Oh, my favorite — sausage for breakfast!"

The female voice roused Deputy U.S. Marshal Bear Haskell from a deep sleep. It wasn't only the voice that had roused him. A stirring in his lower regions woke him, as well. Not just a stirring but the warm, wet sensation of . . . .

Haskell opened his eyes and lifted his head.

He groaned. She was at it again, raising and lowering her blond head down there just south of his belly.

He groaned again. He didn't know that he'd ever been awakened from a deep sleep so pleasantly.

"You're tireless," he rasped.

"Mmmmm . . . hmmmm . . ."

Haskell laid his head back on his pillow in the bedroom of his three-room suite at the Larimer Hotel in Denver. He and the girl had arrived in town late last night. They'd met on the Kansas Pacific flier from Kansas City, where they'd both boarded but hadn't become acquainted until they were a couple of hours out of Denver.

They'd warmed to each other fast, even daring to swap a little spit in their plush seats at the rear of the rocking and rattling coach car, since most of the other folks around them had been soundly sawing logs. When they'd come into Denver, Haskell had asked the girl — Allie was her name, if he remembered correctly — to join him for a drink in the Larimer Hotel Saloon and was roundly surprised when she'd accepted.

She hadn't seemed the type — a golden-haired, lightly freckled young Kansas girl with an angelic face and china-blue eyes that seemed born to reflect the Sunday morning light streaming through the stained-glass windows of a midwestern Lutheran church surrounded by wheat fields and cottonwood trees jostling in the clean summer wind. He wouldn't have suspected that she'd ever drunk anything stronger than communion wine and maybe some of her grandpap's dandelion wine just for fun from a thimble on the Fourth of July.

But in the Larimer's ornate saloon, she'd matched Haskell drink for drink — straight Kentucky bourbon — and hadn't staggered any more than he had when they'd climbed the stairs together to his room here in the posh Denver hotel. Just as he'd never expected the blue-eyed Kansas princess ever to have imbibed, he also hadn't expected that she'd done much more in the way of boy-girl communion other than tongue wrestle a time or two with a second cousin out behind Grandpap's barn, or possibly given one of the boys from school a peek at a ruffled fringe on her drawers.

Boy, had he been wrong in that regard, too!

Rather than clutter up what was left of the evening with a bunch of fool blather here in Haskell's suite, she'd stripped naked for him right away, and leaped into his bed with a delighted, tinkling laugh, as though she were swinging from a rope into a warm Kansas stream. Haskell followed suit and soon found himself wrestling a love-hungry Kansas catamount snarling from the spring-time itch.

They'd gone at it so hard, making so much noise, that someone threw a shoe against the wall from the next room, bellowing something unintelligible beneath Haskell and the girl's love moans, but which Haskell assumed was a plea for ratcheting it down a notch.

The fellow was probably just jealous, Haskell thought. He knew he would have been if it had been any other man in here, getting what he'd been getting — hot and heavy and without surcease, her teeth digging bittersweetly into his shoulder while she hammered his buttocks with her heels.

Now her lips, her tongue, were slow and gentle as they slid up and down his engorged manhood. Spittle oozed out around her lips, making soft crackling sounds.

She slid her mouth off of him and asked, "You like?"

"Hate it. But, uh . . . don't stop." Haskell grinned down past his flat belly at her, marveling at her waifish beauty, her schoolgirl charm. Her hair was a lovely mess about her shoulders. It swirled down to caress her firm paper-pale breasts the size of young cantaloupes.

She licked him, teasing, and said, "You're funny. And gentle . . . for such a big man." Her eyes smoldered as she looked up at him from over the top of the rock-hard member she held in her small, pale fist.

She raked her eyes across his bull neck and broad shoulders, the steel-like slabs of his chest lightly tufted with dark-brown hair, the same color as the curly locks swept back over the top of his head and curving around behind his ears. "I've never been with a man as big as you."

She licked him again, her cheeks dimpling delightfully, blue eyes sparkling in the first light angling through the tall windows. The wet caress of her tongue after the slight pause was like a delightfully sharp ice pick to his heart . . . in a good way.

"How old are you?" A question he'd forgotten to ask last night, due in no small part to the girl's quick, firm hold on him when he'd first spied her sitting alone in the rocking coach car. He'd instantly found her receptive, inviting.

"Nineteen."

Haskell reached down and gently slid a lock of her hair away from her cheek, and tucked it behind her ear. "You sure know how to fuck for nineteen — pardon my farm talk."

She sucked him awhile longer and then lifted her head again, licked some spit from her bottom lip, and said, "I've had some experience." She canted her head slightly to the left and beetled her brows with admonishment. "Promise not to tell?"

"A gentleman never tells."

"I teach at a country school. Back in Kansas. Well, there's this boy . . . he's only a year younger than me. His name is Vincent. He's built like you. Well, not quite as big." She squeezed his cock and grinned. "Anyway, Vincent and I . . ."

"Good lord, girl — you fraternize with your students?"

"Only Vincent! And only on Wednesdays and Fridays, and I told him we had to stop last week after Mary Francis McGuire came back to the school because she forgot her reader, and almost caught us doing it doggy-style on the floor by the wood box!"

Allie snickered.

Haskell laughed.

"Besides," she said, crawling up his body, slowly, almost menacingly, like a beautiful cat stalking its prey, "if it wasn't for Vincent . . ."

She straddled his belly, rose onto her knees, and reached down between her and Bear to grab his cock in her right hand and slide the swollen mushroom head against the hot pink folds of her dew-wet pussy. "If not for Vincent, I wouldn't know how to do all I've learned, and" — she slid slowly down on top of him, and Haskell gritted his teeth and curled his toes in pleasure — "we wouldn't be having all the fun we had last night and are continuing to have this morning."

She dropped her hips to his belly, sliding

him farther and farther inside her. She groaned, shuddering with pleasure, and squeezed the bear claw necklace that lay across Haskell's broad chest. She squeezed some of his chest hair entangled with the bear claws, and the pain somehow pointed up the wash of poignant sensations storming through him, centered down around his staff plundering the girl's snatch.

She moved on top of him, up and down . . . up and down . . . with excruciating slowness, prolonging his bittersweet misery.

Half because he was curious and half because he wanted to distract himself so not to spill his load too soon, for he wanted to prolong the wonderful agony as long as possible, he asked her, "Is Allie your full name, Miss Allie?"

She spoke slowly, grunting softly, head canted to one side, eyes squeezed shut. "No, silly — it's Allison."

"Allison what?"

"Let's not."

"Not what?"

"Not get that personal. I'm Allie. You're Bear. That's all we need to know."

Haskell chuckled to himself. He knew a beautiful young Pinkerton agent who was partial to the same secrecy. At least, she had been when he'd first met her, two strangers meeting in the night at a backwater hotel in the bowels of West Texas, only to find out later and with plenty of ear-reddening embarrassment that they'd been assigned to the same case. That they'd be working together.

Arliss Posey was the Pink's name. Haskell suspected he'd run into Miss Arliss again soon — or so he hoped. He'd never known a Pinkerton quite so talented, and he didn't mean just her detective skills, either.

At the moment, however, he was thoroughly satisfied to have this beautiful young Kansas succubus hauling his ashes, as the old saying went, in his suite here at the Larimer.

Miss Allie began moving with a little more vigor now, shaking her hair back and canting her head to the other side. "Oh . . . oh, god, Bear . . . oh, god . . . !"

Haskell groaned, sucking a sharp breath through gritted teeth. His blood was getting hotter and hotter. His passion was starting that quickening rise to its crest. In an attempt to slow its progress, he said, "Forgive me for pryin', Miss Allie, and you don't have to tell me if you don't want, but what do your folks do out there in Kansas? Just for the sake of conversation an' not rushin' things here, if you get what I mean."

He squeezed her hips in his hands, then slid them up her soft belly to cup her breasts, the bud-like pink nipples deliciously raking his palms.

She giggled, stretching her perfect pink lips back from her perfect white teeth and placing her hands over his, atop her breasts. "I see. I savvy your drift, Bear. But you really don't want to know what my folks do."

She half-turned and leaned back, planting a hand over his right knee. "It's all so boring . . . my life out in Raintree." She snickered. "Poppa is a Methodist preacher."

"Preacher?"

"Mm-hmm. That's right. Preacher. Momma plays the organ. We live in the parsonage behind the church. Oh, Jesus. Oh, Mary — you feel good inside me, Bear! That's where I was born, and . . . if Momma and Poppa have their way, that's where I'll die, too. A miserable, trussed-up old woman. Oh, god . . . oh, god . . . oh, Jesus . . . oh mercy, you fuck good!"

"Ah, hell!"

"What is it?" she asked, snapping a concerned gaze down at him.

Haskell groaned, chuckled, drew a sharp breath through his teeth again, and rolled

Miss Allie to his left, brusquely throwing her back on the bed; then, keeping the head of his member inside her juicy, clutching portal, he draped both her long, porcelain-white legs over his shoulders and pinned her knees up behind her ears.

She squealed in delight, slapping her hands to both his buttocks and digging her nails in deep.

"You were right from the start, Miss Allie. We never shoulda started talking!"

"Why — what happened, Bear?"

"I imagined you in a frilly pink dress, sitting there in church hearing Poppa preach, and — oh, may the good lord have mercy on my wicked soul! — that pretty much blew my dam wide open, Miss Allie! Oh, ahhhhhhhhhh . . . Kee-RIIISTTTTTTTTTT!"

Allie threw her head back and screamed as though she were being murdered with a hatchet.

CHAPTER 3

When Haskell rolled off the girl, panting in the wake of their torrential coupling, he glanced at the clock on the wall by the bedroom door.

Seven-forty-five.

"Holy shit!"

He threw the covers off and rose, stumbling over his and the girl's clothes strewn across the floor, where they'd dumped them last night in their carnal haste, and headed for the marble-topped washstand.

"What is it?" the girl asked, rolling onto her side and propping her love-flushed cheek on the heel of her hand. "I suppose you gotta run off to a job or some such, eh, Bear?"

"I sure do, Miss Allie. I'm supposed to be in my boss's office at eight o'clock sharp. He gets his drawers in one hell of a twist when I'm late, an' I'm late enough!"

"Oh, not fair!" Allie pouted. "I was hopin'

we could have us maybe one more good roll in the hay. I've never been with a man like you, Bear. So big an' sweet an' gentle. I'm gonna be sad to see you go."

"Me, too, girl — believe me." Haskell chuckled as he splashed cold water from a pitcher into the enamel washbasin, and soaked a cloth. "That was one hell of an unexpected night. You just stay there. Go back to sleep if you want, and leave when you're ready."

He soaped the cloth and ran it under his armpits, across his chest, and over his crotch, scouring away the leavings of his and the girl's passion. He wasn't worried about leaving her in the suite alone. He didn't know her very well, but he didn't take her to be a thief. Besides, he didn't have anything of any value to steal except his guns, which would be on his person. He'd seen no reason to clutter up his life with a bunch of possessions when he spent most of his time out in the tall-and-uncut, hunting bad men.

He said, "You know your way around town, all right, do you? You ever been to Denver before? You're here to see your grumpy old uncle — is that what you told me last night?" He cast a grin at the girl over his shoulder. "My memory's a little blurry. You're sort of like a tornado that turned my whole night upside down."

"I'm glad. I gotta admit, I was a little worried that I'd have trouble pleasing a man like you. Me — just a country girl from Kansas, and you a big masculine fella from the city." She frowned. "Say, what is it you do, anyway, Bear?"

"Ah, nothin' all that interesting," Haskell said, quickly toweling himself off, then casting the towel aside and scrambling around to gather his clothes. "I don't have time to go into it, and even if I did, it would sound like a lot more than it really is. Let's just say that I do a lot of travelin', and I'm likely about to be sent to some far-flung little backwater halfway across this dusty frontier — for how long is anyone's guess."

"Well, I'm sure what you do is more interesting than what I'm here for. I finally get to see Denver again, but it's just to go to a stupid ole funeral with my boring ole uncle."

"A funeral, eh?" Haskell was stepping into his canvas trousers. "Well, I'm sorry to hear that. You lose someone close to you, did you, Miss Allie?"

"No one special. Just my Aunt Sally. She was persnickety, nasty-mean. She once told me that only girls of loose morals and weak characters wore their hair in anything but tight buns, and to never trust a man with a mustache."

Allie chuckled dryly. "I was supposed to travel here with Momma and Poppa and my Aunt Gertrude, but just a couple of days ago both Momma and Poppa came down with the flu. They decided to send me with Aunt Gertrude, who would act as my chaperone, but wouldn't you know that Aunt Gerty got sick the very night we were to board the train? Momma and Poppa didn't think they should send me alone, but I convinced them I would be fine, and that" — she paused briefly to snicker devilishly — "my honor as well as my virginity would remain intact."

Haskell had sat down on the side of the bed to button the cuffs of his red and black calico shirt, chuckling at the girl's story. Allie wrapped her arms around his neck from behind and nibbled his left earlobe. The sensation made him warm in the crotch, though he couldn't believe his equipment would be operational down there again for another day or two, after all the strain of late.

"Don't go temptin' me into another tussle, Miss Allie," Haskell said, gently wrestling out of the girl's surprisingly powerful grip.

"I gotta get to work, or start *lookin'* for work, an' since there aren't no more Rebels to fight or buffalo to hunt, I'd be in a pickle!"

The big, shaggy-headed lawman rose from the bed, thumbing his suspenders up over each broad shoulder, then wrapped his brown leather holster and shell belt around his lean waste.

The holster bristled with Haskell's Smith & Wesson New Model No. 3 Schofield revolver, which he positioned for the cross-draw on his left hip, angling the fine, nickel-plated, top-break revolver's polished walnut grips toward his flat belly, within a quick, easy reach.

Bear could feel the girl's eyes on him, watching with mute interest as he wrapped yet a second shell belt around his waist and buckled it, just above the first one. He'd hated it when, long ago pinned down against more owlhoots than he could count, he ran out of cartridges, so he now kept a good supply on his person — both for the .44 Schofield as well as the .44-caliber, sixteen-shot Henry rifle, sheathed in a leather scabbard lined with lamb's wool, that he always carried with him while stalking owlhoots.

He found one of his cavalry-style, low-heeled, mule-eared black boots under the bed, where he must have kicked it last night in his haste to disrobe and get down to business between Allie's spread knees. The other boot was on a chair.

He reached into the right boot and pulled out his lone hideout weapon, which was a "Blue Jacket" .44-caliber pocket revolver manufactured by Hopkins & Allen — a beautiful piece with gutta-percha grips and a leaf motif scrolled into the nickel finish. Usually when the Blue Jacket was necessary, the other two weapons were either out of service or out of reach, and his life was hanging by a thread. The Blue Jacket had pulled the lawman out of a tight spot more than once, so he always made sure it was loaded and in its boot holster where it belonged.

He broke the little popper open and spun the cylinder, happy to see all five chambers showing brass.

Watching him intently, hooking her bare feet together over her succulent pink ass, Miss Allie said, dubiously, "You go around armed for bear — don't you, Bear?" She snickered at her joke.

Haskell looked up at her as he slipped his right foot into the boot in which the Blue Jacket was snugged down into its specially sewn sheath in the well, and said, flushing a little, "Yeah, well, in my line of work, you just never know, Miss Allie."

She turned her head to one side and furled an admonishing brow. "I didn't just spend the night with a bank robber — did I, Bear?" She raised her voice with excitement, sitting up a little, revealing her splendid breasts still mottled from his nuzzling and kneading. *"Do you ride with Frank and Jesse James?* I've read all about them — late at night when Momma and Poppa are asleep and my grading and lesson plans are done, of course — and I just read in the latest issue of *Policeman's Gazette* that . . ."

She let her voice trail off as Haskell, dressed and rigged out now save for his hat, leaned down to close his mouth over hers. He savored the taste of this delightful girl, mingling his tongue with hers, noting the pliant way her silky soft lips moved against his.

When he pulled his mouth from hers finally, he said, "I don't ride with the James brothers, Miss Allie. I'm sorry to disappoint you."

Her eyes crossed as she looked up at him from beneath her thin blond brows and said, "You didn't disappoint me in any way, shape, or form, Bear. I just wish you didn't have to leave so soon. Maybe, when I make

41

it back to Denver someday, we can do it all again."

She grinned with delight at the prospect, and so did he.

"I'd like nothin' better." Haskell walked over to where he'd dumped his hat on a table. He donned the bullet-crowned, black felt topper with a braided rawhide band and winked at her. "You know where to find me."

"I surely do."

Haskell walked to the door, opened it, and said over his shoulder, "You take your time and let yourself out when you're ready, Miss Allie."

"Goodbye, Bear."

Reluctantly, wanting nothing more than to hurry back to the bed and take Miss Allie in his arms once more, but knowing if he did, he'd likely be swamping out saloons until the cows came home, Haskell raked his gaze away from the beautiful, naked blonde in his bed, went out, drew the door closed behind him, and trudged off to work, grumbling.

Haskell whistled as he turned off the boardwalk running along Denver's Colfax Avenue, on Capitol Hill, and mounted the federal building's broad stone steps.

His mood had improved since he'd left Miss Allie in his suite at the Larimer. It was a beautiful, sunny Rocky Mountain morning, and the First Front of the Rocky Mountains stood proud and glowing to the west, the stone peak of Mount Evans tipped in the ermine of a fresh, late-summer snow.

A late-night rain had scoured the Denver air clear of coal smoke, leaving it with the tang of a fine apple wine. City folk bustled toward work, knicker-clad street urchins hawked the *Rocky Mountain News* on nearly every street corner, and street vendors sold breakfast burritos wrapped in old newsprint out of their rickety wooden handcarts.

Dogs were barking, men were laughing, and distant train cars were loudly coupling while cattle lowed in the stockyards down by the tracks. Wagonloads of coal were being hauled by clopping Percherons east toward the gallant mansions decorating Sherman Avenue, where the moneyed lived far from the unwashed crowds dwelling in relative hovels down along Cherry Creek.

It was hard to stay in a sour mood on such a vibrant Denver morning, especially after Haskell had enjoyed such an adventurous night. And who knew? Maybe he'd see Miss Allie again sometime, and they could repeat their sexual high jinks. He doubted it, but there was no reason not to keep the possibility alive in his mind.

At the top of the federal building's steps, he took a last, long puff of one of his favored Indian Kid cigarillos, drew the peppery smoke deep into his lungs, then flipped the smoldering stub back down the steps and into the well-churned dust of the street, along which a hansom cab was just then passing, heading west toward Union Station, several dogs barking with devilish delight at its high, churning wheels.

Haskell snorted a laugh, then pushed through the heavy oak doors and strode up the building's stately marble steps to the official-looking and -smelling second-story corridor. At a door whose pebbled glass upper panel announced CHIEF U.S. MARSHAL HENRY DADE, WESTERN DISTRICT, in high-handedly neat gold-leaf lettering, he paused for one more fleeting reflection on his recent carnal adventure. Haskell then opened the door and stepped into the chief marshal's outer office, where Dade's dowdy secretary, Miss Lucy Kimble, daughter of State Senator Luther Kimble, was busily playing the infernally loud type-writing contraption at her desk to Haskell's left.

"Good morning, Miss Lucy," Haskell said

as he tossed his hat on the tree to his right, just inside the door. "What a lovely morning it is, too — wouldn't you agree?"

Haskell suspected the dowdy young woman was quite the beauty beneath the several layers of dreariness she seemed to apply each morning, the layers of which included wearing old-lady glasses halfway down her pert nose and drawing her brown hair into a severe, round bun atop her head — a bun so tight it resembled a fist clenched in anger.

Then there was the dark-wool attire aged widows usually wore to funerals . . .

Her only response to the deputy U.S. marshal's greeting was a brief cessation of the clattering of her infernal machine and a cool glance over her right shoulder as she said, "Oh, is it? I hadn't noticed. The chief marshal is waiting, Deputy Haskell. He'll no doubt remind you that you are seven minutes late."

Her voice dropped several octaves on those last words, and then she turned her head forward and resumed hammering away at the annoying typewriting machine that must have been invented by a deaf person — or by someone who promptly went deaf after he'd invented it. Haskell had never known such a machine to destroy the quiet of an otherwise peaceful Rocky Mountain morning in quite such a cacophonous way. Why, he'd rather go down to Union Station and hear the cattle bawl and the freight trains couple like maniacal dinosaurs than hear the racket of the girl's fool machine!

It made him wince and gnash his teeth.

"Progress," Haskell supposed they called such an abomination. Well, they could have it. Give him a quiet pencil or a pen and a bottle of ink any day of the consarned week . . .

"Bear, leave Miss Kimble alone and get your ass in here — you're late again, as usual," Henry Dade said, poking his gray head out his office door and turning his bespectacled gaze on the big deputy. "And . . . uh . . . pardon my farm talk, Miss Kimble."

She merely dipped her chin in acknowledgment of the old apology and kept on typing.

As Dade ducked back into his office, Haskell kept his eyes on the understatedly alluring secretary and said, "I don't understand how you don't break your pretty little fingers on that horrible contraption, Miss Lucy." He turned his head forward as he stepped into his boss's office.

At the same time, the typewriter stopped

46

its wretched, deafening prattle.

Haskell stopped and leaned back into the outer office. Miss Kimble was staring down at her hands, pensive. She jerked her head toward Haskell, and a barn-red flush suffused her pale cheeks and ears. Haskell grinned.

She turned back to the machine in horror, and resumed playing the devil's waltz.

CHAPTER 4

"You're late. Again," Chief Marshal Henry Dade admonished his senior-most deputy.

"Ah, hell, I'm sorry, Chief," Haskell said, wagging his head sheepishly. "All I can say is I got in late last night from one assignment only to get a note from you telling me you wanted me in here at eight o'clock sharp. Even I gotta sleep some time!"

"You don't look like you got much sleep. You look like hell." Dade had walked around behind his large, messy desk over which his gray eyes scrutinized his deputy, who stood a full head and several inches taller than his whittled-down boss.

Haskell flushed, opened his mouth to speak, but the chief marshal cut him off with a wry chuff and a twinkle in his right eye. He plucked an ever-present stogie from an ashtray on his desk, and poked it into his mouth. "What was her name?"

Haskell flushed redder, grinning. His boss

48

knew him too well. "Now, Chief, you know I don't talk out of school." Under the circumstances, he liked the irony of that, not to mention the pun. "Let's just say she was a pretty little, blue-eyed blonde from Kan—"

"Stop right there," Dade said, plopping down in his high-backed, leather, rocking swivel chair, which seemed to swallow him whole. "Do you know what an erection would do to a man of my advanced years and with my logy ticker? If I could even manage one, I mean. I wouldn't know. It's been too damn long. Besides, we don't have time to palaver. You'll be heading north on the flier in a half hour."

"What's up, Henry? Must be serious."

"It is." Dade stopped, then frowned. "Say, speaking of your last job, where's your report? I didn't see you hand anything to Miss Kimble except your usual lusty leer."

Haskell frowned, incredulous. "I just got back from the last outing last night, Henry!"

"Yes, and we know what you did with your night."

"A fella's gotta have a little leisure time, Henry! Besides, as detailed as you want me to write these reports, I need some time. I ain't Mister Shakespeare, for pissin' in the king's ale!"

"No, you surely aren't. I've read your reports. All right, all right. When you finish with this next assignment, you'll owe me two detailed reports complete with a precise accounting of all expenses."

"You got it, Chief. So what's the next report gonna be about?"

Haskell dropped into the uncomfortable chair positioned in front of Dade's desk. It was a hard wooden armchair without an ounce of padding. You'd have a hard time finding a chair harder, more stiff-backed or straight-armed. It was like something out of an old-English torture room — maybe something King Robert the Bruce of Scotland would have reserved for King Edward's English invaders dragged howling off the battlefield at Caddonlee, when Robert the Bruce wanted to have some nasty Scottish fun with them.

It was all part of Henry Dade's scheme to make sure his visitors didn't linger. Henry was a busy man not given to prolonged bouts of chinning about the beef market or the weather. He was a crusty former Texas Ranger, a lifelong bachelor who lived alone and preferred to work alone.

"The next report is going to be about an escape from the Colorado Territorial Pen."

"Someone broke out of Trinidad?"

"Not just someone." Dade sank back in his chair, removed the fat stogie from his mouth, and blew a heavy plume out over his desk, adding more smoke to the heavy, eye-burning cloud hovering over his desk and the green and gold Tiffany lamp. "The son of Conway Lockhart."

Haskell jerked his head back, scowling in disbelief. "Con Lockhart has a son in the Colorado Pen?"

"You didn't know, I take it."

"I've worked with Con Lockhart several times over the years. A good man. Sheriff of Sedgwick County based in Julesburg. Never heard about his son bein' locked away in Trinidad. Can't quite imagine it, as a matter of fact. Lockhart walks the straight and narrow tighter'n any man I've ever known."

"I know you've worked with Lockhart, but I'm not surprised you didn't know about his son. It's a tough story, and one that's sort of taboo out that way. Con's a highly respected sheriff and rancher. Folks look up to him, just like they looked up to his pa, who built up a ranch in Sedgwick County long before the war. Came from down south. Fought Comanches tooth an' nail, and died with an arrow in his chest, ole Wat Lockhart did.

"Here it is in a nutshell about Lockhart's

51

oldest son. Jamie killed the woman his father, Con, was going to marry."

"No shit?"

"Not enough to smudge a preacher's ass."

"That's a mouthful, Henry. About Con's son, I mean. Not the preacher's ass."

"I know. I got it stuck in my throat." Dade sank back in his chair and punched his chest.

"Why did he do such a lowdown nasty thing?"

Dade puffed his cigar, blowing another heavy, fetid plume at the ceiling. "This is a little murky. Con Lockhart got a tight rein on the whole story pretty quick, but what slithered out at the trial was that Jamie Lockhart was in love with his pa's betrothed. A young Mexican girl who still lived at home with her family. Apparently, they'd planned on running away together. She backed out at the last moment, told Jamie that she was going to marry his father, and Jamie beat holy hell out of her with an axe handle."

"Ouch."

"Yeah."

"He must've been some mad."

"Con found her in the old trapper's cabin she an' Jamie had been meeting in. He found Jamie there, too. Jamie ran."

"Must've been a helluva scandal in that little town," Haskell said.

"In the whole damn county. Got bigger when Lockhart himself led up the posse that hunted Jamie down in the Dinosaur Rocks south of his ranch, and brought Jamie to justice, but only after wounding him. Head wound. Nearly killed him. Jamie survived, went to trial, and the judge sentenced him to thirty years in Trinidad. Since there were no eyewitnesses to the murder, just plenty of circumstantial evidence, the judge didn't see fit to play cat's cradle with the kid's head. So he sent him to Trinidad, where he's likely been turning big rocks into little rocks for the past ten years."

"And now he busted out."

"Yeah, he must've got tired of wielding that sledgehammer."

"Anyone with him?"

"There was a guard. The same one who helped bust him out. True to character, Jamie bashed the guard's head in with a rock as soon as they were over the outside wall. Then Jamie lit out."

"This Jamie is one nasty *hombre,* I take it."

"The nastiest."

"Was he always that mean?"

Dade shrugged. "I don't know. Lockhart

has a son and a daughter. All I know for sure is that Jamie *turned* mean enough to take a hatchet to his father's bride-to-be and kill three men in Con's posse as he was tryin' to get away. Cunning, slippery devil. Ten years in prison has no doubt made him even more cunning, slippery as a snake."

"When did he escape?"

"Two nights ago."

Haskell tapped the file on his knee. "You want me to run him down, I take it."

"Not exactly."

Haskell frowned. "What, then?"

"I want you to wait for him."

"You want me to wait for him." Haskell twisted around in his chair as though to look for clarification behind him, then raked his befuddled scowl back to his boss. "Where would you like me to wait for him, Henry? Over at the Larimer? That'd be just fine, since I got me a pretty little miss over there, sleepin' like a cat." He grinned.

Dade was having none of it. "I want you to ride over to Julesburg and pal around with Con Lockhart for a few days. I got every reason to believe Jamie Lockhart is headed back that way. Might even be there now."

"Why would he return to Julesburg, Chief?"

"Because as they led him out of the courtroom after his sentence he told his father — shouting at the top of his lungs, no less — that he'd be back to fill him full of lead. I was there. I saw the look on that kid's face, and no one else, including Con himself, seemed to take him seriously. But I knew. I didn't say anything, but I knew that one day Jamie Lockhart was going to find a way to bust out of Trinidad and go back to Julesburg to make good on his threat. I just knew."

Thoughtfully, the chief marshal puffed his stogie.

"I see." Haskell stared at his boss, both of them thinking it through. "Any other law headed that way? The prison must've sent out a posse."

"They all headed south, because that's where most escapees head. Toward Mexico. I don't know if they're still out there or not. I haven't heard from the warden yet today. I'll likely get an update soon. I'm not expecting much. I'm expecting that if you head over to Julesburg, you'll likely run into Jamie Lockhart sooner or later. If he isn't already there."

Dade pinned Haskell with a dark look.

"I take it Con Lockhart's been notified."

"Oh, yes." Dade nodded slowly. "I just

55

hope he's taking the threat seriously."

"You want me to hightail it over there and make sure he is."

"That's right. And take down Jamie Lockhart before he can make good on his threat." Dade nodded again, slowly, narrowing his eyes knowingly. "That's where he's headed, all right. A smart man would head south to Mexico. But Jamie Lockhart is one angry young man. Big chip on his shoulder. He vowed to kill his father, and I just know from that look of the devil I saw in his eye — I just know, damnit! — he's gonna give it a try."

"All right, Henry. You got me convinced. When's my train leave?"

Dade looked at the clock on the wall to his left. "Eight-forty-five."

"Don't leave me much time. Lucky I stowed my gear down at the station last night. Figured I'd be heading back that way after the ticket agent passed me your note." Haskell rose, the file in his hand. He turned toward the door, thought of something, then turned back to his boss. "Say, Henry — why did that guard help Lockhart escape? What was in it for him?"

"It's a mystery. The warden doesn't know. He said the guard's been working there at the pen for eight years. Spotless record. A

56

bachelor. Kept to himself, mostly. Not much is known about him . . . other than he had some gambling debts. Jamie must've offered him money to help him escape, though where Jamie came up with any money at all is anyone's guess. The guard killed three other guards in helping Jamie. If anyone else helped in the escape, they haven't been identified. Funny thing . . ."

Dade let his words trail off with the smoke he'd expelled while voicing them.

"What's a funny thing, boss?"

"The only tracks found within a mile of the pen were those of Jamie Lockhart hightailing it into the wash a hundred yards east of the prison. After that, Lockhart seemed to have faded on the wind."

"He covered his tracks."

Dade said, "Either he or someone else did. The guard must have intended on hightailing it, too. He likely realized he'd be implicated, since he was only one of three men who had a key to the Hell Hole grate. That's where Jamie was when he busted out — in the Hell Hole."

"Ah, the famous . . . er, *infamous* . . . Hell Hole," Haskell said. "Don't doubt it a bit."

"I reckon we'll find out who helped Jamie escape . . . and why . . . when you run him down." Dade looked at Haskell gravely. "So take him alive."

"I'll do my best."

"Now, get out of here. You got a train to catch, and I've got a missing niece to run down." Dade mashed his stogie out in the overfilled tray on his desk.

Haskell arched a brow at him. "A *niece*? Henry, I never knew you to have any family at all, much less a *niece.*" But, then, he couldn't remember him and his boss ever having talked about their personal lives — outside of a few brief mentions of Bear's experiences during the war and Dade's experiences as a captain in the Texas Rangers.

"Oh, well, yes . . . yes, I have a niece." The chief marshal looked up at the clock again, and tapped a finger against his lips. "She was supposed to get in last night." Suddenly, he turned to Haskell who stood with his back to the door. "Say, you came from Kansas City. She likely would have been on the same train you were on."

CHAPTER 5

Haskell's heart fluttered.

Suddenly, his tongue felt a little swollen.

He sagged back against the door as he said, "Your . . . your niece would have been on . . . the same train *I* was on, Chief?"

"She was due in last night around eight. She'd hopped the westbound flier from Kansas City the day before. You might have seen her — a young blonde. Nineteen, I think, or thereabouts. Cute little thing. At least, she was cute as a button the last time I saw her. A little shy, but, you know, a small-town girl. Her father's a Methodist preacher. My sisters are all a bit persnickety."

Haskell stifled a cough.

"A young blonde," he raked out slowly, his tongue continuing to swell and his heart picking up speed. "Around nineteen. Hmm."

"Yeah, around nineteen. I think she's

nineteen. I haven't seen her in a few years. You see, my brother's wife died — wicked woman, I should not have added at such a time — and my two sisters and brother-in-law from Raintree decided to take the train out here with my niece, Allison, for the funeral. The last cable I got said that all three adults had taken ill, but Allison wanted to come, anyway, so they let her. Very trustworthy young lady."

Dade leaned forward and spoke behind his hand, as though imparting a state secret. "Butter wouldn't melt in the girl's mouth. I'm a little afraid she's going to be an old maid. A schoolteacher, you see, but . . ."

The chief marshal frowned at Haskell from behind his round-rimmed spectacles. "Bear, what in the hell is the matter with you? You're as pale as parchment!"

"I — I am?"

"Pale as a mushroom after a long rain. Did you have anything to eat this morning? All that fornication on an empty stomach — or a stomach filled with only cheap whiskey — looks to have played you plum out." Henry Dade, Miss Allie's grumpy uncle, shook his head in disgust. "Good lord, man — the way you live. Did you two come up for any air last night *at all*?"

Haskell swallowed down the knot in his

throat, making a face with the effort. "You know, Henry, I think you're right. I'm feelin' poorly. Why, I haven't had anything to eat in hours!"

"At least, you probably haven't eaten any *food.*" The chief marshal turned his head to one side, winked, and grinned wolfishly.

"That's right, Chief," Haskell said, trying to chuckle, hoping against hope his knees didn't buckle. He turned with effort toward the door, fumbling with the knob. "I think . . . I think I'd best grab a sandwich or a burrito or some such on my way down to Union Station."

"Hold on, hold on."

Haskell glanced back at his boss in dread. Henry Dade narrowed a suspicious eye at him, studying the big deputy closely.

A diamondback of dread flipped its button tail in Haskell's belly. "Y-yes, Henry?"

"You haven't told me if you saw my niece. On the train. Same one you were on. Pretty blonde. Yay-high, I'd say, by now." Dade held his right hand up to his shoulder.

Haskell swallowed again. He was hot and flushed. Sweat was beginning to pop out on his forehead.

"Pretty blonde. Yay-high," he said.

Against his will, he remembered the girl's blond head bobbing up and down over his crotch, his fully erect mast causing her pretty, smooth cheeks to bulge in turn. He squeezed his eyes closed, stifled a near sob, and said, "You know, Henry, I was so dang tired after that last assignment, I closed my eyes as soon as I boarded the train in Kansas City and didn't open 'em again until we pulled into Union Station."

Dade continued to study the deputy suspiciously, like a father wondering if he should believe his son's story about arriving home so late. "I see, I see." A pregnant pause. "So where did you meet the young lady you fucked seven ways from sundown last night, Bear?"

Haskell swallowed down another sob that threatened to burst up out of his guilt-heavy chest. "In the, uh . . . in the uh . . ."

"Oh, in the Larimer Saloon, no doubt," Dade said, nodding knowingly. "Because of course, that's where you would have stopped first as soon as you hit town. Needed to wet your whistle, cut the trail dust. And there she was . . ." He grinned again, coyote-like.

"That's right, Chief. You hit the nail on the head! I'm feelin' so peaked from hunger that I can't even think straight. But there you have it. I met her in the saloon. Took her up to my room. Fucked her seven ways from sundown."

Haskell wrapped his shaking hand around the doorknob, then opened the door against his boot. He slid his boot out of the way, and opened the door again, farther. "I hope you find your niece, Henry. I'm sure she's just fine. I didn't hear about no trouble on the train."

"Well, I'm going to head on home," Dade said. "She might have got turned around in one of the stations between here and Kansas City, during a water stop, and had to take the milk train into Denver this morning. Might even be waiting at my boarding house now."

"That's probably it, Henry. The milk train. Be seein' you, Chief. I got a train to catch!"

Haskell hurried out of the office so fast that he startled Miss Kimble, who glanced up from her ghastly typewriting contraption to gasp with a start. She handed a pile of travel vouchers to Haskell, and the deputy grabbed them as he nearly ran past her desk, skip-hopping in his haste.

He'd just gained the hat tree when Henry Dade poked his head out of his office and cast one more skeptical glance toward Haskell, who was sure he was going to have a heart stroke before he could gain Colfax Avenue and freedom, sweet freedom.

"Bear?"

"Yes, Chief?"

"I hope this makes you reconsider your ways."

Haskell's heart thundered in his ears as loudly as the consarned clattering of Miss Lucy's typewriting machine. "Wh-what ways are those, Chief?"

Dade glanced at Miss Kimble, who kept her head down as she played her typewriter, then mouthed discreetly behind his hand, "Whiskey and women."

"Oh, that," Bear said, trying to smile. "You got no idea how it has, Henry!"

He chuckled lest he should scream, fumbled the door open, and fairly sprinted into the hall.

Evangeline Lockhart negotiated the well-worn path leading to the small cemetery at the top of a low knoll and opened the gate in the white picket fence.

Gray picket fence, rather.

Most of the white had worn off, leaving only the gray, worn boards of the pickets. If the fence didn't get some paint soon, it would likely rot and fall. Since it was doubtful anyone would ever paint the old fence surrounding this remote cemetery housing the moldering bodies of twenty-some dead soldiers, most having died during a typhus epidemic twenty years ago, the others killed by Indians and, in one case, a grizzly bear, the fence would rot and fall.

The old cavalry outpost, lying in a hollow amongst the low bluffs only a hundred yards away, was long-abandoned and forgotten by most everyone in Sedgwick County except Evangeline Lockhart herself, who was the only person still dwelling there now that her father, Zack Lockhart, was dead.

Her father was buried here in the cemetery — the only civilian, as far as Evangeline knew. At least, the old cemetery register book didn't identify any other civilians. It hadn't accounted for her father, either, until she herself had scribbled his name in the register, on the last used page of the book, under what was likely a coffee stain and possibly a soldier's snot smear.

Evangeline had found the dusty, water-stained ledger in the old sutler's store her father had taken over once the army had left, and turned it into a whorehouse, saloon, and mercantile situated near a freight and stage trail skirting the south bank of the South Platte River. She'd perused the book from time to time, fascinated in her dark way, reading the twenty-eight names of the dearly departed written in faded, often smeared blue-black ink, thinking of them rotting in their murky graves, wondering what was left under those rocky mounds.

She'd added her father's name two weeks ago, just after his death, in her own looping, feminine hand in clear indigo.

She didn't think the old, dead soldiers would mind having Zack Lockhart out here. While Poppa had never served, the soldiers buried out here had become like family (even though they were dead, of course) over the years that he and Evangeline had lived here, in the old sutler's store, making their own, hard way in the world as best they could. Now Poppa was joining them — a foster father of sorts. Maybe his presence would add a father's comfort to the dead young men buried here, most of them not having reached even thirty years before they'd breathed their last.

Now Evangeline walked along the path amongst the crude, splintering wooden crosses. Some leaned to the southeast, the way the wind had blown them; many were overgrown with needle grass, brome, and prickly pear. A snake had coiled itself around one — a bizarre lover's embrace — and it tightened its coil, directed its flat gaze, and shook its rattle as Evangeline passed not ten feet away.

66

"Oh, stop, Gus," Evangeline said. "Go back to sleep. Gonna be a hot day, one of the last of the summer."

She glanced at the high sun just now beginning its slide from its noon zenith, and stopped at the fresh grave she herself had dug beneath a sprawling, half-dead cottonwood at the far back of the little boneyard. The grave was mounded with rocks, like all the others. Only, she had mounded the rocks over this one. The others had sunk into the ground over the years. This one, still fresh, humped up as though in defiance of the ravages of weather and time.

"Good afternoon, Poppa." Evangeline stooped to set a small spray of wildflowers down at the base of the cross she had fashioned herself from two willow branches and rawhide. "I'm sorry they're wilted. I picked them just after lunch, down by the river, but you know how long wildflowers last in this heat."

Gus shook his rattle at her again. It was a soft sound that rose, just noticeable, above the rushing-rattling of the cottonwood's dull green leaves. Ignoring the viper, Evangeline said, "The paintbrush is still lovely, though, however wilted." She lifted the spray in her hands and brushed the tip of her index finger down the stem of the Indian paint-brush.

She set the flowers back down at the base of the cross. She placed one hand on the top of the cross, closed her eyes, and began to recite "The Lord's Prayer," which she had just started doing a few days ago, having run out of anything else to say up here at her father's grave.

Mostly, her days were uneventful. There'd been the coyote she'd discovered one night pillaging the keeper shed, but after that her days had dragged by like the dry, hot summer breeze — a steady sigh of time's flat drift.

Like God's slow, weary exhalation.

She'd just spoken past "Give us this day our daily bread" when she stopped the recitation and lifted her head abruptly.

She'd heard something.

She looked around now, squinting into the distance down the backside of the low bluff. Only when she removed her hand from the cross and used it to shade her eyes from the sun's brassy glare did she see the lone rider coming down the old freight and stagecoach trail from the southwest.

The horse and rider were a good half a mile away, thus little larger than a thumbnail from Evangeline's vantage, but his figure and that of the horse he was riding grew gradually, separating, as the horse trotted along the trail meandering between the buttes tufted with brome grass, prickly pear, sage, and occasional cedars and greasewood shrubs.

Evangeline's heart quickened.

She rose, standing, to stare at the approaching rider. He was nearly straight south of her now. He had his head turned toward her, facing her. She could tell by the pale oval of his face beneath the black smudge of his hat. He booted his horse, a sorrel, ahead at a faster clip.

Evangeline's heart beat faster. Her fingertips tingled with a sudden rush of blood. An instinctive fear seized her.

She swung around and began to retrace her steps across the top of the cemetery hill, automatically avoiding the graves with their bristling, moldering crosses. As she strode, increasing her pace with every step, Gus gave his shrill rattle again and struck at her, missing her boot by only six inches. Evangeline's gaze was so intent on the rider, she did not notice.

She pushed through the rickety gate in the dilapidated fence and continued along the path resembling a pale slender snake trailing off down the hill toward the old fort and the mercantile, which was what she called the old sutler's store now, though she wouldn't have sold much there these days even if she'd had much on her shelves to sell. Most folks continued their journey on into the nearby town of Julesburg when they needed food or supplies, a shot of cheap whiskey, or a quick poke from a willing whore. The few freight teams still using the road — and they were getting fewer and fewer because of the railroad — rarely stopped here anymore but just passed the motley collection of old fort hovels overgrown with brush and cactus, and kept rolling toward town.

As she strode purposefully along the trail, reaching the bottom of the hill, Evangeline looked over her right shoulder.

The rider was closer now, loping his horse along the base of the rise the cemetery was on. She studied him closely, her heart thumping anxiously, as she continued toward the old sutler's store dead ahead of her, fifty yards away, set back off the trail and to the right of the windmill from which she acquired her water, to the left of the old post commander's hut.

Evangeline slowed her pace, staring curiously toward the approaching rider. She studied him even more closely than before.

She could see him more clearly now, though not clearly enough to discern whether she'd seen him before.

"Jamie?" she whispered, a thickness in her throat.

Then, loud: "Ja-Jamie?"

The rider, whose eyes she could not see because of his hat brim, grinned. She could see the white line of his teeth between the wide-drawn lips. He hunkered low in the saddle and urged the sorrel on faster.

His mouth opened wider, showing more teeth — as well as gaps between those teeth — and he gave a wild yell that was like an ice pick to Evangeline's heart.

She screamed, turned her head forward, and lunged into an all-out run.

When she'd gained the steps of the high front veranda fronting the mercantile, the stranger thundered up behind her. The sorrel whinnied shrilly as the stranger checked it down and leaped out of the saddle. Evangeline dashed across the veranda, fumbled with the door in her frantic haste, and ran up the stairs that split the rambling building in two equal halves, with the saloon to the left and the mercantile to the right.

The stranger gave a wild scream as he hammered across the veranda behind Evangeline, who screamed again as she reached

71

the second floor. He stormed loudly up behind her.

As she turned to the second-floor hall, she glanced briefly over her shoulder. He was a dark specter closing on her fast, with merciless relentlessness and bizarre humor, taking the stairs two and three steps at a time, placing a hand on either wall to steady himself. He dashed up the steps, his hat still hiding his eyes but not his spread lips and gap-toothed, laughing grin.

Evangeline dashed down the hall, but not before he dove for her, swiping a hand across her right ankle, tripping her. She hit the hall floor hard, with a groan. She gave another clipped scream, sure her heart was going to explode with terror, as she scrambled to her feet and continued running.

The second door on the right was open. That was her room. She tripped over a water pail she'd left in the hall, and fell into her room, again hitting the floor hard. The specter was long-striding behind her. She could hear his ragged breathing, feel the reverberations of his powerful foot thuds through the boards beneath the rug padding her bedroom floor. She rose onto her hands and knees and crawled as fast as she could to the rifle leaning in the corner just ahead of her.

He gave a loud, strangled-sounding grunt and dove for her again. His body hit the floor with an explosive *bang!* and he hooked an arm around her feet just as she flung her right hand up for the old Spencer carbine leaning in the corner between her brass bed and dresser.

She screamed.

The man bellowed ribald laughter as he pulled her back by her ankles. She struggled out of his grip just long enough to grab the rifle, pulling it down to the floor with her. She hastily worked the trigger-guard cocking mechanism, racking a .56-caliber round into the action, and twisted around, aiming the old carbine straight down the line of her body from her right shoulder.

He lay before her, one arm wrapped around her ankles, grinning up at her. He was so close, the sun so intense through the window over her left shoulder, that she could see every pore in his round, sweating face, the nose pink with sunburn. The eyes were brown and bright with humor. His thick lips were pulled back from his teeth. He was missing two — on the top right, another on the bottom just left of center.

"Get out," she croaked, her heart turning somersaults in her chest. "Get out! Get out! Get out!" she sobbed, trying to steady the cocked rifle in her hands.

The two brown eyes staring up at her narrowed slightly, the brown brows knitting. "Oh, Evvy . . . don't you remember me?"

She quickly sleeved a tear from her cheek, then resumed gazing down the barrel of the slightly quivering rifle in her hands, drawing a bead on the stranger's right cheek, just below his eye. "I remember who you were."

"Oh?" He canted his head quizzically to one side. "Who's that, now?"

"Jamie Lockhart. My cousin."

"I'm still Jamie Lockhart, Miss Evangeline Lockhart." Again, the smile played across the thick lips.

"No," she said, her thin voice barely audible to her own ears in which her blood was thundering. "No, you're not. You're someone else. Different from Jamie. You look like him. You smile like him. But there's a strange look in your eyes. You ain't Jamie no more. Not the Jamie I remember. Please, leave here, sir. This is my house and I will defend it to the last." She spoke that last through gritted teeth.

"What's that mean?" the specter she once knew as Jamie said. "Does that mean you're gonna shoot your cousin in the eye with that old rifle of your pa's, Miss Lockhart?" A taunting, mocking grin revealed those two

74

strange gaps in his jaws around which the other teeth were badly discolored. One was chipped. He winked. "After all we meant to each other at one time?"

Evangeline kept the rifle aimed at the specter's cheek. Her head swam, thoughts stabbing her like fishhooks raking weeds at the bottom of the South Platte.

"After all the things we meant to each other . . . once," the specter said, his voice slow and insinuating, his eyes now leering at her, brushing across the two firm mounds of her breasts.

He was hugging both of her ankles against his chest.

He reached up and slid his free hand beneath the hem of her dove-gray and brown print dress. He walked his fingers up her naked calf.

"Don't," Evangeline said.

He didn't stop. He kept walking his fingers up the bare inside of her leg.

And then he flattened his hand against the inside of her thigh, squeezing her gently.

Evangeline drew a deep breath. The rifle sagged in her hands. His hand was hot. Almost as hot as a skillet on a freshly stoked stove.

"You're home — ain't ya, Jamie?" she

breathed. "You really are home."
The hot hand slid higher on her thigh.

CHAPTER 6

The brakes of the Union Pacific coach car gave a tooth-gnashing screech as the train, east-heading out of Cheyenne, jerked and sputtered and jounced over rail seams, gradually slowing and waking the big deputy U.S. marshal slouched sideways against the window, the brim of his black, bullet-crowned hat pulled down over his eyes.

Haskell lifted his head, thumbing the hat brim off his forehead, to see that the train was pulling into Julesburg, a dusty settlement situated on the south bank of the South Platte River, on the gentling rolling scrubland of the northeastern Colorado desert. Just now the relatively new, wood-frame depot building shouldered up alongside the tracks. Its brick platform was adorned with several women in brocade gowns and ostrich-plumed picture hats, as well as a half-dozen or so gents decked out in three-piece suits and bowler hats, several smoking stogies — all waiting for the train that would carry them east to Nebraska, Iowa, maybe Chicago, or, hell, all the way to New York City.

Haskell gave a wry chuff at the thought, silently marveling at the drift of time, the flow of events, how much he'd seen in his relatively brief time on the rock called Earth.

He'd grown up dirt poor in the Pennsylvania hills. During the war, which seemed a lifetime ago but was only twenty years back, he'd fought with the Zouave of the 155th Pennsylvania Volunteers. "Silas's Sonso'bitches," they were called, under the command of Colonel Silas Sanders. The wild-assed guerrilla fighters ran dangerous missions behind enemy lines, blowing up trains, bridges, and ammo dumps, occasionally assassinating Confederate muckety-mucks.

Haskell had been a young first lieutenant who'd fought alongside his old friend Lou Cameron, a wise old sergeant, though only five years Haskell's senior. After the war, the two came west together and hunted buffalo. Back then the bison fairly peppered the plains, thick as lice in a mountain man's beard.

Haskell and his old pal Cameron, now dead, had been part of the horde of hunters and hiders who'd nearly exterminated the bison herds and many of the Indians, who'd depended on them, right along with them. The hunters and soldiers had made way for the glistening Iron Horse, and one of those former buffalo hunters wondered now about the many similar train platforms scattered throughout the west. On how many of these platforms were there now ladies in plumed hats and men in three-piece suits waiting for their own trains, fanning themselves and smoking, on land where only a few short years ago the horseback Indians had followed the bison, pitching their bleached-hide tipis and running wild upon the land.

Around the same time Haskell and Cameron had ventured west after the war, Julesburg had been the site of a storied stagecoach station. In revenge for the Sand Creek Massacre, a thousand Cheyenne, Arapaho, and Lakota warriors had attacked the town and the station, burning the whole kit and caboodle to the ground and killing sixty soldiers and fifty armed civilians.

Since then, the Indians had either been exterminated along with the buffalo, or hazed onto reservations. Julesburg had not only been rebuilt in grand fashion but had grown to become a sprawling, rollicking frontier town complete with saloons by the dozens, fancy hotels, gambling parlors, opera houses, and hurdy-gurdy houses storied throughout the west.

Civilization, the lawman thought. *Built on the blood and bones of the dead.*

"Leave him be," said a voice nearby. "He is deep in reverie."

As the coach rocked to a final stop in front of the depot building, Haskell turned his head from the window and poked his hat brim further off his forehead. He drew a slow breath as his gaze locked onto that of the woman sitting directly across from him, her knees nearly touching his from beneath a long, spruce-green skirt owning a crisp metallic sheen.

Rarely had he stumbled so unexpectedly upon a woman of such mind-numbing, exotic beauty. It was an almost aristocratic beauty, though the aristocratic beauties he'd mingled with, however few and far between they'd been, hadn't been blessed with eyes so frank, openly curious, and vaguely ironic as were the shimmering chocolate eyes regarding him now from only a few feet away, under the brim of a felt burgundy hat adorned with a spruce band and a thin spray of goose feathers.

"I beg your pardon for the intrusion," the

woman said, her voice vaguely hoarse and raspy. She turned to the younger woman sitting beside her and said, "Let's let the other passengers detrain first, Sylvie. I don't want to get caught up in the rush."

The younger woman to whom the first woman had spoken still stared at Haskell, unabashed fascination glistening in her blue eyes. She was a sandy blonde with a cherubic face, who appeared a few years younger than the other woman, whose hair was nearly the same black as her long, slanted eyes.

The young blonde lifted a white-gloved hand and pointed at Haskell's broad chest. "Pardon the query, sir . . . but is that . . . that . . . ?" She let her voice trail off as though words had failed her.

Haskell flipped his necklace with his left index finger, and smiled at the girl. "Grizzly claws."

"Sylvie, you're impertinent," said the dark-haired woman, blinking once slowly, but then turning to Haskell and frowning, as though wondering if she'd heard him correctly. "Grizzly *bear* claws?"

"That's right." Haskell slid his gaze between both women, including them both in the conversation. "Killed that griz back near Clark's Knob on Blue Mountain. Near the old home farm in Pennsylvania."

"I hear they're enormous!" intoned the blonde, slapping her pale hand to the bodice of her yellow, white-edge traveling frock.

"This one wasn't the biggest I've ever seen. But I don't care to have one any bigger eyeing me like a kid eyes a piece of hard-rock candy in a glass jar on a mercantile shelf."

"Did this one . . . eye you . . . like a piece of candy . . . on a mercantile shelf?" asked the black-haired beauty. Her sensuous red lips rose with an amused, vaguely incredulous grin.

Haskell leaned forward, forearms on his knees, as though he were relating a campfire tale. "It was late at night, see? I got turned around between two creeks, lost my way in the dark. That ole griz come at me across a beaver dam. All I heard was a tremendous roar. The roar of a piss-burned god, if you'll pardon my French."

Neither woman batted an eye but appeared to be riveted.

"A tremendous roar and the creaking of the beaver dam under the bruin's enormous weight," Haskell continued. "He must have weighed as much as two horses. I could see starlight flashing on that griz's coat, in his eyes, in his teeth! I headed for the first big tree and climbed for all I was worth. It was all I could do, and it was little enough. See, that big old bruin grabbed ahold of that tree like a long-lost love it hadn't seen in a coon's age, and started shakin' it.

"I tell you, that bear wagged me every which way. I was floppin' around like a leaf in the wind, hangin' on for dear life! I lost my knife, my powder horn, my caps and shot — everything but my rifle, which was slung around my neck. The rifle was an old Hawken. Single-shot muzzleloader. Fortunately, it was loaded. But I had only one bullet with which to keep myself from becoming that bear's supper!"

"Oh, my gosh!" Sylvie gasped.

"What on earth *did* you do?" the dark-haired woman said. Her exotic face with its long, near-black eyes was calm, but a flush had risen, darkening her natural almond color.

"Well, that tree was losin' all its leaves and half its branches . . . not to mention me, as well, almost! I don't know how I hung on, but I did. Out of pure fear, I reckon. I've never been so afraid. The trunk of that tree was crackling and popping as the bruin wagged it from side to side. I could see it splintering! Knowing I had about ten seconds before I and the tree would go tumbling to the ground and likely right into that beast's choppers, I unslung ole Jeremiah — that's what I called my rifle, after the old mountain man who gave it to me — and took aim.

"One shot, you understand. I had one shot, and I had to kill the beast with that one shot while I was being wagged like a puppy dog's tail!"

Sylvie's eyes were glistening silver, nearly popping out of her head. "What happened? What *happened*?"

"I took aim at his right eye. I'd heard tell that the only way to kill a bear with one shot was either through the heart or through the eye. Just shootin' him in the head would be like slingin' a rock at a boulder. Forget it. But if you shot him in the eye, the bullet would turn the eye to jelly and slam into his brain. So, bein' shakin' from side to side, havin' my *own* brains scrambled for me, I aimed just as steady as I possibly could under such horrific circumstances at the snarling, raging griz's right eye."

Haskell curled his upper lip. "And you know what happened?"

The dark-haired gal glanced at the younger one, smiling in appreciation of her traveling companion's unabashed delight in the yarn.

"What happened?" Sylvie squealed. "Oh, please, don't tease us! *What happened?*"

Haskell's lip was still curling that grin as he said, "I shot him in the left eye."

Sylvie covered her mouth with both hands and howled in delight.

"And that's how I come about this grizzly-claw necklace," Haskell said, winking at the dark-haired woman. He extended his right hand. "Bear Haskell, ladies."

Now the dark-haired gal was plainly skeptical. She narrowed one eye as she said, "Bear?"

Haskell grinned again. "No pun intended. That was my given name. After my great-grandpa who fought in the Revolutionary War and who, also, so the story goes, killed his own bear and wore its claws around his neck for the rest of his life. So I wear this one, too. Sort of a wink and a nod to ole Grandpappy's spirit, wherever he may be."

The dark-haired gal shook Haskell's hand. "I'm not sure which of those two stories I like more. I'm Monique. This is Sylvie."

"Please to make your acquaintance, Miss Monique," Haskell said before giving Sylvie's little hand a friendly squeeze. "How do you do, Miss Sylvie?"

"Much better now, thank you . . . um . . .

Bear," Sylvie said, her blue eyes riveted on his.

"Very nice to meet you, Bear," Miss Monique said, rising and taking the younger woman's arm in her hand. "Come, Sylvie. Time to detrain."

Haskell rose and hurried to say, "Monique. That's an intriguing name." Everything about the woman was intriguing. He found himself very much wanting to get to know her better.

"Not unlike *Bear,*" she said, giving him a fleeting, dismissive smile as she ushered the younger woman into the now-vacant aisle.

"Going to be in town long?" Haskell called after her.

She glanced over her shoulder at him. Those delicious lips quirked another captivating half-smile. "Oh, for quite some time, I would think. I live here."

"You don't say."

She smiled as she and Sylvie left the train.

CHAPTER 7

Haskell gave the ladies a moment to de-coach ahead of him.

He didn't want to hurry off and make them suspect he was following them, possibly stalking them. Of course, he wanted to hurry after them. He'd found himself under the intriguing Monique's spell, and he very much wanted to know where she was off to, where he might find her again. But he suppressed the urge.

He was a big man, physically imposing, and he knew he could seem a threat to some women until they got to know him. He wasn't wearing his badge but merely carrying it in his wallet. He usually didn't wear it, as he liked to travel incognito.

Also, the nickeled tin moon and star made an awfully shiny target.

He sat back in his seat and plucked an Indian Kid cigarillo out of the pocket of his calico shirt. As he struck a match to life on the heel of his boot, he saw he wasn't the only passenger left on the coach. There were three other men milling near the car's far end, behind Haskell and near the rear door.

Two were seated facing each other. The third was standing, facing the two seated men. All three were speaking in low tones, casting angry, suspicious glances Haskell's way.

They were dressed in rough trail garb. The one standing wore heavy leather chaps and two pistols.

Now, as Haskell returned their gazes with a curious one of his own, the one standing said just loudly enough for the lawman to hear, "Yeah, it's him, all right. Sure as shit."

The other two cast another quick glance Bear's way, then rose, and the three men left the coach through the rear door, muttering.

Haskell felt the cool fingers of apprehension walk across the back of his neck. Obviously, he'd been sharing his coach not only with one pretty young lady and one very beautiful woman, but with three strangers who didn't like him. Didn't seem to like him a bit. And they were in town now. He'd have to keep that third eye in the back of his head skinned for as long as he was in Julesburg, lest he wind up with a bullet in his back.

He was accustomed to such dangers. You weren't a lawman for as long as Haskell had been without having crawled a few men's humps and gotten their drawers in a twist.

He rose with a fateful sigh just as new and old passengers, some who'd just detrained to stretch while the locomotive took on water, began to enter through the doors at both ends of the coach. He grabbed his gear — saddlebags, war bag, bedroll, and Henry rifle — from the luggage rack and side-stepped his way past the milling passengers, out the coach's front door and onto the platform.

Rolling the Indian kid from one side of his mouth to the other, taking an occasional puff and blowing the smoke out through his nose, he balanced his gear on his shoulders as he made his way into the depot station and out the other side, nodding to the ladies as he did.

Beyond him stretched the broad, dusty, sun-washed main street of Julesburg, which, he judged after a few moments' gander, had grown more than a little since his last visit. The street was dustier with passing horse and wagon traffic. It was louder, too, with the voices of men and the clatter of wagons and the clomps of horses and the intermittent barking of dogs mingling with the patter of piano and fiddle music ebbing out from what he assumed were saloons and probably a few brothels.

The town even had a hansom cab, Haskell saw now, as the cab stopped in front of him, pulled by a fine, high-stepping, head-tossing Arab stallion.

"Take a load off, mister," said the top-hatted, frock-coated, mustached gent on the high seat. He grinned down, his monocle winking in the sunlight. "Where you headed?"

"Oh, not all that far," Haskell said, frowning as he tried to get his bearings, gazing down the street from over the Arab's sweat-slick back. "Just over to Lockhart's place. That's ain't far, is it?"

"Lockhart's place?"

"Yeah. What the hell's the name of it again? I haven't been to Julesburg in two, maybe three years . . ."

The hansom cab driver grinned again and made the monocle flash once more. "You mean Sheriff Lockhart's Big Saloon!"

Haskell laughed now as he remembered. "The very one."

"It's two blocks east on the left. Can't miss it. It was the biggest saloon in town until the Union Pacific Hotel went up nigh on a year ago now, a little farther down Union Pacific Avenue here and on the right. That's where the moneyed stay when they come to town. Are you moneyed, sir?"

"Nope," Haskell said, chuckling. "Poor-eyed!"

The driver laughed. "Just the same — why don't you hop aboard? No use walking under all that gear when you don't have to."

Haskell shook his head. "Thanks just the same, but I've been sittin' since Denver. I'd like to walk and get the lay of the land, and this gear don't weigh much."

"Well, you'd have the shoulders for it, even if it did." The cab driver pinched his hat brim to Haskell. "Good day, sir!"

Haskell bade the man good day, then stepped around the Arab and out into the street. He headed east along the street's right side, in the shade of the awnings over the boardwalks but avoiding the boardwalks themselves.

The walks were crowded with milling folks of both sexes and even a few dogs, some folks hurrying busily along, getting chores out of the way, while many were content to chin at their leisure, some sipping from frothy beer mugs in front of saloons. A few men here and there were chinning with soiled doves painted up and outfitted in as

91

little as possible, the doves laughing a little too loudly at something their prospective clients were saying.

"Hello there, big fella — got time for a poke?"

The voice had come from above and to Haskell's right. He didn't think the proposition had been directed at him until the same voice said, louder and in a peevish tone, "Hey there, mister — can't you hear, or you just tryin' to play hard to get?"

Haskell turned, and the young lady leaning on the rail of a second-floor balcony pouted, twisting a lock of her hair, and said, "Oh, all right — I'll give you a poke for five dollars. That's a dollar off my usual rate. Take it or leave it!"

She gave him a wolfish half-grin.

She was topless. She wore two strands of what Haskell assumed were fake pearls down over and around her perky, pale breasts. She was a comely, henna-rinsed blonde with half of her hair up and half of it down, and she had a heart-shaped tattoo on the left side of her pale neck.

"I'm sorry," Haskell said. "I didn't realize you were talkin' to me."

"Well, I was. I thought maybe you was uppity." She feigned another pout.

"No, I ain't uppity, but I unfortunately

don't have time for a poke just now. If I did
— believe me, girl, I'd set you a-howlin'!"
Haskell grinned.

She snickered. "Braggart."

"What's your name? Maybe I'll look you
up later."

"Just ask for Melody at the Frenchman's
Delight."

Haskell dropped his gaze to the sign over
the narrow, three-story building on whose
second-story veranda the girl stood. Sure
enough, the Frenchman's Delight, it was
called.

"All right, then, Miss Melody," Haskell
said, dipping his chin to her. "I'll see you
later . . . to see what delights a Frenchman."
He winked.

She smiled, flushing. "Say, you have my
name. What's yours?"

"Bear."

"Pshaw!"

"No, really."

She looked him over saucily and said,
"Well, it fits you — that's for sure."

Haskell grinned, swung forward, shifting
the gear on his shoulders, and continued on
his way, feeling a little tight in the pants.
That was the third good-looking woman
he'd run into in Julesburg so far, and the
most recent one had been bare-breasted. A

fine pair of hooters, too. He'd thought his tussle with Henry Dade's niece — knowing he'd fucked his boss's kin still made his ears turn hot — would have appeased him for at least a week.

But he'd been wrong. Obviously, Bear was ready for another mattress dance.

First, business.

To that end, he trudged on up to the high, wide veranda fronting Sheriff Lockhart's Big Saloon, which was exactly what the half-story-sized, gold-painted lettering sprawled across its high, green false façade announced the name of the establishment to be. Several men, probably freighters, with their bushy beards and clinging aroma of wheel dope and mules, chinned on the front veranda.

Haskell nodded to the mule skinners, pushed through the scrolled batwing doors — big, heavy, oak doors with lions' heads carved into the facing panel of each — then stopped and looked around before walking down the big, broad drinking hall, sparsely populated this early in the day, to the long, ornate bar with a glistening backbar mirror at the room's rear. Halfway to the bar, he was not at all happy to see the same three men he'd spied in the coach car just a few minutes earlier, casting him the wooly eye-ball.

Haskell must have become distracted, spying the three obvious hardtails at the bar ahead of him, because his left boot hooked a chair leg, and he stumbled.

One of the three at the bar, tightly grouped toward the left, caught Haskell's misstep. He directed his partners' gazes with a tip of his head, and muttered, "Clumsy fuckin' oaf," loudly enough for Haskell to hear.

Haskell winked and grinned at him, then dropped his gear near the brass foot rail running along the base of the bar, all except the sheathed Henry, which he set across the bar before him. Then he turned to a red-bearded barman swabbing out a schooner nearby.

"The sheriff around?" he asked.

"Ain't seen him today," the bearded barman said.

The man's beard was incredibly carefully trimmed. Such a trimming must have taken the man a good twenty minutes each morning, the lawman silently opined for no other reason than his busy mind often noted such things. But the impeccably trimmed beard still did not make the barman a very handsome man at all, which seemed a shame when you thought of all the time it cost him

95

to trim it — time he would not get back when he needed it most.

"He's still kickin', I take it," Haskell said, raking a big hand down his own face, which he hadn't shaved in three or four days. He himself was an every-other-day shaver. He'd even let it go three or four days sometimes. As with the barman, his beard, or lack thereof, really didn't make much difference in his overall appearance. He was a big, hulking bastard, just the same.

"Yeah, he's still kickin'. Why wouldn't he be?"

"Never mind. Is he due in this afternoon?"

"Maybe, maybe not."

"What's that mean?"

"Sometimes he comes in and sometimes he don't come in, if he's got law work."

"I see."

"Who're you?"

"An old frie—"

"Bear Haskell," one of the three men to Haskell's left said, a good twenty feet away. Two other men, well-dressed townsmen, stood between them and Bear.

Haskell glanced in the backbar mirror at the trio of hardtails. Two were looking down at their drinks on the bar, blushing. The third — the one who'd spoken — met his glance in the mirror, then smirked and looked at the others.

He snorted a laugh.

The barman slid his scowling gaze uncertainly from Haskell to the three hardtails, then back to Haskell.

"There you have it," Bear said. "I'm an old friend of Lockhart's. Why don't I wait for him here since I don't feel like lugging this gear over to the courthouse, and I've been castigated for using government pay vouchers for such luxuries as hansom cabs when I'm an able-bodied man with two good feet. While I'm waiting, why don't you set me up with a shot of good bourbon — at least, pour from a labeled bottle and leave the snake venom on the bottom shelf where it belongs — and a big, tall glass of good, dark ale. As I remember, you fellas brew passably good beer here."

"We do."

"Just what the doctor ordered."

The three to Haskell's left, beyond the townsmen, were snickering and muttering, casting furtive glances at Haskell in the backbar mirror. Haskell could tell they were making the two townsmen nervous. The townsmen seemed as though they didn't like where they were standing just now, between the big bruin in the bullet-crowned black hat and with the Henry on the bar, and the three snickering hardtails.

The barman didn't look one bit comfortable, either. As he poured a glass of bourbon, then filled a schooner at the tap, brushing the excess foam off with a flat stick, his own cheeks reddened above his impeccable beard, and he cut nervous glances between Haskell and the cutthroats.

When he'd set both drinks down in front of Haskell and collected his coinage, he asked, "You, uh, in town on business?"

"The man's a lawman," said the hardtail who'd spoken before. He'd spoken louder this time. Loud enough to be heard even out on the noisy street, in fact. He slapped his hand down on the bar top, hard. It echoed. "The man rides for law and order, don't ya know!"

The two well-dressed townsmen glanced from the three tough-nuts to Haskell, looking a little constipated and wanting to leave, but not sure how to make a graceful exit that wouldn't leave them looking like scurrying rats.

Haskell looked over the two men to the three farther down the bar and said, "If you don't mind, I'll answer for myself, thank you very much." To the barman he said with a faint, slit-eyed smile, "I'm a lawman. I ride for law and order, don't ya know."

He lifted his shot glass between the thumb and index finger, and sipped.

"The fella's a goddamn killer, is what he is." This from one of the other three hardtails. The shortest of the three, Haskell thought. He hadn't made the accusation loudly, but loudly enough for everyone on this end of the saloon to hear.

Haskell took one more slow, savoring sip of the whiskey, winked his approval at the bartender, then set the glass back down on the bar. He looked over at the hardtails again.

The man who'd just spoken was short and baby-faced, but he had mean little pig eyes. He'd stepped back away from the bar so he could see around the two well-dressed townsmen, and both his mean little pig eyes were focused on Haskell.

Haskell turned around with a sigh, brushing his left hand over his Schofield and releasing the keeper thong from over the hammer. He rested his right elbow atop the bar, hand dangling near his belly, positioned for a fast plunge for the pistol angled for the cross-draw on his left hip. "Okay, you little fucker," Haskell said. "Why do you insist on crawlin' my hump?"

CHAPTER 8

The little man pointed at Haskell and narrowed one dung-brown eye, yelling, "You're the federal dick who killed my cousins, Raymond and Wilson Longshanks, in Missouri three years ago. Said they was sellin' whiskey an' not payin' taxes, an' you was wrong."

"All right — just for the sake of argument and since you seem to have your drawers in such a twist about it, let's say I was wrong. That don't discount the little matter that they were about to lynch two deputy U.S. marshals from the Missouri-Arkansas district when I rode up on them. I gave them ample opportunity to surrender, but they chose to slap iron, so I went to work with my Henry.

"Made short work of 'em, too, in fact, though I don't like to brag about killin'. When I've done killed you, you little pip fart, I'm gonna stomp on your head an' piss on your brains, and then I'm gonna roll you into the street right along with these two plug-ugly sonso'bitches who seem to be backin' you, because neither one appears to have a lick more sense than you do."

The two other hardtails at the bar, both also facing Haskell now, had grown white as linen bed sheets drying in the October wind.

The two well-dressed townsmen stood pressed tight to the bar, deathly afraid of getting caught in a cross fire. Finally, one turned to the other one and said, "I'm getting the hell out of here!" He threw back his whiskey shot and bolted for the door.

The other looked at Haskell, muttering something unintelligible; then he, too, ran to the door, but not before tripping over a chair, falling onto a vacant table and having to right himself with some trouble, cursing. Limping and pressing a hand to one knee, he pushed through the batwings.

Now it was just Haskell and the short man standing about seven feet out from the bar and the two others standing nearer the mahogany, side by side, facing him. All three had their hands hovering over their holstered six-shooters.

Keeping his eyes on the short man, Haskell hardened his jaws and snarled, *Draw!* His deep voice thundered around the room. "That hogleg ain't doin' you any good in the leather, pip fart! *Draw the damn thing!*"

All three jerked with starts, but did not touch their hoglegs. One of the two at the bar had given a little yelp when Haskell had yelled, and he'd taken one halting step back. Now he cleared his throat as though to cover his trepidation.

Bear waited. The pip fart just stared at him, his little pig eyes growing wide with apprehension. The other two stared at him, hard-eyed, but they were both pale and growing paler. Their faces had turned to stone. One's hand was shaking as it hovered over the walnut grips of his Colt .44.

"Slap iron, you damn peckerwoods!" Haskell bellowed, twice as loud as before. "*Go ahead,* less'n you're yellow. *Go ahead,* so I can pump you all so full of lead not even your mother will recognize you when they pour you into the box. No. No boxes! I'm just gonna drag all three of you tinhorns out back of this place and let the dogs and coyotes have at ya. Shit, you'll be strewn from here to Christmas come tomorrow mornin'."

Bear glared at the man whose hand was shaking. "I can see your jawbone now, boy — all bloody and with just a little bit of meat left on it, bein' carried high and proud by that collie mutt I seen when I first rode into town. Sure, he'll parade it before the others, teasin'-like!"

None of the three said anything until the smallest one slowly raised his right hand to point at Haskell. Slowly and with building volume, he said, "Y-you're fuckin' crazy. P-p-pure fuckin' . . . fuckin' *crazy!*"

"He is, ain't he?" said the one with the shaking hand, his voice high and quavering. "He's crazier'n a tree full of owls in a light-nin' storm!"

"I heard tell it was true," said the third one, to the left of Shaky Hand. "Now I see it for myself. Pure *loco* as a peach-orchard sow!"

Haskell lowered his voice and pitched it hard with danger. "If you three aren't gonna jerk iron, haul your cowardly asses out of here. If I see you again — catch even a glimpse of any one of you three privy snipes anywhere near me again, I'm gonna kill you, and I'm gonna feed you to that collie I was tellin' you about."

The short man slid his fear-bright gaze to the other two. "Come on. There ain't no dealin' with a crazy sonofabitch like this one here."

"No there ain't," Haskell said. "You're right there, pip fart."

"No need for name callin'!" cried the little man as he turned away, his eyes indignant now.

He beckoned to the other two, and they fell in behind him. The three filed out of the saloon like reprimanded schoolboys ordered to the woodshed for a hard paddling.

When they were gone and the batwings were shuddering back into place behind them, slow applause rose. A tall, gray-haired, gray-mustached man stepped out of the shadows to the left of the batwings, clapping his large, black-gloved hands together in front of his chin. He wore a gray suit with a paisley, gold-buttoned vest, a gold watch chain dangling between vest pockets. His hair and mustache were impeccably barbered, his black-silk string tie impeccably tied.

A long, slender, black cheroot dangled from his mouth, curling smoke up in front of his dark-brown eyes.

"Well played, Bear," said Sheriff Con Lockhart, laughing and striding forward. "Very well played, indeed, sir!"

Haskell scowled at the man moving toward him. "I hope you were ready to *back* my play, Sheriff, 'stead of just watchin' from the shadows."

Lockhart stopped before Bear. "Those

were the Rankin boys. Bill's the short one. Albert and Leonard were the other two. Albert was the one with the palsy. Small-time criminals — rustlers, mostly. If you'd had to, you could have blown their wicks before they got those hoglegs even half out of their holsters."

Lockhart grinned his admiration. "Turned out you didn't have to. I appreciate your not spilling those men's blood on my floor." He glanced down, prodding the shiny puncheons with his boot toe. "Just had these boards sanded down and varnished last winter."

"Glad to not dirty up the place."

"You should consider settlin' down and takin' up local law-dogging sometime, Bear, where words sometime work better than bullets. You'd be right handy at it."

"Pshaw." Haskell snorted. "You know me, Con. Don't like the feel of grass growin' under my feet. It itches, don't ya know."

Lockhart laughed and extended his hand, which Haskell shook. "Welcome back to Julesburg." He narrowed a suspicious eye. "Did Henry Dade send you?"

Haskell nodded.

"Shouldn't have. There was no need. I'm a big boy. Besides, I have two very capable deputies with their eyes skinned for my son, if you'd like to call him that. I stopped calling him a Lockhart a long time ago, when I ever call him anything. Try not to talk about him at all."

"Don't blame you. Just the same, Con, he could be headed this way. Henry says he swore to exact revenge right after his trial, when they were leading him away."

Lockhart glanced at the barman with the perfectly trimmed beard and said, "George, bring over a bottle of my best bourbon and two glasses." To Haskell he said, "Let's have a seat and a libation. You came a long way for nothing."

"Let me grab my gear."

When Haskell had taken his rifle and other possibles, he followed the sheriff over to a table against the finely papered and wainscoted wall, beneath a large elk trophy, which Bear remembered Con had said he'd killed himself in the breaks of the Arkansas River just after he'd followed his father to this northeast Colorado country from Oklahoma, where he'd been born and raised. The sheriff sat in a chair with his back to the wall. Knowing Haskell would want to do the same, he positioned his chair at an angle to the table, so they wouldn't be sitting side by side but sort of half-facing each other.

Haskell piled his gear on the floor flanking him, set his Henry on the table, and dug another Indian Kid out of his shirt pocket while Lockhart lit another of his slender black panatelas. George brought a bottle of Old Reserve and wrestled out the cork. He splashed bourbon into two shot glasses, filling each to the brim, then nodded to his employer, who nodded back, and drifted on back to the bar.

Haskell held the glass of good hooch up to the light, admiring the rich amber color. "You think I came all this way for nothin', eh, Con?"

"Indeed I do. Jamie . . . er, that thing I once called my son . . . won't return here. Oh, he might have tended the stove of his fury for the first three, four, maybe even five years. After that, he'd just want to get free of those granite walls, not risk getting sent back. He'll head to Mexico."

Lockhart threw back half the shot, swallowed, then threw back the rest, savoring the smooth, well-flavored busthead as it went down. Haskell sipped his own drink and looked at the sheriff sitting to his right. Lockhart was staring straight across the bar, toward a tall English clock in a heavy wooden cabinet. But he wasn't looking at the time. He seemed to be gazing into space, pensive.

There was something in the man's demeanor, as well as in his tone of voice, that hinted to Haskell that Lockhart might not be as certain in his convictions as he wanted to seem.

"I have to admit, I sort of thought the same thing," Haskell told him, taking another small sip of his bourbon. "But Henry seemed to think otherwise."

"And he's the boss — right, Bear?"

"Henry's the boss." Haskell drew deeply on the Indian Kid and carved gray ashes off the end into the heavy brass Mohmeaks tray on the table. "And he seems dead certain Jamie will be heading here. Said it was something he saw in your son's eyes as he was being led out of that courtroom, the way he glared at you."

"Well, he was mad," Lockhart said, shrugging. "I was the one who hunted him down in the Dinosaur Rocks south of here." Emotion shone in his eyes and made his voice quiver slightly as he added, "After killing my wife-to-be."

"Why was he so damned mad? You were the sheriff — right, Con? Who did he expect would run him down?"

Again, Lockhart shrugged. "I have a feeling it was more the *way* I ran him down.

Relentlessly. I outlasted most of the rest of my posse, several of whom that *thing* killed — shot 'em out of their saddles as they rode after him. That's what piss-burned him so bad. And the fact that I wounded him — creased his skull with a forty-five pill — and then half-dragged him back to town for trial."

"Half-dragged him?"

"Shit, yeah. Wasn't gonna let him ride. Made him walk!" Lockhart slammed his hand down flat on the table so hard, he nearly upended the uncorked bottle of Old Reserve. It would have gone over if Haskell hadn't grabbed it and cast his drinking partner an incredulous glance.

Lockhart stared straight across the room at the old English clock as he continued with: "He walked twenty-five miles, a rope tied around his wrists, the other tied to my horse's tail. I wanted that son of Satan — I'm sorry, but that's how I see him now — to think long and hard about what he did to me . . . to my betrothed. To our future together, mine and Lucia's."

He turned to Haskell and showed nearly every one of his large, square, yellow teeth as he said, *"How he shamed me!"*

A voice said, "Good lord — take it easy,

Poppa, or you're gonna give yourself a heart stroke!"

Both Haskell and Lockhart jerked their heads toward the batwings. Haskell's breath caught in his throat. His heart fairly blossomed in his chest as through the batwings strode the pretty young Sylvie from the train.

Behind her was none other than the exotic dark-haired, long-eyed beauty Haskell knew only as Monique. She was following young Sylvie toward his and Lockhart's table.

CHAPTER 9

As Monique approached Haskell and Lockhart's table, her gaze locked with Bear's. She wrinkled the skin above the bridge of her nose in puzzlement, which must have been a pretty good reflection of the expression on the federal lawman's own features.

"What's this all about, Poppa?" Sylvie asked, opening her arms and fairly flinging herself into Lockhart's lap. She kissed the sheriff's cheek and said, "We're back from Cheyenne, in case you hadn't noticed." She glanced at Bear. "We met Mister Haskell on the train — didn't we, Bear?"

"Indeed we did, uh . . . Miss Lockhart." Haskell gave his chin a cordial dip, then glanced at Lockhart. "I had no idea . . ."

"You've probably never met Sylvie," Lockhart said, giving his daughter a heartfelt hug, pressing his cheek to hers. "The last time you were here she was probably back east, where we often send the precocious one. She's quite good at the piano, the guitar, the banjo, and even several wind instruments."

"I prefer the piano," Sylvie said. "But more than anything, I prefer to read and write. Literature, you know." She beamed with self-satisfaction and unfettered pride.

"Quite masterly with all of the arts, this one," said Monique, walking somewhat shyly up to the table and smiling down at the pretty blonde. "You should see her oil paintings. Astonishing. Miss Gerard says so herself. She thinks we should send her to Europe, where she could get the tutoring such a talent deserves."

"Europe?" Lockhart said, smiling fondly at the daughter in his lap. "Never! I thought I'd die with Sylvie only gone a week. Did Miss Gerard treat you well, dear girl? Did she teach you lots? She certainly should have, given what I'm paying her."

"An art teacher?" Haskell asked.

"Yes." Sylvie reached for her father's shot glass, which he promptly removed from her hand. "She's French. Quite accomplished in her own right. Her husband is a muckety-muck with the railroad. They moved to Cheyenne from New York City. They'll be going back soon, however. Oh, Poppa, I'm going to miss getting together with Mrs.

Gerard twice a year," the young blonde pouted, pooching out her rose-red lips and tightening her hold on her father's neck. "She's one of the rare few I actually enjoy conversing with out here."

She glanced a little sheepishly at Monique and hurried to add, "Except for Monique, of course."

Monique glanced down with a slight flicker of injury in her deep brown eyes.

Lockhart hugged his daughter lovingly and said, "We'll find you another teacher every bit as good as Mrs. Gerard, Sylvie. I assure you." To Haskell, he said, "Since you've met my daughter, I take it you've met her governess, as well."

"Yes, but I had no idea she was Sylvie's governess," Haskell said, rising from his chair and tossing his hat down on the table. He did so with an awkward self-consciousness not at all like him — at least, not like him in the past twenty years or so. The hat caught the bottle and would have knocked it over had Lockhart not grabbed it.

Sylvie tittered a laugh.

Chuckling nervously and gazing at the striking dark-haired beauty before him, Haskell said, "I don't believe I was given the honor of learning Miss Monique's last name."

"Oh, it's not all that much of an honor, Mister Haskell. It's Bataille."

"Monique Bataille. Has a pretty ring to it."

She brushed a stray lock of her coal-black hair back from her cheek. "I'm a Jew with roots in Austria and France."

She spoke that last sentence hurriedly, as though it had been a confession cursorily made, to get it out of the way so as not to leave anyone wondering about the exotic young woman's origins. She was obviously accustomed to negotiating the prejudices historically directed against her race.

To Haskell, she asked, frowning, "You're . . ."

"Bear's a deputy U.S. marshal," Lockhart said for Haskell, who was having trouble coordinating his tongue and vocal cords. "He's here on routine business." The sheriff had added this with a pointed look at Bear, obviously not wanting his daughter to know the real reason Haskell was in town.

Before Haskell could say anything else, Miss Bataille extended a gloved hand to Sylvie and said, "Come, Sylvie. The cab is waiting." To Lockhart, she said, "Sylvie wanted to stop and see if you were here. You know how she misses you when we're away, Mister Lockhart." To Sylvie again: "We'd best get on home and get you cleaned up after the train ride. Judith is also probably wondering where we are, and I'm sure your father and Mister Haskell want to get back to business."

"Yes, yes, you'd better go on home and see Judith," Lockhart said, hoisting his charming, precocious young daughter up out of his lap with a grunt, pecking her cheek. "She'll no doubt want to hear all about what you've learned. Probably also has a warm bath waiting."

"Judith?" Bear asked.

"My older sister," Lockhart said. "Since you've never been over to my house, you've probably never met her. She's been living with me for a good fifteen years. I brought her out here from Oklahoma after her husband died of a cancer. Judith helped me raise Sylvie." The sheriff smiled at the governess. "I lured Miss Monique all the way out here from Philadelphia to file the western edges off my dear daughter" — then he added, turning to Sylvie — "and to inoculate her with all the culture she's been dying for."

Bear returned his gaze to Sylvie's regal governess. "It was a pleasure getting acquainted, Miss Bataille."

"She's beautiful, isn't she?" Sylvie was standing beside her governess now, glancing from Bear to Miss Bataille. She tittered a faintly mocking laugh. "I think Bear is quite taken with you, Monique."

"Yes, I think he is!" Lockhart intoned, grinning up at the big lawman.

Haskell's cheeks and ears turned as hot as a skillet on a freshly stoked stove. Monique glanced at him, and then she, too, blushed. She quickly took Sylvie by the arm and led her toward the doors.

"Goodbye, Poppa," Sylvie said as she was being rushed through the batwings. "Goodbye, Bear!"

When they were gone, Lockhart turned to the still flushed Haskell and said, "Fancy her, do you?"

Haskell shrugged and threw back the rest of his shot of Old Reserve. "What's not to fancy?"

"I think she might fancy you. She's been Sylvie's governess now for nearly two years, and in all that time I've never seen her glow like that. Not once . . . till now." Lockhart cleared his throat. "Kind of a sad sort. Maybe it's on account of her bein' a Jew so far from her roots."

"I take it she doesn't have a suitor?"

Lockhart shook his head and blew out a plume of panatela smoke. "Oh, I've seen a few men ride by the house from time to time, craning their necks, a couple stopping to chin with Miss Monique when she and Judith ride into town for groceries. As far as I know, Miss Bataille's never stepped out with any of them. Not that Judith would have let her had she wanted to. Judith runs a pretty tight ship, and she's quick to quash any possible influence on her niece that isn't what she would call entirely wholesome. Took quite some convincing to get Judith to agree to allow a Jew to live in our house, let alone tutor and entertain Sylvie. To Judith, a former preacher's wife, Jews are heathens, don't ya know."

Lockhart chuffed an ironic laugh, looking down at the whiskey he was swirling in his hand.

Haskell poured more whiskey into Lockhart's glass, then into his own. "Judith doesn't approve of heathens, I guess?"

Lockhart chuckled again. "Especially Jews. She thinks they're the same as gypsies. Thinks both are decidedly unclean."

"Doesn't appear to be one unclean thing about that young woman," Haskell said, holding his full glass in one hand up near his shoulder while he glanced outside, hoping to catch one more glimpse of Monique Bataille. But the hansom cab had rambled away.

"The only unclean think about Miss Monique are your thoughts!" Lockhart threw his head back and roared.

Haskell snorted a laugh and sipped his whiskey. "You can't blame me for that, I reckon." He frowned. "Must be kind of hard, havin' a pretty young woman like that livin' under your own roof, Con. I mean, kind of hard not to . . ."

"Oh, Judith wouldn't allow any kind of dalliance in what she considers her house. Like I say, Judith runs a tight ship. Sails always in trim. Besides, I'm old enough to be the woman's father. Not only that, but . . ."

Lockhart let the sentence trail off as he turned around in his chair to stare pensively out the window between him and Bear, flanking them. "Ever since Lucia was . . . since she died . . . and maybe *how* she died . . . I haven't been much of a mind to set my hat for anyone else."

Haskell studied the older man. Lockhart was in his early sixties, but somehow he looked even older. The years had not been good to him. Despite being outdoors a lot, exposed to the harsh eastern Colorado sun, his face appeared gaunt and pasty, with burst veins putting an unhealthy, blue-red flush in the nubs of his cheeks, beneath the paleness, as well as down his long, broad nose. Haskell had last seen the sheriff of Sedgwick County two years ago, but by Lockhart's aged appearance, it could have been five or six.

Haskell suspected the cause of the man's seeming infirmity and premature ripening was the murder of his betrothed by his son. Which made Haskell think twice about the question he wanted to ask but ended up asking anyway, his natural and professional curiosity overriding his discretion.

"Didn't you have any idea, Con? I mean . . . about Jamie and Lucia. They must have been carrying on for quite some time behind —"

Lockhart turned to him abruptly and said crisply, "I don't want to talk about that. I'm sorry, Bear, but it's a topic I've been trying to clear out of my head. Under the circumstances, I'm sure you can understand."

Chagrined, Haskell nodded. "I can. There it goes again — another flare-up of my hoof-in-mouth disease." He sipped his whiskey and drew on the Indian Kid, his shame making him look around the room instead of at the man he'd obviously offended. He was surprised that when he finally did manage to slide his gaze back to the sheriff, Lockhart was sitting back in his chair, sort of slumped down and grinning across the table at him, his brown eyes bright with a boyish delight.

"You, on the other hand, are right up her alley — age-wise, I'm talking."

It took a moment for Haskell to realize that Lockhart had returned to the topic they'd been on before Bear had tried to turn the conversation to something darker. Since Lockhart seemed to be having so much fun, Haskell decided to play along. "How old is she, anyway?"

"Twenty-six, I believe. I'm not entirely sure. Miss Monique is rather private, rarely offers any personal information about herself. All I know is that her father had been in banking back east but something bad happened. I think he must have lost everything and thus made it necessary for Monique to provide for herself."

Lockhart arched an amused brow as he raised his glass once more to his lips. "Twenty-six, though . . . now, that's only a few years younger than you, young man."

Haskell grinned around the Indian Kid he was chomping on, in one side of his mouth. "So, what are you saying, Con? You want to set me up? I can't say as you'd have to bend my arm too hard. Then, again, what's the point?"

"What do you mean — what's the point? Even though your journey here was pointless, you can't very well turn around and take the next train home. You're going to have to put on a good show for Henry Dade — stay at least to the end of the week. Why not spend a little of that time romancing my daughter's governess?"

Haskell chuckled. "Why are you so eager to see your governess romanced, Con?"

"The woman's . . . well . . . she's so awfully serious. I think she needs to let her hair down a bit. I just don't think it's natural for a girl of her fairly young age not to mingle at least a little now and then with the opposite sex. I've told her as much . . . as much as I've been able to tell her anything, since she doesn't indulge in much personal chatter. I even told her I'd get Judith out of her way, but" — Lockhart bunched his lips and shook his head — "she seemed to want nothing to do with the topic of conversation. I do, however, think it would do her good . . . make her a little more cheerful, if you will . . . if she could go out and get her ashes good an' hauled by the right *hombre*!"

Lockhart threw his head back again and laughed.

Haskell laughed, as well. Then he said, "What if your governess were to go off and get married on you, Con? What would happen, then? It looks to me like Miss Sylvie is pretty attached to her."

"Well, I wouldn't have to worry about that if you sparked her — now, would I?" Lockhart arched both brows and widened his mouth in a wolf's grin "The roguish deputy U.S. marshal who lets no grass grow under his feet . . . ?"

"You got a point, Con. You got a point there — I admit it."

"What do you say, then?" Lockhart mashed the stub of his cigar out in the ashtray and squinted through the smoke billowing between him and Haskell. "Come over to supper tonight? I'll have Judith slow-cook a roast. She's not much of a cook, against her own opinion, but she can cook a roast well enough — if she lets Monique help in the kitchen, which is rare. Judith sees the kitchen as strictly her own domain . . . unfortunately."

He grinned enticingly.

"I'm not sure I'm not afraid of Judith," Bear said.

"Oh, you have every reason to be afraid of

Judith. But I'll trim her teeth and keep one of her ankles chained to the table. Then you'll only have to put up with the snapping and snarling." Lockhart winked. "Maybe you and Miss Monique can go out for a walk in the starlight after supper. Just what the girl needs."

"Hell, it's just what I need." Haskell chuckled, feeling a warming in his loins as he imagined what her hand would feel like in his.

"Say six o'clock?"

"Six o'clock it is."

"Drink to it." Lockhart leaned over the table to refill Haskell's shot glass.

CHAPTER 10

Jamie Lockhart felt the explosion building again quickly, and managed to roll onto his side, lower his head, and direct the spewings from his tumultuous bowels into the porcelain pot on the floor beside the bed. The bucket was already half full with such detritus, which had racked him sporadically since dawn.

The convulsions were growing less and less frequent now as the sun kited high in the window to Lockhart's left, beyond ragged curtains shrouding dirty glass streaked with bird droppings.

"Christ," he wheezed.

Lockhart ran his bare forearm across his mouth. He saw a half-empty bottle on the table beside the bed, and grabbed it. It stood beside another, empty, bottle, which had been the first bottle he'd consumed last night here at Evangeline's saloon/mercantile.

He accidentally knocked the second bottle onto the floor as he lifted the half-empty one to his mouth and took a healthy pull. The empty bottle struck the floorboards with a thud and rolled, making a hollow sound before resting up against the wall. Lockhart did not swallow the whiskey but merely swished it around in his mouth before spitting it into the bucket, trying to clear out the sour, dead taste on his tongue.

Footsteps sounded on the stairs. They were abnormally loud to Lockhart's tender ears. Each step resounded around inside his alcohol-battered brain like a hammer whacking an exposed nerve.

They grew louder. Someone was coming down the hall.

Lockhart looked at the Remington revolver bristling from the holster resting on the table near the bottle but resisted the urge to reach for it. In his condition, he probably wouldn't be very accurate with the weapon even if he needed it, which he likely didn't.

He was safe here. Probably as safe here as anywhere except Mexico, which is where he hoped the prison posse was looking for him. He hoped they were at least looking for signs of him having crossed the border. He'd taken care to cover his tracks thoroughly when he'd ridden away from the prison, heading northeast toward Julesburg. He'd known how important it was to do so. Not only would he not go back to Hell Hole, but he would not be swayed from his current endeavor.

The bedroom door opened. Evangeline looked in, wide-eyed.

"Are you all right, Jamie?"

Lockhart looked at her. She stood in the doorway dressed in a loose flannel shirt and blue denims. She wore no shoes or socks. The tails of the shirt hung down her shapely thighs. Her breasts pushed out the shirt in two enticing, round mounds. She wore her sandy hair down. She'd brushed it recently and thoroughly; it shone like liquid gold in the harsh light from the windows. She was still holding the tortoiseshell brush in her hand.

Evangeline followed his glance to her breasts, then flushed slightly. She was not a beautiful girl. Some might not even call her pretty. Her features were a little raw, her nose a little too doughy, chin too imperfectly defined. She had a very small mole to the outside of her right, hazel eye.

Her body wasn't perfect, either, but it was fine. He remembered how she'd writhed beneath him and rocked away on top of him only a few hours ago — as though she'd been as desperate for such a coupling as he'd been — and he felt the old stirring down between his legs again.

"Christ, go away," Lockhart growled. "You look too damn good, standin' there."

He grinned to show he hadn't meant it.

Evangeline's mouth quirked a brief smile. Slowly, she came into the room, climbed onto the bed, and curled a leg beneath her. She leaned forward and smoothed a shock of Lockhart's hair away from his forehead. "How you feelin'? Any better?"

"Remind me not to go downin' a bottle and a half of whiskey after I've spent the last ten years in the pen."

Evangeline giggled and brushed her nose against his. "Okay, I'll do that."

He caught her staring into his eyes again in that weird way she'd done last night. "What is it?" he asked.

"What's what?"

"That way you're lookin' at me."

"I don't know what you mean."

As she looked away, Lockhart frowned. "Why did you run from me yesterday, when you saw me comin'?"

"I didn't know it was you comin', Jamie. How would I have known?"

"Yeah, but when I got closer. I could see

your face, so you must've seen mine. Then you screamed and ran inside. Why?"

"Oh, that." Evangeline looked down at her hands entwined in her lap. "I guess I was . . . afraid."

"Afraid of me?"

She nodded. "I wasn't sure how it would be — seein' you again."

Lockhart sat up a little, wincing at the pain in his head. He eased himself back against the brass headboard. "Wait a minute — you didn't know I was gettin' out, did you?"

"Oh, no. Of course not. I couldn't have been more surprised to see you. And pleased, of course. You know how I've always felt about you, Jamie. But . . . then I saw that look in your eye." Evangeline hiked a shoulder, a bit sheepishly. "Sort of a goatish look, I suppose you'd call it."

"Goatish" Lockhart ran a hand down his face and chuckled. "Yeah. I don't doubt it a bit."

"I don't blame you. After ten years, an' all. You know . . . without . . ."

"Yeah. Believe me. I know. I gotta admit, when I saw you I went a little wild." Lockhart reached for her arm and started to pull her down toward him but stopped and stared at the inside of her arm. It was mottled blue and red. "Did I do that?"

He grabbed her other hand, then turned it.

"Ow," she said.

There were even more bruises on the inside of that arm.

Lockhart leaned forward, sliding her hair back away from her neck. More bruising.

"Christ. It's just that you . . . you were the first woman I'd seen in ten years."

"It's all right," she said, looking directly at him now. "It doesn't hurt much this morning."

"I'm sorry, Evangeline." Lockhart turned and dropped his feet over the side of the bed, sitting on the edge of it. "I probably shouldn't have come here." He glanced over his shoulder at her. "I didn't come here for that. I mean, when I saw you, I went a little crazy and couldn't think of anything else. After ten years without a woman . . . But, I came here because I remembered how it was with us, before . . . before . . . you know . . ."

Evangeline scuttled closer to him, placing her hand on his back. "I'm glad you came. I'm really glad you came here, Jamie. You can stay as long as you want."

"It could be dangerous."

"I don't care. How long will you stay? I

mean, you can stay as long as you want. Forever . . ." She gave a sheepish hike of her shoulder and glanced at him sidelong.

Lockhart shook his head.

"Why?" she asked. "Why did you come back, Jamie?" Of course, she knew why. In fact, she'd bet ten thousand dollars that this is exactly where he'd come. But she wanted to hear the reason from his own mouth. She didn't want him to know that she was involved, however. She wanted him to believe that what he was sure to do would be his own idea, uncorrupted by anyone else's influence.

He turned his head forward to study the plain pine-board wall on which hung an oval tintype of Evangeline and her father, Zach Lockhart. He recognized the furnishings around their posed figures as belonging to the only photographer in Julesburg.

"I don't know why I came." It was a lie. He had come back to kill his father. He'd been in such a hurry, having yearned to do it for such a long time. But he suddenly didn't feel in such a hurry anymore. He was going to take his time. He had a few ghosts — one, in particular — he had to get right with first. And even then he was going to take his time. He wasn't going to make it easy on Con Lockhart.

He turned to Evangeline once more, frowning. "Do you have any idea who busted me out of there? Who put McGeehy up to helping?"

"Who's McGeehy?"

"Right." He nodded. "How would you know McGeehy? Whoever busted me out had offered the son of a bitch ten thousand dollars. They staked two horses across the wash — one for me." He wouldn't tell her about how he'd killed the guard. "Both horses were fully rigged. There was a full set of clothes in the saddlebags."

He looked at the Remington, then pulled it from the holster with a little snick of metal against leather. "This gun. And a Winchester. They'd even thought to wrap the hooves of both horses with burlap, so I couldn't be followed so easy."

Pensively, he thumbed the hammer back to full cock and then, holding it, squeezed the trigger and eased the hammer benignly against the firing pin.

"Why, do you suppose?" he said just above a whisper, half to himself. "Why?" He turned to her, studying her closely.

"Why ask why?" Evangeline pressed her cheek to his back, just below his neck. He could feel the swells of her breasts against him. She wasn't wearing anything under her shirt. She placed her hands on his shoulders. She felt warm and supple and very female against him. "Now you're out. You're free. If you're careful, you'll never have to go back."

"Oh, I won't go back." Lockhart flicked open the Remington's loading gate and slowly turned the cylinder, hearing the resolute clicks of the wheel. All six cylinders showed brass.

"What are you going to do, Jamie?"

"I don't know."

"Are you going to kill him?"

Lockhart started to open his mouth to speak but closed it again. He didn't want to tell her his intentions. He supposed he was just being superstitious, but he didn't want to jinx himself. Besides, she didn't need to know.

He reholstered the Remington, then lay back again on the bed. He drew her head down to his bare chest. "What happened to your pa? Uncle Zach. You said he was gone. When? How?"

Her voice grew thick with emotion. It quivered as she said, "This spring. Last winter, the doc said he had a stroke. He was bound to the house at first. He drank and cursed his luck, his fate. Then another stroke bound him to his bed. I cared for him for two long months like that. Then he died. I buried him in the soldiers' cemetery. He wasn't a soldier, but they don't mind, I don't think. At least, I haven't heard any stirrings."

"Stirrings?"

She nodded her head on his chest. "When they're upset about something, I hear them sometimes. They'll prowl around. They'll throw tumbleweeds or they'll prowl the house, knocking pots and pans around. They moved the privy off its hole once." She snickered softly. "Pranksters. When they're upset, the wild cats will disappear until everything is right again. With the soldiers, I mean. Then the cats return. Gosh, I wonder where they go."

Lockhart looked at her. Her face was turned away. He placed his hand on her head. "Evangeline, have you been alone here since your father died?"

She nodded again. "It's okay, though," she said. "I reckon you know a thing or two about bein' alone — don't you, Jamie? But you're here now. That's all that matters."

She moved her head. He felt her warm lips against his belly.

A long, tender kiss.

Hours later, near sunset, Lockhart rode out

of the old draw he remembered so well, stopped his claybank gelding in a copse of cedars and scattered pines, and dismounted. Leading the horse, he walked slowly forward through the trees, trying to make as little noise as possible.

At the edge of the trees, he shoved a branch aside and peered into the yard of a small ranch, scowling.

The ranch's main house was a little adobe *casa* of one and a half stories, with a falling-down front porch that hadn't been painted in years. Weeds had grown up around it. Lockhart remembered the yard as being packed hard by the feet of cattle and horses, but now prickly pear had moved in.

The stable and corral sat off to the left. The gate had fallen and now lay in pieces. Pigweed and bunchgrass had grown up inside the corral. Horses hadn't milled there in years.

It appeared that no one had lived in the house in years, either. It showed no more signs of habitation than the rest of the yard.

Where had they gone . . . ?

Lockhart mounted up and rode into the yard, scowling incredulously as he looked around. He'd expected to find Lucia's family here and, thus, the need to sneak around behind the place in order to visit her grave, in the de Larra family plot.

Obviously, sneaking around was no longer necessary.

He rode around to the rear east side of the house and stared at a boarded-up window. It had been the window of Lucia's room. He'd come here several times, tapped lightly on the window with his fingers, and then walked out into the buttes east of the shack. He'd waited for a time, sometimes up to a half hour. She'd never disappointed him. She'd always come, sandals clicking softly against the soles of her brown feet.

She didn't say anything at first. She just walked up to him, her hair pulled back, a *serape* drawn about her shoulders. She placed her smooth hand on his cheek and whispered, *"Mi amor."*

"Lucia!"

"Shhh. Keep your voice down, foolish *gringo* boy," she admonished him, placing two cool fingers over his lips and glancing toward the house where her family — mother and father and younger brother, Ramon — were likely sleeping in their beds. "This is foolish. We have to stop this, Jamie."

He took her wrist in his hand, squeezing gently. "You know I can't."

"We must!"

"Shhh. Keep your voice down, foolish *se-*

135

ñorita." He smiled, stepping forward to kiss her.

She stepped back. "No."

"Yes."

"I am getting married, Jamie. You know that."

"You can't. You can't marry him, Lucia. He doesn't love you. He just wants to possess you like he possesses everyone, every-*thing* else. I *love* you!"

"He does love me. He told me." She paused, glancing down with a pensive air. "Besides . . ."

"Look, I know why you feel you have to marry him. He's promised to help your family. That's no reason to marry a man you don't love when the man you really love is his son!"

Lucia stared up at him, the moon over her left shoulder gilding her left cheek, glinting in her hair. Her eyes were dark, her brows furled. "I love him, Jamie."

"Do you really?"

"Yes."

Jamie placed his hand against her cheek, then slid it slowly back through her hair. "Does he touch you like I touch you?"

"Yes, he does."

He slid his hand down against her neck. "Do you feel the same when he touches you as when I touch you?"

Looking down, she nodded.

Jamie placed two fingers beneath her chin, lifted her mouth to his, and leaned toward her. "Do you feel the same when he kisses you as when I kiss you?"

He pressed his lips against hers. She held hers together. He managed to work them loose with his own, tasting the moistness within. He drew his face away from hers and whispered, "Do you?"

She looked up at him. Suddenly her dark eyes were silvery with tears.

He slid his hands up inside her *serape,* instantly feeling the warm smoothness of her skin. She wore nothing beneath it. He slid his hands upward until he was cupping her breasts in his hands. Her nipples pebbled against his fingers. Her breasts swelled. She gave a soft cry of pleasure.

"Oh, Jamie."

He kissed her again while he massaged her breasts. Finally he picked her light body up in his arms and, kneeling, gentled her to the ground. Just as she wasn't wearing anything under the serape, she wasn't wearing anything south of it, either. Her legs were bare.

"Hurry," Lucia urged, stretching her arms toward him while he stood and unbuckled his pants. "Hurry, Jamie. Please, hurry. I've been waiting for you, my love!"

When he had his pants down to his ankles, his hard-on swaying like a branch in the wind, he sat down beside her, lay back, and drew her onto him. She straddled him, reached down, grabbed his mast in her hand, licked her other hand, and smeared the spittle onto him.

Finally, her breath quickening, she lowered herself down on his cock, groaning softly, holding up her *poncho* so he could knead her breasts while she rose and fell atop his thighs, impaled on his staff.

They came together, quivering, trying for all they were worth not to scream out with their crested passion.

His heart slowing gradually, Jamie rested his head back against the ground.

Lucia sobbed. She lowered her head to his chest. He could feel her tears through his shirt. "Oh, Jamie!" she breathed, and convulsed with sorrow.

CHAPTER 11

Jamie brushed a tear from his cheek with his fist and closed his eyes as though to retain the memory in his vision, to hold onto the sweetness of a few fleeting moments of his past.

But they were gone just as the window before him — the window of her room in her family's shack — was gone. There were only the weathered gray planks batted over it. In the gap between two of the planks, a black widow spider scuttled slowly, spinning a web. The delicate web was buffeted by the dry breeze rising now at dusk.

"Lucia," he heard himself mutter in a voice thick with grief.

He heeled the horse away from the shack and looked to the west. The sun was just then sinking behind the hills, trees and rocks standing in silhouette against the large, orange ball.

A little cemetery stood on a broad knoll

beyond the yard. One twisted cedar stood atop the knoll. Scattered beneath the cedar were several leaning wooden crosses — all black against the orange-red ball of the descending sun.

Lockhart booted the clay across the yard. He rode between the corral and a dilapidated hay barn and up the hill. Halfway to the top, he stepped out of the saddle and dropped the reins. The horse snorted incredulously. Absently, studying the graves beyond, Lockhart ran his hand down the clay's sleek snout, then walked slowly up the knoll toward the cedar.

He moved past the half-dozen graves marked with crumbling wooden crosses to the one marked with a large, upright, granite stone. It was a virtual monument. Already the chiseled markings were time-worn, faded. Lockhart had to bend down and lean forward to make them out.

Lucia Mariana de Larra
1856–1874
El Amor Nunca Termina

"Love never ends."
Lockhart brushed his gloved hand across the chiseled words, then slid his hand away in distaste. His father had likely paid for the

stone, which meant he had ordered those words chiseled into it. His words.

His lies.

Jamie Lockhart hadn't seen the stone until now. When his father had found him kneeling with Lucia's body in the old shack near Arapaho Creek and accused him of her murder, Jamie had run. He hadn't even tried to explain himself, for he'd seen the cold fury in his father's eyes. He knew from past experience there was no reasoning with that look in Con Lockhart's eyes.

Now, here she was after all these years.

Lucia.

Lying here beneath this stone in the cold darkness. What marked her grave was a lie. A lie in the form of a monument to try to prove to the world that Con Lockhart had still loved her despite her betrayal — her love for his son. And that he hadn't killed her. Couldn't have killed her. That his son, her lover, had killed her.

Lockhart gritted his teeth. He palmed the Remington. "Goddamn you to hell, you murdering bastard!"

Lockhart fired the six-shooter into the monument. Chips blew from the rock. He fired until the hammer clicked onto the firing pin. Slowly, he lowered the smoking pistol.

"Liar," he repeated. "Goddamn liar! *Son of a bitch of a mother-fucking liar!*"

Heavily, he stepped back, stumbled, and fell onto his butt. He sat there facing the monument and the grave.

He looked around. He remembered riding through the de Larra family cemetery long ago, when he'd been on his way to summon Lucia from the shack. There'd been three graves here then. He'd assumed they'd been the graves of Lucia's grandparents, who'd established the small ranch long ago, and the grave of the brother Lucia had lost when the child was barely a year old.

Now there were two more graves. They were marked by only the crude wooden crosses leaning toward the southeast from the heads of two rocky mounds.

Lucia's parents, most likely. Dead from grief?

Her younger brother must have moved on after they'd died, not wanting to live here with the bitter memories, with the ghosts of his murdered sister and grief-haunted parents.

Lockhart reloaded the Remington, then slid it into its holster strapped to his right thigh. He secured the keeper thong over the hammer. A breeze gusted, blowing his hat off his head. He caught it tumbling down his shoulder, and studied it.

A cream Stetson. Similar to the one he used to wear. The same broad brim and Texas crease. He looked at the clothes he wore — the dark-blue wool work shirt, the knotted red neckerchief, the crisp blue denims. The boots were Justin's. Hand-sewn, expensive. Like the rest of his attire, the boots were similar to those he'd worn before he'd gone into Trinidad Pen.

Whoever had freed him had known him before he'd gone into Trinidad.

Who were they?

Why had they wanted him set free?

Did they know he was innocent of the crime he'd been convicted of and were just doing a good deed? Or did they know that the first thing he would do when he was out of the pen was to kill his father?

Surely, Con Lockhart had plenty of enemies. Few men who'd been lawmen for as long as the elder Lockhart had didn't have bitter antagonists. A man like Con Lockhart — powerful, brutal, arrogant — would have even more men hungry to see him kicked out with a cold shovel.

Was Jamie Lockhart merely a pawn in someone else's game?

If he was, so be it. The game was his now.

"So be it," he said aloud now as he heaved

143

himself to his feet. "So be it!"

He laughed, hearing the insanity in the words but not caring.

Who wouldn't be insane after spending ten long years in Trinidad, every minute anticipating finally being free so he could kill his father?

Jamie looked around in the gathering darkness. The sun was down now, scalloped black clouds trailing away in a fading watercolor sky toward a blood-red horizon.

He looked around as though his benefactor were here somewhere, shadowing him.

"Whoever you are," Lockhart said, "I'm about to show you just how much I appreciate what you did."

He tipped his head back, curved his hands around his mouth, and bellowed, *"Thank you!"*

He tipped his head farther back, laughing.

He stopped laughing when he heard the thud of distant hooves.

He scowled off toward the southwest. That was where the sounds were coming from. They drifted away quickly, fading to silence.

Lockhart stared in the darkness. Inexplicably, cold fingers of dread walked across the back of his neck. He shuddered.

What the hell . . . ?

Who'd been out there?

Ignoring his lingering sense of trepidation, he walked over to his horse, grabbed the reins, and looked around to get his bearings. He mounted up and rode toward Julesburg. As he did, he put everything else out of his mind except his one, sole, bloody purpose.

Bear Haskell turned his rented buckskin gelding off the north side of the eastern trail out of Julesburg, and reined the horse to a stop.

He wanted to get a look at Con Lockhart's house, since he'd never been out here before, less than a quarter-mile outside of town. Here Lockhart resided, though his sprawling ranch lay in the bluffs and valleys north of the South Platte River, roughly fifteen miles from Julesburg.

Lockhart had been a rancher before he'd become a lawman, but in the years after becoming sheriff, he'd come to rely on a manager, several foremen, and a couple dozen waddies to run his ranch while he dwelled closer to town, making it easier for him to perform his lawman's duties out of the Sedgwick County Courthouse. Haskell had always figured a man's house reflected the man, that it said a lot about him, but now he was beginning to question his theory.

Lockhart's house sat on a low knoll about a hundred yards off the main trail. It was not the sprawling lodge house Haskell had expected. It was, indeed, quite modest — a two-story structure with leanings toward the Victorian but with little of the Victorians' ostentation.

Without the broad front porch wrapping around at least three sides, it would resemble nothing much more than a large square box to the left, with a mansard roof, and a long, low rectangular box to the right. Clapboards had been nailed to the house's wood framing.

A white picket fence surrounded the place, and there were a few plantings here and there, but overall the yard was nearly as plain as the house. Three or four large cottonwoods stood to each side and to the rear, near a stable and buggy shed, and they offered some relief from the vast, open prairie and overarching bowl of sky engulfing the place.

Haskell had figured that a prevailing businessman and commanding county sheriff, one of the most powerful men in all of Colorado, let alone in Sedgwick County, would live against a picturesque rimrock wall in a veritable castle surrounded by transplanted trees and irrigated gardens, with outbuildings here and there housing his blooded horses and his hired help.

So far, it appeared the federal lawman had been wrong.

Maybe Lockhart really was the simple stockman he'd always professed to be, or maybe he just didn't want to stick out, out here where men with money were vastly outnumbered by those without. He was a politician as much as a lawman, after all. As a politician, he had to campaign for reelection every four years, just like presidents and judges. High-living politicians weren't so easily kept in the good graces of the unwashed masses upon whose votes they depended.

Haskell booted the buckskin on up the two-track drive, which curved gently toward the house on the right and whose windows were lit against the approach of sunset.

He pulled up to the two simple wooden hitch racks that stood on either side of the picket fence. Lockhart had had plenty of visitors here over the years. Both racks were worn down to the size of small branches in some places, from all the reins that had been tied there. There were deep indentations in the ground around the hitch racks, where buggies and wagons had been parked.

Haskell dismounted, looped the reins over the tie rail, opened the picket fence, and strolled along the gravel path to the front porch. As he mounted the porch, the front door opened, revealing a stocky figure standing inside the screen door and wearing a knotted red bandanna.

The figure was concealed by the dimness inside the house, but it appeared to be wearing pants, a fact seemingly incongruous with the raspy but definitely female voice that said a moment later, "Bear Haskell, U.S. marshal. Big, tall son of a bitch with shoulders like a plow horse and hands like pig roasts."

The accent was definitely Oklahoma.

Haskell, who'd stopped dead in his tracks atop the porch, looked at his open left hand.

"I'll be damned," he said. "I reckon they do look like pigs . . . in a certain ray of light."

"Get over here, you big rascal." The screen door opened and the stocky woman, clad in men's shirt and pants, came out with her chin dipped coyly toward her chest, which was about the only thing besides her voice that was not manly about her. If Haskell's hands were the size of pig roasts, then this woman's breasts were the size of two prize-winning pumpkins.

She wrapped her arms around Haskell's waist and hugged him as though he was her long-lost son come home to her so long after the war. Haskell didn't know what else to do, so he hugged her in kind.

"Miss Judith, the pleasure is all mine."

She stepped back and looked up at him in shock. "You know my name!"

"Of course. Con told me all about you."

"He did, did he?" She posed angrily, planting a liver-spotted fist on her hip. "Well, don't you believe all of it. I ain't half the bitch he prob'ly told you I was!"

"I wish I would have known that, gall-dangit," Haskell said, extending a handful of garden daisies and black-eyed Susans toward the mannish, stout-hipped, full-busted woman, whose brown hair, which she wore in a fashionably short coiffure, likely came from a bottle. "I stopped by Mrs. Peterson's hothouse on Third Avenue for these little beauties just in case he was tellin' the truth. Now, I wish I woulda saved my jingle!"

"Oh, how lovely!" Judith took the flowers with delight. "She does have the best flowers in town. She says her secret is sheep dip." She sniffed. "Sure enough, sheep dip. But the bright colors make up for the stench." She tittered her girlish laugh, holding the flowers in one hand and splaying the fingers of her other hand against her bosom.

Footsteps sounded, echoing, and Con Lockhart stepped out of the shadows behind Judith to poke his head out the screen door. "Ah, I seen you've found my sister, Bear. Er . . . she found you. Leave it to Judith to go hunting the biggest man in Julesburg. Be careful of her. She likes big men. The bigger, the better. Her husband was half again taller than you."

"Oh, you go on, Con!" Judith scolded without heat. "He was not. In fact, I think Bear here — how appropriately you were named, darlin'! — is a full head taller than my dearly departed Lon. Lon was orphaned as a child and lived for a time with the Osage, don't ya know, until the good Reverend and Missus Amelia Brown took him in and raised him up a proper Christian. He, too, became a minister, Lon did. Anyway, let me go in and find a vase for these flowers. I'll set them on tonight's supper table. They'll add some badly needed color. Why don't you two go in and listen to Miss Sylvie play the piano? She does so like an audience. I believe it's something by that Italian she likes so much."

To Bear, Judith added in a mock-furtive

whisper behind a raised hand, "I don't even try to say his name, because Sylvie gets so mad when I mispronounce it. The child thinks I'm a literal barbarian!"

Laughing, Judith tramped back inside and down the hall, disappearing through an open doorway.

"Ain't she a caution?" Con said.

"I like her."

"She'll like you as long as you don't take the lord's name in vain. We were raised by the Golden Rule, spanked with the Bible, and she married a preacher. You can say all the 'fucks' and 'shits' and 'sonso'bitches' you want." Lockhart wagged a mock-admonishing finger. "Just don't say any 'goddamns' or you might just get shown the door."

Haskell laughed. "Good to know."

"Good to see you again, my friend." Stepping out onto the porch, Con extended his hand, which Bear shook. "Did you land a good room in town?"

"The McGregor House. As good as Henry Dade will allow. That old bastard's tighter'n the bark on a tree."

Lockhart laughed, then stepped to the porch rail, staring back toward Julesburg, the roofs of which the last salmon light was touching. Smoke from cookfires hung like fog.

"No sign of him, I take it?"

"What's that?" Haskell asked.

"My son." Lockhart emphasized "son" as though it were a bad piece of meat he was expectorating.

"I thought you didn't think he'd head this way," Bear said, hooking his thumbs behind his suspenders and studying the older man quizzically.

Lockhart continued to stare over the prairie toward Julesburg and the river skirting its southern edge. "Oh . . . you never know. I suppose there's a chance he might head this way. Doubtful. But I am hopeful. I ran him down once." He turned his sly, canny gaze toward Haskell. "I reckon I could run him down again."

"Sounds to me like you wouldn't mind the chance."

"Can't say as I would. After what that boy did. To my love. To me. To my family and my career."

"Career?"

"All that was quite a scandal. My own son meeting my . . . betrothed . . . on the side. Of course, it became well known after he killed her." Lockhart lowered his gaze and shook his head. "Killed her in such brutal fashion. Beat her . . . beat her with an axe handle."

He shook his head again.

"Sounds to me like you miss her somethin' awful, Con. Like you might still love her."

"She was special. I took it hard, what she did. What they did together. I loved her, and I thought she loved me as much. She said she did. I still think she did. I think he confused her somehow. Used her to get back at me. He was a good-looking boy. And he was quite the talker. Also . . ." The sheriff let his voice trail off as he glanced once more toward Julesburg.

"Also . . . ?" Bear gently prodded.

"Also, he had it in for me. He'd had it in for me for years."

"Why?"

Lockhart continued to stare toward Julesburg. The light was fast leaving the sky, the gray and brown smudge of the town growing darker by the second.

Finally, Con shook his head again. "No. I don't want to talk about it. It's just too hard. I'm sure you can understand, Bear." He placed his hand on the federal lawman's back and ushered him toward the door. "Come. Let's give my daughter the audience she's been waiting for. And I'm quite certain you wouldn't mind seeing Miss Monique Bataille again, as well."

He gave a mischievous wink.

"Can't say as I would," Haskell said, stepping through the screen door that his host held open for him. His heart hiccupped with anticipation. "Nope, not one bit."

CHAPTER 12

As Haskell was ushered by Con Lockhart into the parlor dominated by a snow-white baby grand piano, Sylvie stopped playing and, her face brightening like a newly risen sun, clapped her hands together three quick times. "Marshal Haskell! Bear! Come! Do enjoy!"

She gestured toward a short leather sofa angled in front of the piano. Between the piano and the sofa was a low table on which a cigar smoldered in a glass ashtray. A snifter of brandy as well as a stout, cut-glass decanter sat on the table near the cigar.

As Haskell and Lockhart moved into the room, Sylvie continued playing very softly but adeptly — to Bear Haskell's unschooled ears, anyway — what sounded like a finely measured piece from the classical past. His sisters back home in Pennsylvania, before he'd joined the Army of the Potomac, had played something similar but with not nearly the grace. As Haskell walked over to the couch, his eyes met those of Monique Bataille, who sat behind the piano with Sylvie, on the same bench, slowly turning the pages of the music from which the precocious young blonde was playing.

Haskell held the young woman's gaze a tad too long. Sylvie must have been playing down near the end of the page, for the blonde gave her governess a fleeting but crisp look of impatient condescension and scolding, which Monique answered by quickly flipping the page and flushing with embarrassment.

She glanced once more at Haskell, then returned her gaze to the music, nodding her head to the rhythm of her charge's recital.

Lockhart settled into the sofa beside Haskell and held up the snifter. Haskell nodded. Lockhart filled a tumbler and slid it over to him. Then both men settled back into the couch, sipping their brandies, Lockhart smoking and listening to Sylvie play.

The child was in her element now, Haskell saw. She lived for an audience and was pleased as punch to be able to show off for a new listener. For his part, Haskell wanted like hell to give her his full attention as well as his appreciation, but it was not his kind of music and he found his attention, as well as his gaze, wandering to the dark-eyed, exotic countenance of the young woman slowly but steadily turning Sylvie's pages.

Good lord, had he ever seen a more uncannily beautiful creature?

She was dressed now in dark-blue velvet, gold buttons trailing down from the gown's bodice, between full, inviting breasts. The tops of those breasts moved faintly whenever Monique Bataille leaned forward to flip a page, and Haskell found himself imagining cupping both orbs in his hands, burying his nose deep between them, and sniffing.

He glanced up from the woman's bodice to see the woman herself casting a quick, sharp-eyed glance. Shit! She'd caught him ogling her. But as she returned her gaze to the music before her, Haskell thought he saw a smile pluck fleetingly and almost imperceptibly at her mouth.

Or was it just his imagination?

Sylvie played three rather long songs before Judith bellowed from the kitchen, "Come and get it — it ain't gettin' any hotter!"

Sylvie stopped playing the song she'd just started to look over the music at Haskell and say with a twinkle in her young blue eyes, "That is not how I like to have one of my recitals punctuated — by Aunt Judith bellowing like a chuck-wagon cook — but at least she didn't hammer away on her iron triangle like she often does, and the succulence of her roasts do so much make up for her lack of etiquette."

She shifted her gaze to Con. "Wouldn't you agree, Poppa?"

Lockhart threw his head back, laughing and clapping in delight as he said, "Sylvie, girl, I don't know half of what you're saying most of the time, but by god if you don't sound and look good sayin' it? Eh, Bear?"

Clapping politely, Haskell said, "I didn't know the girl was adopted, Con. You never told me."

To which Con threw his head back again, and laughed harder.

Sober-faced, Monique Bataille rose from the bench, walked to the door, and, the pleats of the long, blue gown swishing about her legs, stopped to allow her charge to leave the room ahead of her. She turned her head as though to cast a glance back over her bare right shoulder at their guest but then seemed to think better of it.

She turned her head forward, cast her dark-eyed gaze to the floor, and followed Sylvie into the hall and away.

Con Lockhart had been right about his

sister's culinary skills. The roast was juicy and tender and spiced just right. There was also a dark, rich gravy to go over the potatoes, which had been cooked with the roast along with a goodly portion of onions and wild asparagus that Judith had foraged herself.

They ate in a dining room as plainly, unpretentiously furnished as the rest of the house. It had a sideboard and a large oil painting, done by Judith, of cows in a pasture. The table was covered in oilcloth. The plates and even some of the wine glasses were chipped. There were two doors — one to the kitchen, one to the hall.

Judith sat at the end of the table nearest the kitchen. There being no maid, she did all the serving. In fact, just as Monique had mentioned, the kitchen appeared Judith's domain and her domain alone. Neither Sylvie nor Monique Bataille, it appeared, were required — or maybe "allowed" was a better word — to help with the food. They were never asked, and they seemed to know not to offer.

The conversation was dominated by young Sylvie, but with promptings from her obviously adoring aunt and father. The girl held court, as it were, about her travels to both coasts to meet with some of the best music and art tutors in the country. She spoke of her cultivated experiences with the air of a spoiled but charming princess.

For her part, Monique Bataille, seated to Sylvie's right, said not one word through the entire meal. She seemed to automatically defer all attention to her charge, smiling when Sylvie told something amusing, frowning when she mentioned something less so.

At the end of the meal, Judith served coffee from a big speckled pot with a scorched bottom, which she sat on a wooden trivet on the table center. She also served pie with generous dollops of freshly whipped cream, cursorily apologizing for the peaches in the pie being dried.

"Nothing wrong with a dried peach pie," Haskell said, dropping his fork onto his empty plate and smiling at Judith, sitting to his right, "especially when it's baked as expertly as that one there. I don't ever recollect a crust so tender and flavorful."

"Pshaw!" Judith said, dipping her chin and batting her eyes, blushing. "You're far too generous, you charming man. That said, I thank you kindly. Why don't you and Con adjourn to the parlor? I'm sure you have some business to discuss . . . whatever the business is that has brought you here,

Marshal Haskell . . . ?"

Obviously, Lockhart hadn't told her about Jamie. Haskell wasn't about to spoil the surprise.

"Oh, I think we've wrung that rag plum dry." Haskell slid his gaze to Monique Bataille and worked up his courage to say, "I, uh . . . I was thinkin' that perhaps Miss Bataille and I could get a bit of air?"

Judith sat back as though in shock and looked at the governess, who averted her gaze to her half-eaten slice of pie. "Oh, you did . . ."

Sylvie snickered. "It's no surprise. He's smitten, Aunt Judith. Haven't you seen the way he hasn't been able to keep his eyes off Monique all evening?" With gentle chiding, she looked at Bear and added, "I wonder if he heard a single note of what I played earlier . . ."

"Sylvie, please," Monique said gently.

"Yes, Sylvie, hold your tongue," Con Lockhart said from his end of the table, to Haskell's right. "I think it's a fine idea — Bear and Monique having a chat out on the porch, it bein' such a lovely night an' all. The two young folks should get to know each other. Monique gets out little enough."

"Oh, good heavens — it's pitch dark out there!" Judith intoned. "Nothing good can

161

happen between a young man and a young woman after the sun goes down. My husband, the pastor, always said so." She narrowed a shrewd eye at Haskell, sliding her vaguely lascivious gaze across his shoulders. "Especially when it involves a young man so . . . so *masculine* and obviously . . . *smitten,* shall we say?"

She glanced at the fully flushed Monique, then threw her head back, laughing. "No, no, no — I don't think such a tryst would be prudent. What kind of an example would we be setting for our dear Sylvie? If you'd like to step out with Miss Bataille, Bear, you may do so in the light of the afternoon. Say, tomorrow . . . or the next day . . . ? I'll serve tea and cinnamon rolls. My rolls are as good as my pie. Sylvie will be happy to play Mister *Chop*-in for you. Light, charming music. You can sit on the porch and listen through the window."

Sylvie rolled her eyes. "It's Show-*pan,* Aunt Judith. How many times do I have to tell you?"

"Oh, whatever those foreigners decide to call themselves!"

"Besides," Sylvie chimed in, "Monique needs to help me with my bath this evening. It is time for my bath, isn't it?" She glanced at a clock on the wall near the kitchen door.

"Yes, it's nearly eight-thirty. Time for my bath, all right!" She slid her self-satisfied smile from Bear to Monique and back again, tittering softly.

"Well, it looks like you've been foiled, old boy," Lockhart said, scowling. "I'm sorry. I did my best, but the women run the coop while the rooster cowers in the shadows." He chuckled into his napkin.

Judith looked sidelong at Bear, and winked. "You devil."

"All right, then," Haskell said, trying not to look as crestfallen as he felt. *What would it take to have a word alone with the Jewish beauty?* To the governess, he said, "Perhaps another time, Miss Bataille?"

She slid a furtive glance toward Sylvie, who studied her critically, then hiked a noncommittal shoulder and said "Perhaps" without fervor.

Sylvie snickered once more, devilishly, and Haskell entertained a fantasy of bending her over his knee and slapping her bottom till it was as red as a smithy's forge.

Sylvie and Monique rose from their chairs. Politely, they each thanked Bear for coming, told him how wonderful it was to make his acquaintance, and then excused themselves, Monique dutifully following her charge out of the dining room. A moment later, Haskell heard the creaking of their footsteps on the stairs overhead.

While Judith cleared the table, Haskell and Lockhart retired to the parlor for a nightcap. Lockhart was obviously tired, and he didn't seem to want to talk any more about his son's escape from the pen. That was fine with Haskell. He didn't feel social anymore, since the only one he would have enjoyed being social with was upstairs, helping the devilish Sylvie with her bath.

Mostly, he felt frustrated in his plight to get to know Monique Bataille better.

He was quick to thank Lockhart for the brandy and the evening, to pinch his hat brim, telling the sheriff he'd let himself out, and to stride to the house's front door. He'd just reached the door in the dark foyer when he heard a creak on the stairs behind him.

He whipped around, instinctively placing his hand over the grips of his holstered Schofield. There she was, lit by the moonlight angling through two windows on either side of the door behind Haskell. Her slight, dark-haired figure was on the stairs, walking slowly down the steps, one hand trailing along the banister.

Haskell stepped forward, reaching the stairs as she stopped two steps up from the bottom, so that her head was even with his.

"Bear . . ." she whispered.

Haskell's heart danced. His knees were warm.

He tried to find words, but they wouldn't come. Instead, without thinking about it, he placed his hands on her arms, drew her to him, and leaned forward, finding her lips awaiting his.

He pressed his mouth gently to hers, then gradually more firmly. Their tongues flicked against each other, hungry but testing.

Haskell groaned.

Monique placed her hands on his arms, gently pushing him away from her.

"Monique," he said. "I . . ."

"No." She shook her head. "It's not possible. You don't understand. She won't allow it." She glanced around cautiously. "If she knew I was here . . . with you . . . there would be trouble."

"I don't understand. You're a woman. I'm a man."

Monique shook her head again. "Don't even try. Just go. Please."

"Can I see you?"

"There's no point." She paused, staring at him, her face both shadowed and lit by the moonlight, which glistened in her hair. "Goodbye."

She started to turn away. Haskell grabbed

165

her again, pulling her to him brusquely. Again, she did not resist but returned his kiss hungrily. He reached up to touch her breast. She gasped as if with an amalgam of both pleasure and horror.

"No," she whispered, pressing her forehead to his. "No," she added more firmly. "Just go. Please. Don't come again."

Monique turned and strode quickly but quietly up the stairs and out of sight.

Haskell listened to the creaks of her movements dwindling on the second floor.

Then, befuddled and frustrated, he let himself out.

He walked outside, crossed the porch, and strode along the path and through the gate. Inwardly shaking his head, thoroughly befuddled, he mounted up and rode back to Julesburg. He was happy when he could hear the off-key pattering of the pianos and the phony laughter of the whores. They were a nice distraction from the frustration and mystery of Monique Bataille, a woman who had stolen his heart when it had so rarely been stolen before.

Especially not before he'd exchanged much more than three words with the gal.

The faint clomping of hooves behind him was a nice distraction, too. Normally they

wouldn't be. But tonight they were.
Someone had followed him into town.

wouldn't be the tonight, he were
Someone had followed him into town.

CHAPTER 13

Haskell had heard the rider following him
since just after he'd left Lockhart's yard and
turned onto the main trail. The man was
cagey. He'd stayed a good ways back, and
he'd kept Haskell's pace, not wanting to get
too close and give himself away.

But he had come too close a time or two.
Bear had heard the faint clomps of the
horse's hooves and, once, the faint jingle of
a bit chain. Bear had stopped twice on his
way into town. Each time the rider had
stopped, as well, but not before continuing
several telltale steps toward Haskell and
making the lawman conclude he was, indeed, being shadowed.

The man behind him wasn't on his trail
by accident.

Haskell rode on into Julesburg, the din of
reveling drinkers and painted ladies growing louder as he approached saloons on
either side of the street, the clamor dwin-

dling as he rode on past. When he reached a side street, he turned sharply left and booted the buckskin into a gallop for a few yards, until the shadows of the dark street had consumed him.

Then he turned the horse back around to face Union Pacific Avenue.

Hugging the shadows along the side street's right side, near a warehouse hulking against the starry sky, he backtracked slowly until he had a good view of the avenue but was still concealed by the darkness, and stopped. He waited, staring straight ahead, waiting for the man who'd been shadowing him to show himself.

He didn't have to wait long.

The man rode into sight from Haskell's right, moving to his left. He was looking around, turning his head slowly but purposefully from left to right and back again. When he turned his head toward where the lawman waited in the darkness, Haskell hunkered low, making himself as small as possible. There'd been no need. He was obviously well concealed from the vantage of Union Pacific Avenue.

The rider rode on.

When he'd just ridden out of sight, Haskell heeled the buckskin back to the corner of the side street and Union Pacific.

Now he could see his shadower dwindling off to the west, still turning his head, looking from right to left. He was a black silhouette against the oil pots burning in front of hotels, brothels, and saloons.

Slowly, Haskell followed the man. He had to know who he was. The shadower could very well be Jamie Lockhart. The killer might have been skulking around the Lockhart house, trying to discern the big visitor's identity. Maybe overhearing the conversation enough to ascertain that Bear was a federal badge-toter, the younger Lockhart had decided to scour him from his trail and leave his father to stand alone against his revenge-hungry son.

Haskell held a good block behind the single rider.

Suddenly, the man stopped his horse and hipped around in his saddle, peering behind him.

Haskell jerked back on the buckskin's reins, and winced.

Fortunately, he'd stopped the horse at a relatively dark place in the main street, between lighted windows. He didn't think he could be seen here, but he wasn't sure. His heartbeat quickened as the man ahead of him held still in his saddle, staring.

Slowly, Haskell slid his hand across his

belly toward the Schofield. He halted the movement when the man ahead of him turned forward and heeled his horse on down the street.

Haskell followed even more slowly than before. He watched as the rider turned his horse to the right and stopped in front of two hitch racks at which at least a dozen saddled horses were tied. Beyond the horses lay two large saloon windows, brightly lit and casting jouncing shadows of the inside revelers out onto the boardwalk fronting the place.

Haskell watched his man step down from his saddle, tie his horse at a rack, glance around once more, and then mount the steps leading to the raised boardwalk fronting the saloon. Now the windows lit him slightly and briefly. He wore a red-checked shirt and a brown holster on his right thigh. That was all that the lawman saw before the man pushed through the batwings and disappeared into the saloon.

Haskell hurried up to the same hitch rack his shadower had tied his horse to. Bear tied the buckskin, then loosened the Schofield in its holster and mounted the boardwalk.

He pushed quickly through the batwings and stepped to one side. The saloon was filled to brimming with men of all stripes, including a couple of black men and a few soldiers in dark-blue cavalry tunics and sky-blue slacks. Painted ladies worked the room, some with trays of drinks, others looking for someone to take upstairs, judging by how they were swinging their hips and clinging to their prospective jakes.

The air was stifling. It was a cloying mix of man sweat, cheap perfume, and even cheaper whiskey.

Haskell continued to survey the crowd, blinking against the thick tobacco smoke. Then he saw his man.

He stood against the horseshoe bar running from the back of the broad-floored saloon toward the front. The saloon careened out halfway to the front windows, where a roulette wheel was being spun and a rotund woman with purple-dyed hair was reading tarot cards for a couple of pie-eyed waddies. Haskell's shadower had one boot propped on the bar's brass foot rail. He was just now tossing coins onto the counter before him, on which a fresh shot of tangleleg sat.

The barman was scooping the coins off the bar and tossing them with aplomb into a coin box, muttering his thanks with a smile and a friendly nod.

Haskell strode forward, sidling between

men and ladies, wending his way around tables. A couple of men grunted angry scoldings when he jostled their beers. Haskell approached the bar, grabbed the arm of his shadower, and jerked him around until he faced him.

"What's the . . . ?" Incredulity caused the sentence to die on his lips. The man facing him was Bill Rankin, shortest of the three Rankin boys who'd shaken him down in Sheriff Lockhart's Big Saloon right after he'd ridden into town. "What's the idea, Rankin?"

Bill Rankin stared up at him, lower jaw hanging, flustered.

"This is the idea, you big sonofabitch!"

In the backbar mirror, Haskell saw two men rushing toward him from behind. Now as he spun, unsheathing the Schofield, Albert and Leonard Rankin both closed on him, raising revolvers of their own. They must have been outside and had followed him into the saloon, just as he'd followed Bill.

Now there was no mistaking their cold intent, their faces bunched with fury as they brought their pistols up fast. Haskell had no choice but to raise the Schofield and shoot the bespectacled Leonard in the face from ten feet away. As Leonard jerked back, he triggered the Colt in his right hand.

Haskell was vaguely aware of a groan behind him as he slid the Schofield slightly to his right, clicking the hammer back, and shot Albert a quarter-second before Albert fired his own Smith & Wesson, the bullet curling the air over Haskell's left shoulder and taking out a pyramid of clean shot glasses atop the bar before shattering the backbar mirror.

A girl screamed. The barman shouted.

The men around Haskell and the Rankins leaped over one another and even over a sporting girl as they desperately tried to flee the field of fire.

Albert jerked back and dropped to a knee, clapping his left hand to his bloody right shoulder. Haskell had shifted to his own left, so he could get Bill back in his field of vision. As Bill sagged back against the bar, apparently no imminent threat, Haskell turned back to Albert just as Albert yelled, "You are one hell of a son of a bitch!" and raised his Smithy once more.

Haskell aimed at the man's forehead and fired.

The bullet slammed into a heart-shaped, dark-pink birthmark just below the line of the man's scalp. The back of Albert's head vomited blood and white specks of brain and bone, which careened across a table and onto one of the men still scrambling toward safety. The man bellowed his revulsion, then tripped on an overturned chair and hit the floor, causing two others to go down on top of it.

Albert dropped to his knees, his empty head wobbling like a hollowed-out gourd in the wind, and dropped his pistol.

A girl screamed "Bear!" somewhere near Haskell.

Instinctively, he jerked back toward where Bill Rankin was clinging to the edge of the bar with one hand, apparently shot by his own brother, Leonard, and with his other hand trying to raise a Colt that looked way too big for his fist.

Haskell drilled a pill through Bill's heart.

"Oh, fuck!" Bill grunted, the Colt dropping from his limp fingers.

He made a face, tipping his head back on his shoulders as his knees buckled and hit the floor. He looked up at Haskell through eyes turning bleary with a fast-approaching death, and said, "You go to hell!"

He fell face forward, not breaking his fall at all, and quivered as he died.

The crowd had grown silent. The sea of revelers had parted widely, giving a broad space to the three dead men on the floor near the bar and to Bear Haskell, who stood about four feet out from the bar, facing the carnage, Schofield still extended. Smoke curled from the barrel. The crowd gazed at the scene of the killings as though they were in an opera house, gathering their wits after a particularly dramatic and shocking final act.

Looking around quickly, Haskell saw the henna-rinsed blond whore, Melody, from the Frenchman's Delight, standing down the bar a ways, staring at him in horror, flicking her shocked gaze to the Schofield smoking in his right fist.

"You, uh . . . you all right, Bear?" she asked, glancing at the dead Rankin brothers scattered on the floor around him.

Haskell's heart was still beating wildly. Now, as it started to slow, he swallowed and tried a grin at the girl, who might have just saved his life. She wore a skimpy, ruffled red dress, black fishnet stockings, and black stilettos. Her dyed blond hair was loosely piled atop her pretty head.

"Better than these fellas, anyway," he said with a sigh, and holstered his pistol.

"You sure put a damper on the damn night, and it was a good one, too," said the bartender as he poured Haskell the beer and whiskey shot he'd ordered.

Haskell noted the crowd spilling out through the batwings, casting wary, distasteful glances his way and at the three dead men sprawled in thickening blood pools on the floor.

"Sorry, partner," Haskell said. "Didn't see any other way — outside of exchangin' places with that beef down there, I mean . . ."

He let his voice trail off when boots thundered on the raised boardwalk outside, and then Lockhart's two deputies pushed through the batwings, one carrying a Winchester, the other a double-barreled shotgun. Haskell knew both men — Matt Delaney and Karl Haugen — from previous trips through Julesburg. He counted them both as good men, seasoned deputies. Lockhart had other deputies stationed in other, smaller towns about the county, keeping an eye on the county's peripheries.

To these two, Haskell raised his drink, and said, "Sorry for the mess, fellas. I suppose I have some paperwork to fill out. I don't see as how these three is worth the paper and ink, but come on over. I'll buy you a drink and sign an affidavit, just to make everything legal-like."

Delaney and Haugen both knew the

Rankins' reputations, so the deputies wouldn't have doubted Bear's story even if they hadn't known *his* reputation as an above-board law-bringer. So when they got the legal foofaraw out of the way, and Haskell had signed his name to an affidavit, which both deputies witnessed, and the undertaker had come to haul the bodies away, Bear bought him and the sheriff's deputies another round.

"So what brings you to our fair city, Bear?" asked Matt Delaney, poking his hat brim off his ruddy forehead and rocking back in his chair. He was a tall man with a hound-dog face and a nose like a doorstop — an ex-freighter who was pushing fifty and who moonlighted during the day as a bartender in one of the local brothels.

Haskell touched a match to the end of an Indian Kid, and, blowing smoke out his nostrils, said, "Lockhart didn't tell you?"

"Didn't tell me nothin'," said Karl Haugen, an ex-stock inspector whom Haskell had once known back in his buffalo-hunting days. Haugen had had a reputation as an expert skinner, and he'd gone on to supply game to the railroad before turning to law enforcement. He was a short, stocky, red-faced German, who still had a slight accent after growing up among first-generation

Germans in Iowa. "But then, ole Con — he don't talk as much as he used to."

"You know about his son breaking out of jail, right?"

"What?" Delaney slapped the table in shock.

Haskell gave a wry chuff. Lockhart hadn't told them, after all.

He told the two men the story and also that the breakout was why he was here — to find Jamie Lockhart before Jamie could settle up with his father.

The deputies gazed across the table at each other, scowling their befuddlement.

"Damned odd that he didn't tell either one of you," Haskell said, sitting back in his chair and rubbing his chin in speculation.

Haugen turned to Bear. "He ain't what he used to be."

"How so?"

Delaney said, "Hell, look around. He ain't here. Used to be that when a gun went off in Julesburg, he was there. I mean, he was *there*! Before the echoes of the shots had died."

"Now, he leaves the night work to us," Haugen said.

"Hell, he leaves the afternoon work to us," said Delaney. "I start at three. That's when the old man goes home."

"Old man," Haskell said. "He does look old now, don't he?"

Delaney took a dainty sip from his shot glass. "He's been aging five years for every one, last few. Ain't that right, Karl?"

"Matt's got it right," Haugen said. "I don't know — I think it's the business with the kid. Jamie. Shit, how couldn't it be?"

"That was ten years ago," Haskell said. "You'd think he'd have moved on by now."

"How do you ever move on from your boy killin' the girl you was gonna marry? On account o' he was jealous. On account o' she'd been carryin' on with him — Jamie, I'm sayin'!" Delaney crossed his arms on his chest and shook his head.

Haskell sat back in his chair and blew a smoke plume toward the batwings. "I reckon you're right. How could anyone get over somethin' like that? Poor bastard."

He turned his half-empty shot glass in a circle on the table, thinking it through. Wondering where Jamie was now. He'd felt so certain it had been Jamie behind him earlier. He wished he'd been able to take one of the Rankin boys alive so he could have asked them what their plan had been, to ask them if Bill really had followed him all the way back from the Lockhart house.

Maybe someone had followed him to the

edge of town and had then skinned away when he — Jamie? — had seen other men were already waiting for him, apparently to ambush him. Maybe Bill had followed him and Leonard and Albert had circled around to either side, to catch him in a whipsaw, but he'd managed to sashay out of their trap.

"Another drink, fellas?" Haskell asked, lifting the bottle.

"Nah," Haugen said. "We're on duty. We'd best get back to it, Matt."

"I reckon we'd best."

"You fellas keep an eye skinned for Lockhart's son, will you?"

"You really think he'll head this way?" Delaney asked as he heavily gained his feet. He wore the air of a man who worked far too hard for his age.

"My boss seems to think so," Bear said, throwing back the last of his drink. "Even if Con don't. I'm gonna hang around a few more days, just in case."

The deputies thanked him for the drinks, and headed out.

Haskell found himself sitting alone at the table in the near-empty saloon. The bartender was hard at work trying to scrub the blood out of the floorboards, grunting and occasionally cursing with the effort.

A couple of drummers chinned over beers

near the back, where three billiard tables were lined out. An old drunk sat swilling whiskey and talking to himself near the front, calling the empty chair across from him Betty. He and Betty seemed to be having a mild disagreement, the drunk chuffing and shaking his head from time to time and saying, "Jeepers, Betty!"

Haskell dropped a silver cartwheel on the table, donned his hat, and rose from his chair.

"That there's for your trouble," he told the barman, down on all fours to his left.

"Those bastards musta bled out before the undertaker got here!"

"That's the problem with bastards," Haskell said as he strolled toward the batwings. "They'll bleed dry every time."

"What was that?" the barman called.

"That was the wit and wisdom of one Bear Haskell. Comes with the cartwheel."

"You're peculiar!" the barman yelled as Haskell stepped out into the night.

"Yes, I am," Haskell said to no one in particular.

Footsteps rose on his left. He touched the walnut grips of the Schofield as Melody from the Frenchman's Delight stepped out of the shadows, holding a cape about her otherwise bare shoulders. "Don't shoot. It's me. Melody. I came back, hopin' I'd find you here."

"I thought you worked over to the Frenchman's Delight."

The henna-rinsed blonde hiked a shoulder. "Sometimes I work over here." She smiled. "I came back for you."

"You did, did you?"

"You sure know how to run off business!" she said with mock scolding.

"I tend to do that."

"I never took you for a lawman."

"Really? What'd you take me for?"

"I don't know. Maybe a track layer or a game hunter." Melody grinned again. "Right now I take you for a man who could use a Frenchman's Delight."

She snuggled up close to him, placing her hand on his belly.

Haskell groaned. "Ah . . . that I could. That I could."

"Where you stayin'?"

"Come on. I'll show you."

He untied the buckskin's reins from the rack, mounted up, then extended his hand for the girl. She placed her hand in his, and he pulled her up behind him.

She wrapped her arms tight around his belly, and they rode off in the night.

CHAPTER 14

"Hold it down over there, will ya — I'm tryin' to concentrate!" Haskell bellowed at the wall behind Melody's slowly bobbing head.

The pretty young whore lifted her mouth off of his fully erect and throbbing member to squeal a little laugh and run the back of her hand across her lips.

On the other side of the wall, which was composed of thin pine planks, the raucous sounds of lovemaking ceased and a man's voice said, "Uh . . . sorry about that, pardner!"

"Don't mention it," Haskell grunted.

In the adjacent room, a girl laughed. Melody was about to close her mouth over Haskell's cock once more, but then she stopped and glanced, frowning, over her shoulder at the thin wall, the cracks between the planks visible in places behind the torn paper. Through the cracks Bear could see a shadow — or maybe two shadows — jostling.

"Maggie, is that you?" Melody called.

"Yeah," Maggie said. "Is that you, Melody?" She had a dewy Southern drawl.

"Yep sire," Melody said with a tittering laugh. She touched her tongue teasingly to the swollen head of Haskell's organ. "I'm with Bear. A big son of a buck in more ways than one! Who you with, Miss Maggie?"

"I don't know," Maggie called, her voice strained now as the sighing of the bedsprings on that side of the wall resumed. "He won't tell me his name. Shy, I reckon." She laughed softly and then groaned as the wood was thrown to her once more.

"Some are like that," Melody said, then looked up over Haskell's flat belly to meet his gaze with an intimate one of her own as she slowly slid her mouth down his shaft toward his balls. She pulled her mouth off of him to say, "You ain't one bit shy — are ya, Bear?"

She pumped him twice, hard, with her hand, drawing the foreskin up over the head, then lowered her mouth over him again.

He grunted his negative answer, resting his head back against the pillow but looking down his chest and past his belly as the girl

185

administered one of the best blow jobs he remembered.

His shaft made a large, perfect "O" of her sweet mouth. Her eyes were closed. Each cheek bulged in turn, as she turned her head this way and that. She groaned as she worked very purposefully, with the adroitness of a seasoned *dove du pave.* Her loose, henna-dyed hair felt silkily against his chest and hips.

Haskell felt he had a good handle on the meaning of Frenchman's Delight and silently opined that all men of all nationalities should experience something similar at least once in their lives. There would probably be a lot less war and general male-oriented high jinks.

Melody slid her mouth up and down his cock, swirling her tongue against the rigid staff, for a good two or three minutes. And then, as though sensing she was working the big lawman perilously close to his climax, she pulled her mouth off of him and sucked on one of his balls, taking half of his big sack into her mouth.

She sucked until the sucking grew painful. Then she eased up for a time, waiting for his blood to cool. As though knowing exactly when it had cooled to well below the danger zone, she kissed the head of his cock and then slowly, ever-so-excruciatingly slowly, slid her mouth down his rigid shaft once more.

Her mouth felt like warm mud slowly engulfing him.

Her saliva crackled and popped.

Haskell groaned, stretched his lips back from his teeth, and curled his toes.

Melody slid her mouth so far down his cock that he thought he could feel its swollen head snuggling against her vocal cords. She made soft strangling sounds as she mashed her face against his crotch, bathing every inch of him in her hot saliva, teasing him with her tongue.

"One hundred," Haskell wheezed out. "Ninety-nine, ninety-eight . . ."

He wanted to prolong the bittersweet agony for as long as he could.

He made it to ninety-seven but not quite to ninety-six.

Just as Melody slid her mouth up off his wand and then back down toward his belly once more, the dam inside him burst with a fury.

Bear had been so absorbed in his own rapture that he hadn't realized the din from the next room had resumed, as loud or even louder than before, and that now, as his own passion crested, the passion in the next room seemed to crest, as well.

At least, judging by the love cries of both involved over there . . .

For her part, Melody kept her mouth on Bear's dong for as long as she could stand it. Then, so as not to drown on his jism, she lifted her head and finished him with her hand, smiling down at him and rubbing the pearlescent spurtings around on her breasts, massaging the milky substance around on her large, pink areolas.

When Haskell had ceased spasming, Melody crawled up to straddle his chest. His heart was still racing. His chest glistened with sweat. It rose and fell as he breathed.

The pretty whore smoothed his thick, tangled hair back from his temples, smiled sweetly down at him, and opened her mouth to speak but stopped when on the other side of the thin wall Maggie said, "What are you gonna do with that big gun, darlin'? I didn't see any rats in here for a change . . ."

Haskell looked up at Melody, who was frowning over her shoulder toward the paper-thin wall. As she turned her head back toward Haskell, saying, "What on earth do you suppose — ?"

Her question broke into a scream as Haskell sat bolt upright and hurled himself and the girl to his left off the side of the bed, his big body sort of wrapping, cocoon-like, around hers as they rolled off the bed to hit the floor with a heavy *thud!*

At the same time, Maggie screamed on the other side of the wall, a half-second after Haskell heard the ratcheting click of a gun hammer being cocked and had seen an eye peer through one of the cracks in the wall.

A gun roared.

Covering the screaming whore with his own body, Haskell glanced over his left shoulder to see a bullet blast a hole the size of a silver cartwheel in the wall beyond the bed, over a rickety dresser. The blast knocked a picture off the wall just before the gun roared again, blasting a hole just right of the first one.

Another blast, another hole. The bullet plunked into the bed where Bear and Melody had been entangled a moment before.

Another blast, another hole.

Another bullet plunked into the bed.

Maggie continued to scream as the gun continued to roar until there was the metallic ping of the hammer dropping on an empty chamber.

"What the fuck?" Maggie screamed.

Haskell's sentiments exactly.

Before the bastard in the other room could reload, Haskell grabbed his Schofield from the holster hanging from a chair back. He told Melody to stay down, though she didn't appear to be in any hurry to get up, then rose and aimed the cocked Smith & Wesson toward the wall in which six holes shone, giving a clearer but still obscured view of the next room.

In his fury, Haskell nearly squeezed off a shot before realizing he might hit Maggie.

"Shit!" he bellowed and then lowered the Schofield and ran straight ahead, never mind that he wasn't wearing a stitch, and bulled into the papered wall, sort of following his lowered left shoulder.

He hit the wall with a thundering crash and bulled right on through, breaking out the spindly wood as though it were no more substantial than glass. He hit the floor of the other room, wood and bits of paper raining down around him. Maggie screamed as Bear rolled twice, then came up on his right knee, raising the Schofield and quickly trying to get his bearings.

As he did, he caught a quick glimpse of a naked girl cowering in a corner and of a figure leaping through a window on the far side of a badly rumpled brass bed.

Haskell fired the Schofield once, twice, three times at the retreating figure. The screech of breaking glass filled the room, drowning Maggie's screams. There was the heavy thud of a body hitting a roof below and then scrambling sounds as the fleeing son of a bitch apparently continued to flee.

Haskell leaped onto the bed and peered out the broken window, unable to see much because of the darkness and the lamplight pushing around him from behind. He was probably staring out over an alley. He couldn't see a thing. What he could hear was the fast-retreating footsteps of the ambusher running away.

Then silence.

The son of a bitch was gone.

Even if Haskell hadn't been naked as a jaybird, it was too damned dark to follow the bastard. He depressed the Schofield's hammer, then walked over to where Maggie sat on the floor against the wall, her bare knees drawn up to her bare breasts.

"Easy, there, girl, easy," Haskell said, wrapping an arm around the sobbing girl's shoulders. "It's all right. He's gone now."

"What on earth was he *shooting* at?" she said, looking up at Haskell with tear-bright, brown eyes.

"I reckon he was shootin' at me," Haskell said slowly, trying to piece together the last two minutes — for that was probably all the time that had passed before the bush-

whacker fired the first shot through the wall
— and lit a shuck.

"Why?"

"That I can't tell you. What did he look
like?"

"Are you all right, Maggie?" Melody
asked, stepping cautiously through the
ragged, roughly man-shaped hole Haskell
had made in the wall. She was still as naked
as Haskell and Maggie were, and she looked
just as scared and befuddled.

"I think so," Maggie said, wiping the tears
from her eyes.

"Did you get a look at him?" Haskell said
as Melody dropped to a knee on the other
side of Maggie.

Maggie blinked at him. "He fucked me,
for Christ sakes — of course I got a look at
him!"

"All right, all right," Haskell said. "Well,
maybe, you could tell me what his face looks
like, anyway, so I can run the bastard down."

"We finished fucking and then he chuckled, and I looked over and he had this big
gun in his hand!"

"I know, I know, but . . ." Haskell let the
question die on his lips when gunfire
sounded somewhere outside, in the far
distance. Men shouted. There was more
brief gunfire and then silence.

Could be separate trouble, could be part of *this* trouble. He had to check it out.

As he rose and Melody took Maggie in her arms, the big lawman realized someone was pounding on the door and demanding to be let in. He was still naked, but he opened the door, anyway. He'd never been overly modest, and it was a man's voice that had been demanding entrance. Besides, Haskell had more to occupy his mind than his big dick, still moist from Melody's mouth, wagging down between his legs.

"What in the hell is going on in here?" bellowed the McGregor House's manager — a middle-aged man named Iver Hendricks. He wore a checked robe and a long night cap, round spectacles hanging low on his warty nose.

He looked Haskell's large, brawny frame up and down. He looked at the two naked girls on the floor. He looked at the broken-out window and the broken-out wall, and with each look his narrow jaw sagged a little lower.

"Just a little foofaraw," Haskell said. "Nothin' to get your drawers in a twist over." He walked back through the hole he'd made in the wall to the left of the bed and into his own room. "Oh, and no charge for making these two rooms adjoining, either. Let's just chalk that up to a perk of my visit."

CHAPTER 15

Haskell dressed quickly, wrapped his Schofield belt around his waist, made sure the .44 Blue Jacket was tucked into the holster inside his right boot, and grabbed his Henry, checking to see that it was fully loaded. He donned his hat and pinned his badge to his chest. Under the circumstances, it was likely best that folks knew he was a lawman, so he didn't get shot by someone thinking he was an owlhoot.

He headed out into the hall. Several people, mostly men, but a couple of middle-aged women as well, were standing in their rooms' open doorways, looking curious and owly. A couple asked Haskell what all the shooting had been about. He told them to go back to bed.

Downstairs, he crossed the dark lobby and stepped out into the night. He heard someone speaking loudly a distance away on his right. Striding in that direction, he saw shadows jostling a couple of blocks away, men running about. One man was yelling for someone to fetch the doctor.

Haskell broke into a jog. As he approached the jostling shadows of the five or six men in the street, he saw that one man lay in the middle of the street, on his side. Another one lay near the boardwalk on the street's right side. The standing men were gathered around the man near the boardwalk, and one was saying, "Hold on, Delaney. Ralph is fetchin' the sawbones."

"Fuck!" Matt Delaney bellowed. "Oh, bloody fuck, that hurts!"

Haskell pushed two men out of his way and dropped to a knee beside Deputy Delaney. "Matt?" he said, breathless. "You all right, Matt?"

"Fuck — do I look all right? Me an' Karl heard shootin' over to the hotel and went runnin'. Someone bushwhacked us. I took a pill to the leg, another one here in my fuckin' arm!" Delaney looked toward the other man humped darkly in the middle of the street. "Bastard killed Karl!"

Haskell looked at the unmoving figure lying to his left, and snarled a curse.

"Did you get a look at him?" he asked Delaney, who'd lost his hat and lay writhing on the ground, kicking his wounded leg and

196

clutching his upper left arm.

"All I seen was three or four flashes, heard three or four gun pops. Two hit me, an' I went down. Karl ran toward the son of a bitch, and the son of a bitch cut Karl down right where he's layin' now. I didn't see the shooter, but the shots came from over there, between Burnside's shop and Maple's Grocery. *Fuck!*"

"Did you see where the shooter went after he shot you?"

"No." Delaney shook his head. "I didn't see nothin' after that."

Haskell looked at the five men standing around, crouched over him and Delaney. "Did you men see where the shooter went?"

They all looked at each other, muttering and shaking their heads.

"We was all drinkin' in the Thunderhead yonder," one of them said.

Delaney looked at Haskell. "You think it was him, Bear? Jamie Lockhart?"

"I don't know. But someone just tried the same thing on me they pulled on you an' Karl." Haskell rose, clutching the Henry in his right hand. "Probably safe to assume it wasn't a coincidence that three lawmen were bushwhacked tonight. You hang tight, Matt. I'm gonna ride out to Lockhart's!"

"Careful, Bear!" the wounded deputy

197

called. "If it's Jamie, he's a sneaky, blood-hungry son of a bitch, and he must have one god-awful plan for his pa!"

Fortunately, the shooting in the street had awakened the livery barn's night manager, so Haskell didn't have to waste precious time pounding on the barn's chained doors. He found the man smoking outside and full of questions, all of which Haskell ignored as he bounded between the barn's open doors and saddled his buckskin.

He shoved his Henry into the saddle scabbard jutting up over the horse's right wither, led the horse outside, and swung up into the leather. The liveryman was still wondering aloud what the dustup had been about when Haskell heeled the buckskin into a gallop back toward the main street.

He rode east out of town like a bat out of hell, crouched low in the saddle. He kept seeing in his mind's eye Jamie Lockhart quietly breaking into Lockhart's house, stealing up the stairs to the sheriff's bedroom, and filling the slumbering sheriff full of lead, making good on his ten-year-old threat. Since he'd ambushed Haskell and Lockhart's two deputies, Jamie had had more than enough time to ride out to Lockhart's house.

The buckskin thundered down the moon-lit trail, stretching its stride and laying its ears back against its head. Haskell turned the horse so quickly off the main trail and onto Lockhart's driveway that the horse nearly lost its footing and went down before regaining its balance and stretching its stride once again toward the big house looming in the darkness, moonlight shimmering on its shake-shingled roof and reflecting off its dark windows.

Haskell looked around quickly, spying no man and no horse anywhere in sight. That didn't mean Jamie Lockhart wasn't here. Blood running anxiously through his veins, Haskell dropped lithely out of the saddle, slid his Schofield from its holster, and ran up the porch steps. He crossed the porch in three lunging strides, opened the screen, and hammered the inside door with his fist.

"Con? Open up — it's Bear!"

He tried the knob. The door was locked.

He slid an ear to the glass pane in the door's upper panel. Inside there was only silence.

"Con? Open up — it's Bear Haskell! Open up, Con!"

He hammered again and was about to ram his fist against the door once more when a light shone from inside. The light grew.

Someone was approaching the foyer with a lamp.

Relief washed over Bear. He stepped back as a key was turned in the lock, and the main door was pulled open. Judith stood just inside the door, her bulky body clad in a cotton nightgown and flannel shawl. Her hair was down, and she held a hurricane lantern high in her left hand. The light reflected in her wide, startled eyes. Her pale cheeks were drawn from sleep.

"Good lord, Marshal! What on earth is the meaning of *this*?"

"Everything's all right?"

"What? Why . . ."

"Everything's all right here? No one has tried to break in."

"*Break in?* Why, no. Of course not. Why would they?"

Footsteps rose behind Judith and Con Lockhart's gravelly voice, said, "Judith, who's there? For crying out loud, what is going on?"

Judith turned to look behind her. As she did, she lifted the light to reveal Con Lockhart striding heavily — shuffling, would be more accurate — into the foyer. He was fully dressed, though his clothes looked rumpled, as did his hair. He held a chipped goblet in his right hand.

"Oh, Con," Judith intoned. "Are you still up?"

Her glance dropped to the glass in her brother's hand. Haskell's gaze dropped in the same direction. Then he looked into Con Lockhart's eyes. They were drawn and blurry, as though he'd been by fits sleeping and drinking in a chair. Probably in his office or in the parlor.

"Bear," Lockhart said, stopping beside Judith and scowling incredulously at Haskell. "What the hell has gotten into you?"

Another light appeared at the top of the stairway flanking Judith and Haskell. This one was held by Monique Bataille, who wore a heavy dark shawl over a frilly cream nightgown. Her hair was also down for bed, brushed across her shoulders. It glistened like polished ebony in the light of her flickering lantern. Her eyes were as dark as her hair. They stared curiously, anxiously, down at the three gathered in the foyer.

"I think he's here," Haskell said, letting himself inside, easing the screen door closed behind him. "In Julesburg."

"Who?" Both Judith and Con said at the same time.

To Lockhart, Haskell said, "Jamie. I was bushwhacked in my hotel room. After the shooter jumped out a window, he ambushed

201

your two deputies. Karl Haugen is dead. Delaney took two bullets. Looks like he'll live, but he'll be out of commission for a while. I think Jamie wanted anyone who might have stood between him and you out of the way."

"Jamie?" Judith said, jerking her head back in shock.

She swiveled her head to look up at her brother. "What is he talking about, Con?"

Staring in befuddlement toward Haskell, Lockhart said with a vague, absent air, his tongue thick from drink, "My . . . my son . . . he busted out of the pen. Bear is here because he . . . because he thinks Jamie might have returned home. To kill me."

Judith gasped. Quickly, she swung full around, took a heavy step toward the stairs, then, seeing Monique standing at the first landing, said, "Check Sylvie's room, Miss Bataille. Hurry!"

Haskell, Judith, and Lockhart waited as Monique hurried up the stairs and into the second story. Haskell heard a distant door latch click. Hinges squealed softly. There was another click as the door was latched, and then Monique walked down the stairs holding her lantern, turning her head toward the foyer and saying, "She's in bed. Sound asleep. She's fine."

"Thank god!" Judith said, slapping a hand to her heavy bosom.

Lockhart turned to Haskell. "There. See? You got it wrong. Whoever bushwhacked you and my deputies wasn't Jamie." He shook his head with stubborn defiance. "Probably had a beef against you, and my deputies got in the way. Haugen's dead, you say? Well, I'll be damned. Oh, *Christ*!"

Lockhart's glass had slipped out of his hand. It hit the floor with a loud thump, spilling brandy over the varnished puncheons.

Judith gasped again, then turned a reprimanding look on her brother. "Con, you're drunk. Off to bed with you. You know you shouldn't be up this late! What has the doctor told you?"

Lockhart opened his mouth to defend himself, but there was no resisting Judith's commands. "Off!" she fairly yelled, snapping her fingers and pointing at the stairs. "Off with you this instant, Con Lockhart!"

Lockhart flushed with embarrassment and then shrugged at Bear and moved slowly, wobbling on his feet and nearly losing his balance, toward the stairs. He grabbed the rail and began climbing heavily. Monique met him halfway and helped him the rest of the way.

When the governess and the sheriff were gone, their footsteps creaking in the ceiling as Monique helped him to bed, Judith turned to Haskell. "Tell me it's not true. Tell me that that . . . that . . . *killer* has not been turned loose to wreak havoc here again!"

"I'm afraid it's true." Haskell glanced toward the ceiling. "Does he often sit up this late, drinking like that?"

Judith drew a deep breath, then released it.

"Come," she said, and retreated into the parlor where they'd sat hours before listening to Sylvie play the piano.

She sat in an upholstered armchair, setting the lamp on a table beside it.

"Sit," she said, indicating the short leather sofa.

When Haskell had doffed his hat and sunk into the sofa, Judith tucked her feet, which were clad in silk slippers with pink ribbons, beneath the chair, crossing her thick ankles. She folded her hands in her lap. Her eyes were red-rimmed, cheeks puffy.

She was far from the hale, hearty woman who had greeted him earlier. She looked like the dead version of her former self, and he could tell by the way she had trouble meeting his gaze that she felt self-conscious about her appearance.

Still, she wanted a word with him in private.

"He's not well," she said straight out, letting the words hang there as though for him to absorb.

"Well, I didn't think so, but —"

"He had a slight heart stroke a little over a year ago. He had another one earlier this summer. He doesn't want anyone to know. In fact, he's sworn me to secrecy, and if he knew I'd told you, he would absolutely explode!"

Her eyes did not show fear, though. Haskell could tell Judith felt in full command of the situation. Her not telling anyone about her brother's condition had probably been as much her decision as Con's. She knew how important appearances were. Haskell doubted that Judith was afraid of anyone or anything.

"Should he be drinking like that?"

"Of course not. But I can't stop him. He tells me he's going to bed and then later I'll find him sitting in his study . . . just sitting there . . . staring out the window or into space . . . drinking. Drinking and smoking his infernal cigars, which the doctor has also forbidden."

"Why?"

"He's a deeply wounded man, Bear. No one but I will ever know how deep a wound his son and that . . . that *woman* inflicted. My god, the humiliation. Add to that the fact that his son beat the woman to death in a jealous rage when she told him she was going to go ahead and marry his father."

"I can imagine."

"Oh, why did that have to happen? A little Mexican whore — that's all she was! Merely vowing to marry Con for his money and then . . . then . . . *carryin' on* with his son!"

"We never know which way the wind's gonna blow — do we?" Haskell said.

"That horror made him drink and smoke all the more. And it weakened his heart. I've been trying to get him to retire, or to at least hire a couple more deputies. He's really incapable of fulfilling his duties. He needs more help. Julesburg is a growing town, Sedgwick a growing county. He has deputies in the outlying areas but, still, it's too much work for a man in Con's condition."

Judith drew another deep breath and released it slowly, staring at the floor and fatefully shaking her head.

"He is Con Lockhart," she said. "Sheriff of Sedgwick County. A strong, admirable man. He doesn't want to give up the crown or betray any tarnishing whatsoever. I'm sure he'll die with that badge pinned to his shirt."

She lifted her gaze to Haskell. "Maybe sooner rather than later if what you say is true. If Jamie has escaped . . . and he's here."

"He's here, all right," Haskell said. "I'd bet on it. I think he followed me from your place to town earlier." He knew there was a chance it could have been one of the Rankins, but his sixth lawman's sense told him it had been Jamie. "I think he followed me to scrub me off his trail and to make sure there was no one to interfere in his vengeance quest. Which tells me that he really does have it out for his father — in a big way."

"Oh, yes . . . I've no doubt about that," Judith said, sitting back in her chair and staring darkly at the windows looking out at the still, black night.

Haskell studied her. "Is there some other reason he's so angry? I mean, one that goes farther back?"

CHAPTER 16

Judith stared at Haskell, though he could tell she was thinking about something else. Finally, she said, "I'm going to go make some coffee. I'm sure the range is still hot. Would you care for a cup?"

"Sure, I'll take a cup. If it's all right with you, I'd like to stay here tonight. I'll stay outside, keep an eye on the place."

Judith rose from her chair, wringing her hands together, worried, glancing at the night-dark windows once more. "That would be wonderful, Bear. Thank you." She paused, staring out the window, no doubt wondering if her nephew was out there somewhere, stalking his father.

Finally, she strode to the door. "I'll be back in a few minutes."

"I'm gonna take a little walk around outside," Haskell said, rising and donning his hat.

When Judith had gone into the kitchen,

he walked outside and shucked his Henry from his saddle scabbard. He took a slow stroll around the perimeter of the yard, looking around, scrutinizing every shadow, stopping and listening.

It was a quiet night. There was hardly any breeze. He heard nothing more than coyotes yammering in some distant coulee, likely crowing over a fresh kill, and a lone dog answering their revelry from town.

When he'd walked completely around the property, he led the buckskin into Lockhart's stable, and unsaddled, fed, and watered him. He walked outside, stood in front of the closed stable doors, and watched and listened for another five minutes.

Still nothing. Now not even the coyotes were yammering.

It was so quiet, Haskell thought he could hear his own heart beating.

The house sat about fifty yards ahead, pale in the moonlight. He started walking toward it. There was a thump behind him.

He stopped and wheeled, levering a cartridge into the Henry's action.

A high-pitched squeal tore through the quiet night, causing the lawman's heart to quicken. There was the windy creak of flapping wings, another desperate peep. Staring off to the west of the stable, Bear saw the shadow of a nighthawk winging off toward town, moonlight catching in its dark feathers, the squeals of the baby rabbit in its talons gradually fading with distance.

Haskell loosed a relieved breath and eased the Henry's hammer down.

He walked to the house and climbed the porch steps. He'd just taken a seat in a wicker chair facing the direction of town when the front door opened and Judith came out, holding a tray with two steaming coffee cups and a china server. She set the tray on the table beside Haskell's chair and sat in the second wicker chair.

"We're alone out here, I take it . . . ?" she said, her voice trilling with unease.

"So far. You're really afraid of him, aren't you?"

Judith filled the two cups from the server. "Wouldn't you be, after what he did? The promise he made as he left the courtroom? The glare he gave his father! I was there — I saw the whole thing!"

"Yeah, my boss, Henry Dade, was there, too, and said the same thing."

"Awful boy. A man now. Who knows what those ten-plus years in prison did to him."

"If it's what they do to most men, it's not good." Haskell lifted his cup, using both hands, afraid he might break the dainty china. Blowing ripples on the surface of the coffee glistening in the moonlight slanting in under the porch roof, he said, "You were going to tell me what made Jamie so angry at Con. Besides being sent to prison . . ."

Judith sipped her own coffee, then held the cup on her thigh. "I wasn't sure I should speak of it. No one has. At least, neither Con nor I have spoken of it outside the family. I'll tell you now, Bear, so you know what fuels Jamie's resentment . . . so that you don't underestimate him."

Haskell sat back in the chair, holding the uncomfortably dainty cup in both his big hands, waiting.

Finally, Judith sipped her own coffee once more, swallowed, and, staring off to the west, said, "There was an accident long ago. One Con blamed Jamie for. It involved Con's first wife, Jamie's mother."

"I didn't realize he'd been married twice before . . ."

"Yes. Jamie and Sylvie have different mothers."

"I didn't realize that, either."

"Sylvie is from Con's second wife, Meredith, who died the day after Sylvie was born, from a hemorrhage. His first wife was Nell Sackaway, daughter of a businessman from Kansas City. A bright, beautiful young

211

woman filled with good cheer and vigor. I've always believed that a very large part of Con — maybe the best part of my brother — died along with Nell. Anyway, when Jamie was ten years old, his father punished him severely, whipped him, after finding out that Jamie had stolen rock candy from the mercantile in town. Jamie said that other boys had dared him into it.

"Enraged, humiliated, and filled with self-righteous indignation — he could be a very headstrong, melodramatic child, Jamie could — he saddled a horse and rode into the Dinosaur Rocks country. A storm came up — one of those late summer monsoons we get out here. Against Con's wishes, Jamie's mother, Nell, rode out into those rocks looking for the boy.

"While she was gone, Jamie returned to the ranch soaking wet and scared. His father sent him out to the ranch's original shack — a ten-by-ten-foot hovel back in the trees by a wash. Con used it as a jail of sorts, when he didn't know what else to do with the boy." Judith gave a ragged, fateful sigh. "Anyway, when Nell didn't return that stormy night, Con and several of his men rode out looking for her. They found her where she and her horse had fallen after being struck by lightning. Killed."

"Jesus."

"She was badly burned. Charred. Con brought her home. In his grief and rage, he carried her out to the shack in which he'd locked Jamie, and showed the boy his dead, badly burned mother, raging at him the whole time, telling him that he was responsible."

"Christ almighty . . ."

"Con blamed Jamie, a boy of only ten years, for his mother's death."

"That's hard."

"That's Conway Lockhart, I'm afraid, Bear. I love my brother deeply. He can love like no other man I've ever known — with all his heart. But he can hate the same way. There are many different sides to the man, and some, I dare say, I do not care for much at all. His hardness. His coldness. His stubbornness. His temper. He is, as we say in Oklahoma, like a cyclone picking its own path, an' the devil may take the hindmost."

"Jamie's likely the same way. Is that what you're saying?"

"I saw it in his eyes that day, after the judge had read him his walking papers. Condemned him to life in the territorial pen."

Haskell nodded, thinking over what he'd learned. "Thanks, Judith. I'm sure that was a hard story to relate. I appreciate it. I feel like I know Jamie better now . . . as well as his father."

"Don't judge Con too harshly. Our father was much the same way, his father before him. I even have a little of that hot blood myself, unfortunately."

Judith lifted her chin, filled her lungs with the fresh night air, and turned her cold eyes on Haskell. "As far as Jamie goes, however, you'd best kill him as soon as you see him. He's pure bad. Has been since he was a boy. Whether it's all Con's fault is debatable. But he was bad ten years ago — rotten bad — and ten years in prison likely turned him into an enraged mountain lion. If he truly has returned to Julesburg, I'm right about him, and you must kill him on sight."

Judith rose, the wicker creaking beneath her. "I'm going to go in now. I doubt I'll sleep another wink this night, but I'm getting cold. Fall's on the way, I reckon." She topped off Haskell's coffee cup, chuckling when she saw he'd only slurped down a couple of sips. "I'll bring out another mug. One you won't be so afraid of."

Haskell gave a wry chuff. "Thanks, Miss Judith. I'll be right here. If you hear or see anything, let me know."

"I'll feel better with you here."

Judith set the server on the tray, and picked it up.

"Oh, Judith," Haskell said, another thought occurring to him.

The woman had turned to the door, but now she stopped and turned back around. "What is it, Bear?"

"Do you know of anyone in town here — in the county, maybe — who would want to see Con dead? Someone he might have graveled more than most?"

"Well, his being a sheriff, you know . . ."

"I'm trying to figure out who might have gotten Jamie out of Trinidad Pen. Whoever they were had to have a good reason and enough money to hire someone inside the pen to help."

"Hmmm . . ." Judith stared off, pensive. "The only one I can think of . . . would be . . ." She shook her head quickly, dismissing the thought. "No. Couldn't be. He's dead and his daughter . . . no. Never mind. It's just late and I'm weary."

Haskell put his hand on her arm. "Please. Tell me who you're thinking of, Miss Judith. Couldn't hurt."

Judith hesitated, pensive, then slowly sank back into her chair.

There wasn't much of the night left after

Judith had gone back inside. She brought Haskell fresh coffee in a large mug and told him the pot would be on the range's warming rack inside if he wanted more. He slurped down two more cups as he prowled around the yard and sat on the porch, wrapped in the blanket Judith had also provided.

At dawn, he dozed.

He awoke when the front door opened to his right. The movement startled him, and he reached for the Henry, which he'd leaned against the house behind him.

"No need for the sixteen-shooter," Con Lockhart said, stepping out onto the porch and easing the screen door quietly closed behind him. "Just me."

Lockhart stopped before the door and sipped from the steaming stone mug in his hand. He was fully dressed, and he wore a fur-lined, deer-hide jacket with its collar raised around his neck. His polished silver sheriff's star was pinned to the jacket's left breast. He also wore a crisp pearl Stetson. Haskell saw a holster poking down from beneath the hem of the jacket. It was strapped to his right thigh.

The sheriff looked only slightly better than he had last night. Age lines formed deep crevices around his mouth and his eyes. His pale cheeks sagged like aged parchment. His nose was a striking purple-red. He owned a vaguely sheepish look as he sipped the coffee, then lowered the mug, staring out over the porch rail at the broad, flat yard that the rising sunlight was just now finding, causing shadows to lengthen.

"A quiet night?"

Haskell nodded. "A liver-colored puss came sniffing around. Didn't much care for seein' me out here."

"Feral," Lockhart said. "Sylvie feeds him. He was likely looking for an early breakfast."

"Sleep well?"

Lockhart hiked a shoulder and sipped his coffee. "I heard you and Judith talking out here."

"Oh."

"So . . . now you know my sordid past. Dead wives, logy heart, an' all."

"Your past is no more sordid than most folks', Con."

"I'd appreciate your not spreading any of that around."

"You know I wouldn't."

Lockhart walked over to the porch rail, set his coffee cup on top of it, and stared off over the rolling, salmon-streaked prairie toward the rooftops of Julesburg obscured by the smoke of breakfast fires.

"You going in today?" Haskell asked him.

Lockhart nodded and continued staring toward town. "I have a job of work today. Have to bury one deputy, check in on the other one, and look for a couple more. I'm not worried. I know a couple of stock detectives I can deputize until I can hire two more permanent men. In the meantime, I have to get after that bushwhacker."

"Jamie."

"No." Lockhart shook his head, keeping his head aimed toward the west. "The shooter wasn't Jamie. I know you and Henry Dade believe it was. But it wasn't." He paused. "You know how I know?"

"How's that?"

"If Jamie was here, I'd be dead by now." Lockhart glanced over his left shoulder, casting Haskell a grim smile. "But you go on and keep lookin' for him. That's fine by me." He threw back the last of his coffee, set the cup on the rail, and walked to the porch steps. "As for me — well, the sheriff of Sedgwick County has a long day ahead of him. I'd best get started. You have a good day now, Bear."

Lockhart headed off around the house to the stable flanking it.

"All right," Haskell said, staring incredulously after the man. "You, too, Con."

When Lockhart had ridden out on a fine Appaloosa stallion, Haskell rose and picked up his rifle. He intended to have one more look around before saddling his buckskin. But then the house's front door opened again, and he turned toward it.

A schoolboy flush rose once more in his cheeks when Monique Bataille stepped out.

CHAPTER 17

Monique held a steaming plate in one hand and a steaming mug of fresh morning mud in the other hand. Haskell quickly stepped up to help her with the screen door.

"What's all this?"

"Breakfast."

"For me?"

"Of course. Here — take it. The coffee is burning my hand." She laughed.

Haskell grabbed the coffee mug, then took the plate from her, as well. "I don't know what to say."

"Yes, we seem to have that trouble — don't we?"

Haskell blushed. "You, as well?"

She smiled, pressing her lips together and dimpling her cheeks. She wore a flannel nightgown and wool slippers. Around her shoulders and waist she held a striped wool blanket. "Cold out here." She shivered. "Sit and eat before it gets cold. It's probably not very good. I rarely get the opportunity to cook around here."

"Why is that, anyway?" He set his cup on the table before the other empty one, and hungrily dug into the plate of scrambled eggs and bacon and two baking powder biscuits slathered in bacon gravy.

"Judith told me when I first got here that she wouldn't tolerate me in the kitchen. I guess a friend of hers back in Kansas had a Jewish maid, and the family got sick. They all attributed the illness to a Jew in the kitchen, so they forever forbade the woman to cook."

Haskell laughed ironically.

"Please, do eat," Monique said when she saw him hesitating. "I don't want it to get cold."

"Have a seat, then," he said, indicating the chair to his left, which Judith had occupied the night before.

He went ahead and took advantage of her invitation. He dug into the breakfast like a starving man who'd walked a hundred miles across a desert for a meal. He hadn't realized how hungry he was. Not more than two minutes had passed between his first bite and the last bit of grease-soaked biscuit he shoved into his mouth.

Glancing sheepishly at Monique, he set

his fork quietly on his plate and set the plate onto the table. "Uh . . . sorry you had to witness that."

She was leaning forward, huddled in her blanket, her eyes aglow as she watched him in unbridled delight. "I don't think I've ever seen a man eat so heartily."

"Like I said, sorry —"

"I bet you make love the same way."

Haskell's heart thudded. He stared at her, aghast.

Monique laughed and flushed, as though embarrassed at what had escaped her mouth. "Never mind." She shook her head and looked at her feet. "I enjoyed watching you eat." She sat back in her chair and crossed her legs under her nightgown. "I rarely have the company of men. I was raised with brothers, and I miss them."

Haskell sipped his coffee. "Judith keeps a pretty tight rein, I reckon."

"It's more than that." Monique looked away, vaguely troubled. She didn't appear sure she could continue.

Haskell reflected that the folks who lived here at the edge of Julesburg sure seemed to have a lot of things they had trouble talking about.

He didn't prod Monique. He didn't know her well enough, nor she him. But she must have decided to go ahead with what she'd started, because suddenly she turned to him and said, "She watches me sometimes. Through a keyhole in my washing room door." She glanced down as though with shame. "When I'm bathing."

Haskell let a breath out slowly. "I see."

"Do you?"

"Sure. I've been around the block a few times, known plenty of other women like that. She's jealous."

"I gathered that. And for that reason, she keeps me close to the house. I certainly don't know of any other reason why she would. I am twenty-six years old, and I should be allowed private time. Her excuse, however, is that she doesn't want me setting a poor example for Sylvie. I wouldn't stand for such treatment, but I need this job. There isn't much I can do."

"There is something you could do."

Monique arched a dark brow at him.

"Haul your freight. Leave."

"Where would I go? I've no home. My parents are dead. I came out here from Philadelphia for this job. I don't know of any other way to support myself."

"You could support yourself the same way in Denver. More and more families — wealthy families in need of housekeepers and governesses — are pouring into Denver. Why, you could have a job in a matter of days. Hell, I know men who work in the government. Powerful men with connections."

Monique looked startled, a little frightened. "Oh, Bear, I . . ."

Haskell got up and dropped to a knee beside her. He didn't feel one bit foolish, because he didn't have time to reflect on it. His feelings were moving him along at a frantic pace. He took her right hand in his. "What the hell is going on with us, anyway? I've never felt this way about a woman before . . . so soon after just meeting."

"I don't know." Monique laughed, gazing down at him with open delight once more. "I must say I've never been so taken by any man." She studied him closely through slitted lids. "I don't . . . I don't quite know what to make of you, Bear."

"I don't quite know what to make of you, either, Monique. But I'm not asking you to marry me or nothin' like that. I'm not the marryin' sort. But I think you could do better somewhere else, better than being talked down to by a spoiled brat like Sylvie. I like Miss Judith just fine, but you obviously don't feel the same way about her as she does you, and it ain't right, her not letting you live your life."

"I'm still not sure what you're saying."

"I'm saying come to Denver with me. I want to get to know you better, and I think you'd like to get to know me better. I could help set you up in a better life. Maybe not the kind of life a woman like you deserves, but better than what the Lockharts are offering here."

Haskell could resist the temptation no longer. He took her in his arms and kissed her. Hungrily. Like she was the first woman he'd ever kissed. She returned the kiss in kind.

Reluctantly, he disentangled his tongue from hers. She seemed reluctant to break the kiss, as well. He had to gently push her away from him.

"Think about it," he said. "Think long and hard on it, Monique. It might be better in Denver, it might be worse. I'm not guaranteeing anything. But it'll be different. And we can get to know each other."

Slowly, he rose, towering over her. She looked up at him, befuddled, breathless. She swallowed, then nodded. "All right. I'll think about it."

He pinched his hat brim to her, smiled, and winked. "I have to get to work. I'll be back."

225

Haskell grabbed his rifle, shouldered it, and walked down the porch steps and into the yard, angling toward the stables in back. His boots felt like lead. He didn't want to leave Monique. He felt an almost overpowering pull toward her.

But he had to run down Jamie Lockhart before he found his father and killed him.

After all, that was why he was here.

At the southeast edge of Julesburg, Haskell crossed the South Platte via an old wooden bridge, turned the buckskin onto the old stage and freight road, and headed southwest. He rode along the river for a ways, the sunlight shimmering on the tea-colored water, then drew away from it and over a low rise of buttes, the trail twisting up them and down the other side.

When he topped another rise, he drew the buckskin to a halt and stared at the rolling prairie ahead of him. There it was — the old cavalry fort. It sat in a broad bowl of fawn-colored ground about a quarter-mile south of where the river made a broad, horseshoe-shaped bend. Twenty or so mud-brick, sod-roofed shacks of various sizes ringing a parade ground roughly a hundred yards long by fifty yards wide.

The old flagpole remained standing in the

middle of the parade area. No flag had likely hung from the pole in years.

The parade ground was grown up with sage, buckbrush, greasewood, and prickly pear. Gophers peeped from the brush, dashing from hole to hole.

The only building that appeared to still be in use was the largest one sitting off a ways by itself, south of the parade ground and the other shacks. It was flanked by a barn and corral and several other, smaller outbuildings including a privy. Like the others, the main building was constructed of mud bricks, and it had a dilapidated porch sagging off its front wall. The building's shake shingles and wooden window casings were badly timeworn. Many of the shakes were missing.

The only thing that made the structure appear occupied was the thin curl of smoke rising from the brick chimney poking up from the building's southeast side, and the curtains Haskell could see hanging in some of the windows.

Otherwise, this building — which Judith had told him was the former sutler's store and saloon — was nearly as shabby as the outpost's other derelict quarters. Another thing that gave the place an air of habitation was the fact that a person stood atop the nearly barren hill to the west of it. The person was a girl, judging by the dress she wore and her long hair blowing in the warm, dry breeze.

Around her bristled a good dozen or more leaning wooden crosses. The top of the hill was marked off by sun-bleached stones. Near where the girl stood rose a large, twisted cedar.

As Haskell watched, the girl appeared to kneel down. She knelt there for a time, then ran her hand over the top of the wooden cross protruding from the ground before her. She straightened, then turned and started down the gently sloping hill toward the old sutler's store. She took long, light-footed strides, keeping her head down.

Her long hair winged out behind her in the breeze.

Haskell clucked to the buckskin and started down the hill he was perched on, northeast of the fort and the old store. He booted the horse into a lope, dropping smoothly down the hill and then out across the flat, the old sutler's store moving up on his right, still a good distance away, the fort spreading out behind it.

When Haskell followed the trail's curve to the right and came within a hundred yards of the store, the girl must have heard his galloping hoof thuds. Still moving down the cemetery's easy rise, she swung her head toward him as though with a start. She stopped, raised a hand to shade her eyes, and held her head still, studying him.

Haskell continued loping toward her and threw a hand out to signal he was friendly. She didn't seem to take the gesture as friendly, however, nor the man who'd given it. She continued down the hill at a fast walk, swinging her arms stiffly at her sides, keeping her head forward.

"Hello!" Haskell called as he drew within a hundred feet of her.

She jerked another look at him and then broke into an all-out run.

"I'm friendly!" Haskell yelled, slowing his horse to take some of the apparent menace out of his approach. "Name's Haskell. I'm a deputy United States marshal!"

"Go away!" the girl screamed as she crossed the yard and then took the steps of the porch two at a time. She crossed the porch, opened the rusted screen door, reached inside the store, and pulled out an old-model Winchester. She stood back against the crumbling brick front wall, holding the rifle up high across her chest.

"I just want to palaver," Haskell said, walking the buckskin up toward one of the well-worn hitch racks fronting the place. "I'm a deputy United States marshal. See?" He brushed his gloved left thumb across the moon and star he wore on his calico shirt.

"Anyone can cut a badge out of an airtight tin," the girl said, scowling across the porch at the newcomer.

She was plain in a rustic sort of way, though not ugly. Her long hair was straight and brown. Her face was vaguely heart-shaped, the nose blistering from sunburn. Her light-brown eyes were cast with a wolf-like malice as she rubbed her delicate thumb across the Winchester's hammer.

At first, Haskell had thought she was young. Maybe around fifteen or sixteen. But now he realized that it was merely a youthful impression she conveyed. The lines around her eyes, the texture of her skin, said she was probably a good ten years older than her demeanor said she was. Maybe in her middle twenties.

"You're right, you're right," Haskell said, glancing down at the badge again. He slid his hand back toward a rear pocket of his canvas trousers. "Want me to show you my bona fides?"

"You're *what*?" she barked, angrily pumping a round into the Winchester's breech.

"No, no, no, no," Haskell said, chuckling and holding both his hands up, palms forward. "Nothin' like that. Bona fides is an official identification."

"Look, mister, I don't care who you are. I'm a young woman alone here, and I don't appreciate strangers. Especially strange men. Especially strange men as big as you are!" Her gaze slid across his broad shoulders.

"I thought you ran a saloon."

"So what if I do?"

"You must get a few men like me comin' around for a glass of busthead once in a while."

"Rarely these days."

"That a fact?"

"Most of my customers are regulars. Men who live up and down the Platte. On little shotgun ranches or placer diggin's. I know 'em. They know me. As for strangers — I don't see that many no more, since the railroad came and no one uses the freight road anymore."

"How about if I buy a drink from you, Miss Evangeline? Hell, I'll even buy you one. When two people share a drink you really can't call 'em strangers anymore — savvy?" Haskell fashioned a winning, good-humored grin.

She wasn't having any of it. When he'd said her name, the skin above the bridge of her nose wrinkled, and her gaze grew even more wary. She tilted her head to one side and asked suspiciously, "Who told you my name?"

"Judith."

"Con Lockhart's sister." The girl said the words tightly, wrinkling her upturned nose slightly, distastefully.

"That's right."

"What're you talkin' to her about me for?" The air of suspicion around the girl was like a heavy, invisible veil.

"Her nephew broke out of Trinidad Pen."

She didn't say anything for a moment. "What's that got to do with me?"

"Nothin'."

She tilted her head to the other side. "Then what are you doin' here?"

"To tell you the truth, Miss Evangeline, I was just out ridin' in circles since Jamie hasn't shown himself in town. I've already decided he's likely in Mexico by now, and I wasted a trip to Julesburg from Denver. I just followed the old freight road, seen your place sittin' way out here, and thought I'd stop for a drink."

"You said you was talkin' to Miss Judith about me."

The girl didn't miss much, Haskell thought. She sensed he was lying. He'd have to lie better if he thought he was going to get her to let her guard down. As well as that Winchester . . .

"Your uncle had a bad night. I sat up with Judith. We talked pretty much about everything, including her favorite color. You know what that is?"

"Black, most likely."

Haskell laughed. "You know Judith."

That got her to smile, though she tried hard not to.

"Her favorite color is yellow."

"So it is," Evangeline said, her tone softening.

"You know what mine is?"

"How would I know that?"

"Green. What's yours?"

"I don't have one."

"Okay, we know one thing about each other now. My favorite color is green, and you don't have one. How about you let me step down from my saddle without drillin' me a third eye, and let me buy us each a drink?"

She stared at him.

"Come on." Haskell turned his head to glance at the cemetery capping the low hill in the west. A breeze picked up some dust there and swirled it. It shone tan in the brassy sunlight.

Bear turned back to the young woman and said, "Must get damned lonely out here — don't it?"

She stared at him for several more seconds.

"All right," she said, depressing the Winchester's hammer and lowering the weapon. "But just one."

CHAPTER 18

Haskell doffed his hat and hung it on a hook in the wall beside him.

He was sitting at a table in the small saloon area of the old sutler's store, which was now the Evangeline Lockhart residence. He imagined that the dozen or so small tables fronting the plank board bar at the back of the low-ceilinged room had likely been filled to brimming most nights of the week, back when the fort was occupied.

The old floor puncheons were scuffed and gouged where the soldiers' spurs had probably scraped them when they'd been carousing, staggering around drinking, full of soldiers' blather, dancing with the pleasure girls the old sutler had probably housed in cribs in the second story and paraded down the stairs each night, painted up and dressed in the colors of exotic birds.

Now there were just the tables. Cobwebs. Mouse shit near the baseboards. Dust-streaked windows. A few dusty deer and elk heads mounted on the walls, above the wainscoting and where the old faded red print wallpaper was peeling. A piano sat in the corner under a thick layer of dust.

"Quit studyin' my housekeepin' or the deal's off," Evangeline said now as she splashed amber liquid from an unlabeled bottle into two shot glasses on the bar, back where the light from the windows barely reached.

"Sorry," Haskell said, and averted his gaze to his own table, into which the initials C.G. and K.L. had been scraped with a knife, on either side of a crudely carved heart.

"I see no reason to keep up appearances when I get so few visitors," the young woman said, dragging the heels of her low black boots as she tramped over from the bar, holding a shot glass in each hand.

"Don't blame you a bit." Haskell glanced through the dusty window on his right. "That your father you were visiting when I rode in?"

"Yes."

"How long's he been dead?"

"Judith prob'ly didn't tell you that. Maybe she doesn't even know Pa's gone. Or the sheriff, neither."

"I wouldn't know. You're right — we

236

didn't discuss it."

"No discussion about Pa at all." Evangeline had set one of the shot glasses down in front of Bear, the other one on the other side of the table. She sagged into a chair sideways, curling her left leg under the right one, beneath her plain, homespun dress, smiling knowingly and without a bit of humor at her sole customer. "Now, ain't that sweet?"

She made her voice syrupy with ironic, barely bridled anger.

Haskell sipped the whiskey. It was definitely of the bottom-shelf variety, but he tried not to make a face. He let the toxic sludge — probably from the bottom of a vat on which a dead diamondback had lolled — roll back over his tongue, and swallowed, clearing his throat slightly against the acidic burn, and said, "Your pa and Con Lockhart didn't get along — I take it?"

That was what Judith had told him. There was no point in Evangeline knowing that, however. She was naturally wary, which was understandable, and Haskell didn't want her to know he was here for any other reason than the coffin varnish and a little polite conversation to while away the better part of a boring morning.

He didn't want her to suspect the real

reason for his visit just yet, anyway.

"Get along?" Evangeline mocked him, rolling her eyes and wobbling her head. "No, they didn't *get along.* Not because Pa didn't want to get along with his brother, but because Con Lockhart was an asshole from the day he was born, and he'll be one till the day someone puts a bullet in him."

She picked up her shot glass using only her thumb and index finger, and threw back half the shot. She swallowed and sucked a breath through gritted teeth, then smacked her lips together. She was used to the stuff. Her cheeks didn't even flush like Haskell was sure his own had.

Tough gal.

An angry one, too.

"You don't like your uncle very much," Haskell said.

"Why would I? He killed my father, the son of a bitch! Pa died two months ago, and it was Con Lockhart who killed him . . . long before."

"How so?"

She opened her mouth to speak sharply but had second thoughts. She closed her mouth and scowled across the table at him, suspicious again. "Forget it. It ain't important." She threw back the rest of her shot, then set the glass back down on the table.

"I should get back to work. Cold weather will be here soon, and I got to get some wood hauled in."

Wanting to stay right where he was, Haskell threw his own shot back, tried and failed to stifle a choking cough, and slid the glass toward Evangeline Lockhart's side of the table. He dangled a baited hook with: "I was only askin' because I like Con myself. Him and me have worked together from time to time, on several cases, and I always thought he was right upstanding."

He nudged the glass another inch toward her. "Another round? On me."

"You don't know Con Lockhart very well at all, then, if you think he's upstanding. Upstanding, my ass!" She rose, swiped both shot glasses off the table, and strode back over to the bar.

She tossed another angry scowl Haskell's way and popped the cork on the same bottle she'd poured from before, making Bear's gut wince. "He and my pa are the only two brothers that made it through the war. There was five, but three died. Con an' Pa came back and aimed to prove up on Granddad's ranch. But Pa wasn't the rancher Con was. My pa was slower moving. He wasn't greedy. Oh, he'd put in a day's work, but then he wanted to have a little fun. He said he wanted to enjoy his life, since we all only got so much time on this side of the sod."

She refilled the two shot glasses and brought them back to the table, retaking her chair but sitting on her other leg this time. "Con got on Pa's case about it. Was forever rawhiding him. Finally, they got into a fight an' Pa told Con he could buy him out. So Con did. But he cheated him bad, gave him only half of what his interest in the ranch was worth. Pa fell for it because he was tired of working for Con. Pa bought this place with the money he made on his portion of the ranch. It was a good bet, too, for two whole years, when a stage was comin' through three times a week and mule teams were pulling through here from either Denver or Council Bluffs nearly *every day.*"

"But then the railroad came."

"But then the railroad came. An' Ma got sick. That wiped us out. My brother, Ned, went bad. He's in jail down South some-wheres. An' Pa had two heart strokes and then another one in his brain. The last few weeks of his life he was like a toddler. I had to hand feed him and change him like a baby. He didn't talk but only babbled. Half the time I don't even think he knew who I was. The other half of the time he realized what had happened to him, and he cried. Howled like a coyote till I couldn't take it and had to run outside till he stopped."

She lowered her head and sobbed quietly, tears oozing from her eyes to dribble down her cheeks.

"I'm so sorry, Evangeline." Haskell reached across the table and closed his hand over hers. "Now, you're all alone."

"That's right." She lifted her head, sniffed, and looked out the window on her left, staring toward the hill. "I'm all alone. Just me an' the dead soldiers. An' Pa . . ."

"Your hatred of Con Lockhart is understandable."

She chuffed ironically at that. "Of course, it's understandable."

Haskell took another reluctant sip of the whiskey, and when it had done its damage inside him, he rubbed his fist across his mouth and sat back in his chair, hooking his thumbs behind his suspenders. He studied the girl sitting across the table from him, staring out the window toward her father's grave.

"You haven't said anything about Jamie, Evangeline."

She turned to him, frowning, her eyes still slick with tears. "What?"

"I mentioned Jamie bustin' out of Trinidad several minutes ago, an' you didn't have much of a reaction to that. How come? Judith said you were close, growing up together out at the ranch . . ."

Evangeline just stared at him, suspicion beginning to germinate again in her eyes.

Haskell said, "Did you know about Jamie swearing he'd kill his father someday? After the trial . . . ?"

"Who doesn't know about that?"

Haskell canted his head to one side. "Do you know how he busted out of Trinidad, Evangeline?"

A long pause. Her gaze was flat, skeptical. "How would I know anything about that?"

Haskell continued to study her. She was harboring secrets. Of that he was certain. But whoever had helped Jamie escape from Trinidad Pen had money. It would have taken a good amount to pay off a guard or two to spring a prisoner from Trinidad, likely much more than Evangeline could have got her hands on.

She certainly had the motivation, though. Her hatred of Con Lockhart was obvious. Knowing that Jamie would likely ride back here and make good on his promise to kill his father would probably have made Evangeline one very happy niece. She'd have seen it ironically fitting, too, to have kept the killings all in the family, since she fully believed that her own father had been murdered, albeit indirectly, by his brother.

Haskell looked around at the cobwebs hanging from where the square-hewn support posts met the ceiling, the dust on the battered piano, the mouse dung speckling the floor near the baseboards.

The only problem with Bear's theory was money. There just wasn't any here. At least, it sure as hell didn't look that way.

Haskell threw back the last of the whiskey, put his fist against his mouth, stifling a strangling cough, and rose from his chair. "If you see Jamie, greet him for me, will you? I mean, I know you and him were close. If he's around, you an' him will likely meet up sooner or later . . . don't you think?"

She stared up at him with grim defiance, and twisted her mouth snidely. "If I see Cousin Jamie, I will most certainly greet him for you, Mister Lawman. You greet my uncle for me. Tell him that if Jamie's around, he's likely to get a big heaping shovel full of just desserts."

Her eyes glittered with wry humor. Keeping her gaze on Haskell, she picked up her shot glass with her right thumb and index finger, extending her pinkie as though it were her middle finger, and threw back the entire shot as though it were warm tea and honey.

She must have a cast-iron stomach. But that was all that was cast iron about her. She acted tough, but she really wasn't. She'd been beaten to a pulp by life.

By life and, apparently, Con Lockhart.

Haskell felt deeply sorry for her. But he was also suspicious of her. He hoped she hadn't had anything to do with Jamie's prison break. He didn't want any more bad to come down on her. She'd had enough bad. She lived alone here with the mice and the ghosts of her father and a dozen dead soldiers.

Haskell pinched his hat brim to her. "Good day, Miss Evangeline. Nice to have made your acquaintance."

"Likewise, I'm sure," she said through a faint sneer.

He walked outside, took a slow look around the grounds of the old fort, then swung up onto the buckskin and rode back the way he'd come.

He was aware of Evangeline's gaze following him as he rode away from the old sutler's store.

■ ■ ■ ■

To cleanse his palette of Evangeline Lockhart's tarantula juice, Haskell drew half a shot of labeled bourbon into his mouth and swished it around before swallowing. He smacked his lips and splashed more of the Old Reserve into his shot glass, then plucked an Indian Kid from his shirt pocket and scratched a match to life on the table here in Sheriff Lockhart's Big Saloon.

He touched the flame to the cheroot. He drew the smoke deep into his lungs, blew out the match with a smoke plume, and tossed the lucifer onto the empty plate before him. He'd had a cheese sandwich and a bowl of chili, having stopped here for lunch after leaving the old sutler's store. He'd taken a ride around town. All had appeared relatively quiet for Julesburg at midday in the middle of the week. He'd seen no sign of Lockhart or a man who might have been his son.

Hunger pangs eventually lured Bear to Lockhart's saloon. Eventually, Lockhart would probably show. Bear didn't really care if he didn't, though he supposed the only way he was going to run Jamie Lockhart down was to stick close to the heels of his father and hope to catch the killer before he did what he'd come here for.

Haskell sat back in his chair and took another drag off the Indian Kid.

He was in a sour mood. It had soured when he'd gone over to the old sutler's store and met Evangeline and learned the kind of life she lived, her father dead, her now living alone in isolation, alienated from her extended family.

Haskell thought that if he were she, he'd likely want Lockhart just as dead as she did.

As though the thought had summoned the man, Haskell heard footsteps and looked up to see Con Lockhart himself striding into the room from the swinging batwings. He was heading toward Bear's table, looking grim, vaguely sheepish.

"I thought maybe you'd gone back to Denver." Lockhart gave a shrewd half-smile. "Having trouble admitting defeat?"

"Defeat?"

"Yes, Jamie isn't here. Matt Delaney didn't get a good look at the man who'd bushwhacked him and Haugen, but he thought it might have been a freighter they arrested last month for beating up a whore in a Chinese cathouse down by the river. In fact, by the time I left Matt at the doc's office, he was convinced that's exactly who it was. I'm on the scout for him now. Bernard Colson. Slender, bearded fella with one lazy eye. Around forty. Has a slight limp. I've run down several of Colson's acquaintances, and they think he's still in Julesburg."

"Slender fella with one lazy eye."

"I think it's the left one. If you insist on remaining here in Julesburg, keep an eye out for him, will you? I don't have a deputy hired yet, but I've got my feelers out for a couple. Matt's going to be out for at least a month. We're going to bury Karl this afternoon."

Lockhart started to turn and walk away but stopped when Haskell said, "I just had a visit with your niece."

Lockhart scowled. "What's that?"

"Evangeline Lockhart. Remember her? She lives alone now at the old sutler's store at the fort." Haskell took a drag from the Indian Kid and studied the coal as he blew out the smoke. "Alone, she says, because of you."

CHAPTER 19

"Evangeline's alone?" Lockhart said. "I don't understand."

"Your brother's dead."

Lockhart sat down slowly in the chair across from Haskell. "That doesn't surprise me." He motioned to the bartender, who nodded, and then Con turned to Bear. "My brother wasn't well. Hadn't been well for years. How . . . how is his daughter . . . Evangeline . . . how is she doing?"

"You should ride out and see for yourself."

Lockhart stared at Haskell. It quickly became a glare, the man's cheeks and ears turning red. "How dare you judge me!"

"Everyone judges."

The bartender approached tentatively due to the sudden loudening of the conversation, and just as tentatively set a tumbler on the table in front of Lockhart.

The sheriff didn't seem to notice the man but, wrapping his right hand around the glass and squeezing until Haskell thought it would break, kept his angry gaze on Bear. With his other hand, he filled the glass from the bottle of Old Reserve. "Just because you come here and find out things about me . . . about my boy . . . his problems . . . about my trouble with my brother . . . you think you know me. Well, you don't!"

He slammed the bottle back down on the table.

"Ambition has a downside, Con." Haskell lifted his glass, sipped, and set it down slowly. "That downside can come back to nip you in the ass. Jamie is here. Sooner or later, he's going to show himself, and when he does, all hell is going to . . ."

He let his voice trail off when he spied movement out the window — a carriage approaching the saloon behind a galloping cream mare. Several pedestrians ran to get out of the way, and a man on horseback reined his mount out of the carriage's path just in time to prevent getting bulled over. He cast a sharp look at the carriage, cursing angrily.

Haskell blinked, waited until the carriage rolled closer, then blinked again. His heart quickened. Judith was wielding the mare's reins. She wore a man's hat and a string tie, which blew back over her shoulder in the wind. Monique sat beside her, hatless, wrapped in a brown shawl.

"What is it?" Lockhart asked. "What's out there?"

He could hear the angry shouting of another man on the street whom the mare had nearly run over before Judith had jerked back on the reins, stopping the sweating mare in front of the broad steps leading up to the saloon's front veranda.

"That hell I was talking about?" Bear said, sliding his chair back and reaching for his Henry leaning against the wall beside him. "I think it might have just broke."

"What?" Lockhart leaned forward, turning his head to see over his left shoulder. "What in god's name . . . ?"

Judith was yelling for Lockhart.

Haskell hurried out of the saloon, pushing through the batwings and stepping onto the veranda. "What is it?" he asked. "What happened?"

Lockhart strode out behind him, scowling incredulously at his sister. "Judith . . . ?"

"Con!" Judith yelled, red-faced. She tried to speak but her lips only trembled and then she gave a bizarre-sounding wail, tears rolling down her swollen cheeks.

Monique looked at her, then turned her own anxious gaze to Lockhart and Haskell.

"It's Sylvie! She's been taken!"

"Taken?" Lockhart stumbled backward. His knees seemed to buckle.

"We thought she was just sleeping in," Monique explained. "When I went up to check on her, she was gone. I found this on her bed." The governess held up a scrap of notepaper, which ruffled in the breeze. "It says you can find her at the old fort!"

"The old fort?" Lockhart looked both astonished and skeptical. "Who . . . ?"

"Who do you think?" Haskell said, clomping down the porch steps and ripping the buckskin's reins from the hitch rack.

As he swung up onto the horse's back, he glanced at Lockhart. The man was coming down the steps, as well. His face was pale. He looked like a deeply befuddled old man.

"Hold on," he said to Bear. "Wait, now. Wait for me." As he heaved himself into the saddle of his fine Appaloosa, he turned to Judith sitting in the buggy beside Monique, looking horrified.

"Go on home," Lockhart told his sister. "I'll have her home soon."

"It's him, isn't it?" Judith said, her voice dull with shock. "Oh, god!"

"Go on home!" Lockhart barked, then reined his horse away from the hitch rack.

He and Haskell booted their mounts into

trots, heading toward the west edge of town, weaving their way through the midday traffic. A dog ran out from an alley mouth and nipped at the hocks of Lockhart's Appy. The sheriff didn't seem to notice. He looked like a man in a trance, his eyes wide and glassy, lower jaw sagging, cheeks pale, his nose bright red. Haskell was afraid he'd have another heart attack.

At the edge of town, Bear nudged the buckskin into a gallop. Lockhart followed suit. They crossed the river and tore up the trail, following the slow curves, for a while hugging the broad Platte, but then following the trail in a wide curve to the southwest.

When they topped the last hill and started down the other side, riding hard, Lockhart now barking at his mount for more speed and whipping its hindquarters with his reins, a scream sounded from the old sutler's store ahead and on their right.

"Poppa!" came Sylvie's screeching cry, just audible beneath the thunder of the lawmen's galloping horses.

"Good god!" Haskell heard Lockhart mutter, riding just off his right stirrup.

Haskell studied the sutler's store, the sprawling, mud-brick structure moving up on his right now, the abandoned parade ground ringed with derelict barracks flanking it, the whole place baking in the harsh, midday sunlight. He saw no movement anywhere around the store. No one in the cemetery atop the hill to his left, either.

"Poppa!" Sylvie cried again as Haskell and Lockhart approached the store at a full gallop.

The cry had come from inside the shack.

As he checked the buckskin down hard, Haskell glanced at Lockhart, who was halting his Appaloosa.

"It's a trap," Haskell warned, stepping smoothly down from the buckskin's back.

Lockhart didn't say anything as he swung gingerly but quickly from his saddle. He unholstered the Colt .44 from its holster strapped to his right thigh, and clicked the hammer back. Haskell stepped up to the man's left side and unholstered his Schofield, scrutinizing the store's front windows, expecting to be fired on at any moment.

"Poppa!"

"I'm here!" Lockhart lurched into an unsteady run toward the steps leading up to the front porch.

Haskell ran up behind him and leaped onto the porch, left of the steps, swinging around in front of the sheriff.

"Con — let me go in first."

He didn't wait for a reply. He turned to the door, pricking his ears, listening for movement inside, and tripped the metal and leather latch. The door sagged on its leather hinges. Haskell nudged it inward, extending the cocked Schofield straight out in front of him. The pent-up smell of the place pushed against him. Along with the musty smell came the smell of fresh cigar smoke.

He stepped quickly inside and to the right. Lockhart stepped in behind him and didn't bother avoiding the bright sunlight framed by the door. He strode into the saloon's murky shadows, looking around and barking, "Sylvie? Sylvie?"

"Hold on, Con," Bear urged.

Haskell's eyes had adjusted to the dimness enough that he could see the girl at the back right side of the room, at the bottom of the wooden staircase. She was dressed in a frilly nightgown, and that was all. Her legs and feet were bare. She stood on a chair back, about three feet off the floor. A rope was wound around her fine, pale neck and tied off somewhere straight above her, unseen, likely on the stair rail in the second story.

She shifted her little pink feet on the top of the curving chair back. The chair wobbled beneath her weight, the wood creaking, the uneven legs thumping and scraping against the floor. Sylvie was sobbing and wincing against the rope drawn taut against her throat. Her hands were tied behind her back.

"Help me, Poppa!"

"Sylvie!" Lockhart lunged toward his daughter.

As he did, a figure rose leisurely from the stairs behind Sylvie — a shadowy figure wearing a Stetson and holding a Winchester. The sunlight brushed only part of him. His face was round and unshaven, the eyes a cold, dark blue. A slender, tan cigar poked out from one corner of his mouth, drooping slightly, gray smoke curling up beneath the brim of his hat.

"That's far enough, there, Poppa." The man loudly leveled a round into the Winchester's action and held the rifle straight out from his right side, aiming over the downward slanting stair rail at Lockhart, who stopped abruptly.

Haskell had moved forward, but he stopped, as well. He was several feet behind Lockhart and to the man's right, but he could see the sheriff's lower jaw sagging in shock.

The man holding the Winchester grinned, eyes flashing cruelly.

"Miss me, *Poppa*?" He bit that last word out through gritted teeth, eyes instantly going flat and cold.

"Jamie, for god's sake!" Lockhart took another step forward.

The rifle crashed. Flames lapped from the barrel.

Sylvie screamed and nearly lost her balance on the chair.

The bullet slammed into a table just right of Lockhart. The sheriff stopped dead in his tracks, glancing at the hole in the table.

"I'll put the next one in your belly, *Poppa*," Jamie said.

"She's your sister!"

"*Half*-sister. Besides, why should she have it so good? I spent the last ten years in Trinidad."

"If you're going to kill me, kill me," Lockhart said, spreading his arms. He still had the Colt in his right hand. "But cut Sylvie down. She has no part in this."

"She does now."

"What do you mean?"

"She's gonna be the jury."

"What jury?"

"A trial needs a jury," Jamie said. "That's what we got us here. A trial. A new one. For both me and you. Let's see what verdict our jury of one comes up with . . . once she's heard all the evidence."

Before Lockhart could respond, Jamie Lockhart said, "But, first, I'm gonna need the bailiff. Evangeline?"

Boots scraped and thumped behind Haskell.

"You called?" the young woman said as she walked through the open door.

"I'm gonna need you to take these fellas' guns. No guns in the courtroom, please, fellas." Jamie looked very pleased with himself as he straightened the cigar in his mouth and the coal glowed red as he drew on it. He kept the Winchester aimed at his father.

"No sudden moves now, fellas," Jamie said as Evangeline walked deeper into the room. "Either of you so much as coughs, you might startle young Sylvie here, and she might fall off that chair and break her delicate neck. Or" — he aimed the rifle at the young blonde's head and said with menace — "I might shoot her."

"You're an animal," Lockhart said.

"Yes," Jamie said, grinning again. "Yes, I am. Thanks to ten long years in Trinidad for a crime I didn't commit."

"Didn't *commit*?"

Meanwhile, Evangeline had walked up to Haskell. She held her rifle on him with one hand and extended her free hand for his pistol. She gave him a sneering look and snapped her fingers.

Haskell depressed the Schofield's hammer and set the piece in her hand.

She set the gun on a table behind him, near the bar, then walked over to Lockhart. He held his Colt out without looking at her. He kept his gaze on his son holding the rifle on him from about five steps up the stairs, and on his sobbing daughter trying to maintain her balance on the chair.

Evangeline placed Lockhart's Colt on the same table as Haskell's, then sat down. She aimed her rifle over the table, covering both the sheriff and Bear.

Jamie slid his rifle toward Haskell. "Did you have a good time last night, big fella?"

Haskell hiked a shoulder. "Until it started rainin' lead."

Jamie chuckled. "Why don't you have a seat?" With his rifle, he indicated a table near Bear. "This courtroom needs an audience. A deputy U.S. marshal audience, all the better."

His eyes grew hard as they slid, along with the Winchester, back to Con. "As for the accused — you just stand there."

Con gave an angry, caustic chuff. "The *accused*? What're you talking about? You're mad. Just shoot me and be done with it and cut your sister down!"

"No, Poppa!" Sylvie cried.

Lockhart held his open hands out to the girl, pleading with her. "Stay still, Sylvie. Stay still. It's gonna be all right!"

"I'll cut her down just as soon as you confess your sins, old man."

"*My* sins?" Lockhart shook his head. "Jamie, I have no idea what you're talking about?"

"Still lyin' after all these years." Jamie hardened his jaws and glowered at his father. "I didn't kill Lucia, and you know it. You wouldn't listen to reason back then. Back then, I didn't know why you wouldn't. I didn't know why you were so bound and determined to believe I killed her, an' wouldn't listen when I told you I didn't do it. I thought it was just because you still believed I killed Ma, and this was your way of gettin' back at me. It didn't take me long after I got to Trinidad to figure it out, though."

"Figure what out?"

"That *you* killed her, you son of a bitch! You knew we were going to meet in that shack, the same one we always met in, by Arapaho Creek. You rode out there, found her waiting for me, and you beat her to death in a rage. You rode off, saw me comin'

259

to meet her, and circled around. You rode up on me after I found her . . . beaten to death with that axe handle.

"You stormed after me, determined to kill me. I could see it in your eyes. The same look you had when you brought the lifeless body of my lightning-struck mother to that shack you locked me in! When I saw you were gonna blame me for Lucia, too, I mounted up and hightailed it, and you gathered that posse and ran me down and shot me like a calf-eatin' coyote in the Dinosaur Rocks! And you dragged me back to town for a kangaroo trial! Well, I'm back, *Poppa*! How do you like me now, you *murderin' son of a bitch*?"

Jamie snapped the Winchester to his shoulder and pressed his cheek to the stalk, aiming at Lockhart, who stood before him with his arms spread wide, eyes squeezed shut.

"No!" Haskell shouted.

The rifle thundered.

CHAPTER 20

Haskell jerked with a start, the rifle shot resounding throughout the saloon. He frowned toward the stairs.

Jamie fell back against the wall on the opposite side of the descending rail, cursing and inadvertently triggering his Winchester up into the stairwell.

Haskell glanced to his right. The shot had come from outside. There was a hole in a near window with cracks spidering away from it. On the other side of the glass, a stocky figure was pumping another round into a rifle breech.

Sylvie and Evangeline screamed at the same time.

"Jamie!" Evangeline cried, bounding to her feet, raising her Winchester, and taking aim at the window.

There were two more rifle barks as Haskell took two running steps to his right and then hurled himself over the table Evangeline had just evacuated. As he flew over the table, he grabbed his Schofield. He rolled up off his right shoulder and lifted his head above the table as Jamie heaved himself to his feet and aimed his Winchester at Con.

The elder Lockhart had turned toward the window from which the first shot had come.

Haskell aimed quickly and fired just as Jamie triggered his Winchester into his father.

Con grunted and staggered backward.

Jamie dropped the Winchester over the stair rail and flew back against the wall once more, falling and rolling down to the bottom of the stairs.

At the same time, Evangeline fired her third or fourth round out the window — Haskell had lost count in the sudden, explosive chaos — and turned to Lockhart, screaming. She fired at the sheriff from ten feet away, jerking Lockhart around and sending him stumbling back toward the stairs. Lockhart dropped to his knees, groaning, and picked up his son's Winchester.

He pumped a round into the action and looked at Evangeline walking toward him and cocking her own rifle.

"Bastard!" she cried. *"Bastard!"*

"Devil!" Lockhart bellowed back at her,

aiming Jamie's rifle at her.

"Stop!" Haskell bellowed.

Evangeline fired her rifle into Con.

The sheriff screamed and jerked backward, firing into Evangeline, still closing on him.

She yelped as she flew back over a chair, dropping her rifle with a clattering thump.

Con sagged down to the floor at the bottom of the stairs, near where his son lay unmoving.

"Sylvie!" a woman screamed somewhere behind Haskell.

Haskell turned to see Monique run into the saloon, heading for the stairs. Haskell's heart thudded when he saw Sylvie dangling in midair, bare feet kicking as she strangled. She'd apparently lost her purchase on the chair, which now lay on its side below her feet.

"Sylvie!" Monique screamed again, tripping over a chair and nearly falling before she reached her charge.

Sylvie made gagging, strangling sounds as she twisted in the air beneath the stair rail, her face swelling and turning red.

Haskell heaved himself to his feet and ran toward the stairs.

"Grab her legs!" Bear yelled at Monique.

As the governess hugged Sylvie's lower

legs and lifted, trying to ease the tension in the rope, Haskell leaped over Jamie's still, bloody body and ran five steps up the stairs. He looked up. The rope was tied over the second-floor rail several feet above his head. He jerked up the Schofield and fired four rounds, the fourth one finally tearing through the rope's last strand.

Monique gave another scream as Sylvie's body dropped. Together, the two hit the saloon floor, Sylvie on top of Monique.

Haskell dashed back down the stairs. Monique was rolling out from under Sylvie and pulling the noose up over her head, tossing it away.

"Sylvie?" Monique yelled. "Oh, Sylvie!"

The girl opened her eyes and drew a deep breath into her lungs. Immediately, she started sobbing and calling for her father. Lockhart pushed away from the wall encasing the stairwell near where Sylvie had been hanging. He'd been shot several times, blood oozing from wounds in one arm, his chest, low on the right side of his belly, and his left hip.

Haskell couldn't believe he was still alive.

"Sylvie," he said, grunting with agony. "Oh, lord . . . Sylvie!"

The girl sat up and threw her arms around her father's neck. "Poppa!"

Haskell rose and glanced at Monique. She stared, wide-eyed in shock, at Lockhart's bloody visage. Haskell touched her shoulder reassuringly and then went over and stared down at Jamie lying in a twisted pile at the bottom of the stairs. The younger Lockhart stared straight up past Haskell, his eyes glazed with death.

Haskell walked over to where Evangeline lay beside an overturned chair. She was on her side, facing the saloon's front wall. Bear dropped to a knee and turned her over. She, too, stared back at him through death-flat eyes. Lockhart's bullet had taken her through the dead center of her chest.

"Christ . . ."

Haskell walked outside. He strode heavily along the front veranda, where Judith lay with her head resting back against an awning support post. Her eyes were open, heavy bosom rising and falling slowly. She'd been shot two or three times in her chest.

Haskell dropped to a knee beside her, shaking his head, thoroughly puzzled. "Why?"

Judith winced as pain spasmed through her stout body. She groaned, shifted her position, and stared at Haskell. Her expression was sad and forlorn. A tear bubbled out of her right eye and dribbled down her cheek.

All at once, it dawned on Haskell.

"It was you," he said barely above a whisper. "Not Jamie. Not Con."

Scraping, hammering footsteps rose from inside the saloon.

"Why?" Haskell again asked the woman lying only half alive before him.

The footsteps grew closer. Haskell glanced over his left shoulder. Con Lockhart shambled out of the saloon and headed toward Bear and Judith. Blood matted his entire upper torso. Sylvie walked beside him, one arm around his back, the other around his belly, helping him. Her father's blood stained her now, as well.

Monique walked behind them, one arm crossed on her belly, her other hand across her mouth, muffling her sobs.

"Judith," Con said, approaching. "For god's sake . . . Judith . . ."

Haskell straightened and moved to one side, giving Lockhart room.

The sheriff dropped to a knee near his dying sister. Sylvie knelt beside her father. She was sobbing quietly, tears streaking her cheeks brushed with her father's blood.

"I killed her, Con," Judith raked out. "I . . . killed . . . that girl."

"What?"

"I killed Lucia."

Lockhart only stared at her, eyes wide and dull with disbelief.

Judith shook her head. "I followed him there . . . discovered where they were meeting. I intercepted a note . . . learned when they were going to meet again . . . and I rode out ahead of him. Wanted to . . . to talk to that girl. I only wanted to convince her to leave you both alone. She wouldn't listen. Said she loved . . . him. I went into a rage . . . couldn't control it."

"You . . . ?" Con said.

"I hit her once . . . with a . . . with an axe handle. Something snapped. I couldn't stop. I left when I heard him coming. Then you came, found him there."

"I got suspicious, followed him that day," Con muttered. "Oh, Jesus . . . Judith."

"I should have told you right away. But I didn't . . . and then the train had left the station." She gave a somber, fateful sigh. "I was just . . . just tryin' to help, Con. Keep them . . . from makin' a fool of you. From committing such a *sin*!" She laughed again, bizarrely. "I reckon I'll burn in hell." Coughs raked her. "I reckon . . . it's better than . . . than what I . . . deserve."

She convulsed once more, spasming.

Her eyes rolled back into her head. Her head slid slowly down the support post to rest on the veranda floor. Her stout body gave another jerk and lay still.

"Judith," Lockhart said.

For nearly a minute, his face was a mask of mute horror.

All that had happened. All he had done.

All he had done to his son . . .

He sagged slowly backward. Both Haskell and Sylvie caught him, but he was dead before they eased him down to the veranda floor.

Sylvie threw herself over him, wailing.

Haskell looked at Monique, and for several seconds they commiserated silently, sharing each other's shock and disbelief.

EPILOGUE

The funeral for the four dead Lockharts was well attended. In fact, it was probably the largest funeral Sedgwick County had ever seen.

Businessmen, drovers, drummers, bartenders, saloon swampers, city councilmen, county commissioners, freighters, prospectors, drifters, even a few gaudily clad parlor girls — nearly everyone in Sedgwick County came to the boot-hill boneyard on the outskirts of Julesburg, in a broad bend in the north bank of the South Platte River.

They stood gathered in a sprawling semicircle amongst the tombstones and crude wooden crosses, some shaded by the few cottonwoods standing sentinel there, listening to the preacher recite a few prayers, say a few words, and then toss the obligatory handful of dust on the four coffins lined before him glistening in the lemon afternoon light of the high plains of eastern Colorado.

Haskell didn't hear what the sky pilot said. He'd always been uncomfortable with funerals, rarely attending them, so he stood back near the gate of the fence that encircled the cemetery, near the horses. He leaned against the fence and smoked an Indian Kid, letting the breeze tear the smoke from his lips and nostrils.

"Terrible thing, what a family can do to each other."

He jerked his head around. He hadn't realized anyone else was back here with the horses, but he'd been wrong. Matt Delaney was sitting in the driver's seat of a rickety-looking buckboard maybe twenty feet away. The leg that had taken one of Jamie Lockhart's bullets was stretched out before him, propped on the wagon's dashboard. The leg of his denim jeans was sliced to accommodate the heavy bandages. His left arm was in a sling.

He looked pale and worn, his nose red from the sun angling in from beneath the broad brim of his Boss of the Plains Stetson.

Haskell flicked the Indian Kid away and walked over to the deputy.

"I didn't realize you were back here, Matt."

"I thought it best I stay here," Delaney

said. "I don't get around so well."

"Much pain?"

"Yep." Delaney reached inside his deerskin jacket, producing a leather-wrapped traveling flask. "Fortunately, I come prepared for the random spasm." He extended the flask to Haskell. "Sip?"

Haskell hiked a shoulder and took the flask, grinning. "Just to be polite."

He took a sip of the whiskey, then handed the flask back to Delaney.

"Yeah, families," Haskell said, turning back to watch the crowd just now beginning to break up on the other side of the cemetery. "Hard to figure 'em sometimes."

"Especially that one. Imagine that whole mess on account of Judith couldn't control her temper. Or tell the truth. Her, the wife of a preacher."

"Too proud."

"I reckon they all were."

"There's no tellin' about folks."

"Nope."

"Just like there's no tellin' how Evangeline Lockhart ever got enough money to bust Jamie out of prison," Haskell said. "Assumin' it was her who did it, that is." Leaning against a wheel of Delaney's wagon and staring toward the slowly dispersing crowd, he added half to himself, because it had confounded him no end, "But if not her, who?"

"Oh, it was her, all right," Delaney said, taking another pull from his flask. "Of that I'm certain."

Haskell glanced up at him, narrowing one eye. "Oh? Why?"

"I reckon you haven't heard."

"Heard what?"

"The banker in Julesburg, Ralph Wayne, mentioned to me after church last Sunday what a shame it was Evangeline hadn't used her inheritance to light a shuck out of Sedgwick County, like Zach had wanted her to."

Haskell turned full around to the deputy now, scowling up at him incredulously. "What're you talking about, Matt?"

"I asked Ralph the same thing. I reckon he figured I knew, though I don't know how I or anyone else but him would."

Delaney offered the flask to Haskell again, but Bear waved it off. The wounded deputy took another couple of small pulls, then screwed the cap back onto the flask and returned it to his shirt pocket, saying, "Zachariah Lockhart managed to save ten thousand dollars over the years. Mostly from gambling, which he was a pretty fair hand at. Always had been. Whenever he made a little extra, he squirreled it away with Wayne, in a special account at the bank. That account was for Evangeline. He wanted to make sure that after he died, she was taken care of. That she had enough money to hightail it out of here. He couldn't leave when he was alive. Too deeply rooted, I suppose. But he wanted to make sure Evangeline had that opportunity after he was gone."

"Holy shit," Haskell said. "But she didn't use the money for that."

"Nope."

"She used it to bust Jamie out of Trinidad," Haskell said, his voice hushed with skepticism. "So he could exact revenge for them both. I'll be damned."

He stared at the coffin four men were now carrying away from the other three, toward the undertaker's wagon. Evangeline would be buried with her father at the fort. Several men from town who'd known her and her father had thought it only fitting.

Haskell agreed.

He stared at the coffin, wondering at the size of the anger and hatred of the girl lying dead inside. Then he wondered at the fury that had been seething for so long inside the entire Lockhart family.

They could all rest easy now. All except Sylvie, that was. She was the sole survivor.

Haskell switched his gaze to the young blonde now. Monique was just then helping her into a chaise about fifty feet away from where he stood with Delaney.

The other mourners were slowly making their ways to their own rigs and saddled horses, murmuring amongst themselves. Haskell could smell the men's bay rum and the ladies' perfume, hear the horses snorting in anticipation of moving on.

Sylvie Lockhart was dressed in black widow's weeds complete with black felt hat, a black veil, and long, black gloves. Her curly hair looked especially blond in contrast to her grave attire. She appeared barely able to walk by herself. Monique walked along beside her, half-carrying her. One of Lockhart's cowpunchers was helping.

When they'd gotten the bereaved girl into the buggy, Monique glanced around, her gaze settling on Bear. As she started walking toward him, clad in a black dress that clung invitingly to her high-bosomed figure, a beaded black reticule dangling from her right wrist, Haskell pinched his hat brim to Delaney and walked up to meet Monique near the cemetery gate.

"I wasn't sure you came," she said, looking up at him with her liquid dark-brown eyes. The feathers adorning her small, black-

274

and-gray hat ruffled in the breeze. "I'm glad you did."

"I'm not much for funerals, but I thought I'd pay my respects."

"I suppose you'll be leaving soon."

Haskell had spent the last three days helping the county commissioners seat a temporary sheriff — one of the stock detectives Lockhart had often deputized when he'd needed an extra hand.

"Tomorrow morning," Haskell said. "First train out."

"Back to Denver?"

Haskell placed his hands on her shoulders. "Join me?"

Monique studied him for a moment, a faint longing in her eyes. Then she quirked a bittersweet smile. "Sylvie needs me more than ever now."

"What's she going to do?"

"I'll be taking her to live with some of her mother's family back East."

"You don't look unhappy about that."

"Only that I'll likely never see you again, Bear. I feel a strong pull toward you." Monique shook her head, smiling curiously. "I don't understand it. We're each from such different worlds."

"Kindred spirits," Haskell said. "I felt it right off." He gave her a sad smile. "If you ever change your mind, you know where to find me. I work out of the federal building on Colfax Avenue."

She returned his smile.

He squeezed her arms with affection and leaned toward her, glancing around a little self-consciously. "May I?"

"If you don't, I'll be deeply offended."

Despite the crowd milling around them, mounting horses and buggies, Haskell took the exotic beauty in his arms, tipped her head back, and kissed her. He savored the taste of her lips against his own.

Then he let her go.

"Goodbye, Bear," she said, brushing gloved fingers lightly down his cheek. She turned away.

He watched her go, his heart thudding heavily, sadly, in his chest.

But that wasn't their last goodbye. Unexpectedly, Monique knocked on his hotel room door late that night in Julesburg, when he'd been scratching out a detailed report for Henry Dade. He let her in, frowning curiously, wondering if something had happened to Sylvie.

"No," Monique said, smiling and shaking her head. She wore a long wool coat and black shoes. Her black hair spilled across her shoulders, shiny with a recent brushing and smelling like the cool night air tinged with woodsmoke. "Sylvie's fine."

"What is it, then?"

"I thought it only proper that two kindred spirits have a proper goodbye."

With that, she kicked off her shoes and opened the coat, letting it fall.

Haskell's breath caught as he looked down at her.

She wasn't wearing a stitch.

■ ■ ■ ■

BULLETS, BRUINS, & A LADY CALLED CHANCE

■ ■ ■ ■

CHAPTER 1

The old government tracker Stumpy Gibbs spat a stream of Taylor's Pride over the side of his saddle — though most of the raisin-colored chaw dribbled into his long salt-and-pepper beard already stained with the sun-baked remnants of his last three meals — and said, "That's it right there. That's the ghost town I told you about. I just know that's where them owlhoots are holed up! The last two of 'em, anyways."

As the buckskin-clad oldster checked down his sweat-lathered chestnut, pointing over the lip of the wash they were in, Deputy U.S. Marshal Bear Haskell halted his own sorrel. He'd requisitioned the mount at Fort Steele, sixty miles to the south and the last vestiges of civilization in this godforsaken part of east-central Wyoming. If any lowly outpost — especially the hard-bitten Steele — could be called civilized.

The only life Haskell had seen since leaving that louse- and rat-infested perdition was his partner, old Stumpy himself, a handful of jackrabbits, a diamondback rattler that had nearly sunk its fangs into his sorrel's left hock — threatening to set its rider afoot or to Stumpy mercy's, which amounted to the same thing — and three mangy coyotes fighting and yipping over a bloated-up brindle steer lying sun-seasoned in a shallow ravine.

Haskell blinked against his and his partner's dust catching up to them.

He followed Stumpy's gaze up over the lip of the wash and across a hundred or so yards of bunchgrass, sage, and prickly pear toward the old ghost town of Atlantic City, or so the town had been known at one time. Apparently the settlement once had high hopes for itself. Unfortunately, the final result was a dozen or so ragged, gray, wind- and sun-battered, gap-boarded shacks, crumbling adobes, and false-fronted business buildings standing out in the sandy prairie, listing badly in the same direction and looking as though the next stiff wind whistling down from the Bighorns looming in the north would pick it all up and toss it like matchsticks scattered by a Texas cyclone.

According to Stumpy, who knew the area better than Haskell — the tracker had scouted for the frontier army after he'd reluctantly exchanged his Confederate gray for Yankee blue — no one had lived in the town for ten years, give or take. The last person, an old whore named Arabella Lovely who had weighed around four hundred pounds at the last, hadn't left afoot but had merely died in bed. She likely wouldn't have been found if a pilgrim stopping for water at the town well hadn't sniffed the stench of death on the wind and risked a walk up the whorehouse's dilapidated staircase to investigate.

"How come you're so sure they're here?" Haskell bit out, swinging down from the sorrel's back and tossing the reins over a branch of a scraggly cedar. "You sure as hell didn't track 'em here . . . though that's what you're gettin' paid for — *trackin'*!"

"You consarned catamount!" Stumpy slouched down from his own horse's back, glanced cautiously toward the town, then cast a glare up at the head-taller Haskell, and wheezed, "You can't track when there ain't nothin' to track. That dust storm wiped all sign of them owlhoots . . . between Broken Buttes an' here."

"Then why are you so sure that this is

where they came from?" They'd run four of the six train robbers down in Broken Butte where they'd been buying trail supplies. The four were being tended to by the local undertaker. Two were still missing. Stumpy had opined the now-dead four had probably driven into Broken Butte from this lost, long-forgotten ghost town, and assumed the last two were still here.

"This is where they came from 'cause it's the only place *out* here!" Stumpy rasped, his craggy cheeks glowing as red as a smithy's forge beneath his natural russet skin tone, honed by twenty years lived out under the western sun. He sucked his overlarge false teeth back into his mouth, and said, "If they're holed up somewheres like you think, ya big galoot, then this is where they're holed up. It's the only shelter in a hundred square miles, and it's the only water in twice that far. Leastways, the only water that ain't rank as a dead man's sock. In case you ain't seen, this whole damn valley is one big alkali flat!"

"All right, all right — don't get your drawers in a twist," Haskell said, sliding his Henry repeater from his saddle sheath. "I was only askin'. Makin' sure."

"You young pups think you know everything an' us who's older'n more experienced don't know our asses from gopher holes!"

Stumpy had slid his old, military-issue Sharps repeater from his saddle sheath, and now he climbed the ravine's bank, stopping to slump prone against the bank about two feet from the lip. He angrily doffed his battered old hat and tossed it down, exposing the egg-shaped crown of his liver-spotted skull to the sun.

Haskell moved up the slope, as well, and dropped to his hip and shoulder when he could edge a look over the crest toward Atlantic City. He also removed his hat, lessening his chances of being seen if anyone was looking his direction.

"All right, all right, you cussed ole grayback," Haskell said with genuine chagrin. "I apologize. You know better'n I do."

Stumpy stared off toward the ghost town. "I sure as hell do!"

Haskell studied the oldster's hawk-like profile complete with long, hooked nose and deep-hollowed cheeks above his patchy beard. The lawman thought the old tracker was taking his ribbing a little more indignantly than usual. In fact, he looked a little pasty around the eyes, Stumpy did.

"What's the matter, Stump?" Haskell said. "How come it's so easy for me to climb your hump today? Ain't you feelin' well?"

"I feel fine," Stumpy groused snootily, keeping his gaze on the town.

"Ah . . . I know what it is," Haskell said, grinning. "You feel guilty on account o' that whore you tangled with last night in Broken Butte. The half-breed that was young enough to be your great-granddaughter."

The federal lawmen playfully nudged the old tracker's spindly shoulder with his own.

"No, that ain't it at all," Stumpy grumped. "Old Lou Ellen don't mind me cavortin' with whores. In fact, she encourages it to keep me from pawin' around on her — tuggin' on her apron strings, as she calls it."

Haskell scanned the town with his lawman's keen-eyed gaze, seeing nothing moving but a whole lot of high-desert sunlight steaming down from a westerly angle over Atlantic City. It was unseasonably warm for so late in the year — Christmas was only a couple of weeks away — but the days were short. The sun would be down in an hour or two.

"You didn't lose your shirt playin' poker last night, didja?" Haskell continued to prod his brooding partner.

Stumpy didn't say anything. He just continued to scowl off toward the ghost town, worrying a gloved thumb against his Sharps's hammer.

Haskell frowned. "Ah, shit."

"What?"

"That's it, ain't it? That's what's got your shorts in such a twist."

"No, it ain't," the tracker said without conviction.

"How much did you lose?"

"Not a damn dime!"

"How much, Stump? How bad is Lou Ellen gonna come down on ya? Should I hire an organist?"

Stumpy scowled at him, narrowing one pale-blue eye beneath a caterpillar-sized, salt-and-pepper brow. "Organist?"

"For your funeral."

"Pshaw!"

"How much?"

Stumpy stared toward the town — a dozen or so log cabins, adobe brick shacks, and the backs of a half-dozen long-retired business establishments slowly being swallowed up by the Wyoming desert. Tumbleweeds nearly obliterated some of the slouching hovels and moldering stock pens.

"How much?" Haskell asked again as he surveyed the town before him.

"My, uh . . ." Stumpy paused. When he spoke again, his voice was thick and crackly. "My last paycheck from Henry Dade."

"Get out of here!"

Stumpy flinched, pooched out his lips, and sucked his dentures.

"The one you just cashed before we hopped the flier to Cheyenne?"

Stumpy flinched again and fluttered his lips.

"Not only that," the old tracker said. "But I gave up that silver watch Lou Ellen gave me for our fifth anniversary." Stumpy had married the former Lou Ellen Cole, a farmer's widow, seven years ago. Lou Ellen was Stumpy's sixth or seventh wife. Haskell had lost count.

"You bet away your entire bank roll *and* your watch?"

"And I had to write an IOU to Sullivan Wilkes for twelve dollars on account o' that's how much he staked me." Stumpy turned to see Haskell's horrified scowl. "I had to try to win back the watch — don't ya see! Lou Ellen would skin me alive if I come home without that watch she done had engraved for me an' all . . . for our fifth anniversary. That's the longest I was ever married up to that point, Bear. It was one hell of a milestone!"

"You're a dead man, Stumpy. I'm starin' at crow bait right now. The man before me is as dead as a big fat turd in a milk bucket."

"Do you think I don't know that? Ah,

hell!" Stumpy sucked back a sob, lips fluttering, dentures clattering, as he stared bleary-eyed toward Atlantic City.

Haskell sighed, sleeving sweat from his brow. He imagined Stumpy heading home to his and Lou Ellen's little frame shack on the outskirts of Fitzsimons, a mile or so northeast of Denver, and having to relay the information he'd just born witness to, to the churlish Lou Ellen. Bear gave an involuntary shudder, as though a ghost had just catfooted across his grave. He felt almost instant relief, however, when he reminded himself that it wasn't he — thank god! — who was married. Stumpy's situation was a good reminder of why he hadn't — *and why he'd vowed to never* — walk down that long, dark, perilous church aisle and mutter, "I do."

"All right," Bear said with another sigh, again sleeving sweat from his brow. "What's done is done. Shed it from your mind. We got a job to do here, Stump."

The government tracker gave a wheezing sigh of his own and blinked his eyes rapidly as though to clear them of the image of Lou Ellen bearing down on him with an iron skillet or a freshly sharpened axe. Haskell had a feeling Lou Ellen could move right fast for so large a woman.

"All right, all right," Stumpy said, mostly to himself. "Time to focus here. We got two more train robbers to take down."

Haskell looked at him, placing a gloved hand on the smaller, older man's shoulder. "You gonna be all right? I'm going to need you clear-headed, partner. I don't want you goin' and gettin' your head blown off because you're imagining Lou Ellen with a butcher knife."

Haskell snorted a chuckle.

Stumpy jerked his shoulder. "Get your hand off me, you big, ugly blue-belly!" In the older man's opinion, Haskell had fought on the wrong side of the War of Northern Aggression, since Bear had fought with the Zouave of the 155th Pennsylvania Volunteers. "Silas's Sonso'bitches," they were called, under the command of Colonel Silas Sanders. These wild-assed guerrilla fighters ran dangerous missions behind enemy lines, blowing up trains, bridges, and ammo dumps and contributing in no small part to Lee's surrender.

"Now, how do you want to do this — since you know so much more than me!" Stumpy asked.

Haskell pulled the Henry's loading tube out from beneath the sixteen-shooter's barrel, making sure the long gun was fully loaded. "Let's swing wide around the town, on foot. I'll come in from the south. You come in from the north. We'll each head down the main street, see if we can pick up any sign . . . or movement. Maybe we can spot their horses, at least, and that'll tell us if we're on a wild goose chase or not."

Haskell snapped the tube back into place, then shucked his Smith & Wesson New Model No. 3 Schofield revolver from its soft, brown leather holster positioned for the cross-draw on his left hip, and broke the big, top-break pistol open. He filled the chamber he normally kept empty beneath the hammer, so he didn't shoot his pecker off, with a .44-caliber bullet from one of the two cartridge belts he customarily wore around his lean waist, and which supplied both the Schofield and the Henry as well as the "Blue Jacket" .44-caliber pocket revolver manufactured by Hopkins & Allen — a beautiful piece with gutta-percha grips and a leaf motif scrolled into the nickel finish — housed in a small sheath sewn into the well of his right, low-heeled cavalry-style boot.

"We'll meet in the town's center," he continued. "Just remember to keep your head down. You don't want to cheat Lou Ellen out of having the honors of shooting it off herself!"

He couldn't help snorting another laugh.

"Disrespectful pup!" Stubby donned his hat with a curse and slipped back down the bank. Quickly, he removed his spurs from his boots and dropped them into one of his saddlebag pouches. He fired another furious glare at Haskell, cursed again, and ambled up the wash, heading north, the mule ears of his high-topped boots jostling as he strode.

"Remember," Haskell called after him, keeping his voice low, "if them two owlhoots are here, one or maybe even both could be keeping watch, since the other four are likely late getting back. If they intended to head back, that is," he added to himself, "and the gang wasn't just splitting up."

Stubby threw up a dismissive arm and disappeared around a bend.

Removing his own spurs so the trilling of the rowels wouldn't give him away, Haskell snorted dryly and shook his head. "You'd think the damn fool would learn."

CHAPTER 2

Haskell shouldered his rifle and jogged south along the wash. When he was roughly fifty or so yards south of the town, he climbed out of the ravine. He took another careful look around, crouching in the shade of an old post oak, and then started striding straight ahead. Gradually he adjusted his course so that it would take him to the town's southeast corner.

He still had a ways to go before he reached the first outlying shack, which was half-dug into the sandy soil and sporting a tawny brush roof.

He looked to his right, toward the open country on the far side of the town. A slender shadow was moving over there, roughly parallel with his own position. Squinting, he could see Stumpy a little clearer. The oldster was striding quickly, sort of crouched over his rifle, stumbling and kicking rocks. He had his hat tipped low over his eyes.

Haskell snorted. The old fellow was used to a horse doing the hoofing for him.

A sudden whipcrack split the silence wide open. The rifle report's echoes chased one another skyward, dwindling.

Haskell threw himself down behind a small hump of ground spiked with prickly pear, and looked around wildly, trying to locate the shooter. The crack came again. Haskell winced, then turned to stare off to the north. His heart lurched when Stumpy's slender shadow dropped to the ground.

"Stumpy!" Bear raked out through gritted teeth. "Shit!"

He stared at his partner's prone figure. The old man appeared to be moving. The rifle spoke again. Dust plumed near where the old tracker lay, apparently writhing, or maybe crawling, toward cover.

Haskell stared at Atlantic City, scrutinizing every building, heart racing. The whipcrack cut through the dry air once more, a quarter-second after hot lead spanged off a rock two feet to Haskell's right. He winced, ducking, then jerked his head up and saw powder smoke wafting up from the second-story balcony on the backside of a business building in roughly the heart of town. A figure knelt on the small balcony at the top of a weathered staircase outside a second-floor door.

From this distance of maybe a hundred and fifty yards away, the shooter was little more than a dark stick figure.

Smoke puffed around the figure. Another bullet chopped into the prickly pear in front of Haskell, sending two prickly ears bouncing off his hat crown, sand slashing at his face. The whipcrack followed, shrill with menace.

"You son of a bitch!" Haskell pumped a cartridge into his Henry's breech, pressed his cheek to the stock, aimed, and fired. He fired again, again, and again, his brass cartridges pinging onto the sand and gravel behind him.

He squinted through his wafting powder smoke. The shooter rose from his crouch, swung around awkwardly, and ran back through the open door of the building behind him.

Haskell heaved himself to his feet and took off running straight north.

"Stumpy, goddamnit . . ."

He ran as fast and hard as his six-foot-four-inch, two-hundred-thirty-pound frame would allow, his bear claw necklace dancing across his chest clad in red-and-black calico. He wasn't wearing his badge but had stowed it in his saddlebags, for the silver-washed nickel made just too damned nice a target.

His big body was enough target out here in this high-country sunlight.

He found that out for certain when a bullet sang off a rock just behind him, followed again by the rifle's shrill bark. By now, Haskell was approaching a small stock pen flanking a mud-brick cabin nearly buried in tumbleweeds. He dove forward as another slug cut into the dirt behind him. He hit the ground and rolled behind the stock pen.

Another bullet plunked into the pen. He rose and ran to the pen's other side. He stopped, doffed his hat, and edged a look around the corner, then pulled his head behind the pen again fast.

No bullet came.

He held his hat out to his right, drawing it in quickly as a slug screeched through the air and drilled the dirt several yards behind him. As Haskell jerked another look toward the business buildings a hundred yards to the south, he saw smoke puffing, then the shooter's silhouette standing in a break between two buildings.

Lifting his rifle's barrel as he cocked it, Haskell snapped the Henry to his shoulder and sent several rounds caroming toward the break. Dust puffed from the rear of the building to the shooter's left. The shooter jerked back into the break, out of sight.

Haskell rose to his feet and took off running toward Stumpy, pumping his arms and legs. The shooter had been nearly straight south of the stable. Now Bear was putting the son of a bitch behind him, over his left shoulder. As he ran, he traced a zigzag course, weaving around more stock pens, rock piles, hillocks, discarded farming implements, piles of trash, and moldering lumber.

The shooter fired on him, but the bullets were landing farther and farther away until he could see the narrow, shallow ravine in which his partner lay. Stumpy peered around the side of a pumpkin-sized rock. The shooter had a clear field between him and Haskell now, and two bullets curled the air perilously close to the lawman's head while a third clipped the edge of his pounding boot heel.

Finally, he dove forward, hit the ground as another bullet sliced the dirt two feet behind him, and rolled into the shallow cut and nearly onto his fallen partner.

"Stumpy!" Haskell bellowed, breathless, turning to the hatless old man who lay on his back now, moaning. "How bad you hit?"

"I'm a goner."

"What?"

"I'm a goner for sure. Hit . . . hit bad, Bear!"

Haskell rose onto his left hip and shoulder. "Where?"

"My leg, for chrissakes! You blind as well as stupid?"

"Let me see. Take your hand away!"

"I'm losin' blood fast!"

"Take your goddamn hand away!"

"I'm a goner, Bear!"

The shooter hammered several more shots at the ravine. All bullets plowed short of the cut or sailed just beyond it to plume dirt on the other side.

Haskell removed Stumpy's right gloved hand from the tracker's right thigh. Blood oozed up from a ragged hole in the side of his leg. Haskell lowered his head and took a good look, sliding his head around to see the backside of the old man's skinny leg, spying the bloody hole in back of the tracker's dirty buckskin trousers.

Haskell laughed.

"What's so damn funny, you heartless son of a bitch? Why should my demise tickle you so? Must be the Yankee in you. I'm just another dead Rebel to you!"

"Oh, quit your caterwaulin', you mossy-horned old fool. You got nothin' to worry about." Haskell removed Stumpy's faded red kerchief from around his leathery turkey neck. "You'll be back in the lovely . . . albeit somewhat piss-burned . . . Lou Ellen's arms again in no time. It's just a flesh wound, you old coot. The bullet went through the side of your leg — the very far *outside* of your leg. Little chance it even grazed the bone."

He wrapped the neckerchief around the tracker's leg and tied it tight. "There — you'll be good as new in no time!"

Stumpy blinked up at him, nonplussed. "I will?"

"You bet you will."

"Certain-sure?"

"Certain as I am that Lou Ellen's gonna chop you up in tiny little pieces and —"

"Oh, shut up about that, you smart-ass son of a Yankee bastard!"

Haskell gave another snort and picked up his Henry. "You just keep your head down. If you'd done that in the first place, you might not have taken one in the leg."

"I aimed to stick to this ravine here until I got up closer to the main street, as the cut hugs purty close to town, but it's teemin' with vipers. One of them nasty sand rattlers almost sunk its fangs into my ankle back there a piece!"

"Snakes, huh?" Haskell looked into the shallow, twisting, gravelly bed of the wash. "Shit. Nothin' worse than a damn rattler." He turned to stare toward the backs of Atlantic City's tall business buildings, all brightly painted at one time. But now the paint had dulled so that they resembled nothing so much as aging debutantes in dresses from seasons past, forever waiting for the ball that would never start again. Not for them, anyway. They were fated to slouch lower and lower against the sandy Wyoming wind and blazing sun, tumbleweeds piling high around their once-pretty legs.

"Say, you hear that?" Bear said.

"I don't hear nothin' but the wind."

"That's what I mean. That shooter finally stopped shootin'."

Stumpy tipped an ear, listening. "Say, you're right. S'pose he's out of bullets? He capped a whole passel!" He winced against a pain spasm and clamped both hands more tightly over the kerchief-wrapped hole in his leg. "You don't have no whiskey on you, do you, Bear?"

"You're shit out of luck, old-timer," Haskell said, rising from his knees and casting another cautious look at the gap from which the shooter had last fired. "You sit tight. We'll get you back to town soon, and then I'll buy you a bottle or two of thunder juice, since you're down to nothin' but lint in your buckskins. Crazy coot. Never seen a man with such a passion for stud poker and so little talent."

Bear left Stumpy cursing a blue streak behind him as he made a mad dash down the shallow ravine, crouching to keep his head behind the lip of the cut while keeping an eye skinned for sand rattlers. He spied two. It was the second one that would have sunk its fangs into his right leg if he hadn't seen it in time and leaped up out of the ravine in one, long, bounding stride.

He heard the tooth-gnashing buzzing of the viper behind him as he fell to one knee atop the ravine's bank, cursing.

He heaved himself back to both feet and ran past the rear of what appeared to be a long-abandoned livery barn, its rear paddock grown up with weeds, and pressed his left shoulder against the side of a three-story, mud-brick building facing the broad main street. A large wooden sign high above his head announced HOLDEN'S GRO-CERY & DRUGS, though the red letters were so badly sand-blasted, they didn't so much announce anything as merely whisper it.

Holding his Henry straight out from his right hip in his right hand, thumb caressing the hammer, Haskell strode along the side of the building, heading south. At the building's front corner, he stopped, staring off across the tumbleweed- and trash-littered main street to the other side.

No movement amongst the abandoned buildings over there.

He swung around the corner, mounted the splintery boardwalk, and started walking south, keeping to the boardwalks fronting the business buildings on the street's east side. He moved slowly, glancing into glassless windows, keeping his ears pricked for sounds. His boots thumped softly on the whining boardwalks, most of which were missing more than their fair share of slats.

Haskell stopped roughly midway through town, looking around at the ghostly, skeletal structures slouching around him. He read old, faded signs identifying a harness shop, a furniture store/undertaking parlor, Ben Crawford's Law Office, Emmett Keel's Tonsorial Parlor, and a large, sprawling structure that a half-fallen shingle on the second story announced as E. M. DANIELS MERCANTILE COMPANY & STOCK SUPPLIES.

But for the wind moaning under the eaves

and causing a loose shutter to tap softly against a wall, there was only silence. Dust blew up in the streets, jouncing the tumble-weeds a bit and sending an old newspaper pirouetting like some disembodied dove's wing down the street to the south.

Haskell swallowed the knot of tension in his throat, and continued walking.

He'd taken only two steps when the loud, raucous patter of a piano exploded from a building just south of the mercantile. He lurched with a start and stepped back into the shadows of an alley mouth, raising the Henry high in both hands, clicking the hammer back.

He followed the din back to a saloon — the Wyoming Sporting House — which slouched behind a partially caved-in awning and a rubble-strewn boardwalk. The piano notes continued to assault the air, as though the ivories were being hammered by a mad pianist in a fervent attempt to bring the ghosts of Atlantic City back to life for one more shindig.

The hair on the back of Haskell's neck stood on end. Damned eerie to hear such a sound here, in this dead town. It was like someone fiddling a jig in a cemetery, but worse. The black, gaping mouths of glass-less windows and doorless doorways leaned out toward Haskell with silent but lethal menace.

Cold sweat, like icy snowmelt, trickled down his back.

The piano's din ended anticlimactically with a clatter of riotously off-key notes and then a ping, followed by silence.

Haskell held his ground, staring over the Henry's barrel at the saloon — a narrow, wood-frame structure three stories high. No sounds came from there now. The silence on the leeward side of the piano was nearly deafening.

The piano was of the self-playing variety. Still, someone must have set it to playing . . .

He drew a deep, calming breath, stepped tentatively away from the alley mouth, then leaped forward, springing into a run across the street, aiming the Henry straight out from his right shoulder. He slipped into a narrow break between the sporting house and the mercantile, and paused to listen.

No sounds came from inside the saloon.

Slowly, he stepped out of the break and onto the boardwalk fronting it. He crouched beneath the perilously hanging awning, then turned to the large, broken-out window to the right of the door, squinting as he stared inside, aiming the Henry, his right finger taut against the trigger. Heavy shadows hovered over a badly scarred floor littered with trash, dead leaves, and sand. There appeared no furniture in the place — none, that was, except a bar running along the back. Stairs rose to the right of the bar, angling back toward the front. In the well beneath the staircase sat the piano beneath a large, rectangular swatch of faded red wallpaper where a painting had likely hung.

Haskell moved to the door from which the batwings and inside door had been pillaged. He walked inside, litter crunching beneath his boots. The air was rife with the smell of moldy leaves, bird and mouse shit, and rotting wood. Bones lay on the floor, as well — the bones of small creatures, rabbits or squirrels, that had probably been dragged in here by a coyote or fox, and consumed.

The lawman looked around carefully, swinging his Henry from left to right as he walked toward the piano. When he reached it, he looked down at the solid oak upright caked with dust and cobwebs and marred with two ragged bullet holes. A scrolled brass plate over the ivories bore the name *Frederick Keogh, London,* which meant nothing to the big lawman. He tapped the piano, above the keys. Nothing. He nudged it with his hip.

Immediately, it started playing, the keys rising and falling quickly as though manipulated by a ghost that had stepped out of a wall.

Wincing against the near-deafening and misplaced din, he glanced at the stairs above his head. Whoever had nudged the piano before he had, either intentionally to draw him in here or unintentionally, watching him from the window and hoping he'd stay away, was likely upstairs. He tapped the piano again, hoping to stop the infernal cacophony, the reverberations of which he could feel through his boot soles. That didn't work. He had to wait until the blasted thing stopped of its own accord, in much the same anticlimactic but welcome fashion as before.

Gradually, the keys stopped resounding and the echoes died.

Haskell walked from beneath the stairs and, tipping his head back to look up into the murky shadows of the second story, moved around the newel post to the bottom of the stairs. He stepped onto the first riser, wincing when it groaned beneath his weight. He raised his other foot, then stopped.

A board had squawked in the hall above him, which he couldn't see from this angle. All he could see were shadows and a swatch of pale ceiling. A hat crown appeared. Then a face beneath the brim.

Then a rifle barrel angling downward, the round, black maw yawning at Bear.

Haskell snapped his own rifle to his shoulder and fired, shouting, *"Noo!"*

The shooter fired her own weapon a wink after Haskell had fired, only she'd fired hers into the ceiling above her head as she flew backward with an anguished, terrified scream. Haskell had shouted to himself as much as to his assailant, and he'd shouted too late to keep himself from squeezing the Henry's trigger.

He'd seen the girl's face beneath the hat when his bullet was already on its way.

Slowly lowering the smoking Henry, Haskell stared up in shock at where he'd seen the girl's face only a moment before. A girl. Just a girl — a fair-skinned, brown-eyed girl.

Up there in the shadows, she groaned.

"Christ!"

Haskell ran up the stairs two steps at a time, and paused. She lay before him, about six feet back from the top of the stairs. On her back, one leg turned beneath the other one, she was dressed in rough male trail garb, complete with brush-scarred leggings and stockmen's boots.

Her hat lay on the floor beyond her. Her dark-blond hair spread out on the floor beneath her head. She groaned and coughed as she rolled from side to side, blood bubbling up out of the hole Haskell had hammered into her chest. The blood bibbed her cream blouse, behind her open wool coat, and dribbled onto the floor underneath her, the pool growing steadily.

"Ah, shit," Haskell wheezed, dropping to a knee beside the girl. "I'm sorry, little miss!"

Staring down at her smooth, heart-shaped face, he judged she wasn't more than fifteen or sixteen years old. He placed his hand over her chest, wanting to stop the flow of her precious blood, but there was no way. He'd punched one through her heart, and there was no taking it back.

She blinked rapidly as she turned her head toward him. Her gaze found him staring down at her, and she opened her mouth several times, showing her small white teeth, before she got the words out.

"I'm dyin' . . . ain't I?"

"Why in tarnation, little miss?" Haskell said, shaking his head in revulsion of what he'd done. "Why are you here?"

She gave a shudder as though deeply chilled. "My . . . my brother, Jory . . . is in there." She rolled her eyes toward a door partway open on Haskell's left. He glimpsed a body on a brass-framed bed. "He's dead," the girl choked out. "Took . . . took a bullet . . . when . . . when we was hightailin' it away . . . from the train. I tried to doctor him . . . but . . ."

"You're one of them?" Haskell said, staring incredulously at the girl's sweet, cherubic face. "You're one of the bank robbers?"

"Hell, yeah." She coughed, quivering. Blood oozed up into her mouth and she spat it to one side. A fleeting smile flickered across her bloody lips. "Held . . . held my own, too. Woulda . . . woulda buried Jory an' . . . an' got clean away" — she scowled up at the lawman hatefully — "if you hadn't showed up."

"Ah, hell," Haskell said.

"The others," she said, breathing hard, trembling in Haskell's arms. "Are they . . . ?"

"Dead."

"Damn." She laughed a little. Tough girl. But her eyes were terrified. She gave a long, gurgling sigh. Her body shuddered violently, briefly.

Gradually, the light left her eyes and she fell slack in Haskell's arms.

CHAPTER 3

"Melissa Sue Wiggins," Chief Marshal Henry Dade read aloud from a typewritten sheet in his federal building office on Capitol Hill in Denver. "Born in Buffalo, Wyoming Territory. Rough family. Mother a prostitute, father a drunk. Melissa Sue was known to run with her brother, Jory, who was twenty-two at time of death, a known horse thief haunting the area from the Buckskin Buttes to Cheyenne. Was known to sell stolen horses in Wyoming and Montana. Did a year in Deer Lodge from age nineteen to twenty. Melissa Sue started running with Jory after their father died, when she was thirteen. At time of death, she was sixteen years old."

Dade dropped the paper onto the short stack of other papers comprising his file on the Wiggins family and the holdup of the Burlington Northern express car that had sent Haskell and Stumpy Gibbs to Wyoming in the first place. The chief marshal, a compact, gray-haired, gray-mustached little man, looking every bit the feisty former Texas Ranger he was, plucked a fat, moist, half-smoked Cuban cigar from his ashtray, stuck it into his mouth, and puffed.

Dade nudged his little round spectacles up his slender nose, sat back in his high-backed leather swivel chair, and blew smoke across his desk at Haskell, who slouched, head bowed, in the chief marshal's notoriously uncomfortable visitor's chair. Bear's bullet-crowned black hat with its braided rawhide band was hooked on the big lawman's right knee.

"Those are the words of Ralph Bidwell, editor of the *Cheyenne Leader*. He's been covering young Jory's exploits for a while now. Bill says all of eastern Wyoming will rest a little easier, knowing the kid was taken out of action. With every passing year, he was getting more and more uncivilized. Turning into a regular hardtail. Had to be if he was runnin' with the Bolan Boys, I reckon."

The Bolan Boys were the gang of four that Bear and Stumpy Gibbs had taken down in Broken Butte.

"Only sixteen," Haskell said, turning his

hat on his knee. "Won't live to see seventeen."

"You had to pull the trigger, Bear. It was you or her. Hell, she'd already put a bullet in Stumpy's leg. Lucky she hadn't killed him."

"I realize that, Chief. But you didn't see the look in her eyes when she was starin' up at me. Just a kid. Trying to be brave, but she was scared as hell."

"A sixteen-year-old girl can kill you just as dead as a full-grown man."

"Yeah."

"Shake it off."

"Ah, hell — I will. Just gonna take some time's all."

"I gave you three days," Dade said, blowing another smoke plume over his desk. The air in the chief marshal's office was already as soupy as San Francisco was foggy when the tide rolled in. He kept a stogie burning pretty much all day, every day. "I was hopin' you'd go out and drink and gamble and fuck to your heart's delight. Somethin' tells me you just stayed in your room over at the Larimer Hotel and brooded for those three days. Am I right?"

Haskell shrugged, sheepish. "It's just that she reminded me of the kids I killed during the war. Young men. Some even younger than her. There's nothin' like killin' young men. It haunts you deep inside. There's something . . . well, there's somethin' *sacrilegious* about it. Know what I mean, Henry? It haunts your sleep at night. At night, you see their faces, hear their screams. Up till last week, I'd never killed a girl that young."

The big lawman ran a hand brusquely through his thick, wavy, dark-brown hair, jerking it out from beneath the collar of the buckskin mackinaw he wore against the wintery, high-country chill. "I keep seeing those eyes of hers. Those dark-brown eyes. The fear in 'em. It was a cold, lonely fear, deep as the deepest damn well on earth." He held his arm half out away from him. "And when I held her, I could feel that fear deep in her bones. She gave a last shudder. Her heart had been beating fast. Fast as a little, wounded bird's heart. Then suddenly it wasn't beating anymore, and she just sagged there — so damn still — in my arms. I tell you, Henry, I can't get her off my mind!"

Haskell lowered his head and ran both hands through his hair, grabbing thick fistfuls of it and tugging as though to pull it out by its roots.

"Ah, hell, Bear," Dade said. "It was either you or her. What were you supposed to do

— toss away your rifle, throw up your hands, and let her shoot you? No doubt she would have done just that."

"No doubt about it, Henry," Haskell said. "Still, I shot that girl, and I can't get that haunted look in her eyes out of my head."

"Only one thing to do, then."

Haskell looked up at his boss, hopefully. "What's that?"

"Send you up to Dakota Territory. Way the fuck up there where you'll have far bigger problems to contend with than the killing of an outlaw, even if said outlaw was young and purty."

Haskell turned to the window just right of the ticking Regulator clock. A recent snow had fallen, dusting roofs jutting into view from the federal building. Beyond those roofs, the first front of the Rocky Mountains stood in snaggle-toothed glory, cloaked in the soft ermine of a recent mountain snowstorm. It was a cold day in Denver — all across Colorado Territory, in fact — and smoke from wood and coal fires hung thick and gauzy over Capitol Hill.

Haskell shivered. "It's December, Henry. You're joshin' about sending me to Dakota. You know me an' cold weather ain't exactly two peas in a pod. It's cold here. Hell, in Dakota it's likely below zero by now!"

"See? You've already forgot about that girl!"

"You are just joshin' me, right, Chief?"

"Not a bit. You're headin' for Dakota. The Burlington flier pulls out in one hour, so you don't have long to pack an extra pair of winter-weight balbriggans and wool socks. You might want to throw in a muffler or two. You got a lot of hair, but you still might freeze your ears off. Brrr!" Chief Marshal Dade leaned forward, hugging himself as though deeply chilled. "Cold up there!"

He wheezed with laughter, thoroughly pleased with himself. Gray cigar ash spilled onto his brown wool vest mottled with stubborn food stains likely from years gone by, and more than a few cigar burns. Dade was a reputable veteran lawdog and lifelong bachelor for whom his attire had never been his primary concern.

Giving the ash a cursory brush with one hand, he plucked a file folder off a teetering stack beside his ash tray, and tossed it onto Haskell's side of his desk, beyond the green Tiffany lamp beneath which the chief marshal's cigar smoke hung like spiderwebs.

"There you go. That's the file that details the killings in a small town way up there close to the Canadian-fuckin' border." Dade chuckled again, shaking his head at his

315

perceived brilliance. "This is the perfect job for you at this particular time, Bear. I have a feeling that in a day or two, you'll be thanking me for the distraction."

"I'm already distracted, Chief. And you must have gotten yourself distracted by some young parlor girl or some such while me an' Stumpy were up in Wyoming. What'd you do — have some young Chinese walkin' on your back in pink velvet stilettos? Dakota Territory has its own marshals running out of Bismarck. The chief up there is —"

"I know who the chief assigned to Dakota Territory is. Phil Copenhagen. Good man. He's also incredibly *under*manned. One of his deputies was recently fed a twelve-inch steel blade he couldn't digest. Two more are chasing whiskey runners with the Mounties in Canada. Two more are down with the flu, and his last two, being Texans and this being their first winter in Dakota, defected back to their home state when the first stiff wind blew down from Manitoba."

"Don't blame them a bit!"

"That's why Copenhagen asked me to send someone to help out on this particular assignment. In fact, he mentioned you by name. Now, I know you and cold weather mix about as well as an unheeled cur and the parson's wife, so I was going to send

Warren Snodgrass, seein' as how Warren grew up in western Minnesota an' all, and is accustomed to cold weather."

"There you go," Haskell said, excited. "Send Warren. Hell, his mother shitted him out in a six-foot drift on the way to the sawbones. He told me himself!"

"Right, right. I would have sent Warren, but seein' as how your head is all screwed on backwards due to your justified killin' of this outlaw girl, I'm sendin' you."

"That's addin' insult to injury, Henry!"

"Call it a trip to the woodshed or a Sunday-go-to-meetin'. Call it whatever the hell you want." Chief Dade leveled an icy, gray-eyed look at his big, senior-most deputy. "But there you have it."

"Ah, shit." Reluctantly, knowing Henry Dade well enough to know when the old marshal had his mind made up, Haskell plucked the file off the desk, plopped it into his lap, and peeled back the cover. "Well, give me the high an' low, Chief. Since you're so bound and determined to freeze my head clear. You know how I hate to read almost as much as I hate the winters north of El Paso."

"Two citizens in the little town of Sioux Camp, north of Bismarck, were killed last month. Both gunned downed at night."

"Which takes it even farther out of our jurisdiction . . . that not bein' anything close to a federal offense."

"Shut your pie hole an' let me finish." Dade took another quick puff from his stogie. "Two weeks after that, another man was killed. The sheriff of Bennett County. He'd gone to Sioux Camp to assist the town marshal with the investigation into the killings. He was shot from bushwhack."

"We're getting closer," Haskell grudgingly allowed as he ran his gaze over the file's typewritten pages.

"Two weeks later, the Sioux Camp postmaster was murdered in his office. Late at night. Well after hours. Shot in his arms and legs and finally put out of his misery with a bullet to the head."

"Ah, shit."

"That's not the only thing that makes the problem in Sioux Camp a matter of federal concern."

"Pray tell."

"You remember that deputy U.S. marshal I mentioned — the one who was fed a steel blade he couldn't digest?"

"Yeah," Haskell said darkly.

"He was fed that knife late at night, just after arriving in Sioux Camp. Someone grabbed him, dragged him into an alley, and stabbed him once in the back before slitting his throat."

"Shit."

"He'd just stepped off the train in Sioux Camp, and that's all she wrote."

"That's even shittier."

"That's about as big a federal problem as you can get without shooting the president."

"I get the idea, Henry."

"So watch your back up there."

Haskell closed the file with a sigh. "Any idea who the culprit is? The motive for these men gettin' drilled and sliced?"

"None. Everything you need to know is in the file there, but there's not much more than what I just told you. Some names and contact information, folks you might interview. As soon as you leave here, I'll make sure Copenhagen knows you're coming. He'll likely inform the Sioux Camp town marshal. Can't remember his name, but it's in the file there. It's a three-day trip, so you'll be gettin' started today. Miss Kimble has made all the arrangements, as usual."

"What would we do without Miss Kimble?"

"Fortunately, there's a spur line from Bismarck, so you'll be in the comfort of Burlington and Great Northern rolling stock the whole damn way. When I was wearin' that deputy's badge, I had to horse-back it or freeze my ass in a horse-drawn sleigh."

"Yeah, I know," Haskell said, climbing out of the uncomfortable chair, which always made his joints ache, "we whippersnappers take all the perks of civilized society for granted."

"You do!" Dade stubbed his stogie out in his ashtray, coughing and saying, "Miss Kimble has your travel vouchers all drafted. I've authorized two weeks' expense money. Keep your accounts in order for a change. None of this per diem nonsense, either. Washington busts my ass over per diem. All your expenses must be accounted for in clean, legible handwriting, and said expenses do not include firewater or doxies. Do I make myself clear?"

Dade leaned far forward over his desk and poked an admonishing finger at the big bear of a man standing near the door. His round spectacles glinted in the lamplight.

Haskell scowled at him. "Wait a minute. If Miss Kimble already has my paperwork drafted and expense money ready to go, you must have known all along you were sending me to Dakota for Christmas."

Dade flopped back in his chair, his self-satisfied smile in place. "If it takes till

Christmas, a whole week away, it's your own damn fault!"

"You were going to send me to Dakota all along!"

"Yeah, but now I have a good reason. That cold up there will be just the distraction you need. Have a nice trip, Bear!" Dade grinned a tobacco-stained grin.

Wagging his head, Haskell pulled the door open and stepped into the outer office, where the lovely but prim Miss Lucy Kimble was playing her infernal typewriting machine, lifting a din that always made Haskell gnash his teeth. She stopped playing as Haskell moved up to her desk.

Turning toward him from her typewriter desk facing the wall, she nudged her old-lady spectacles up her fine, clean nose, and said with customary crisp formality, "You'll be wanting your traveling papers and expense money, Marshal Haskell."

"I reckon I will, Miss Lucy."

"They're all here, ready to go." The pretty girl, daughter of state senator Luther Kimble, who by all accounts lived a rather sheltered life in her family's fancy Sherman Avenue digs, scooped a manila envelope off her desk and held it up to the big man before her. She glanced at him briefly, all business as usual, then lowered her gaze demurely to her desk, an ever-so-slight blush painting her fair cheeks.

Haskell accepted the package with a sigh. "Thanks, Miss Lucy. We'll be seein' you." He walked to the door, picked up his Henry rifle leaning against the wall beside the hat tree, and reached for the doorknob.

"Marshal Haskell?" Miss Kimble called behind him.

Haskell turned to her, one brow arched. "Mm-hmm?"

"Is . . . is . . . uh . . . is" — she cleared her throat — "is something wrong, Marshal?"

"Huh? Oh . . . well . . . I reckon I'm feelin' a little off my feed, is all." Haskell frowned. "Why do you ask, Miss Kimble?"

"Well . . ." The pretty girl — Haskell thought she was around twenty-three, though she tended to dress like a fifty-year-old spinster schoolmarm — cleared her throat again, cheeks flushing beautifully. "Well . . . it's just that you usually . . . have a few words for me . . . on your way in and out of the chief marshal's office. You know . . . you usually compliment me on my . . . my hair . . . or my blouse . . . or ask me about my beau, and . . . well, you know . . . you almost always say something terribly inappropriate." She placed a hand on her breast and shook her head as though in mild revulsion.

"Oh, yeah, I do — don't I? Hmmm."

"I mean, it's not that this . . . this lack of inappropriate commentary on my looks or my dress or my personal life is any bit unfortunate. Quite the contrary! It's just that the sudden contrast — your silence today — is so *stark*." Again, she cleared her throat. "I was just wondering if something . . . if something were . . . wrong."

"Ah . . . no, not really, not really. Like I said, I'm just feelin' a little off —"

"Oh, it's that girl, isn't it? The one you had to shoot — I read your report as I typed it, I'm afraid — up in Wyoming."

"Yeah, I reckon it sort of is."

"I'm sure it couldn't be helped, Marshal. I understand why you feel guilty, but like the chief marshal said, it wasn't your fault. Not that I was eavesdropping through the door, you understand!" she added in afterthought, slapping her hand to her breast once more.

"Oh, no, no — of course not, Miss Kimble."

"It's just that when I changed the paper on the typewriter here, I inadvertently overheard a bit of your conversation, the walls being so thin and all."

"They are thin, aren't they? That's a

government building for you." Haskell gave a dry chuckle. "Rest assured, Miss Kimble, that just like the chief marshal said, my run up to Dakota . . . in the middle of December . . . with snow damn near up to my, uh . . . well, up to my belt buckle . . ."

The poor girl lowered her gaze again, blushing even brighter than before.

". . . I'm sure I'll return to Denver . . . and this office . . . in fine fettle. I'll no doubt be making inappropriate observations all over the place . . . remarking on the cut and color of your blouse and how it flatters this or that . . . and mention how you'd look better with your hair down . . . and I'll probably try to convince you to meet me out for a sip of warm wine some night . . ."

A smile flickered across Miss Kimble's pink lips, and she said, "Oh, that would be wonder . . . ! I mean, that would be inappropriate, of course, but it would seem more in line with how you usually are. It was just a little disconcerting . . . you walking past my desk with nothing more than a simple, 'Good morning, Miss Kimble.' It shocked me a bit — I guess is what I'm saying."

"I do apologize."

"Oh, no need. Like you said, I'm sure the cold Dakota air will make you feel better about things. You'll come back feisty as the proverbial rooster."

"I no doubt will at that." Haskell gave her a weak half-grin and pinched his hat brim to her. "Take care, Miss Kimble."

"Have a safe journey, Marshal Haskell."

"Bye now."

"See you again soon."

Haskell went out.

CHAPTER 4

"Ohhh!" the woman cried.

Haskell jerked his gaze from the crackling fire to see the woman falling before him, having stumbled over one of his boots.

"Here, dearie — I got ya!"

Bear jerked forward over his knees, twisting to his right and thrusting out his left arm. The woman fell into that arm, and he quickly pulled her up against his shoulder as her knees hit the floor of the depot station. Her little black felt hat tumbled down the side of her head. The thick, rich, cherry-red tresses to which the hat was pinned fell from atop her head, as well, spilling in a beautiful tangle over her left ear and across that shoulder.

"Oh, jeepers — I'm sorry, miss. Leave it to me to leave one of my big clodhoppers right out there where someone can trip over it, an' trip you did!"

"Oh, thank you, thank you!" she gasped,

lifting her gaze toward his, her head only about a foot away from his own.

The woman's deep umber gaze, complementing the rich cherry highlights of her hair, took the big lawman by surprise. When he bore witness to the delicate feminine beauty of her face, with its long fine nose, cleft chin, succulent lips, and pale stretch of neck dropping downward into a winter coat containing the matronly lumps of a well-filled corset, he felt a tightening in his throat. Her beauty was enhanced by her smell of lilac blossoms in the early spring, with a very faint hint of licorice.

How surprising it was to find such beauty, out here in the middle of nowhere, northern Dakota Territory, in the midst of a raging blizzard — or, "a churnin' piss-pot of a helluva Canadian kerfuffle," as the engineer of the train had declared it to Haskell, when they'd had to stop in the little town of Oxbow, about sixty miles from the Canadian line. Snow blocked the tracks some miles ahead, where the northern winds cut loose with the fury of a Norse witch, and a crew had gone out to clear it.

With the vehemence with which the gale was still howling, there was no telling how long it would take the dozen-man team of Oxbow volunteers, whom the Oxbow station manager had promised a bottle of the local saloon's best thunder juice and a bucket of malty ale, to clear the tracks enough for the little spur line's passenger and freight combination to chug its way through to Haskell's destination of Sioux Camp.

Haskell found himself gazing into the woman's eyes, which gazed right back at him, as she knelt on the floor between his spread knees. "My, my," he said, throatily, mostly to himself.

Keeping her eyes on his with surprising brashness, her mouth corners lifted a beguiling smile. "My sentiments exactly, Mister, uh . . ."

"Bear."

"Mister Bear?"

"No, uh . . . Haskell. But please call me Bear. That's my name."

"What an appropriate name" — her eyes roamed across his shoulders, over which his heavy, red flannel shirt stretched taut and down which his bear claw necklace hung — "for such an enormous and wild-looking man."

Again, her lips lifted in that mesmerizing smile, little gold specks in her light-brown eyes flashing in the light of the hotel's fire. Fortunately, there was a hotel connected to the depot station — a small, log, crudely furnished, two-story affair — but it was warm and comfortable and appointed with a small saloon only about as large as a farmhouse kitchen. That's where Haskell had bought the tumbler of brandy sitting on the table to his left, off the end of the horsehair sofa on which he was perched, and from which he'd been staring into the hearth's blazing flames when the woman had tripped over his boot.

Haskell felt a warm flush creep into his cheeks, and grinned with embarrassment. "Ah, hell — I ain't no more wild than the preacher's old tomcat."

"No?" She shook her head slightly, staring into his eyes as though she were mesmerized. "But a whole lot better looking, I should think."

She placed her hands on his knees and when her eyes slid from his own, they flicked down his chest toward the large, brass buckles of his double cartridge belts to the fly of his flannel-lined corduroy trousers. It was as though she'd placed her warm hand on his groin.

Instantly, the snake stirred in its hole. A vein pulsed in his right temple. She pushed up off his knees, and he rose to help her, placing his hands on her shoulders to steady

329

her as they both came to a standing position at the same time.

He found his hands cemented to the woman's shoulders, clad in a cinnamon fur coat. He gazed down at her, his broad chest rising and falling heavily as he breathed, embarrassed by the boldness of his stare but unable to look away. She gazed up at him, their eyes locked once more, her own chest rising and falling in time with his own.

"You couldn't have been on the train," Haskell said. "I would have noticed you, Miss . . ."

"Emily Carr. And, yes, I certainly was on the train, Mister Bear," she added playfully, reaching up to the side of her head to unpin her dangling hat from the pretty mess of her hair. "I was seated ahead of you two rows and on the opposite side of the aisle. I glanced back at you several times. You seemed lost in very deep thought."

"I did, did I?"

Haskell felt a twinge of chagrin. He'd been unable to get his mind off of young Miss Wiggins, try as he might. While the Dakota cold might scour such obsessions from his brain, the long train ride had been conducive to nothing so much as brooding, reliving the girl's gut-wrenching demise. Now he realized that he'd brooded right through the presence of the intoxicating young woman before him. One who was unabashedly alive and standing before him now, radiant in her beauty and earthy charm.

He couldn't do anything more at present for Melissa Sue Wiggins. Maybe it was time to put her to bed. He'd likely get back to her in the morning, or whenever he was able to board the train again and continue his journey to Sioux Camp.

"Could I interest you in a drink, Miss Carr?"

"Emily, please."

"Could I interest you in a drink, Miss Emily?"

"Certainly."

"They have a locally distilled firewater, Kentucky bourbon, brandy, and ale. The firewater has a snakehead lolling on the bottom of the bottle, fangs bared."

"I don't doubt it a bit," Emily laughed. "That would be Emil Vossler's old recipe, handed down from his father. I'm from around here, see? My father frequents the saloon here. I'm on the way back to my family's ranch from Cheyenne for Christmas. I'd love a brandy."

"A brandy it is."

Haskell disappeared into the little saloon off the parlor area of the hotel and the old, gray-headed gent with an enormous up-swept mustache, whom Haskell took to be Emil Vossler himself, splashed brandy into a tumbler with a slightly cracked base. He slid the tumbler across the narrow bar toward Haskell, gave his mustache a little twist, glanced into the parlor where Miss Carr sat on the sofa by the fire, and said under his breath, "James Carr's daughter, don't ya know."

He arched an admonishing brow.

"Is that supposed to mean something to me?" Haskell asked.

Vossler hiked a shoulder. "He'll be fetchin' her as soon as the storm's over, Carr will."

"Again . . . is that supposed to mean something to me, friend?"

"James Carr," old Vossler said. "He's always been right protective of his daughter. The only one he's got."

"I'll keep that in mind," Haskell said.

Vossler grunted as Haskell dropped coins onto the bar, picked up the tumbler, and carried it back into the parlor.

"Madame," he said, extending the drink to the young woman with a flourish.

"Thank you, kind sir!"

She'd taken off her bearskin coat, reveal-ing a stylish, metallic black velvet traveling gown with puffy sleeves and lace over the bodice. Her bust was firm, her waist narrow. She'd unpinned her hat from her hair, and the lovely, dark-cherry tresses framed her long, oval face beautifully, and spilled down over her shoulders and across her breasts. She wore a pearl necklace with matching earrings; the pearls twinkled like freshly fallen snow in the light from the dancing flames.

She'd taken a seat very close to where he'd been sitting. She'd curled one leg beneath her and was leaning back against the sofa, extending one arm across the back. An invitation if there ever was one. This girl was not shy.

She sipped her brandy as Haskell dropped down onto the couch beside her, picking up his own glass from the table, and half-turning to his new friend. She slid her gaze beyond him to the fire.

"That's where I was standing a few moments ago."

"In front of the fire?"

She nodded. "And you didn't see me. In fact, I believe you were staring right *through* me."

Feeling another pang of chagrin, Haskell lifted his bourbon to his lips and gave a half-hearted shrug.

Emily Carr placed her hand on his thigh.

"Who was she?"

"Who was who?"

"The girl you were thinking about. A man like you wouldn't be thinking about anything with that kind of concentration . . . except a woman." Emily tipped her head back slightly, showing the tips of her white teeth through a shrewd smile. "Was she special?"

"Special in that I killed her."

Emily arched a cool, cautious brow.

"It's not what you might think. I'm a lawman. Deputy U.S. marshal. I shot the girl, only sixteen years old, in self-defense. She was about to throw down on me with a Winchester rifle."

"A deputy U.S. marshal . . ."

"That's right."

"Interesting. Very interesting. And you are having trouble getting this girl you had to kill off your mind."

"I'll say I am." Haskell took another sip of his bourbon. Then he threw back the rest of it, setting the glass on the table. "She died in my arms. She knew she was dying. She tried to face it with a smile. She didn't want me to know how scared she was. She wanted to show defiance to the bitter end. But she was scared, all right. I could feel her heart beating. It was like to spring up out of her chest. At the very end, her eyes betrayed her. She was as frightened as any girl would be, only sixteen years old, your life being taken from you. All you'd been. All you'd ever be. The husband you might have loved. The kids you might have raised."

Haskell shook his head, then leaned forward, resting his elbows on his knees and turning to face the fire. He wrung his hands together as though trying to press the images from his brain.

"It's all right," Emily said softly, placing a hand on his shoulder. "I understand, Bear."

"Damned embarrassing — this not bein' able to let her go," Haskell said, lowering his head, raking a big paw through his hair. "It's not like she was the first person I'd ever killed. Hell, I fought in the war. I've been a lawman for damn near ten years, a Pinkerton before that. There was just something so heartbreaking in her eyes — the need to look tough even in the face of death. So young. So damn young. And I'm the one who made damn sure she'd never get old!"

Emily leaned forward and pressed her left temple against his thick right arm. "You know what I think, Bear?"

"What's that, Miss Emily?"

"I think we should have another drink. And then — forgive me for being so bold

— I think we should retire to one of our rooms." She glanced toward the saloon, as though to see if Vossler was within earshot. Looking up into Bear's face from the side, she said, "What do you say? I think I can distract you from the thoughts that haunt you so. I won't pretend to be a woman of great experience, because I'm not. I've lived a somewhat sheltered life on my father's ranch. That said, I've been around the haystack once or twice, and I think . . ."

She let her voice trail off when he turned to her, his expression darkly apologetic. "I'm sorry, Miss Emily. You're about as pretty a woman as I've ever seen. And when I first saw you . . . really *saw* you . . . I'd thought I'd died and gone to heaven, but . . ." He paused, searching for the words.

"But not tonight — is that what you're telling me?" Emily removed her hand from his shoulder and looked at it, opening and closing it in embarrassment. Her cheeks colored. "Well, then . . ."

Haskell turned to her, then placed his hands on her shoulders. "Believe me, if it were any other time. I'm just not in the mood for that sort of thing this evening. Somehow, it wouldn't seem right . . . me enjoying the pleasures of the flesh while that poor girl is snuggling with the snakes. I'm

336

sorry." He kissed her cheek, then rose and set his hat on his head. He pinched the brim to her. "Good night, Miss Emily."

She looked up at him, feigned a smile, then looked quickly away. "Good night, Bear."

Feeling like a fool, Haskell headed up the narrow, halved-log stairs to the second story. Snores rose from behind doors in the hall lit by two guttering bracket lamps. Haskell thought there had been five or six other travelers on the spur line coach car when it had rolled up to the Oxbow Station. (That number must have included Emily Carr, though he'd obviously not taken a good look at the young woman, so preoccupied had he been with his own misery.)

Only ten or twelve passengers besides himself had headed north from Bismarck, and the number had dwindled gradually and steadily with each stop along the way. He didn't know how many travelers had secured rooms in the hotel. Judging by the snores, maybe only two or three besides himself and the rancher's daughter.

There was no key for Haskell's door — only a nail and a hasp on the inside of the frame, making the door possible to lock from only the inside. Crude but functional.

The room itself was sparsely but comfortably furnished with a four-poster bed, a simple pine dresser, a spindly chair, a few hooks from which to hang clothes and gun gear, a chamber pot, and a washstand. A small brazier glowed umber in a corner.

Haskell tossed a shovelful of coal into the little fireplace, then got undressed. Despite the heat from the blaze, the room was still cold. He could see his breath as he stumbled around, shivering, taking a quick, bracing, icy whore's bath at the washstand.

Finally, as clean as he was likely to be until he could find a proper tub that would hold his brawny, oversized frame, and clad in only his balbriggans and socks, he poured himself a nightcap from his traveling flask of Old Reserve bourbon, which he'd handily thought to purchase in Denver before heading out to the tall and uncut. He probably wouldn't see good whiskey again for a couple of weeks. Sipping the good-quality skull pop from a dented tin cup from his saddlebags, he dragged the slat-back chair over to the brazier, and slacked into it. It creaked considerably under his weight.

He lit one of his favored Indian Kid cigars and tossed the lucifer into the fireplace.

He sipped the whiskey and smoked the cigar for a long time, staring into the coals, watching individual flames lick up around the coals and run down their sides. He watched the coals glow almost blue, burning through until they were nearly transparent, and he'd be damned if he didn't see Melissa Sue Wiggins's face in every little blaze, brown eyes gazing up at him, smiling at first, then crinkling at the corners and growing bright with the horror of her own demise.

"Jesus Christ, Haskell, you sentimental son of a bitch!" he fairly bellowed at himself, leaning forward and rubbing the heel of the hand holding the cigar against his forehead.

Three light taps sounded on the door, spaced nearly a full second apart.

Haskell tossed the Indian Kid into the fire and reached for the Schofield hanging from the back of his chair. He slid the piece from its holster, raised the barrel, and clicked the hammer back. He finished his bourbon, set the cup on the floor, then rose and tramped in his stocking feet to the door.

Outside, the howling wind threw giant shovelfuls of snow against the log walls and sashed window. The draft made the cheap curtains flutter.

Haskell tipped his head toward the door's worn planks, listening for the telltale click of a gun hammer being cocked. This wouldn't be the first time the lawman had been the target of a bushwhack. Even way out here, in the middle of a raging Dakota snowstorm, there might be someone whom he'd piss-burned at one point in his lawdogging past. Someone who wanted to fill him so full of lead he'd rattle when he walked.

He grabbed the door's curved metal handle and, keeping the nail in the hasp, drew the door open wide enough that he could see through the long, vertical crack between the door and the frame. It was her. Shit. He could see only her silhouette against the candle behind her, but it was her, all right.

"Marshal Haskell?" she said, glancing over her right shoulder, where another door opened a crack and a snooping eye peered out.

"I told you, Miss Carr, I —"

"Marshal Haskell, I have some business to discuss with you. Law business," she added, glancing again toward the cracked door on the other side of the hall.

That door closed with a faint click.

Haskell sighed. He flicked the nail from the hasp, drew the door open, and stepped back. She walked into the room, then pressed her back against the door behind her, latching it. Haskell stared down at her.

She wore a long buffalo robe. Her hair was down. It shone with a recent brushing. Her feet beneath the robe were bare.

"I thought I might change your mind," she said, stepping forward so that her feet were on top of his own. "If not, I will leave your room and you will never see me again."

"Look, Emily, I'm awful sorry, but I —"

Suddenly, he lost the ability to speak. She had slipped the robe off her shoulders and let it drop to the floor. She stood before him, naked. Her full breasts with jutting nipples rose and fell as she breathed. A deep, shadowy hollow lurked beguilingly between the two full orbs. The brazier cast wan red light across the outside curve of the right one. Bear could smell the musk of female sexual desire on her, mixing with the gamey smell of the ancient buffalo robe.

It was wild and intoxicating.

Staring down at her partially shadowed but unmistakably naked figure, Haskell felt a constriction in his throat. He opened his mouth to try and speak once more, but again he could not find the words. He drew a breath. His loins warmed.

"Jesus god," he finally croaked out.

She smiled up at him, eyes flashing in the umber light of the blazing coals. "In that case, I guess I'll be staying."

The howling wind blew snow against the window.

CHAPTER 5

Ever so slowly, Emily ran the tip of her tongue from the base of Haskell's scrotum up over his balls. She paused, pressing her tongue to the base of his staff, which was iron hard and throbbing.

"Oh," Haskell grunted, staring down over his chest and belly, where she crouched, glancing up at him from over his iron-hard member, which she had her right hand wrapped around, as though it were a club.

She smiled. Keeping her eyes on his, she slowly ran her tongue up the jutting organ, pausing every now and then to plant a warm, silky kiss on it. "Oh, Christ," he wheezed out on a mini-explosion of air from his lungs. "Oh, sweet mother of Jesus!"

He grabbed the sheets to either side of his naked chest, grinding the heels of his bare feet into the bed. When her tongue had made it to the tip of his cock, Emily slid it back down the length of him, starting the journey all over again, keeping her eyes on his own. As she did, he gazed at her long, curving body crouched over him, resembling a wildcat poised to pounce.

Her round, porcelain-pale rump was in the air. Her back tapered beautifully from the swell of her hips to her neck buried in all those dark-cherry tresses. He couldn't see her breasts from this angle, but he could feel her jutting nipples softly raking the tops of his thighs and causing gooseflesh to ripple up and down the insides of his legs.

Her tongue, which felt nearly as hot as one of the coals blazing in the brazier, had made it back down to the base of his balls. It lingered there, the warmth penetrating him deeply until he could feel her heat trailing up from deep in his belly to his throat.

Oddly, it made him shiver.

She groaned, pressed her lips against him, still down there at the base of his scrotum, then began the return trip northward. She moved even more slowly this time, gently opening and closing her hand around the upper half of his shaft.

His blood rose.

He opened his mouth, drawing deep, slow breaths.

"Oh, Jesus," he breathed. "Oh, Jesus . . ."

He stared down through the strands of

her dark-cherry hair dangling over his belly at her pink tongue sliding up his shaft. When she got to the top, she winked at him and then slipped her lips over the swollen mushroom head.

"Ohh," he gurgled. "Ohh," he chuckled, shaking his head against the almost unbearable, sweet torture.

She slid her lips down the length of him — warm mud slowly engulfing him. When she'd gone down as far as she could, she stopped and pressed her lips taut against his throbbing shaft, turning her head this way and that, groaning. He could feel the base of her throat expanding and contracting around him. She pressed her head down farther, ramming the head of his cock more firmly against the base of her throat.

She made a little gagging sound, then slid her mouth back to the mushroom head before taking a breath through her nose and sliding down, down, down the length of him once more.

"Oh, shit," Haskell said, reaching down and closing his hands around her slender arms. "Stop!"

She lifted her mouth from him, drew a breath, and smiled up at him, pumping him slowly, methodically with her hand. "That's all right. You just go ahead and spill that seed, big man!"

Haskell felt his blood temperature rise.

Her hand pumped him — slow, hard thrusts, drawing the foreskin up over the swollen red head.

"Oh, Jesus!"

"Go ahead, honey," she said in an intoxicating little girl's voice. "Go ahead and let it go . . ."

Her voice and her hand had worked him to a frazzle. He was still frazzling, his heart racing, pulse throbbing in his temples. Her hand was soft, gentle, yet firm.

And relentless . . .

"Oh, Jesus, here it comes!" he spat out through gritted teeth, grinding the backs of his fists and his heels into the husk-filled mattress sack, curling his toes and arching his spine.

She laughed in delight as his seed spewed out of his jutting manhood. The pearl liquid arced up past his belly to splatter onto the heavy, cinnamon-haired slabs of his chest.

"Oh, Christ," he wheezed as his spasms began to subside, though jism was still oozing out of his cock, which she continued to manipulate with expert precision, milking out every last drop, then running her thumb over the little, puckered hole at the end. She licked the pearl dew from her thumb and dropped down beside him, squirming against him, wrapping one of her legs over his. He could feel the silky hair of her snatch lightly raking his hip.

"Did you like that, *señor*?" she asked playfully, leaning over him and dipping her tongue into the milky substance on his chest.

"*Señorita,*" Haskell said, sweeping his hands back through his hair as he caught his breath, "you done *muy bueno.*"

"I aim to please." She lapped more of the jism from his chest, like a kitten lapping up a pool of spilled milk, her breasts feeling warm and full against his belly.

"You did just that." He lifted his head and scowled ironically at her. "Hey, I thought you said you led a sheltered life."

"I have." She licked several more drops from his left pectoral, drew her wet tongue into her mouth, swallowed, and smacked her lips. "But my father had this cowpuncher a couple summers back. His name was Joe. Joe'd had some experience down in Louisiana, and, while my father usually kept a close watch on me around the ranch headquarters — me being his only daughter, don't ya know, and Pa's been saving me for the son of his business partner, Mr. Melvin Mueller, since I was twelve-years-old — Pa got bit by a spider in the tack room one morning, and took ill. He was in bed with a swollen leg for nigh on a month."

"And during that month, old Joe taught you —"

"The fine arts of tusslin'." Emily chuckled. "That's what Joe called it. *Tusslin'.*" She chuckled again, lustily. "That young man could fuck like a Russian plow pony!"

"So what happened to old Joe?"

"While Joe was right gentle in the haymow and down by the creek with a girl, he was not so handy at poker with the fellas. He lost a game he was playin' in Miss Chance's Parlor House up in Sioux Camp. Joe was drinking, and when Joe drank, he could get madder than an old wet hen. Well, he got mad about having his pockets turned inside out, and went for a hidden hogleg. Before he could clear leather, Miss Chance's half-breed bouncer blew Joe to hell and gone with his double-barreled shotgun . . . . since it was the half-breed, Jimmy Two Eagles, whom he had accused of cheating and been about to shoot."

"Shit, I'm sorry to hear that."

"I was, too," Emily said, giving a guilty little smile, her cheeks dimpling beautifully. "For more reasons than one."

Having cleaned Haskell pretty thoroughly

with her tongue, Emily lay flat against him, breasts down, and stretched her long legs against his own. She lay sprawled atop him — every inch of her beautiful body — and she felt warm and supple and altogether wonderful. Her pussy was a furry glove pressed against his flaccid cock. She reached up and placed her hands in his, and ground her cheek against his chest. "I haven't been with a man since Joe."

"How old are you?"

"Twenty."

"You got time."

"Not much. I'm marrying Melvin Mueller next July. A funny little guy. I doubt he has the woman-pleasing equipment God saw fit to appoint you with, Bear. Oh, why couldn't Melvin be hung like you?"

Haskell laughed. "So I reckon you know he's not?"

"No — not for sure. Melvin wouldn't lay a hand on me till both our fathers, his and mine, as well as the preacher, say it's all right. In other words, not until after the ceremony. He's shy, Melvin is. Standoffish is a more fitting description. Humorless. Doesn't know how to hold a conversation for beans. I'm probably going to have to show him the ropes on our wedding night. Oh, God, it's going to be a long life with

Melvin, Bear!"

Haskell squeezed her in his bear-like arms and pressed his lips to her forehead. "You shouldn't have to marry a man you don't love, Miss Emily. That ain't fair."

"Unfortunately, my father doesn't care about fair. A long time ago, he and Melvin's father agreed that we'd marry one day. In a way, he was sort of throwing me into the pot, enhancing his relationship with Melvin's father. They own two ranches and several mines together. Melvin and his father oversee the mines in Montana. My father overseas the ranches here in Dakota. Melvin will be spending the holidays with us out on my father's ranch. Might even be out there now. He'll probably be with my father tomorrow, when Father rides to town to pick me up in his sleigh. If the storm blows itself out by then. I do so wish I could have found an excuse to remain in Cheyenne."

"What were you doing in Cheyenne, Miss Emily?"

"I have a sick aunt who lives alone there. Or, did. She died last month. She was my mother's sister. I lived with her for the last six months of her life, as her husband, a railroad man, died several years ago. Aunt Margaret died two weeks ago. I helped her only son, my cousin Richard, clean out her house and put it up for sale. So now, unfortunately, I have nothing remaining to keep me away from the ranch . . . and Melvin."

"Jesus, that's too bad."

Emily glanced up at him. "Where are you headed, Bear?"

"Sioux Camp," Haskell said with a sigh. He told her the grim story of what had brought him up this way at such an inopportune time of year.

Emily gave a raspy whistle of surprise. "Townsmen killed up that way, huh? And the county sheriff *and* a deputy U.S. marshal?"

"That's about the size of it."

"I wonder who the townsmen were. Since Sioux Camp is a little larger than Oxbow, my father and I do most of our summer shopping there, even though it's a few miles farther from the ranch than Oxbow is. I probably know those men who were killed. I knew the sheriff — Bryant Johnson. He was a friend of my father's. Any idea who the killer is?"

"Not as far as I know. The town marshal might have some idea by now. I reckon that's one of the first things I'll do when . . . or *if* . . . this storm lets up and I can

351

complete my journey. I'll check in with him."

"Cable Gunderson," Emily said with a sneer.

"I take it you don't cotton much to Mr. Gunderson," Bear said, running the tips of his fingers lightly down her slender back.

"He's a pervert. I caught him peeking through the half-moon in the privy out back of the mercantile one time — when I was the one inside. I couldn't have been more than twelve or thirteen years old." She gave a caustic chuff. "Scum of the earth — Cable Gunderson. He used to sell firewood to the riverboats along the Missouri River, and the only reason he's town marshal of Sioux Camp is that no one else wanted the job. There can be a good bit of trouble up that way. It's only twenty miles from Oxbow, but somehow it's rougher country — maybe on account of it being so close to Canada and being so isolated."

"Doesn't sound like much of a place. Maybe I'll kidnap you and take you with me, Miss Emily, and save you from Melvin Mueller. I'll still freeze my ass off during the day, but I'll be sure to keep warm at night!" Haskell chuckled and rolled the young woman onto her back, climbing on top of her and suckling one of her nipples

352

while thumbing the other one to life.

"Would you?" she asked, hopefully. "I'd much rather spend Christmas with you, Bear!" Her eyes snapped wide, and she gasped. "Good lord — what are you doing down there, Deputy Haskell?"

Haskell had crawled down her belly, nibbling all the way. Now he continued nibbling between her thighs, which he spread wide, laying her open like a clam, so that her pussy bloomed like a rose bud cracking open in the springtime. He slid his face into the silky tangle of her pubic hair, and slid his tongue inside her.

"Oh!" the young woman trilled, jerking as though she'd been struck by lightning.

Haskell paused long enough to say, "Joe might've known a thing or two about *tusslin'*, but ole Bear's been to New Orleans his ownself, and it was there in the French Quarter I learned what a woman enjoys more than just about anything else!"

He laughed and went to work as slowly and methodically as she'd played with him earlier. He could feel her pleasure building inside her. Her breathing became shallow and erratic and she began squirming around beneath him, groaning, reaching down and raking her fingers through his hair as he lapped away like a thirsty dog in a back-eddy pool.

"Oh, god," she groaned, raking her fingers more brusquely through his hair, bending her knees inward toward his head. "Oh, god. Oh, god . . ."

Haskell had pleasured women enough times to know when she had nearly risen to the apex of her desire. Devilishly, he withdrew his busy tongue, chuckling, and slid down the bed to let her cool off a little while he sucked her toes.

"Oh, Jesus," she said, breathless, chuckling with delight, "what are you doing?"

"Letting you get your second wind."

"Why, that's . . . oh my god . . . that's nearly as pleasant as . . . oh, my god, I've never felt such torture, you animal!" Looking down over her heaving breasts at him, she trilled a laugh.

Haskell sucked on her little toe for a while, until she was groaning and mashing her fists against her belly and kneading the bed with her bottom until he thought the posters would give way. Crawling back up the bed, he mounted her. She opened her eyes and stared up at him, glassy-gazed, cheeks as rosy as a summer dawn.

"What're you going to do now?" she said, her voice quaking.

"Grand finale."

Haskell reached down between their bodies.

"No, let me do that!" She slipped her own hand past his and wrapped it around his fully engorged member. She squeezed him until it hurt wonderfully, and then giggled and slid the mushroom head up and down her moist crack, making soft wet crackling sounds.

The maneuver enflamed her desire.

"Oh! Oh! Oh! *Ohhhh!*"

When she could stand it no longer, she slid the head into her pussy, then reached around his big body, splayed her hands over his buttocks, and drew him into her. He was propped up on his extended arms and on the tips of his toes. Now he thrust himself deep, deep into her and held there, turning his hips, grinding.

She threw her head back, snapping her eyes and mouth wide. She would have screamed as though she were being murdered with an axe if he hadn't clapped his hand over her mouth, lest she wake up not only everyone in the hotel but the entire county.

Outside, the wind howled.

CHAPTER 6

Haskell woke at dawn's first blush. It really did appear an embarrassed blush, for the eastern sky was a long, beautiful streak of gradually deepening rose. The storm had blown itself out, and the sky had cleared, making way for a crystal sunrise.

Pretty as hell but as cold as an icehouse.

Haskell had slept so deeply, he'd let the fire die. Now, naked and shivering, he hopped out of bed and hotfooted across the floor, which felt as cold against his tender soles as a knife blade, and tossed a shovelful of coal into the brazier. He bent down and blew at the coals until he could see a red as similar to that widening across the eastern horizon. The stove ticked and groaned, albeit faintly.

Another groan rose from the bed. This one was louder, and anguished.

"So cold . . ."

"Sure as hell is," Haskell said, dancing

across the floor and climbing back under the covers.

"Warm me up, Bear!"

"Don't have to ask me twice, Miss Emily!"

He curled his big body against hers, wrapping her in his arms, and thrilled to the warmth of her breasts mashed against his chest, her long legs entwining around his own. A bayonet blade of desire prodded his nether regions. Instantly, his trouser snake stirred. Emily laughed, feeling it growing down there.

"My god — you're an animal!" she cried, reaching down to fondle him.

Haskell had intended on catching another few minutes of shut-eye while waiting for the room to heat up enough to thaw the water in the pitcher atop the washstand. Such hopes were quickly dashed, however, as the girl, still warm and supple with sleep, squirmed beneath him and took his hardening member into her mouth.

Haskell lay back and smiled at the wet warmth of her lips sliding down, down toward his scrotum.

When Emily had stoked Haskell's own furnace, so to speak, Emily climbed on top of him, straddled him, and hunkered low, keeping the covers wrapped warmly around them both, the sheet and quilts tenting around her shoulders. She made sweet, slow love to the big lawman. She lifted her pretty ass, let it fall — lifted it, let it fall.

She took her time. Neither was in a hurry. The room was still cold. It was cold outside. On the leeward side of a Northern Plains blizzard, it would likely get colder. The train would probably leave in a few hours, if the tracks had been cleared, and Emily's father and beau would likely be coming for her when the sun rose.

But for now, the briefly encountering lovers still had each other, the warmth of their bodies, the fleeting magic of their time alone. The real world would return soon enough — a killer to stalk for Haskell; for Emily, Melvin Mueller to marry. For now, this . . . the young woman toiling slowly, gently on top of the brawny lawman, Haskell nuzzling her rising and falling breasts, his cock sliding up inside her and then down to the edge of her hot blossom.

Up once more . . . slowly . . . oh, so excruciatingly slowly . . .

Later, when he'd dressed and gathered his gear and reluctantly left the room warmed by the brazier as well as their gentle and dreamy lovemaking, Haskell made his way down the halved-log stairs to the saloon.

The small room was filled to the brim with bearded men standing at the bar or sitting at tables, consuming breakfast with the ravenous appetites of hard-rock miners having completed a long shift in the bowels of the earth.

The track-clearers, most likely. Their collective bawdy roar filled the room as they laughed and conversed while forking steak, egg, and potatoes into their hungry mouths, hoisted high the promised pales of frothy ale, and threw back overflowing shots of cheap whiskey. A fire raged in the potbelly stove in the corner, heating the room like a sauna. Mackinaws hung from chair backs or hooks about the room. The air was dense with tobacco smoke, the aromas of Vossler's cooking, skull pop, wet wool, and man-sweat.

So warm and thick was the air down here that Haskell turned up the collar of his thick, wool-lined, three-point capote, and stepped outside, digging an Indian Kid out of his shirt pocket. He fired a lucifer to light on his thumbnail and touched the flame to the Kid. When he had the cheroot drawing to his liking, he chucked the spent match into the snow at the edge of the iron-gray tracks running past the station, from north to south, just beyond the overhanging roof and freshly shoveled brick platform.

He quickly donned the glove he'd removed to fire the Indian Kid. He reckoned from previous experience in these climes that it was well below zero. At that temperature, exposed flesh didn't take long to turn to stone. The train waited on the tracks just ahead and to Haskell's left — a short combination of the requisite Baldwin locomotive and tender car, but with only one passenger car, an express car, a flatcar loaded with lumber apparently headed for Sioux Camp, which was the end of the line, and one more freight car sitting just ahead of the caboose.

The brakeman and engineer were crouched together between the caboose and the freight car, working on what appeared to be the brakes with a pair of wrenches easily as long and stout as one of Haskell's own arms, and a sledgehammer. Their full beards were frozen, gray masks. The men were probably tightening the brake couplings while smashing ice and snow free of the dove prongs to get a workable connection.

"Are the tracks clear?" Haskell yelled into the frosty air and brittle wind, his breath billowing heavily about his instantly frozen cheeks.

The engineer had just hammered a dove prong, which the brakeman had been holding steady. The brakeman leaped back and howled, grabbing his exposed left hand. The engineer whipped around toward Haskell, eyes pinched with rage as he bellowed, "Why, you damn fool — you scared the shit out of me and I almost took Bean's hand clean off!"

"Fuck me — that hurts to blue blazes!" howled Bean, holding his hand in the air with the other, mittened one, and jumping up and down.

"On account o' this big son of a bitch, I missed the prong and hit your hand, Bean!"

"Don't tell me what I already know, Dewey!" cried Bean, still hopping around like a one-legged rabbit.

"Jesus, sorry about that," Haskell said.

"Yes, the tracks are clear," yelled Dewey through the solid gray mask of his frozen beard. His head was swaddled in a visored wool hat and two thick scarves. "You think old Vossler would be buyin' free rounds for the boys in yonder if they hadn't cleared the fuckin' tracks?"

"I admit it was a fool question," Haskell said. "I'd like to ask one more at the risk of getting tarred and feathered on such a chilly day."

"What the fuck is it?" said Dewey in exasperation.

"When will we be pulling out?"

"As soon as the fuckin' fireman has the fuckin' boiler fully stoked and the fuckin' pressure is up!"

"Could you translate that to minutes?"

"An hour or so!"

"Much obliged," Haskell said, waving and grinning. "And I'm real sorry about your hand, there, Bean."

Holding his hand under his arm and leaning slightly forward, Bean cast him the wooly eyeball.

Deciding he'd caused enough trouble out here, and the lashing wind had far too much of an edge for anyone to endure it for no good reason, Haskell pinched his hat brim to the trainmen and retreated back inside the station. Several of the drink- and food-fortified track-shovelers were shrugging into their coats on their way out, one of them yelling something about waking up the doxies at the local parlor house for a mattress dance. That seemed to be the general direction of the entire dozen or so men, whose faces were still flushed from the cold they must have suffered overnight, shoveling the tracks clear.

A couple of tables had opened up, so

Haskell walked into the saloon and sank down in a chair at a table that had yet to be cleared. Vossler was busy at the moment, so Haskell sat back against the wall, ankles crossed on an opposite chair, and smoked at his leisure, enjoying the pulsating warmth of the nearby stove after experiencing, if only for a minute or two, the outside chill. He could feel the menacing cold pushing in from the walls and up through the floorboards, and shivered.

Dangerous damned cold country. Thanks a heap, Henry!

But Haskell had to admit it had washed away his lingering heartache over Melissa Sue Wiggins. Henry Dade had been right. Amazing what ass-splintering cold weather and a hearty romp with a beautiful woman could do for a man's soul!

Haskell chuckled at that.

When the station manager had cleared his table, taken his order, and brought him a thick white mug of hot coffee, Haskell worked on the comforting cup of mud and a fresh Indian Kid until his food came — two platters piled high with ham, eggs, greasy potatoes, and flapjacks swimming in melting butter and fresh maple syrup.

Haskell peeled the tip off his Indian Kid, saving the rest of the cheroot for later, and stowed it in a coat pocket. Then he rolled up his shirtsleeves and got down to business, putting immediate dents in both food platters.

"Oh, Bear — I'm glad to see you're still here!"

Haskell looked up to see Emily striding toward him, smiling, her cheeks rosy from a fresh, cold-water scrubbing.

"Emily!" another man said.

She stopped with a start, eyes snapping wide, and turned to the young man who'd called her name. He stood at the table she'd been passing on her way to Bear's table. Another, older man sat at the same table, his back to the young woman. Both men were looking from Emily to Bear and back again, frowning curiously. The older one wiped his gray mustache and thin lips with a napkin as he stiffly gained his feet and turned to the young woman — his daughter, if he was who Haskell thought he was — James Carr. The younger gent would be Melvin Mueller.

"You, uh, you know this gentleman, Emily?" the older man said, canting his head in Bear's direction.

Emily hesitated, her flush deepening. Then she strode forthrightly forward, her smile returning to her pretty face and flashing eyes, and stopped before Haskell's table and turned to the older and the younger man, extending her hand to Bear and saying, "Indeed I do. This, Father . . . Mr. James Carr . . . and Melvin Mueller, my betrothed . . . is Deputy U.S. Marshal Bear Haskell."

Clearing his throat and feeling his own sheepish flush climb into his cheeks, Haskell scrubbed at his mouth with his napkin, cleared his throat, slid his chair back, and rose.

"Ah, you're the marshal from Denver," said Carr, extending his hand toward Haskell. "I'd heard one was on the way . . . after the unfortunate incident with the man from Bismarck."

Carr was maybe in his early sixties — a crisp, well-groomed, straight-backed stockman type, a little bow-legged from years on horseback, all day every day. He wore a black and white checked wool shirt and suspenders, his sleeves rolled up his forearms. He and the younger man had been eating at one of the tables the snow shovelers had recently vacated.

"Pleased to meet you, Mr. Carr."

"Likewise."

The infamous Melvin Mueller stepped to his future father-in-law, frowning behind round-rimmed, steel-framed spectacles. He was an inch or two shorter than the older man's six feet. He might have been handsome if his face had had a little less flesh on it, and if he hadn't been trying so hard to grow a mustache that was coming up like a few parched weeds in a salty garden bed. His eyes had the surly, priggish cast of the overindulged. He was the type who would look twenty well into his forties, and act like it.

"How do you know Emily, Mr. Haskell?" he wanted to know.

"Deputy Haskell," Emily corrected her beau. "*Deputy United States Marshal* Bear Haskell."

Mueller slid a suspicious glance at her. Oh Jesus, Haskell thought. If the sprout had even an inkling of a tenth of what had transpired upstairs five or six hours ago. Haskell was suddenly aware of the lingering taste of the young woman's nether regions on the back of his tongue, the memory of how her own mouth had felt, sliding up and down his manhood.

"All right," Mueller said, petulantly, "how do you know Emily, *Deputy United States Marshal Bear Haskell . . . ?*"

"We met on the train." Haskell glanced at Carr, then smiled at Emily. "I feel obliged to thank you for spawning such a charming and beautiful young lady, Mr. Carr. She made the, uh, the long train ride over these snowy plains so much shorter than it would have been without her warm and welcome presence."

"Yes, we had a wonderful ride — Bear and I," Emily said, sidling up close to Haskell — too close, in his own estimation and under such circumstances — and wrapped both of her arms around his left one. She beamed up at him charmingly, but not without a good dose of devilry, as well, though he hoped her father and Melvin Mueller would notice only the former and none of the latter. "It was a long storm, and we whiled away the hours quite creatively."

"Oh?" Mueller asked, frowning, his eyes on Bear. "How creatively?"

"I'm just glad you're here," Carr broke in. "Terrible what is happening up in Sioux Camp. It appears someone has waged war on the businessmen up there. As you probably know, two shopkeepers and the postmaster have been brutally murdered — shot from ambush — over the past two months. Tortured with bullets. The sheriff murdered in the same fashion. And then the first federal agent they sent up here got his throat cut from ear to ear. It looks as though the fox is loose in the henhouse, and that fox doesn't want anyone interrupting his feast!"

"That is how it sounds," Haskell said.

"Best watch your back."

"Yeah, you'd better," Mueller added, scowling at Emily's arms clinging to Haskell's.

"Do be careful up there, Bear. It's a rather rough town even when someone's *not* out killing the businessmen."

"Oh, I will, Miss Emily," Bear said, taking the opportunity to remove his arm from her veritable hug. He took her hand in his, patted it reassuringly, and let it fall. "This ain't my first rodeo. I've grown eyes in the back of my head, don't ya know." He turned to her father. "Do you have any idea . . . even a remote suspicion . . . who might be running off his leash up around Sioux Camp, Mr. Carr?"

The rancher shook his head and pursed his lips in frustration. "None whatsoever. I can't imagine anyone wanting those three men dead. They were *good, hardworking* men!"

"You've never heard of them having any enemies? The deadly sort?"

"No more than any other man who's attained some level of success for himself. All three were prominent citizens, highly regarded by the town. Max Weber owned a grocery store. His wife and son are running it now. Sigurd Abel had been a stock detective over in Montana. He moved back here after he took a bullet to the hip, rendering him lame and unable to sit a horse. He moved to Sioux Camp to live with his elderly father, Otto, a gunsmith, who has since passed. Sigurd took over Otto's trade, and lived alone in Otto's little house behind his shop. The postmaster, Burt Hodges, was as mild as a summer rain. He was just getting over the death of his poor wife from cancer."

"I'll talk to Weber's widow, then," Haskell said. "Maybe she'll have some idea who'd want to see her husband pushing up daisies."

"Snow, more like it," Emily said with foreboding, glancing out the window at the cold, blue-white morning. She gave a shiver. "Pushing up snow this time of the year."

"Shall we sit, dear?" Melvin Mueller had sidled up to the young woman and extended his elbow to her, sliding a none-too-friendly glance Haskell's way. "Let's order you some breakfast. Your father and I just started eating."

Emily glanced up at Bear, a wan smile

pulling at the corners of her mouth — a smile rife with sweet memories of the night before and the bitterness of their parting. Haskell nodded at her and smiled, feeling another sheepish flush touch his cheeks and the tips of his ears.

"Maybe see you later, Marshal Haskell?"

Haskell's flush grew warmer and probably brighter. "Well, uh . . . you never know, Miss Emily."

"Perhaps we could invite Bear out to the ranch for supper one night, Father," she said to Carr, arching a brow hopefully, then reluctantly allowing Melvin to lead her away.

"Of course, of course," Carr said to Haskell. "I'll send a man to town when we've decided on a night." He stared at the big deputy, but there was no warmth of a genuine invitation in his eyes. The rancher's gaze had an edge to it — an admonishing sharpness, at once letting Bear know that he was aware an impropriety regarding his daughter had taken place and warning her accomplice that no such impropriety would occur again.

When he was sure the message had gotten through, the rancher gave another lopsided smile, which Haskell returned, and Carr moved over to the table at which Emily and Melvin were just now taking seats.

Haskell dropped back into his own chair with a relieved sigh, damned glad to have the awkward encounter over and done with. Carr was a savvy old-timer — savvy to the natural laws as well as to his beautiful daughter's desires, obviously. Emily didn't seem to realize the old man was on to her. But he was, by god. That was for damned sure.

Haskell gave a little ironic snort as he placed his napkin on his lap and took up fork and knife once more. As he cut into his ham, he glanced over at the Carrs' table to see Melvin Mueller giving him a furtive, menacing stare behind his glinting spectacles, and flaring his nostrils above his dust-smudged mustache.

Haskell amended his previous assessment of those aware of Emily's high jinks to include her betrothed, as well.

Be careful, old son, Haskell silently admonished himself as he ate. *You're liable to get back-shot before you even make it to your destination, and that'll make two federals dead with the killer still running off his leash, but only one having deserved exactly what he got!*

CHAPTER 7

Aboard the train once more, his rump being smacked by the hard wooden seat only thinly upholstered in green plush, Haskell drew deep on the remaining half of his previous Indian Kid, plucked a small notepad from inside his coat, and touched the tip of a pencil stub to his tongue.

He flipped through the worn book, rife with scribblings from previous cases, and found a clean leaf at the back. Puffing the Indian Kid, he wrote the names "Max Weber," "Sigurd Abel," and "Burt Hodges." The names were in the file he carried in his war bag, but he wanted to start keeping his own notes. There was no telling when, going through such notes, something would jog his brain.

He also scribbled "Weber's widow and son," reminding himself that he needed to speak with those two, since they might have some idea who'd wanted Weber and Abel turned toe-down in the cold Dakota prairie.

As an afterthought, Bear scribbled "James Carr," "Melvin Mueller," and "Emily Carr." He didn't know why. He often didn't know why he scribbled certain notes in his book, but it was good to keep a running tally of the folks he met on his assignments, never knowing when one or two such folks might play a bigger part in his investigation than he would have expected. Sometimes patterns revealed themselves only after enough names and random thoughts and intentions were logged, and enough time had passed for his brain to have digested such musings.

Haskell glanced over the sparse notes he'd made so far, then returned the pad and the pencil to the inside pocket of his coat. He looked out the window to his left, feeling the cold air pressing through the glass to slither like a witch's cold hand under his coat collar and inside his shirt and winter-weight, woolen balbriggan top.

He gave a shiver as he stared off across the rolling, snow-mantled prairie. Nothing out there but an occasional tree or two standing alone on the side of a knoll. An icy slough slid into view; the prairie pond edged with the dun spikes of cattails and saw grass. Haskell could see some small, shadowy tracks crossing the slough — likely a pair of traveling deer searching desperately for substance on the lee side of the storm.

A minute later, a shack appeared, dug into the side of a hill, brush poking up from the snow on its roof. A log barn, corral, and outhouse hunched nearby. A man just then walked from the barn toward the shack, a steaming wooden bucket in his right hand. Probably milk from the family cow.

The man was short and stocky, and he was clad in a fur coat, heavy canvas trousers, and fur boots. An immigrant cap and rabbit fur earmuffs topped his head. As he glanced over his shoulder at the passing train, Haskell glimpsed a pipe angling out from the man's salt-and-pepper-bearded face, smoke from the pipe joining with the frost from his breath to plume the air above his head. The engineer blew the whistle, and the thick man tossed up an arm in cursory greeting, then continued trudging through the drifted snow toward the cabin.

A second or two later, he was behind Haskell's left shoulder, the man and the farm dwindling rapidly, merging with the vast whiteness of the snowy plain.

Nearer the tracks, a rough-legged hawk perched atop a telegraph pole. Haskell would have sworn the raptor's gaze had found his own; the tawny-feathered bird turned its head as the lawman, staring out the coach car's frosted window, staring back at it, continued on down the tracks to the north.

"Goddamn godforsaken country," the lawman groused aloud, then took another drag on the Indian Kid.

"You sure as hell got that right." This from one of the two other men in the car, sitting six rows beyond and facing Haskell, on Haskell's side of the aisle. The man, a drummer, judging by his cheap woolen winter garb and ratty bowler hat fixed to his head with a ragged muffler, said nothing more. He just gave an acidic chuff, turned his head to one side, and spat a long stream of chew into a sandbox provided for that purpose.

One of the other men in the car began coughing — deep, raking coughs that lasted until the train had nearly pulled into Sioux Camp — a scrubby collection of log shacks and frame shanties strewn about the white plain beyond the log depot station, on the east side of the tracks. Haskell stepped off the coach car's vestibule, burdened by his gear — Henry rifle, war bag, saddlebags, and bedroll. He'd packed the bedroll out of habit. If he found it necessary to sleep out under the stars in these climes, it would likely be a long sleep, indeed. He'd packed the roll, just the same, so now he had to carry it.

The few other passengers scurried for the warmth beckoning from inside the depot shack, which boasted a gray column of smoke unfurling from its stout brick chimney. Snow was piled everywhere — six- and seven-foot mounds of the stuff in brick-like chunks. Haskell spied a sign in the shape of an arrow with the single word HOTEL hand-lettered in red on its face, and trudged in the direction indicated. The town was small, maybe two-to-three-hundred residents in all, and gathered closely around the depot station, as though all the buildings had sought companionship against the harsh Dakota elements.

The hotel was a rickety frame, two-story building whose sign jutting into the street announced merely HOTEL. But its front porch was shoveled, and a potbelly stove panted in the foyer, so Haskell deemed it sufficient, and secured a room from an egg-shaped gent in pinstriped overalls with a hairless head to match the egg shape of his body. Rather, the top of his head was hairless. He wore a full, steel-colored beard minus a mustache, and little round spectacles perched on the thick, doughy wedge of his nose. He regarded Haskell with suspicion, as was common in jerkwater towns like Sioux Camp.

The lawman doubted informing the gent that he carried a federal badge would assuage the man's distrust. It might even aggravate it. Hell, it might even get him a bullet in his back as soon as he turned around.

Bear left the badge in the wallet residing in the right rear pocket of his flannel-lined corduroy trousers. He carried his gear upstairs, got a fire going in the little monkey stove, then stole a few sips from his traveling flask to fortify himself against the cold he would soon be confronting once again. He wouldn't get to the bottom of the killings in these parts curled up in front of his fire, though he felt a deep inclination to do just that. He'd be damned if his toes didn't feel like rocks — what he could feel of them — inside the high-topped, fur winter boots he'd donned in lieu of his regular cavalry-style stovepipes, which offered no insulation whatever.

"Wretched fuckin' cold," he muttered. "Thanks a heap, Henry."

He went out, leaving his Henry inside the room. No point in hauling the heavy piece around town. In close quarters, his Schofield and Blue Jacket would be his best bet, anyway — if he could get one of his heavy winter mittens off in time to shoot anyone shooting at him, that was.

Cold weather was not conducive to fast shooting. He needed to remember that and think ahead, even it meant frost-burning a finger or two.

In a Scandinavian accent heavy enough to swamp a fjord, the surly hotelier directed Haskell toward the office of Sioux Camp Town Marshal Cable Gunderson. Haskell tramped off into the cold, sticking to the shoveled boardwalks on the street's north side. Business buildings of all shapes and sizes stood around him, looking washed out in the bright, post-storm sun, the wind basting them with already-fallen snow, like handfuls of glittering sequins. The raw breeze felt like sandpaper scraping roughly across the lawman's cheeks.

On the corner where Henderson's Drugstore stood, its front doorbell jangling as a stout woman dressed all in black and gray trudged inside, grunting against the wind trying to wrestle the door out of her hands, Haskell started across the street toward the town marshal's office. It was a box-like stone building with a wooden front stoop and a flat brush roof piled with snowdrifts resembling frozen ocean waves.

A sign announcing SIOUX CAMP

TOWN MARSHAL leaned on its pole against the building's west side, spotted with snow clumps. A rocking chair sat on the stoop, covered in the downy-like fresh snow slithering off the chair as the near-constant breeze nudged it, moaning under the eaves. The stoop hadn't been shoveled. Scuffed tracks marked the heavy powder mantling the steps and leading across the stoop to the front door.

Haskell tramped up the steps and rapped twice on the whitewashed front door with his gloved hand.

No response.

Bear knocked again, and when there was still no reply, he looked around, stretching his gaze both ways along the broad main street. Maybe the marshal was out making the rounds, though it was hard to imagine anyone breaking the law on a day so cold. He stepped back and looked up at the tin chimney pipe poking up from the snow and brush of the roof.

No smoke.

Odd. Even if the marshal wasn't in his office, he'd likely have a fire going with which to thaw himself upon his return.

Haskell tripped the door's metal latch. The door sagged, squawking, on its frozen leather hinges. Haskell nudged it wide, frowning into the shadows. As the door fell back, the bright sunlight pushing in around Haskell's large figure found the red-and-white checked wool shirt of the man hanging from a rafter six feet in front of the door.

The man's pale-blue eyes glistened in the crisp light. They weren't glistening from any life lurking behind them. They were glistening only from the light touching them from the outside.

A five-pointed tin star pinned to the man's shirt reflected the sunlight also, above the pocket from which a pipe stem protruded. The man's gaze was as flat and dead as the man himself, hanging there from a stout noose wrapped two or three times around his neck, the rope curving up over the beam above his head and tied off on one of the lowest bars of one of the four cells behind him, running across the rear of the jail office.

A chair was tipped over to the left of the man's brown leather stovepipe boots.

Haskell moved inside and stopped before the hanged man, scowling up at him in wonder.

"Well, if that don't beat all . . ."

Automatically, not really thinking about it, Haskell bit off his right-hand mitten and reached down to shuck his Schofield from the holster beneath his mackinaw. The only menace he had sensed in the immediate area was the hanged man himself — Marshal Cable Gunderson, Haskell assumed — but he was glad he'd listened to his inner protector's voice and drawn the big pistol when a rifle barked behind him, beyond the half-closed front door. The bullet punched through the edge of the door and clanged off a cell bar.

Haskell wheeled, saw the rifle-wielding figure on the jailhouse's front stoop, and let the Schofield voice his disdain for would-be back-shooters. As the Smith & Wesson's roar rapped Haskell's ears, echoing off the jail's stone walls, the man on the stoop yelped and fell backwards down the snowy steps, dropping his rifle with a muffled clatter.

Haskell clicked the smoking Schofield's hammer back again as he stepped into the open doorway. His bushwhacker was writhing at the bottom of the porch steps, clutching a hand to his upper right arm. Haskell looked around for more possible attackers. He saw no one else on the street except the old woman dressed all in black and gray pausing outside the door of the drugstore, a paper sack in her hand, staring in mute interest toward Haskell and the man groaning and cursing in the street before him.

The lawman quickly scanned the rooftops around him, then returned his gaze to his ambusher, who was now moaning, clutching his right arm with his left hand and shuttling his pain-wracked gaze between Haskell and the rifle that lay with its butt on the stoop's bottom step.

"Don't even think about it," Haskell admonished the gent, who wore a ratty blue wool coat and lace-up, knee-high boots. His fur cap with earflaps had fallen off his head, and thick, pewter-colored hair stood in unruly shocks about his scalp. His face was long and angular, with a jutting chin and a two- or three-day carpet of metal-filing beard stubble. He was probably somewhere between sixty and seventy — hard-earned years, every one. Those years had whittled him down to bone and gristle. He didn't appear to weigh much more than one of Haskell's boots.

He looked at the Schofield that Haskell aimed at him, and said, "Well, go ahead!"

"Go ahead and what?"

"Go ahead and finish me."

"You reach for that rifle and I will."

"You will anyway, you murderin' bastard!"

"Wait." Haskell glowered down at him, one eye narrowed. "What?"

"You're the killer. I knowed it was you all along. You can't outsmart a fox — not one who's been around as long as this old fox has been around!"

"You don't know me from Adam's second whore, you old back-shooter!"

It was the oldster's turn to narrow one eye and lean his head slightly to one side, vaguely skeptical. "I seen you around."

"No, you haven't."

"Yes, I have. It was you who killed Max Weber and Sigurd Abel and poor ole Hodges!"

"No, it wasn't," Haskell said. "What in the hell are you doin' out and about, you old codger? You oughta be in your roomin' house, lettin' the girls spoon-feed you gruel and keep you from muckin' about the streets, shootin' at federal lawmen and makin' a general damn nuisance of yourself."

The old man's eyes gained an uncertain cast. Then, just as quickly, his stubborn resolve returned. "Don't toy with me!" He looked around Haskell at the dead man hanging in the jailhouse behind him. "You killed poor ole Gunderson. Look at him hangin' there!"

"I didn't kill him. He was hangin' like that when I walked in."

The old man just stared at him, his quick eyes growing uncertain again.

Haskell depressed his Schofield's hammer and lowered the weapon. "I'm Bear Haskell, deputy U.S. marshal out of Denver. I'm here to investigate the killings . . . which now appear to include the hanging of Cable Gunderson."

The old man blinked, glancing around, then looked at Haskell. "You, uh . . . you . . . are?"

"I am."

"Law, are ya?" Suddenly, the old codger appeared to have finally realized his mistake. He looked into the jailhouse once more and, still clutching his bullet-torn right arm, said, "Oh, shit!"

"Yeah."

"No — I mean, if it wasn't you who hanged Cable, I know who did, dadgum-mit!"

The old man heaved himself with a curse to his feet and, leaving the rifle where it lay, ambled up the steps. He brushed past Haskell, who eyed him skeptically, and stepped into the jailhouse. "Sure as shit."

"Sure as shit what, old-timer?"

"Sure as shit he's gone. They busted him out an' hanged ole Cable out of pure mean-ness." He looked up at Haskell flanking him.

"Them Thorsons is poison mean!"

"You mean Gunderson had a prisoner in here?"

"In that cell there." The old man pointed at the cell behind the hanging town marshal. "Bradley Thorson was in there last night when I hauled in a load of wood. That's what I do. I cut wood and sell it around town. I was headed here just now to ask Cable how many wagonloads he wanted this week and if he had money to pay for it — I don't work for free, by god! . . . and seen you here. I thought for sure you was the killer. Big son of a bitch, ain't ya?"

He looked from Haskell's boots to the crown of the lawman's black, bullet-crowned hat.

"Who're you?"

"Knute Larson. I live down by Sioux Creek. Cut wood for a livin'." He paused, studying Haskell skeptically. "You're a federal, you say?"

"That's right. Here to investigate the killings."

"You're big for a federal. They're usually skinny little fellas or portly. Too well fed, livin' on the federal dime, don't ya know."

"You're full of opinions, aren't you, Knute?"

"I got a few."

"How 'bout if you tell me who you think hanged Gunderson here."

"I just told you, damn your thick hide! It was the Thorsons. Billy an' Richard musta busted their brother Bradley out an' hanged Gunderson. Musta done it not too long ago. I was stackin' wood for the Widow Avery, an' I seen 'em trampin' through the snow, laughin' and snickerin' an' passin' a jug as they headed over to Miss Chance's sportin' house."

"You mean they're still in town?"

Knute Larson chuffed in red-faced exasperation behind his steel-colored beard stubble. "Ain't that what I just said?"

Haskell scowled up at the dead marshal. "Christ." He couldn't believe his bad luck — having rolled into town minutes after his main contact, the town marshal, had been hanged during a jailbreak. If what old Knute Larson was telling Haskell was true, that was. It remained to be seen.

"Where did you say those bad asses was headed?"

"To Miss Chance's sportin' house. Big red house on Wild Plum Avenue, just down the hill toward the creek a ways. Whorehouse it is. Best in the county. Attracts fellas from far an' wide." He removed his blood-smeared left hand from his arm wound long enough to hold it up to his face and whisper out from behind it, as though voicing a deep, long-held secret, "Run by the purtiest lass in all Dakota — never mind she's a full-blood Injun!"

"Miss Chance, Miss Chance," Haskell muttered, turning to gaze out into the street. "I've heard that name before . . ." He recalled that Emily Carr had mentioned the name. Wasn't it at Miss Chance's place that the young drover who'd schooled her in the ways of "tusslin' " had met his premature demise?

"Most folks around here have heard about Miss Chance," Larson said. "Or they hear about her not long after they pull into town." He chuckled lustily, then sucked air through his teeth sharply. "Damn, this hurts! You shot me, you son of a bitch!"

Haskell turned to him. "You had it comin', you old polecat. Just the same, you better look up the local sawbones and get the bullet dug out before you bleed to death."

"Ah, it ain't that bad. I'm just carryin' on." Larson began shrugging gently but awkwardly out of his wool coat. "Just a flesh wound. I'll wrap it an' have me a few swigs of whiskey and be good as new."

"I reckon I'm off to Miss Chance's Sportin' Parlor," Haskell grumbled, flicking open his Schofield's loading gate. He plucked out the spent cartridge, flicked it into the snow, then replaced it with fresh from his double shell belts. He also filled the chamber he normally left empty beneath the hammer. He spun the wheel, enjoying the precise, solid-sounding whine, then returned the hogleg to its holster and snapped the keeper thong over the hammer.

Tramping down the porch steps, he plucked his mitten out of his pocket and returned it to his right hand before the limb hardened up like a stone at the bottom of a frozen stream. His fingers ached from exposure.

"Miss Chance's Sportin' Parlor — hmm," he muttered, swinging left and heading back in the direction from which he'd come.

Tying a neckerchief around his bloody upper arm, Knute Larson poked his head out of the jailhouse. "Catty-corner from the train station! Be careful — them Thorsons is poison mean!"

CHAPTER 8

Haskell tramped through the snow of Wild Plum Avenue, heading south, puffing an Indian Kid. The cheroot offered meager warmth, in sharp contrast to the steel-like air.

The train station was behind him, over his right shoulder. A shaggy, gray line of trees lay ahead, a hundred yards off. The trees likely marked Sioux Creek. Between him and the creek, a large splotch of red revealed itself around a long curve in the avenue that had become a two-track trail here at the edge of town.

The trail had been well traveled even after the new snow. Several overlying sets of horse tracks angled along the trail only to turn sharply left and carom around to the backside of the red splotch that now cohered into a two-story house of Victorian design, with shutters on the windows cloaked from the inside by gauzy white curtains, a large porch, and gingerbread decorating the eaves. The house was indeed a deep red with white trim and white, ornately scrolled porch posts.

Prim but stately, Haskell thought as he opened the white gate in the picket fence and walked along the recently shoveled, brick path leading to the porch. The house had two stout brick chimneys, and gray smoke fairly gushed from both. Miss Chance, whoever she was, had a couple of nice fires burning. The thought of those warm, dancing flames set up a tingling in Bear's fingers and toes, all of which ached from the cold. As did his nose. In fact, save for the tingle, he couldn't even feel his nose, he noticed, as he stomped up the five porch steps, brushing a mitten across the appendage.

As Haskell moved quickly to the door, he noticed a long list of admonitions in the form of hand-lettered signs nailed to the front wall to the door's right, in a long vertical column — "No Fighting," "No Harsh Talk," "No Spitting on the Floor," "No Drunkenness," "Leave Guns and Boots on Bench By Door," "No Striking Girls," "Payment Up Front," "Not Following Rules Will Result in Lifetime Banishment from the Premises."

Haskell noted there was no admonition against cheating at cards, which had been what had done Joe in, but it was probably just assumed here as elsewhere. He pushed through the door and stepped into a foyer of sorts, stamping the snow from his boots on a large rope mat. Welcome warmth heaved against him, the air tanged with the smell of burning pine. Several pairs of boots and two pairs of men's shoes were lined up on a bench to his right, beneath a row of coats hanging from hooks. There were also several coiled gun rigs. Haskell considered keeping his boots on, reluctant to confront three killers unshod, but then, remembering the crispness of the admonitions, decided he'd best follow the house rules like everyone else.

He would have to ignore the one about leaving his guns, however. He couldn't assume the men who'd hanged the town marshal would follow the rules here any better than elsewhere, especially in the lawman's own office. By way of explanation, he dug the wallet containing his badge out of his coat pocket, and pinned the badge to his shirt. Leaving his boots on the bench and his coat, muffler, and hat on a hook, he walked out of the foyer and into a short hall in which a cabinet clock ticked away the seconds in dolorous, hollow tones.

A carpeted stairs rose straight ahead of him. To his left and right were open doorways. In the room to his left, four men were playing cards at a baize-covered table, near a popping fireplace. Two skimpily dressed, bored-looking girls lounged in separate chairs near the card players. One was reading a magazine. No one seemed to notice Haskell, who, hearing voices in the room off the hall's opposite side, turned to it.

This was a saloon of sorts, dominated by an opulent bar and backbar with a leaded mirror with fancy designs engraved around its edges. The bar lay on the far side of the room. Between the door and the bar were half a dozen tables and chairs. There was also a stout potbelly stove from which welcome heat radiated, and a dancing orange fire could be seen through the cracks around the door.

Running along the edges of the room were plush velvet- and brocade-upholstered chairs and sofas and fainting couches, pie crust tables, polished brass spittoons, and a couple of wingback chairs. The place was tricked out like a private gentleman's club in Denver, the kind Haskell couldn't afford to join. The smell was intoxicating, not only because the aromas of various alcohols flavored it, but because that of women did, as well. It was a mixture of expensive perfume and scented bathwaters and another fragrance that could only be attributed to the female sex itself.

It caused Haskell to remember all too keenly his previous night with Emily Carr, and to suppress a stirring hard-on with a wince and a groan. It didn't help that a comely, black-haired woman stood behind the bar facing him — staring at him, in fact. She held a cut-glass goblet in one beringed hand and an impossibly white towel in the other. Her dark-brown eyes were cool, impassive, as she took his measure. Her gaze flicked to the nickeled moon and star pinned to his heavy flannel shirt, beside his customary necklace of bear claws. Then it dropped to the two cartridge belts buckled around his waist and to the big Schofield holstered for the cross-draw on his left hip.

That she was the full-blood Indian Knute Larson had mentioned, there was no doubt. Her eyes were long and almond-shaped, her cheekbones high and wide, so prominent as to be edging close to severity. Her skin was the deep red of quality brandy. From what Haskell could see of her body behind the bar, she was beautifully shaped, though large of bone. She appeared so Plains Indian

393

that Haskell could see her outfitted in tanned doeskins and a deerskin cloak, maybe a few feathers in her long, coarse hair glistening with bear grease.

As it was, she was dressed in the elegant attire — spruce green velvet gown trimmed in white lace — and flashing jewelry of a top-shelf whorehouse madam. Very much like an Indian, however, her expression betrayed very little of what was going on behind her molasses-black eyes.

A man sat at a table near the bar. This was doubtless Jimmy Two Eagles, the fella who'd kicked poor Joe out with a cold shovel. A shotgun rested across the arms of the chair to the man's right. He was a big Indian in a suit two sizes too small for him, and his left eye listed inward, toward his pitted, hawk-like nose. He'd been devouring a plate of eggs and bacon when Haskell had walked into the saloon, but now he'd stopped, his right hand splayed out on the table near the shotgun — a sawed-off twelve-gauge with a wide leather lanyard. He stared at the newcomer owlishly over his thick left shoulder.

"Jimmy," the young Indian woman said softly, giving her head a quick, resolute shake. "We can make an exception for the newcomer's gun since he has a badge to go with it." She narrowed her eyes skeptically. "A United States marshal?" A faint, mocking smile tugged at her mouth. "Another one?"

"Deputy U.S. Marshal — yes, ma'am," Haskell said, walking toward the bar and glancing around. She and the big Indian were the only two in the well-appointed watering hole. The gamblers' voices pushed through the door behind Haskell. He strode sock-footed up to the bar, liking the heat playing against his back and thawing his toes in his socks. He planted his left elbow on the bar, keeping the young woman and the big Indian with the shotgun to his right. "Bear Haskell's the name."

"That's quite a name." She set the goblet atop a pyramid of other matching goblets on the bar and looked at the necklace hanging down his broad chest. "Is that your totem?"

"I reckon it is."

"Did you kill the bear?"

"Just in time."

"Is that where you got the handle?"

"Nah." Haskell fingered the necklace. "I took these claws on account o' my great-grandfather was said to have done the same thing to a bear that was stalkin' him. Thus he got the handle, 'Bear.' So I guess you could say I was named after Great-Grandad's *nick*name."

Haskell smiled at the young woman, trying to put her at ease. But maybe she wasn't on edge. It was hard to tell. He could usually get a girl's eyes to glitter with his aw-shucks, Pennsylvania mountain-boy demeanor, but so far he'd failed with this girl. Her stony gaze and stiff, albeit wide, sensuous mouth, told him she might be a tough nut to crack.

"Are you the lady called Chance?"

"What if I am?"

Haskell glanced at the Indian, whose hand still lay on the table near the shotgun. He still gazed owlishly up at Haskell through his good eye, the lazy eye staring at the bridge of his nose. He had a face like a large, brown pumpkin with a doorstop for a nose.

"Is that Jimmy over there?"

"What if he is?"

When neither offered anything more, and Jimmy kept his hand too close to the shotgun for comfort, Haskell decided to get on with it.

"Bad news," he said, returning his gaze to the woman probably called Chance.

She didn't say anything, just tossed away her towel and spread her hands on the edge of the bar, leaning forward, a black brow arched in question, prodding him to get on with why he was there, disobeying her rules.

"The town marshal, Gunderson, is dead. He's hangin' over to the jailhouse, trussed up like a side of beef."

She seemed to flinch if only slightly. "Who . . . ?"

"The Thorson boys." Haskell hadn't made the response. Knute Larson had. The old man shuffled into the saloon from the hall, clamping his left hand over the wound in his right arm. He looked washed out and weary, his face framed by the earflaps of his fur hat. He winced as he kicked out a chair and dropped into it. "I sure could do with a bottle, Miss Chance."

"What happened to you, Knute?" Chance asked him, her voice pitched with concern. She grabbed two bottles from under the bar and a shot glass from a shelf behind her. She moved quickly through a break in the bar, heading for Larson's table.

"I shot him."

She stopped halfway between the bar and the old man, scowling toward Haskell. "Perhaps you'd better leave."

"Can't do that. Knute told me the Thorson boys were headed this way. I'm guessin' they're either in the other room, playin' cards, or they're upstairs with your girls."

She stood, staring suspiciously at the big lawman. Jimmy continued to stare at him, too, from where he sat at his table, not eating but only staring, his hand still awfully close to the shotgun.

To Bear, Knute said, "I took a gander around the wolf den." He smiled at the name for the gambling parlor. "They ain't in there. If they're here, they must be upstairs with the girls." He turned to the woman. "I had the bullet comin', Miss Chance. I was too quick with my old Spencer. I thought the lawdog was the killer. It's only a flesh wound." The oldster stared lustily at the bottle she held against her ample bosom. "A few shots of the ole thunder juice oughta fix me right up."

He chuckled.

The woman called Chance raked her gaze from Haskell, then continued to Larson's table. She set the bottles and shot glass before the old man. One of the bottles didn't have a label. The other one did. She popped both corks, splashing whiskey into the glass from the labeled bottle.

Knute said, "Gunderson had Bradley locked up for stealin' that horse from J. D. Kettleson. I seen his two brothers, Billy an' Richard, in town last night. They was over to the Overland, don't ya know. I seen all three of 'em headin' this direction just before I went over to the jailhouse to find Gunderson hangin' like a dead turkey in a keeper shed, this big, curly-headed badge-toter starin' up at him."

Knute glanced at Haskell, shrugged his undamaged shoulder, and emptied his shot glass.

Chance automatically refilled the glass, staring down at the old man as though she had something else on her mind.

"Are they here?" Haskell asked her from the bar.

To Larson, she said, "Take off your coat, Knute. Let me have a look at that arm." She turned to the big Indian. "Jimmy, heat some water and bring some clean cloths and my sewing kit."

The Indian kept his eyes on Haskell as he said: "You sure, Chance?"

She looked at Haskell, her expression implacable. "I'm sure."

The Indian kept his dark, menacing eyes on Haskell as he slid his chair back and stood up. He was nearly Haskell's size. He plucked the shotgun off the arms of the chair to his right, slung it over his back by the leather lanyard, marched heavily behind the bar, and then disappeared through a curtained doorway flanking it.

Chance helped the grunting Knute out of his coat. The oldster cursed under his breath, veins bulging in his forehead. Haskell grabbed a goblet off the bar to his right and walked over to the old man's table. He sat down on the far side of the table from Knute, picked up the labeled bottle, and splashed liquor into his glass.

"Are they here, Chance?" Haskell inquired of the Indian woman once more. She had draped Knute's coat over a chair back and was now kneeling to examine his bloody arm.

She turned to Haskell. "They're here." She stared at him hard, narrowing the corners of those deep, black eyes, the bright sunlight from the windows dancing in them. "If you're going to arrest them, wait until they're done upstairs. I keep this a safe place for my girls. God knows there are few enough of *those* for *them.*"

She began untying the neckerchief Knute had wrapped around his arm.

"I'm in no hurry," Haskell said, rolling the tumbler between his large hands. "Besides, I like the company down here. I might even wait until the Thorson boys leave to run 'em to ground, so's not to offend the woman of the house."

Chance tossed the bloody neckerchief over Knute's coat and turned to Haskell again, frowning skeptically. He smiled and raised his goblet to her. "Your house, your rules."

Knute looked at Haskell, then at Chance, then back to Haskell, and chuckled.

Haskell took a couple of deep sips from his glass.

"I think you got you another admirer, Miss Chance," Knute told the woman, chuckling, showing a mouthful of tobacco-stained teeth and more than a few gaps.

She rolled her eyes and shook her head, but as she glanced at the big lawman again, Haskell couldn't help notice that her fleeting gaze took quick measure of the breadth of his shoulders and chest before she turned once more to the old man. She unbuttoned his right cuff, grabbed the cloth in both hands, gritted her teeth, and began tearing straight up toward his shoulder.

"Please, don't tear my shirt, Miss Chance — why, it's only one of two I . . . !"

But she'd already ripped it all the way up to the hole in the upper sleeve. Knute stared down in mute misery at the torn garment.

"Be quiet, you old coot," Chance admonished him, her tone harsh, but her eyes soft with affectionate jeering. "You were just going to let that wound fester, weren't you? If you hadn't come to me, you'd probably have lost that arm by the springtime. Would've turned black and rotten. How would you have made your living?" She glanced at Haskell, and for once her eyes were not flinty with incrimination but danced with warm humor. "Can you imagine a one-armed woodcutter?"

"Well, I reckon you're right, but . . . this is my favorite shirt."

"You're only missing a sleeve when you could be missing your arm," Chance told him. "Besides, the shirt will do you for summer now." With that, she reached up and flicked his pointed chin with her thumb.

Knute colored up and snickered, thoroughly smitten by the gal.

Haskell laughed, as well, rolling his drink between his hands and staring in unabashed adoration at the woman. If he'd been one to tumble for any woman, he likely would have tumbled for this one already. She had an enigmatic way about her, the woman called Chance did. By turns as serious as a brick wall, then suddenly as merry as a colt dancing in the springtime wildflowers. She had a way with men. That much was obvious. She was probably a dream beneath the covers. Haskell couldn't help wondering if she did any work upstairs herself. Some madams did, some left that part of the business to their staff.

Haskell took another sip of his bourbon and reminded himself why he was here. The three killers upstairs.

Business before pleasure.

He looked at Chance, who was just then soaking a cloth in the steaming porcelain bowl Jimmy had fetched over to the table, and thought: *But after business . . .*

The woman's eyes met his. Her cheeks appeared to turn a shade darker than their natural dark cherry. Was she blushing? She averted her gaze as she wrung out the cloth, then turned back to the old man's wounded arm.

Haskell felt a lusty smile jerk at his mouth corners and desire warm his loins.

But then he heard a peal of raucous laughter and footsteps on the stairs. He had a feeling he was about to meet the Thorson boys.

CHAPTER 9

"Oh, boy," Knute said. "Here we go."

Chance, who was dabbing at the old man's wounded arm with a cloth soaked in water and the unlabeled whiskey, glanced at Haskell.

"Relax," the lawman said, smiling and taking another sip of his bourbon. "No one's gonna go breakin' your house rules, Miss Chance." As the voices and the footsteps on the stairs grew louder, he added, "Perhaps you'd like to make the introductions, real civilized-like . . . ?"

Just then a young man, maybe twenty, appeared in the saloon's doorway, stretching, his yellow hair standing up in spikes all around his head. He was under six feet and scrawny, but with a little potbelly pushing out the longhandle shirt that shone between the open flaps of his blue flannel work shirt.

"Well, hello there, Miss Chance," he said, blue eyes brightening as they found the saloon owner tending Knute's wound. "You sure a pretty this morning. I never knew a woman who could look so . . ." He let his voice trail off as his gaze found the bullet wound Chance was tending. "Say there, Knute, you old devil. What'd you do, shoot yourself cleaning that old infantry rifle of yours?"

He laughed. So did the other two men walking into the saloon behind him, both also looking rumpled and tired from their romps in the proverbial hay — after hanging the local marshal in his own jailhouse. The other two — one taller and thinner, one short and fat — both owned a familial resemblance with the yellow-haired kid, whom Haskell had a feeling was the Thorson brother who'd been locked behind bars — Bradley.

"I did no such thing, you disrespectful pup!" Knute said, indignant. He looked at Haskell. "This fella here did."

The three Thorson boys looked at Haskell. Their laughter dwindled. Their smiles grew stiff. Their eyes flicked toward the moon and star badge pinned above the left breast pocket of the federal lawman's shirt.

"Gentlemen," Chance said, pouring more cheap whiskey onto her blood-speckled cloth, which she held over the washbasin,

"I'd like you to meet a new friend of mine. Bear Haskell, deputy U.S. marshal from Denver, won't you meet Bradley, Richard, and Billy Thorson?"

Bear had been right. Bradley was the first one. The tall one was Richard. The fat one was Billy.

Haskell smiled his friendliest smile and, continuing to roll his bourbon glass between his big hands, said, "Fellas, pleased to make your acquaintance." He dipped his chin as he raked his affable gaze across all three young men staring at him tensely now. "Why don't you all sit down and take a load off. Let me buy you a drink!"

The three flushed, face muscles tightening. They slid their eyes to each other and then to Haskell and then back again.

Knute gave a throaty chuckle.

Chance tucked her ripe bottom lip under her top lip and pulled back a smile that was wanting to spread across her pretty face.

"Uh, well . . . ya see," Bradley said, nudging Richard with his shoulder and then backing toward the doorway, "we'd love to stay an' chew the fat, but . . . but, uh . . . we got an appointment to keep."

"An appointment?" Knute said. "Who you boys got an appointment with? Don't tell me you're finally gonna get yourselves an honest job!" Knute chuckled again, thoroughly delighted by the Thorsons' discomfort.

"Sure, sure, we might," Billy said, backing with the other two men through the doorway. "We got us an appointment with a fella over in Oxbow. Maybe do some freight haulin' for him. Well, it was nice meetin' you, Marshal Haskell."

"Sure was," Bradley said, as he turned and hurried off down the hall to where their guns, boots, and coats waited. "Maybe hold you to that drink some other day!"

"The pleasure was all mine, fellas," Haskell said, waving. "Be seein' you boys again real soon!"

Haskell sat listening to the Thorson boys thumping around in the foyer, muttering among themselves as they grabbed their guns and boots and outdoor gear. He sipped his bourbon with one hand, lowering the other one to his right thigh, placing it near the Schofield in case the Thorsons, having armed themselves, decided to come calling once more, this time with pistols blazing.

But then he heard the door open and close as the Thorsons took their leave.

Knute gave a raspy whistle. "That was close!"

Haskell rose from his chair and walked to

a front window. He stared out at the Thorsons slouching through the gate in the picket fence and then turning north along Wild Plum Avenue, heading back to town on foot. As they walked, they cast several cautious looks behind them, then turned to one another, their breath painting the cold air around their heads as they conferred.

"Nah," Haskell said. "I could tell right away they didn't have it in them to go up against a federal — face to face."

Chance squinted one eye as she threaded a needle, preparing to suture Knute's bullet wound closed. "You'd best watch your back, Marshal Haskell. Those three are known for their back-shooting antics."

"Sure enough," Knute said. "They got crossways with a fella named Henderson Gentry last summer, and it's said they waited for him outside the roadhouse they was all gamblin' at, down along the Missouri River, and they shot him in the back and stole his hoss."

"Don't doubt it a bit." As the three brothers disappeared around the bend in the snowy trail, Haskell turned from the window. "Is there a back way out of here?"

"Sure," Chance said, pouring whiskey over her threaded needle. "Straight down the hall beyond the stairs."

Haskell strode into the vestibule by the door, gathered his gear, and returned to the saloon. Knute was sitting stiffly back in his chair, by turns taking deep gulps from his whiskey glass and grunting as Chance very deftly and purposefully sewed the wound closed. Haskell drew his coat on and started buttoning it.

"It was mighty nice meeting you, Miss Chance," he said.

"Likewise, Marshal." Chance drew the needle through Knute's pinched-together skin and pulled the catgut taut.

"Oh, jeepers. Oh, jeepers!" Knute muttered.

"You don't happen to work upstairs — do you?" Haskell asked the woman.

Knute grinned despite his misery.

The woman turned a cold eye on Haskell, but then she gave a little ironic smile, causing her cheeks to dimple. "Sorry."

Knute chuckled.

Haskell winced. "Maybe, uh . . . well, maybe I could stop back by here, and I could buy you a drink." Haskell dropped some coins on the table. "That there is for what I had out of Knute's bottle."

"Shouldn't you be concentrating on what you were sent here to do, Marshal Haskell?" Chance drew the catgut taut once more, then snipped it off with a small scissors close to the wound. "Instead of pestering a disinterested businesswoman?"

"Ouch," Haskell said. He frowned curiously as he said, "How come you don't talk like an Indian does, if you'll forgive the boldness of my question? I mean, you talk like a white lady talks. Refined-like . . ."

She rolled her eyes, then leaned close to Knute's arm to inspect her handiwork. "Your impertinence is matched only by your audaciousness, Deputy Haskell."

"Chance ain't from around here," Knute explained. "She's from St. Louis. Adopted by a white sky pilot. Brought up Christian, don't ya know. She ain't no heathen like most of her kind in these parts."

Chance flicked her thumb against the old man's chin again, chuckling, then rose and faced Haskell, smiling ironically. "There you have it. I can't imagine a better explanation than Mr. Larson's. Now if you'll excuse me, Deputy Haskell, I have work to do in the kitchen."

Haskell had been hearing Jimmy rattling pots and pans around back there. He and someone else must have been preparing lunch.

"Raised by a preacher, eh?" Haskell brashly swept his gaze across the woman's body, the tight gown revealing all her curves and accentuating the high jut of her bosom. "You sure don't look like you was raised by no preacher."

Knute cackled a lusty laugh. "That's what ever'body says!" Then he added: "Can't blame you for tryin', Bear, but I could have told you you was wastin' your time. Every man with hot blood in his veins in these parts has tried to, uh . . . uh . . . *spark,* Miss Chance here, shall we say? We all been given the same response you just was. She does make your heart ache, though, don't she?"

The old man's eyes glittered like candles on a Christmas tree as he stared up at the Indian goddess standing before him.

Chance said, "I tell you what, Deputy, you come back later and I'll fix you up with one of my girls. It's obvious" — she let her own brash gaze drop to the area just south of his belly — "you're in need of having some sap bled off. I know just the girl to handle a man like you."

"And what's a man like me?" Haskell asked, not sure he wanted the answer.

"Crude," she said, the coldness back in her gaze. Her nostrils flared slightly. "Wanton. Wild. As untamed as the men you hunt."

She arched a brow at him as though to

punctuate the incrimination. Then she added: "One of the unspoken rules of my house, Deputy, is that I don't do business upstairs. I always have Jimmy and his sawed-off twelve-gauge within earshot, in case anyone decides to press the matter. Understand?"

With that, she gathered up her sewing kit, then strode back behind the bar and through the curtained doorway flanking it. Gone.

Bear and Knute stared after her in shocked silence.

Finally, Haskell turned to the old man. "Give it to me straight, Knute," he prodded. "You think I got a chance?"

Knute slapped the table, howling. "You got about a snowball's chance in hell. But, shit, that's more than most of us has!"

Haskell chuckled, donned his hat, picked up his boots, and headed for the hall. "See you later, old-timer."

"You can quit reminding me of age any old time! Hey, where you goin', anyway?"

"Got me some coyotes to lasso."

Haskell headed into the hall. He strode past the carpeted stairs and down a good stretch of hall with a couple of doorways in the papered walls to each side. The rear door was a double-rigged affair — a winter inside door with a curtained window in the upper panel, and a screen door on the outside.

There was fresh snow and bark on the rope mat in front of the door. This was likely where Jimmy hauled in wood to the range in the kitchen, which Haskell figured was behind the near door on his right.

He stepped into his boots, slid the curtain aside to peer out the window, making sure the Thorsons hadn't anticipated his move, then headed outside. He slogged past a couple of snow-mantled piles of split wood and a large stump with a splitting maul embedded in it. He continued straight to the back of the house, between two privies, and then shouldered through snowy shrubs. He was heading straight north, back toward town, but steering far clear of Wild Plum Avenue.

When he'd nearly made it back to the main street, he cut over to Wild Plum Avenue, which he dashed across, as much as the deep snow made "dashing" possible. Then he headed back in the direction of Miss Chance's place, but now keeping to Wild Plum Avenue's far west side. He moved through skeletal winter trees and shrubs. He circled around a springhouse and an old settler's cabin that appeared abandoned — half the brush roof was caved in, and there were no tracks in the snow around it — and slowed his pace.

Maybe fifty yards beyond the cabin lay an old corral and a dilapidated lean-to stable. He'd passed the place earlier, on his right, when he'd been making his way along the avenue toward Miss Chance's place. He'd made a vague mental note of the corral, in the way that men driven toward keen observance by years of danger often did. The deer knows to keep its ears pricked for the sound of stalking wolves. Now Haskell was following a hunch that had come to him when he'd watched the Thorson boys depart the house by way of the avenue.

Stepping under a low-hanging branch of a large, lightning-struck cottonwood, Bear paused and felt a knowing half-smile tug at his mouth corners. His hunch had been right.

The snow had drifted up into a frozen, white, glittering wave over the corral's bottom rail. The drift made perfect cover for the three hardtails hunkered behind it, occasionally lifting their chins to edge looks over the top of the drift and through the corral toward the avenue and Miss Chance's big red house beyond.

The Thorson boys were waiting for their quarry.

Haskell bit off his mitten and winced at the cold nipping his fingers. He lifted the flap of his three-point capote, unsnapped the keeper thong from over the Schofield's hammer, and slid the big popper free of the leather. He loudly clicked the hammer back and snarled, "I'm here, you cork-headed devils!"

As though all three heads were on the same swivel, they jerked toward Haskell. The fat Thorson, Billy, gave a startled screech, and jerked up the pistol in his hand. The Schofield barked in Bear's fist. Skinny Richard sprang to his feet, bringing up his own revolver. The Schofield spoke once more, a dull roar in the cold, clear air, and sent Richard falling back over the corral's top rail.

The rail broke, giving way beneath Richard's writhing body. Richard dropped and rolled, kicking and cursing, into the corral.

Bear slid the smoking Schofield toward Bradley Thorson, the hammer clicked back, but held fire. Bradley's terrified gaze flicked toward the Schofield's barrel and he threw his own gun away as though it were a hot potato, raised his hands, and turned his head, as though to avoid an imminent bullet.

"Don't kill me! Don't kill me!"

"You shot me!" Fat Billy wailed, sitting up and lifting his old Remington once more.

"Billy, don't!" Bradley shouted.

Billy triggered his Remington a quarter-second before Bear punched a puckered, dark-blue hole through his broad forehead, just beneath the red wool scarf his head was wrapped in. The fat kid sighed, sagged back against a corral post, and dropped his chin, as though he'd decided to take a short nap.

Haskell turned toward Richard, who lay just inside the corral, beyond the broken top rail. Richard wasn't moving. The front of his gray wool coat was bloody over his heart. His eyes were half-open but opaque as stones.

"You killed my brothers, you fuckin' bastard!" Bradley Thorson spat out through gritted teeth, slowly lowering his hands, one of which was bare.

Haskell slid the Schofield back toward him. "How 'bout you join 'em?"

"No!" the kid yelped, raising his hands in front of his face, which he turned to one side, squeezing his eyes closed.

Running footsteps sounded from the direction of Miss Chance's big red house.

CHAPTER 10

Haskell started to bring the Schofield around toward the sound of the running footsteps, but then he saw Knute Larson slogging through the snow, coming into view from behind a large cottonwood standing beside the trail. Larson stopped twenty feet away, breathing hard but smiling expectantly at Bear.

"Did you get 'em?"

"I got 'em." Haskell depressed the Schofield's hammer.

Keeping his hands raised shoulder-high, Bradley Thorson turned toward the old man trudging through the snow that rose in some places to his knees. "What's it to you, you drunken old fool?"

Larson walked up to the younger man, curling a wolfish half-grin and flaring a nostril. "Drunken old fool, huh?"

"That's what I said — drunken old fool!"

Larson held a whiskey bottle in his left,

417

mittened hand. His other arm was concealed under his coat. Chance must have outfitted him with a sling for holding the wounded limb stable. He raised the bottle. "You look like you could use a drink, Bradley."

"I sure could use one."

Thorson reached for the bottle but before he could grab it, Larson jerked it back down. Then, holding it by its neck, he gave a grunt and thrust it forward, underhanded, burying the bottom of the bottle in the younger man's crotch.

Thorson yelped. Drawing his knees together, he bent forward and clamped his hands over his crotch, groaning deeply, miserably.

"Oh, you rancid old bastard!" he grunted out, dropping slowly to his knees. His hat tumbled off his shoulder, showing the moth-eaten muffler he wore over his head, covering his ears.

"You feel better?" Haskell asked the older man.

"Some." Larson smiled. "I been wantin' to do somethin' like that to these Thorsons for years. Nasty firebrands is what they always been. Runnin' roughshod over the county. Their pa was a nasty son of a bitch . . . even meaner'n his boys." He walked over and stared down into the corral, where Richard lay deader than last year's Christmas goose, then turned to where Billy sat back against the fence post, chin dipped to his bloody chest.

Smiling up at Haskell again, Knute winked and said, "Say, you do good work!"

"Ah, hell."

Larson looked at Bradley, still pressing his hands to his crotch and moaning, veins standing out in his forehead. "Why don't you kill this little barn rat, too? Be done with these Thorsons once an' for all. Their older brother, Ray, was hanged over to Montana a couple years back. This here one, Bradley, he's the last of that rabid breed."

Haskell holstered the Schofield, then dug a set of handcuffs out of his coat pocket. "I'd love to oblige. Not havin' a prisoner to look after would make my job a whole lot easier. But that'd be against the law."

Bradley glared up at Larson. "You're gonna pay for that, old man. Don't think you ain't. You're gonna pay good!"

Larson wrinkled his nose and shook his head. "I got me a feelin' the big federal here'll be a whole lot better at keepin' you locked up than Cable was. Especially after he seen what happens when a Thorson is free to wreak your nasty brand of havoc. Hangin' the town marshal in his own office. Speakin' of which" — the old man turned to Bear — "I sent the undertaker over to the jailhouse for Gunderson."

"Can you fetch him over here for these two, as well?" Haskell asked. "I'd best get Bradley to the jailhouse." He grabbed the kid by the back of his coat collar, shoving him belly down in the snow. Bradley kicked at him and cursed, but Haskell held him fast to the ground with his knee pressed hard against the middle of his back. "I don't suppose Gunderson had a deputy, did he?"

"In a town this size?" Knute said. "And with as tight as the town council is?" He cackled caustically. "Nope. The only law in town was the sheriff, when he rode through from time to time, and Cable. The sheriff has a handful of deputies, scattered in little towns about the county. But the law here in Sioux Camp has only been Cable."

"Shit." Haskell grabbed one of Bradley's arms and cuffed the wrist. He grabbed the other one and cuffed it, too.

"That's about the size of it," Larson said. "Now you got a prisoner to watch . . . to feed and keep warm, an' such. Not to mention empty the poisonous little viper's slop bucket. All that on top of findin' the killer runnin' amok." He grinned devilishly up at Haskell, and arched his brows enticingly. "Unless you pop one between those nasty little eyes of his."

Bradley was writhing and cursing where Haskell held him facedown in the snow. The federal lawman had to admit that placing the Schofield to the back of the firebrand's head would solve a lot of problems. Besides, only he and Larson would know.

Still, it wasn't something he could do. He hoped he never could.

"Just fetch the gravedigger for me, Knute," he ordered, jerking Bradley to his feet.

"You ain't no fun at all," the old man griped.

Adjusting the set of his fur hat on his head, Larson slogged off through the snow, heading around the far side of the lightning-topped cottonwood, apparently taking the most direct route to the undertaker's.

"I got a better idea," Bradley said, blinking snow from his brows and smiling coldly up at Haskell. "You could let me go."

"Get movin'!" Haskell gave the kid a brisk shove, sending him stumbling through the snow.

"Just hear me out!" Bradley said as he headed for Wild Plum Avenue.

"Shut up."

"Me an' my brothers had us a stake saved up," Bradley said. "How 'bout if I split it with you?" He smiled at the lawman over his shoulder.

Haskell followed, trudging through the snow, close on the kid's heels. "You hanged the town marshal and you think you're going to buy me off?"

"Ten thousand dollars."

"Sorry, kid."

"That's a lot of money!"

"Shut up."

"All right — how 'bout this?"

"Shut up."

"Now, hear me out, dammit!" They were on the avenue now, though it was nothing more than a snow-drifted trail, heading back into town. "I think I know who the killer is. The son of a bitch who killed Weber, Abel, and Hodges and the marshal out of Bismarck, to boot."

"You know?"

Again, the kid grinned over his shoulder at Haskell. "Yep."

"How?"

"I'll not only tell you how, I'll tell you who . . . if you take off these bracelets and turn me loose."

Haskell only chuckled and shoved the young man forward through the snow.

"All right, then, you big fuckin' stupid bastard!" the kid snarled angrily over his shoulder at Haskell. "I ain't tellin' you a goddamn thing, and he's just gonna keep on killin'!"

"Bradley?"

"What?"

"Shut up!"

They turned onto the main street and headed east. There weren't many folks out even now. It was too damned cold. A single saddle horse stood tied before a feed store, and a farm wagon was parked in front of the mercantile. Aside from puffs of woodsmoke unspooling from chimney pipes and flattening out over snow-mantled rooftops, they were the only signs Sioux Camp hadn't been abandoned, the population having hopped the train for warmer climes.

When they arrived at the jailhouse, Haskell shoved Bradley Thorson through the door, left half open when the undertaker had cut Marshal Gunderson down from the ceiling beam, and hauled him over to get fitted for a wooden overcoat. The rope lay on the floor beneath where Gunderson had been hanging. Haskell shoved Thorson into the room's right-most cell, and slammed the door. He gave it a tug, making sure the bolt locked.

"Hey, what about the cuffs?" Thorson held his cuffed wrists out to Haskell.

"What about 'em?"

"Take 'em off!"

Haskell stepped up close to the cell door, and glared through the bars at his prisoner. "Listen up, you little pip-squeak. You and your brothers hanged the town marshal. That puts you crossways with me. So don't go demanding a goddamn thing, you understand? Or all you're going to be fed is an occasional cup of snowmelt, and I'll open this door every now and then to beat you silly with an axe handle. Got it?"

Thorson stared up at the big, shaggy-headed lawman towering over him, glaring down at him like a piss-burned griz. He swallowed and stepped back, sagging onto the cell's single cot. "All right, all right," he said, cowed, lowering his gaze to the floor. "Settle down, big fella . . ."

"That's more like it."

Anger seething in Haskell, he set to work building a fire in the potbelly stove crouched in the middle of the office. It wasn't only Gunderson's murder that had him so grieved. It was also the fact that he now would never know the town marshal's thoughts on the killings — whom he might have suspected, if anyone. Gunderson had been Haskell's lone contact here in Sioux Camp, the sheriff being dead. Now Gunderson was dead, as well. That made Haskell's investigation into the murders that much more difficult.

Not only that, but Haskell now had a prisoner to tend.

Blowing on his fledgling fire in the cold, black stove, Haskell cast another feral glare over his shoulder at his prisoner. Thorson saw the look, winced, and lowered his gaze to the floor once more — a truckling coyote.

As the flames began to dance inside the stove, the cold iron coming awake with creaks and groans, the building warmth beginning to penetrate the icehouse-cold of the marshal's office, footsteps thumped on the snow-buried stoop. The door opened and Knute Larson came in, stomping snow from his boots and shivering. He slammed the door and walked over to the stove, his bottle tucked into a pocket of his decrepit wool coat.

"Gallblastit! Who blew out hell's fires, anyhow? It's colder'n a gravedigger's's ass out there!" He plopped down into a ladderback, hide-bottom chair near the stove and looked up at Haskell. "Always coldest on the lee side of a storm!"

Haskell chunked another couple of split

logs into the stove, closed the door, twisted the latching lever, and sagged into the swivel rocking Windsor chair positioned before Gunderson's cluttered rolltop desk. He swiveled around to face the old man. "Knute, how well did you know Cable Gunderson?"

The oldster hiked a shoulder and reached into his coat pocket for his bottle. This was a fresh one, and it wasn't labeled. "Purty well, I reckon. Me an' Cable was both bachelors, about the same age. We played checkers almost every day right here in this office. I'm gonna miss ole Cable" — he turned to where Thorson sat on his cot in the cell — "thanks to you, you wet-behind-the-ears privy snipe!"

Thorson wrinkled his nose at the old man. He started to open his mouth to speak, but then he saw Haskell's hard gaze and turned away, muttering to himself.

Haskell turned to Larson, who popped the cork on his bottle. "Did you an' Gunderson discuss the killings here in Sioux Camp? Did he mention who he thought might be behind them, or where he was going to sniff around next?"

Larson started to tip up the bottle, then, reconsidering his manners, pulled it back down and offered it to Haskell, who waved it off. Larson took a swallow, then lowered the bottle to his knee, smacking his lips. He shook his head. "He didn't have no idea, Cable didn't. He figured it must've been a customer that Weber and Abel done wrong, and the killer was gettin' back at him. He couldn't figure out why anyone would want to kill Hodges, though. Who kills the post-master? But then the federal, like you, was killed when he'd only just got off the train."

"That could have been the killer just try-ing to protect himself, though he certainly must have realized another federal would show up to take the first one's place." Haskell reached into his coat for an Indian Kid. "And killin' the federal just to cover your tracks — that doesn't add up. I don't see a grieved customer — even a grieved postal customer — goin' to such a great length."

"I don't neither," Larson said.

"You're never gonna figure it out." This from Bradley Thorson in a mocking sing-song.

Haskell looked at him. Thorson sank back against the wall and hooked the heel of one boot over the edge of his cot. "I'd tell you straight out who the killer is . . . just as soon as you . . ."

The prisoner let his voice trail off as

crunching footsteps rose in the street outside the jailhouse. Someone was approaching at a fast clip. Automatically, Haskell slid his right hand across his belly, toward the Schofield, and had just pulled the big popper from its holster when the door opened quickly and a tall, clean-shaven young man dressed in a somewhat gaudy, three-piece business suit poked his head into the room, pale-blue eyes large and bright with exasperation. "Marshal Gunderson, you're needed right . . . !"

He stopped when he saw only Haskell and Larson seated around the stove.

He glanced around, his gaze lingering on Thorson for a moment, then turned back to Haskell and the old man. "Where's the marshal?"

"Dead," Haskell and Larson said at the same time.

"Dead?" The young man — handsome in a prissy way, in his mid-twenties — frowned and shook his head, thoroughly befuddled. "Well . . . my father-in-law has taken very ill, and the doctor, Wannamaker, sent me over to fetch the marshal."

Haskell rose, holstered the Schofield, and slid the unlit Indian Kid into his shirt pocket. "Who're you?"

The young man's gaze followed Haskell's

face from his sitting position to his full height, his lower jaw sagging slightly in awe. An indignant cast entered his sensitive, somewhat superior, pale-blue eyes as he said, "Who're *you*?"

"This is Bear Haskell, Arthur," Larson said. "He's a deputy U.S. marshal out of Denver. Here to investigate the killin's." To Haskell, the old man said, "This is Arthur Rasmussen. He's the loan officer over at the bank. His father-in-law, George Dawson, owns the bank." The old man squinted his watery blue eyes at the younger man. "You say Mr. Dawson has taken ill, Arthur?"

"Oh, my god — it's awful!"

"Where is he?"

"He's at Wannamaker's office!" The young man didn't wait for a response. He wheeled and dashed back out through the door, nearly slipping in the snow on the porch but catching himself against the rail with an indignant wail.

Haskell and Larson exchanged a look.

"I don't think Wannamaker would send for the law if Dawson just came down with a bout of the flu," Knute said.

"I don't, either."

Haskell headed for the door, glancing at Bradley Thorson who stared at him and Larson with mute interest. "You sit tight,

Thorson."

"Don't you be gone long, Haskell." The prisoner cast the ticking stove an anxious glance. "It's colder'n a witch's tit out there, and that fire's gonna burn down fast!"

"Yeah, it will, won't it?" Larson snickered.

He winked up at Haskell and shuffled out into the snow. Haskell followed him, pulling the door closed.

Behind the door, Thorson bellowed, "It's gonna burn down *fast* — you hear me?"

Haskell gave a little snicker himself as he followed Larson into the street.

CHAPTER 11

Haskell angled west behind Knute Larson, heading for the street's far side. Young Rasmussen was several yards ahead of them both, slipping in his little brown business shoes. In his haste to fetch the marshal, he hadn't dressed for the weather, and he slapped his shoulders to keep warm.

Haskell paused to glance at the sky. Only a few minutes ago, the sun had been sparkling with painful brightness on the new snow. Now the sky was leaden and low, and the breeze was picking up, blowing feathery snow against the fronts of the business establishments on the south side of the street.

Bear hoped another storm wasn't blowing in. That would make his job here just that much harder . . . and his body just that much colder.

He continued on to the other side of the street, following Larson, who in turn was following Arthur Rasmussen. They strode past the bank — a two-story building built of sandstone likely quarried from nearby — and into the wood frame building sitting just to the west of the bank and which gold-leaf lettering on a front window identified as the office of M. Emmett Wannamaker, M.D. As he passed the bank, Haskell had noted several faces staring, wide-eyed, out the windows on both sides of the front door.

Immediately upon entering the doctor's office, Haskell heard bellowing cries coming from a room flanking the front one, which was furnished with a large desk, stove, several book cases, and six or seven waiting chairs arranged against two walls.

"Doc!" Rasmussen yelled.

"Back here!" a man's voice shouted above the agonized bawling.

Rasmussen ran through a curtained doorway flanking the desk. Bear followed, striding down a short hall, then turning into an examining room in which an old, balding gent in a business suit like Rasmussen's lay writhing violently on the floor. Another man, nearly as old, knelt over him, trying to shove the first man's shoulders down. Meanwhile, the patient was foaming at the mouth like a rabid dog but howling like a gutshot wolf.

"Oh, my god!" Rasmussen cried, chomping on the knuckles of his right hand.

"God sure as hell ain't here just now," the doctor snapped up at him, a lock of thick gray hair hanging like a wing over his right eye. "But I could sure use some help getting this man back up on the examining table. I can't handle him!"

Haskell dropped to a knee on the other side of the convulsing patient from the sawbones. He grabbed the banker's writhing body, as did Wannamaker and Larson, and they lifted him up off the floor and onto the table.

"Can you hold him while I give him a shot?" the doctor asked, red-faced, breathing hard.

"I got his legs!" Knute said, leaning sideways over the man's knees.

Haskell threw himself on top of the banker's chest, holding him back against the table. "I got the rest!" The banker's writhing body felt like that of a giant snake. Haskell probably outweighed the man by fifty pounds, and he was a good foot taller. Still, he had a devil of a time keeping both himself and the banker on the table. Every bone, muscle, and tendon in the man's body was like a wild horse bent on springing free of its confines.

The doctor scrambled over to a cabinet, fumbled around for a bottle, and then poked a syringe into it.

"What in God's name is happening to Mr. Dawson?" Rasmussen yelled.

"I wouldn't mind knowin' the same thing, Doc!" Knute hollered, grunting as he maintained his precarious hold on the banker's legs.

"Hurry up, Doc," Haskell said. "He's slippin' out from under me!"

The banker writhed and groaned, white foam spilling out from his mouth and down his chin. He was choking on it, and that made him fight Haskell even more. The man's eyes were bright with agony and stark terror. It was as though his own guts were eating themselves, slowly killing him.

"Steady now," Wannamaker said, approaching the table with the filled syringe in one hand.

"We got him!" Haskell yelled.

"No time to cut off his sleeve — I'm going right through his clothes!" Wannamaker grabbed the banker's right arm and pinned it to the table with his own left shoulder. He thrust the syringe into the banker's upper arm and pressed the plunger down.

Almost immediately, the banker's writhing began to ease, if only slightly. Gradually over the next minute, with both the banker and Wannamaker holding the man against the table, the convulsions dwindled. When Dawson was nearly still but groaning behind the spittle in his mouth, the doctor straightened. He drew a deep breath. His ashen features were mottled red. He shook his head as if to clear it, then focused his anxious, worn-out gaze on Haskell.

"Who're you?"

"Bear Haskell, Deputy U.S. Marshal."

Wannamaker nodded dully, then glanced at the examining room's open door. "Where's Gunderson?"

"Dead," Knute said, straightening, as breathless as the doctor. The two men were roughly the same age. "Hanged by the Thorsons when Richard and Billy busted Bradley out."

Wannamaker stared at Knute dully, as though he wasn't quite sure what he'd just been told. Apparently deciding to seek clarification later, he looked down at the banker. "We have to roll him onto his belly so he doesn't drown on his own bile."

Haskell and the sawbones turned the banker over. It was as though the man was dying, going through the death spasms. While he was relatively calm, his eyes were terror-stricken, and his hands and arms

435

continued to jerk. Bile spilled out of his mouth and onto the table. From there it dribbled to the floor.

Haskell stepped back in revulsion. "What the hell's wrong with him, Doc?"

"I second that question," Knute said, running his coat sleeve across his mouth and staring in shock at the patient.

Wannamaker stared down at something behind Haskell and the old woodcutter. Bear turned. The banker's son-in-law had fainted. He sat on the floor against the wall by the door, legs spread before him, head tipped to one side, glasses hanging from one ear.

"Christ," Haskell said, reaching for him.

"Leave him." Wannamaker beckoned Haskell and slipped through the door and back into his office. "He'll be all right. I'll get him up in a bit."

Following the doctor into the main office, Haskell drew a deep breath. He hadn't seen anything so horrifying since the war. "What'd you give him?"

"Straight morphine. Enough to knock out an elephant."

"What happened, Doc?"

Wannamaker staggered around behind his desk and sagged into his black leather chair. It squeaked beneath his weight, which wasn't much. He had that in common with Knute, as well. Haskell thought he might have weighed a hundred pounds dripping wet in his frayed suit, even with his stethoscope hanging around his neck. He had the bulbous red nose of a hard drinker. Long-fingered hands shaking, it was a decanter on a cabinet behind him he fumbled for now.

He turned to hold up the decanter and said, "Need a bracer?"

"I'm braced enough."

"I got my own." Knute patted the unlabeled bottle poking up out of his coat pocket.

"Not me." The doctor splashed liquor into a brandy snifter, threw back the entire shot, then splashed another couple of fingers into the snifter. He turned in his chair, set the snifter on his desk, and leaned forward, elbows on his knees. "Strychnine."

"What?" Haskell said in shock.

"Strych-nine."

"Yeah, yeah, I heard ya." Haskell ran his hand across his cheek.

"You mean he was poisoned?" Knute stood in front of the curtained doorway. Behind him, the banker was still grunting and gurgling.

"I doubt that anyone would voluntarily

consume strychnine." The sawbones grabbed the snifter in his shaky left paw and took a deep sip. Sighing, he set the snifter back on his desk. "Murdered. That's why I fetched Gunderson . . . but got you." He glanced dubiously up at the big, shaggy-headed man in the three-point capote standing before him. "A U.S. marshal, you say?"

"Deputy."

"Didn't know they grew 'em that big."

"Yeah, I get that all the time. How can you be so sure it's strychnine?"

Wannamaker sat back in his chair, his long, pale, age-spotted hands hanging down over the chair's wooden arms. "I've seen it before. Too many times, in fact. You can buy it in any mercantile. It's commonly used by wolfers to poison their quarry. Miners use it to kill rats. Just last year I treated a miner for it, if you can call it 'treat.' I injected the poor sot with a bromide of potassium and chloral, which is supposed to counteract the effect. I gave Dawson the same injection when he first came in, but it's not doing much good. The miner had come to me too late, as well. He died howling and foaming at the mouth, just like Dawson. This man and his partner'd had a falling-out over a whore, and the partner laced his whiskey with the nasty substance. He came to me feeling sick and very, very nervous — pacing to and fro — and ended up just like that poor devil in there."

"Wolfers," Knute said softly, as though talking half to himself.

Bear turned to him. "What's that?"

Larson ran the sleeve of his good arm across his mouth and gave Haskell a direct look of deep gravity despite the drink-bleariness of his eyes. "Remember what we was talkin' about back in the office? Before Rasmussen came?"

"I'd asked you if Gunderson had any idea who the killer might be."

"That's right," Knute said with quiet gravity. He sniffed, sucking snot down his throat. "I said that Cable didn't have no idea. But I did. And I'm even more convinced now" — he hooked a thumb over his shoulder to indicate the examining room behind him — "after seein' that in there."

As though the gesture had evoked a reaction from the room, the banker bellowed incoherently. He yelled again, forming a vaguely coherent, "Here!"

The doctor jerked up out of his chair and strode quickly into the examination room. Bear and Larson followed. The banker still writhed, all the muscles in his body dancing like snakes in a gunnysack. Somehow, he'd rolled onto his side, resting back against one elbow. He threw his other arm out toward Haskell, beckoning.

His eyes were ablaze, as though a fire burned inside his head. Sweat dribbled down his craggy cheeks and into his thick muttonchop whiskers. The poor man looked as though he were burning up inside and out, thick spittle still bubbling from one corner of his mouth. He was at once miserable and terrified. The fire in his eyes bespoke rage.

The doctor and Larson glanced at Haskell, who stepped forward curiously. "You . . . want . . . me?"

As he crouched over the banker, the man hooked his arm around Haskell's neck, drawing the big lawman's head closer. The man's arm shook like a tree limb struck by lightning. The old man garbled incoherently. It was as though his mouth and throat were filled with sand. He winced, closed his mouth, shook his head, and tried again, his blazing eyes staring directly into Haskell's. More incoherence followed as more foam dribbled from his mouth, but finally there was one word Haskell made out: "See!"

"See?"

Dawson nodded, head quivering, then

drew Haskell's head even closer, sliding his mouth toward Bear's left ear. "Suh . . . suh . . . suh . . . sir . . . *see!*"

Then his arm and head dropped, and the man died in one last spasm that would have felled him from the table if Haskell and Wannamaker hadn't thrown themselves on top of him.

"What the hell did he say?" the doctor asked.

Bear hadn't gotten it.

But apparently Larson had. "Circle C," said the old man, his leathery forehead creased with incredulity. "I'm sure that's what he said. Yeah. Circle C."

"Circle C," said Wannamaker dubiously.

Haskell studied old Larson for a time, then turned to Dawson lying belly down and finally, mercifully, still on the examination table. "That's the Carr brand," he said.

"I don't understand that," Larson said, deeply puzzled.

"Understand what?" Haskell prodded him.

"What would James Carr have . . . ?" Knute turned to Doc Wannamaker. "I was thinkin' Ole Kemp."

"Kemp," the sawbones said, snarling out the name. "Oh, him. That devil!"

"What about him?" Haskell said.

441

"Three weeks ago . . . or some such . . . I forget," Larson said, turning slowly to Haskell, his own gaze glinting with building emotion, "he left town drunker'n a skunk and shouting that he would kill every miserable, business-ownin' bastard in sight. Mark his words!"

"That's a direct quote," Wannamaker told Haskell. "I heard him myself. He walked right past my place, drinking from a bottle and shouting so's to be heard as far away as the Montana line. Apparently, every businessman in town had cut off his credit. Kemp is a no-good drunkard. Hasn't worked an honest job in years."

An unfamiliar voice said, "He'd been in the bank that day. My father-in-law had turned down his request for a loan to pay off his bills."

All eyes turned to Rasmussen. The young banker had regained consciousness but remained on the floor, looking as pale as the new-fallen snow. He sat with his back and head against the wall, his long, curly hair mussed. His eyes were glassy as they stared into space.

The doctor crouched beside him. "Do you feel better, now, Arthur?"

The young, stricken-looking man shook his head slightly, the skin above his nose wrinkling as though in irritation at the question. He turned to Wannamaker. "It was him, wasn't it? I had a bad feeling after that day. He sounded so . . . sincere!"

Wannaker glanced at Haskell. "Help me get him up and into my office."

When they'd lifted the young man to his feet and guided him to the doctor's office and into Wannamaker's comfortable chair, Haskell hiked a hip on a corner of the desk, looking down at the loan officer, who kept saying, "What am I going to tell Verna . . . and Verna's mother . . . ? Oh, my god — Mr. Dawson is *dead*!"

"Son, have you seen this Ole Kemp fella in the bank since then?"

Rasmussen turned to Haskell. It seemed to take him a minute to understand the question. Then he shook his head. "No. But Mr. Dawson's office is by the back door. He could have slipped into the office when Mr. Dawson was out, and . . . poisoned one of his liquor decanters with . . ." He turned to Wannamaker. "With strychnine, you say?"

"That's what it looks like," the doctor said, standing beside the banker and squeezing his shoulder comfortingly. "I'll help impart this tragic news to your wife and mother-in-law, son. Don't worry."

The young man stared into space again.

"Thanks, Doc."

Haskell rolled an Indian Kid around between his thumb and index finger as he stared through a near window, thinking over the situation. Finally, he turned to the young man once more. "Does . . . or did . . . your father-in-law drink out of those decanters regularly?"

"No," Rasmussen said, dully. "He's been trying to cut back, but I know this cold bothered him. I bet he made himself a toddy as soon as he got to the bank after lunch today. Oh, god, how horrible! Verna is going to be heartsick!"

Haskell turned to Wannamaker. "Would you be able to tell strychnine by sniffing those bottles, Doc?"

Wannamaker shook his head. "It has no smell. I'm told the taste is bitter, but for obvious reasons, I can't taste it. It can affect you by just getting into your saliva."

Haskell turned to Larson standing tensely on the other side of the desk. "Where will I find this Ole Kemp fella?"

Larson canted his head over his left shoulder. "Six miles south of town. Lives in an old log shack by Cottonwood Creek. Want I should hitch my sleigh? It's over to the livery barn, along with my mule."

Haskell glanced at the wounded arm still

tucked up inside his coat.

"Don't worry about that," Larson said, lifting his bottle from his coat pocket and grinning. "I got me the best pain reliever there is. Haven't felt a twinge for hours now!"

CHAPTER 12

The clomps of the mule's hooves, along with the jingle of the sleigh bells and the soft snicks of the runners slicing through the feathery snow, sounded festive as hell.

Bear Haskell and Knute Larson, holding the leather trace ribbons in his buckskin-mittened hands on the seat beside the big lawman, could have been venturing out to cut a Christmas tree to throw into the sleigh's broad, high-sided box, which had half a chord of wood in it for weight and ballast, as well as several pounds of bark and sawdust — all feathered with snow. The federal lawman and the old woodcutter could have been out here following a snow-drifted trail heading into the buttes and wooded ravines south of town, to cut that tree and haul it back to Sioux Camp's lone church for Sioux Camp's orphans or whores' bastard progeny to trim with silver glitter, candles, colored glass balls, and popcorn strings.

A festive snow was even falling — large, downy flakes tumbling out of a low sky the color of an overripe plum.

Jingle-jingle-jingle, went the sleigh bells jostling down the mule's chest.

Jingle bells, Jingle bells, Jingle all the way,
O what fun it is to ride
In a one-mule open sleigh . . .

It would have been a lot more fun if Haskell could have felt his toes inside his fur-lined boots, his fingers inside his fleece-lined buckskin mittens, and his nose exposed to the raw, subzero air and which felt — what he could feel of it — like a fierce little creature was digging its sharp teeth into it, gnawing gleefully away on it. Now he swiped his mitten across it, and winced.

That hurt like hell!

Larson glanced at him, a grin creasing the old man's crinkled-parchment face with its two- or three-day-old metal-filing beard stubble. He wore his deerskin hat with ear-flaps tied snug beneath his chin. His nose glowed like a locomotive's stoked firebox. He'd just taken a drink from his ubiquitous bottle. He thrust the whiskey toward Haskell, arching a gray brow.

Haskell waved it off.

Larson shoved the bottle against his

shoulder. "Go ahead. Warms the oysters. Not as good as the sweet little gals over at Miss Chance's place, but it'll do in a pinch. And out here at this temperature, I'd say we're in a pinch."

"What the hell." Haskell took the bottle, tipping it back.

The rotgut threatened to burn a hole through the bottom of his belly and expose his pecker to the elements.

"Christ!" he said. "I think that stuff is best used for cleaning bullet wounds!"

Larson shrugged, took the bottle back, and had another liberal pull. He sighed and smacked his lips. "It grows on a fella."

"Like cancer," Haskell croaked, trying to keep the damned stuff down. He glanced behind him. The town was out of sight now. "I hope old Louie remembers to stoke the stove in the jailhouse." He glanced at Knute. "You think he will?"

Louie was the proprietor of the Sioux Camp Federated Livery & Feed Barn. Haskell had paid the man a silver dollar to keep the fire going in the jailhouse until he returned, checking on it every two hours or so. But the old man — a daytime imbiber himself, Haskell could tell — seemed more involved with the new litter of kittens adorning his haymow and which he'd seemed tickled pink over.

Larson shrugged again. "Does it really matter?"

Haskell imagined the sneering, rat-like face of Bradley Thorson, and gave a wry chuckle. "Right." He stared straight out over the mule's twitching ears. A line of gray, which he assumed were trees, grew ahead along the drifted trail the sleigh bounced and swayed upon, sometimes jerking violently from side to side, threatening to toss Haskell and Larson into the snow. "How much farther?"

" 'Bout two more miles." Knute extended the bottle once more. "Have another coupla pulls. It'll make the time fly!"

"And burn my guts to gray ashes." Clamping his mittened hands over the edges of the seat for purchase, Haskell turned to the old man. "You visit Miss Chance's place, do you, Knute?"

"Me? Sure." Larson grinned lustily. "When I feel the fire. Me? I like that little China girl, Li. She's so gentle an' nice, and she don't make a feller feel bad if . . . well, you know, if it takes us old guys a little longer, if you get my drift?" He winked.

Haskell chuckled as he pulled off his mitten, then reached into his coat for an Indian Kid. "What about Miss Chance?"

"What about her?"

Haskell gave a sheepish shrug. "She told me she never works upstairs. That true?"

"Sorry to say it is. Many a man has offered her a pretty penny, but she's turned every one down. I heard tell a muckety-muck from the spur line offered her one thousand dollars one night — one thousand dollars for one hour — and she even turned that down!" Larson shook his head in disbelief. "That there is a lot of money around here, as most places. A thousand dollars would buy Chance a lifetime's worth of them purty dresses she has shipped in from San Francisco."

"She must get her satisfaction from somewhere." Haskell narrowed an eye at the old man. "Jimmy?"

"*Jimmy?*" Knute said, incredulous. "*Two Eagles?* Well, I don't know for sure, mind you. I don't know what Chance and Jimmy do in the privacy of their own rooms, but I sure can't see her entertainin' the likes of that big, ugly Injun."

"Chance is Injun herself."

Still looking flabbergasted, Larson said, "Yeah, but she ain't no big ugly squaw! Chance is a St. Louis-eddycated lady. Jimmy's from south of Bismarck, born and raised in a tipi before his tribe, the Sioux, was shunted off to the reservation. He's Chance's bouncer, bartender, and personal protector, an' that's all."

The old man chuckled dryly. "Hell, no. I hear tell that Chance don't allow Jimmy none of the pleasures of her own parlor. Keeps him away from all the girls. So he goes down to the hog pens Merle Iverson has down around the Buffalo Buttes, north of town about eight, nine miles. An old, abandoned cavalry post. I've heard of fellas seein' Jimmy down there, three sheets to the wind and howlin' like a maniac. Fightin' an' such. Lockin' horns with freighters and market hunters an' bustin' the place up. No, sir. Miss Chance would never put up with that at her place, an' certainly not in her own room."

"She must have somebody," Haskell said, taking a long drag from his cheroot and blowing the smoke out in the cold, gray air, downy flakes catching on his eyelashes.

Larson gave a husky laugh as he glanced sidelong at the big lawman.

"What?" Haskell said, annoyed.

"You're smitten," Knute said. "Just like all the rest of us!" He laughed and shook his head, then hoorawed the mule through a four-foot drift.

Haskell thought he probably would have

felt a flush rise in his cheeks if they hadn't been so damned cold. Just because his chagrin didn't show didn't mean it wasn't burning inside him, making him flinch. He had to admit the woman had worked a spell on him, making his loins ache pleasantly, twitching every time he conjured her dark-eyed, black-haired countenance.

The Indian lady called Chance was right intriguing. There was no denying her sexual attraction. He'd have enjoyed nothing more than spending a night with the pretty lady in her boudoir, removing her clothes very slowly, running his tongue over every inch of that tall, raw-boned, high-busted, bourbon-colored, exotic body, then mounting her only when he'd worked them both into a mewling lather.

The twitching in his own nether regions just now was dampened down by what Knute had told him about her apparent tight-fistedness when it came to sharing her bed. It didn't look like his yearned-for union with the Sioux madam was going to happen. If she'd turned down a thousand dollars from a railroad muckety-muck, she wouldn't have much trouble giving a raggedy-heeled federal lawman the cold shoulder — which she'd already done, come to think of it.

More's the pity, he thought, sucking the rich, peppery tobacco deep into his lungs, liking the way it mixed with the cold air, making him feel a little drunk while also warming his innards, at least until he took another breath of the icy, stony air.

Silently chastising himself for the unprofessional diversions of his renegade mind when he should have been concentrating on business, he shifted his thoughts to the job at hand, at the same time nudging his Henry rifle. The long gun lay on the floorboards behind his feet. He'd wanted to make sure it was still there and hadn't slithered out and into the snow during one of the sleigh's dangerous pitches.

He'd retrieved the gun from his hotel room after he'd investigated Dawson's office at the bank, finding that the man had, indeed, poured himself a bourbon. He'd apparently been drinking the skull pop with a cup of creamed coffee. The cup and the glass had sat together on his desk blotter, beneath a burning Tiffany lamp. He'd drunk all of the bourbon excepting half a swallow, and half the coffee. That must have been when he'd started getting sick, the sickness growing so quickly and violently that Rasmussen had hustled him to Wannamaker's place next door.

There he lay dead. The doctor and Rasmussen were no doubt relaying the sad news to the man's wife and daughter.

And Haskell and Larson were heading out to Cottonwood Creek to investigate the wolfer, Ole Kemp. Of course, many folks in Sioux Camp had free access to strychnine. The poison was commonly used on mice and rats, and some even used it to keep down feral cat populations as well as wolf and coyote populations. But the fact that Kemp had threatened all of the Sioux Camp businessmen who'd refused doing business with him was more than enough to make him Haskell's prime suspect. He must have had the same beef with the postmaster that he'd had with the others.

"Tell me about Kemp," he prodded Larson, who was just then lowering his bottle after another slug.

The old man gave a liquid sigh as he shoved the cork back into the bottle and returned the rotgut to his coat pocket. "What's to tell? A loner. Used to hunt wolves for a livin'. I don't know where he came from. Showed up here a few years ago with a Montana crease in his hat and a Montana brand on his horse. Moved into an abandoned shack on Cottonwood Creek. Never said a word till he was drunk. Then he'd go loco. Gunderson barred him from town more than a few times, but after his banishment was up, here he'd come again, lookin' to get drunk and fuck and pick up a few supplies for his cabin. In that order."

"Did he frequent Miss Chance's place?" Haskell didn't know why that seemed important. Maybe it didn't. Maybe the pretty Sioux madam was just haunting the misty halls of his depraved mind like the fragments of a particularly beguiling wet dream.

"One time. Just after she got here and set up her place, two, maybe three years ago. *One time.*" Larson grinned over at Haskell, the hollows of his cheeks filling with dark shadows, the freshly falling snow sticking to his deerskin cap. "Then he was banned for life. Jimmy threatened to cut him in two with that sawed-off gut-shredder."

Haskell snorted a laugh.

"Here we go." Larson pulled the sleigh off the trail, heading cross-country. The snow was falling hard now and the wind was kicking up. Haskell glanced at the sky. It seemed to be hovering lower and growing more purple. He hoped they weren't going to get stranded out here.

Ahead lay a dip in the snowy land. That must be the course of Cottonwood Creek. Between the sleigh and the dip was a six-foot-high drift of snow, perfectly fashioned with a frozen curlicue adorning its crest. Larson reined the mule to a stop in front of the drift.

"Best stop here," he said. "Otis'll never get through that drift. Not without tipping the sleigh, anyways."

"Where's the cabin?" Bear asked.

"Should be in the ravine, straight ahead."

"Then this is close enough." Haskell reached under the seat for his Henry. He shucked the rifle from its leather, wool-lined scabbard, stepped down from the sleigh, and tossed the scabbard back onto the seat.

Setting the rifle on his shoulder, he strode forward, wading through the drift along its far right side, which appeared the shallowest part. Still, the snow rose nearly to his hips. The cold engulfed him, and he winced against it. "Thanks, Henry," he muttered aloud.

"What's that?" Larson was coming up behind him. He'd taken his injured wing out of its sling and shoved it through his coat sleeve. Now he wielded an old Spencer carbine in his mittened hands, a wool muffler buffeting around his scrawny neck.

"Nothin'," Haskell grunted.

Keeping his voice low, Knute said, "If I didn't know better, Deputy Haskell, I'd say you weren't so fond of our fair climes here in Dakota Territory."

Haskell merely grunted a response to that, and the old man sucked a chuckle through his begrimed teeth.

When he was on the other side of the drift, the lawman saw that he was on the ravine's lip. He dropped to a knee. Larson crouched beside him. Bear could see the cabin about thirty yards out from the ravine's bottom. It was a small gray shack with no window facing Haskell and his crouching partner. To the far left was a log stable and corral. Beyond the cabin and the stable lay the curving course of the creek sheathed in thick trees and brush and mantled with snow. It was frozen up solid, except for maybe a few springs feeding it.

Haskell stared at the brick chimney crawling up the cabin's left side. No smoke issued from it. Odd.

He surveyed the slope dropping away before him. Bramble and winter-dead saplings poked up through the fresh snow while the falling new stuff coated their branches like bits of goose down. Haskell glanced at the sky. It wasn't getting lighter. It looked like the storm was building, and night would be along soon.

"I'm going to head down." He pushed off

his knee.

"I'll come, too."

Haskell glanced at the old man. "No need. You stay here and keep your head down."

"I know Ole. He's odder'n a three-dollar bill, and he don't cotton to strangers. He might start shootin' as soon as he sees you. He won't if he sees me. Leastways, he won't start in right away, but'll let me tell him what we're here for *first*."

Haskell thought it over, then shrugged. "Couldn't hurt." He started down the steep slope made treacherous by snow-covered brush and blowdown. "Watch your step."

"Watch your own step," the old man groused behind him. "I live in this shit."

CHAPTER 13

When Bear and old Knute had finally gained the slope's bottom, both men were breathing hard. They'd had to push forcefully, but with finesse, over and through the deep snow and buried obstacles. Haskell had tripped once over covered vines and fallen hard, getting handfuls of snow down his back for his trouble. Larson had wheezed happily at that. The old man had remained upright all the way down the hill.

Crouching at the base of the slope near a small privy whose slanted roof was capped with a good foot of snow, Larson silently offered his bottle to the lawman. Haskell waved it off. Knute took a sip as Bear strode forward, keeping directly behind the shack and casting occasional, wary glances toward the stable, hoping a horse wouldn't betray his presence. He couldn't see any animals in the corral, however. The wolfer's horse must be locked inside the shelter.

Larson following close on his heels, Haskell made his way slowly around the cabin to the front. He frowned as he stared at the front door, which was abutted on both sides by stacks of split stove wood. More split wood was piled in a rough pyramid shape in front of the door, to the left of the smooth oak handle of a splitting maul angling up out of the snow. The maul's head must have been embedded in a chopping block under the downy white.

What fascinated Haskell most was that the cabin door was unlatched. The breeze nudged it fitfully against the frame, making dull, quiet tapping sounds, occasionally holding it open a quivering foot and then nudging it back against the frame before sucking it out again. Fresh, unmarred snow lay all around the front door, indicating that neither the wolfer nor anyone else had fetched wood lately or even stepped outside. At least, not since the storm of the day before yesterday.

Odd.

Haskell strode along the front of the cabin, quickly passing a small front window. He stopped beside the door, pressing his back to the front logs, and called through the crack, "Mr. Kemp? Ole Kemp?"

No response. The door continued to flutter and jerk and tap against the frame.

Haskell glanced at Knute, who'd come up behind him to stand beside him. Larson hiked a shoulder.

"Wait here," Bear whispered to the older man.

Using the barrel of his Henry, Haskell levered the door wide. He stepped quickly into the cabin, pumping a cartridge into the chamber and sweeping his gaze quickly around the small, cluttered hovel. No one was here. Haskell took another step inside and even looked under the small eating table covered in frozen food scraps and dirty dishes. He walked over to the fireplace, removed his mitten, and poked his hand into the gray ashes mounded on the grate.

They were as cold as the air outside, though a large, blue-speckled pot hung over the gate from a metal tripod.

Bear straightened and glanced again around the cabin. Traps of all shapes and sizes hung from the walls, as did hides of all kinds, including more than a few wolf hides. Clothes hung from hooks. Foodstuffs peppered shelves built into the back wall, above a dry sink and makeshift counter hammered together from halved pine logs.

Larson pulled the door open, stepped inside, and looked around. "Where do you

461

s'pose the rascal is?"

"I don't know." Haskell stepped to the table, brushing his mitten across the scarred wooden surface. "He's been gone long enough for mice to have moved in." Their shit peppered the table as well as the plates and cups sitting on it. The coffee left in a tin cup was frozen solid, which Haskell discovered when he knocked the cup against the table with solid thuds. Glancing at the full plate of what appeared frozen rabbit stew, he said, "Looks like he left just when he'd been about to sit down to a meal."

"Why would he do that?"

Haskell stepped around the old man as he headed outside. He looked around carefully, noticing vague dimples in the snow. At first, he thought they were shadows, but when he raked his moccasins through the snow, large dark-brown patches staining the older snow were revealed.

"What's that?"

"Blood."

"Human blood?"

"Hard to tell."

Haskell continued to look around, following the faint shadows in the snow, occasionally kicking away the new stuff to reveal more of the old blood and scuff marks in the older snow. The course of the sign led him out along the frozen, snow-dusted stream. He continued walking, following the sign, occasionally stepping over fallen trees. He followed a bend in the stream, stopped, and looked around for more sign. He kicked away more snow, uncovering more patches of brown. Finally, his gaze landed on something poking out from beneath some snow-laden shrubs about six feet back from the stream.

Whatever it was, covered in snow, it was curiously shaped.

Haskell lightly brushed his right fur boot against it. Snow danced off of the object, revealing what appeared a human cheek and jaw.

"Holy shit," the lawman raked out.

"What in hell is that?"

Haskell crouched over the object and used his right mitten to clear the face of a man with four or five days' worth of beard stubble carpeting his porcelain-pale cheeks. Porcelain pale with a sickly undertone of deathly blue.

"Jesus fuck!" Larson wheezed, jerking back with a start.

"Is that the wolfer, Ole Kemp?"

Larson stepped forward and crouched down, stretching his lips back in revulsion as he cast his gaze at the dead man's face.

There were several deep scratches on the cheeks, and one of the eyes had been plucked out to hang by the thick, dark-red thread of the optic nerve. The other eye, a murky hazel color, stared at the snow falling from the deep-purple sky. Long, coarse, pewter hair hung to the man's shoulders. One half of his mouth was twisted in a snarl, revealing a couple of cracked teeth and a gap where one was missing.

"Yeah," Larson said, straightening. "That's him. That's Ole, all right. Deader'n a fence post."

Haskell leaned his rifle against a tree. He reached down and found Kemp's right shoulder. He reached lower and felt for the man's arm, around which he closed his mittened hands, and pulled.

"What do you suppose happened?" Knute said. "He get drunker'n a Irish gandy dancer, stumble out here, pass out, and freeze to death?"

Haskell tugged. The body wouldn't budge. It must have been frozen to the ground. Bear wrapped his left hand under the dead man's left shoulder, set his heels, and gave a fierce pull. He uttered a startled oath as the dead man jerked so suddenly free of whatever he had been frozen to that Haskell flew backward, releasing the dead man's arms, and hit the ground hard on his ass.

"Fuck!" he said.

"Ah, Jesus!"

Bear looked up at Knute. The old man stared down at something near Haskell's boots. His face, which had turned the off-white of fresh cream, was creased in horror at the dead man whose head resided between Haskell's spread legs.

"What is it?" Haskell said, sitting up.

He followed the old man's gaze with his own, and his stomach turned a flip-flop. What he stared down at was not quite half a man. All that was left of Ole Kemp was the man's head and chest, and part of his gut. The man's legs were gone. In fact, all that remained below the wolfer's beltline were flaps of frayed red viscera, indistinguishable from the tails of the man's torn wool shirt, and the two bloody knobs of his hip bones. From the hollow look of the man's chest, behind the wool shirt and two snakeskin suspenders, even the man's guts and organs had been removed. Torn out, more like, by the beast that had done him in.

"Bear," Haskell said when he'd climbed to his feet to stare down in horror at the grisly spectacle. "Must've been waitin' for Ole out by the woodpile. Ole decided to get

465

his fire stoked before sitting down to that rabbit stew in the cabin . . ."

"But it was the bear that dined," Larson said.

"On Ole himself." Haskell brushed his coat sleeve across his mouth and nose, sucking in a fresh breath of the chill, bracing air. "Dragged him out here, fed on him, buried him in those bushes to finish later."

Suddenly, Haskell felt the uncanny sensation of being watched. Chicken flesh rose along his backbone, and an icy witch's hand splayed its wrinkled fingers against the small of his back. As if to validate the sensation, a horrific cry rose behind him. The bellowing wail was so loud and jarring, Bear felt himself leap a good foot in the air, heart bounding into his throat. Twisting his body, he dropped back to the ground and found himself staring up at the huge, shaggy, cinnamon-colored bruin standing atop a wagon-sized boulder protruding from the side of the brushy slope maybe forty yards away.

"Ah, hell!" Knute shouted. "I don't think that son of a bitch wants us messin' around with his cache of Ole Kemp!"

The old man's shout was nearly drowned out by the following wail the bear loosed as it opened its mouth, showing its large, razor-edged, white teeth and thrusting its human-like hands straight out in front of it, as though flailing for the objects of its wrath. Its cinnamon fur, dusted with fresh snow, rippled across its broad, thick, lumpy body.

The beast gave yet another enraged wail, shaking its head as though to rid itself of a pesky fly, and then turned and leaped from the top of the boulder to the slope beside it with a great crunching cacophony of trampled brush and snapping branches.

"I got a sick feelin' you're right." Haskell ripped off his right mitten, grabbed his Henry, and levered a round into the action. "Knute, you hightail it up the closest tree and be quick about it!"

"Ah, shit!"

"Move!"

"Ah, hell!" Knute wheeled and ran in his shambling, heavy-foot fashion, casting terrified looks over his left shoulder.

Haskell drew a bead on the grizzly's head as it barreled down the slope, and pulled the trigger. Dust puffed from the bruin's right shoulder. A miss! The bear roared its screeching roar of tempestuous fury, the bullet having merely riled it more, and kept coming.

Haskell ejected the spent round, seated another one, aimed, and fired.

The beast was moving too quickly and pitching too violently around on the snowy slope for an accurate shot. The way the beast's long, light-brown fur separated slightly low on its left side told the lawman he'd again missed the head.

He could pepper the big bruin all he wanted, but the forty-four caliber rounds would likely not penetrate the beast's hide but only aggravate its fury. He needed a head shot.

The grizzly gained the base of the slope and barreled toward Haskell, mewling and bellowing and shaking its head, moving alarmingly fast for a beast so big and lumbering, tearing up great clumps of fresh snow and casting them behind it. Bear aimed, and fired. The bruin didn't even flinch. Haskell aimed and fired again. The bruin kept coming at a slant across the open ground between the slope and where Haskell stood near Ole Kemp's frozen torso.

Ejecting the last spent cartridge casing, Haskell glanced behind him, toward where Larson was clumsily trying to climb a pine tree thirty yards back in the direction of the cabin.

"Get up that tree, Knute! He's comin' hard and fast!"

Larson yelled something too garbled for

Haskell to make out as he racked another round in the Henry's action. Behind him he heard branches snapping and the scuffs of the old man's boots against the pine's trunk as Larson clumsily climbed.

Trying like hell to ignore his instinctive impulse to flee, and to hold his ground instead, knowing that the grizzly could outrun him and that his and Knute's only chance at survival was to kill the beast, Haskell raised the Henry once more. He drew a bead on the bruin's jostling head as it galloped through the snow. It was within fifty yards now and coming hard and fast, sort of skip-hopping, thrusting itself forward through the snow with every lunging leap.

Haskell could smell the wild, sweet, gamey tang of the beast on the chill, snow-stitched wind. It cut through his brain on a knife blade of raw, animal fear . . .

He settled the Henry's sites on the top of the beast's head, between the two upright V's of its ears, and squeezed the trigger. Only, the trigger wouldn't squeeze. It wouldn't budge.

Jammed!

"Shit!"

CHAPTER 14

Haskell tried to lower the rifle's cocking lever. Halfway down it stuck, and then it wouldn't move either up or down. The cartridge was trapped in the action.

"Shoot the goddamn thing, Bear!" Larson shouted from behind Haskell. "What the hell you doin' over there?"

Haskell looked up from the useless rifle in his hands. The bear was twenty yards away . . . fifteen . . .

"Shut up, you old coot!"

Again suppressing the iron-strong urge to flee, Haskell stepped forward and flipped the rifle around, wrapping his bare right hand and mittened left hand around the barrel. Letting his bald-assed fear turn itself to fury, acknowledging that this bruin was out to take his life . . . to chew him up into little bitty pieces and leave little more than what it had left of Ole Kemp . . . he raised the Henry like a club.

He'd killed one before — but he'd been wielding a Sharps Big Fifty in good working order . . .

"Come on, you son of a bitch!"

As the bear bulled toward him, growing as large as a barn before him, he choked back his fear once more and swung the Henry up and sideways, aiming for the beast's head, hoping to at least daze it a little and possibly buy himself enough time to reach beneath his coat for his bowie knife. He was only vaguely aware that it was the only hope he had — and that it was very little hope indeed . . .

Goddamn you, Henry Dade . . .

The rifle's stock glanced off the side of the bruin's head, the power of Haskell's own thrust wrenching it from the lawman's hand and throwing it off into the snow.

"Fuck!" He'd shouted the epithet at the tops of his lungs, crouching, setting his feet wide, and throwing his arms out to both sides, trying to look as intimidating as a man could in such circumstances, knowing that the bear was probably laughing at him far behind those stony eyes.

"Run, Haskell, you crazy bastard!" Knute bellowed from his tree. *"Run!"*

To the lawman's surprise, the bear stopped a mere five feet before him, canting its giant

471

head this way and that, its broad black nose, the size of a wagon's wheel hub, expanding and contracting, scenting him. The brown eyes, each one nearly as large as Bear's clenched fist, glinted with atavistic fury.

The bear stood a full four or five feet taller than the human Bear before it, dwarfing Haskell's own six-and-a-half-foot frame. Still, Bear decided he was going to fight the bear . . . or go down fighting, anyway.

Quickly, he slid his hand down beneath the flap of his coat and shucked the Schofield.

"I may not be able to kill you with this, you big son of a bitch, but I can make you itch somethin' awful!"

"Haskell, goddamnit — run, fool!"

Bear raised the big pistol and fired up into the grizzly's face. He'd gotten two shots off and was clicking the hammer back to fire a third when the big, screaming bear lunged forward and swung its right paw, claws fully extended, toward its opponent. Haskell yelped as the big limb, like a club with blades, slammed into his left shoulder, lifting him a good two feet in the air and throwing him seven feet to his right.

He hit the snowy ground and rolled, piling up belly-down against a snow-covered rock. Gritting his teeth against the aching burn in his left arm, he rolled onto his back. He shook his head to clear the cobwebs. As his vision clarified, horror filled his big body like cold mud replacing the marrow in his bones, turning his joints to cement. The bear was on all fours running toward him through the snow — a blur of brown sheathed in the white of displaced powder.

Haskell wanted to move, but his body had turned to stone. And then it was too late. The massive round head was four feet away, teeth as large as Haskell's fingers bared and snapping and ready to puncture and rend. The massive head was so close that the grizzly's warm, fetid breath bathed the lawman's face, making his innards heave.

As Haskell stared up at it, the head jerked slightly, blood lapping from just beneath the beast's left ear.

The bruin froze. Its dull brown eyes seemed to stare into Haskell's. The light was leaving them.

The head jerked again, more blood lapping from below the ear, near the same place as before. At the same time, what sounded like a thunderclap rose to Haskell's right.

The bear tipped its bloody head to one side, opening its mouth and bellowing its shock and confusion, then lifting up off its front paws. There was another thundering boom, and Haskell saw where the bullet punched into the bruin's left side, just behind its shoulder, pluming the fur and staining it red.

The great beast's entire body jerked and then sagged down toward Haskell's left, twisting around as it fell with a heavy thump on its back, throwing up a great spray of pink snow over Haskell's face. One of the beast's heavy paws slammed down on the lawman's chest, making him grunt as the air was punched from his lungs.

Blinking snow from his eyes, the lawman looked down to see the paw resting unmoving on his chest, palm up, its claws flecked with blood. Bear realized as he began to register the raking burn in his upper left arm and shoulder that the blood on the bruin's claws was his own.

Then he also realized there could have been a lot more of it if not for . . . what?

He lifted his head, turning to his left. The bear lay unmoving not four feet away, teeth bared in an eternal grimace toward the sky. Haskell's brains were scrambled. As he tried to return all his marbles to their rightful pockets and figure out what had just transpired, a woman's voice called, "Bear . . . is that you?"

Now he was hearing things. What would a woman be doing out here?

Still, the voice had sounded familiar.

"Bear?" she called.

Haskell turned his head to peer to his right. He'd been so absorbed by his skirmish with the bruin, he hadn't realized the storm had thickened. He could see only a few yards before him, the trees on the other side of the ravine a gray-black blur beyond the fog of falling snow. A shape moved against the blur of the trees — a figure running toward him.

"Bear?"

She dropped to a knee beside him — a slender figure clad in furs, including a coyote fur hat on her head. He recognized the voice before he recognized the face partly concealed by the hat and tendrils of gold-blond hair dancing in the wind and sliding across the smooth, pale cheeks.

"Emily?"

She swept the dancing tendrils away with her bare right hand. "It is you! I thought I recognized your voice. My god — are you all right?"

He blinked, not entirely sure his brains weren't so badly scrambled that he wasn't imaging this whole thing — Emily Carr showing up here by Ole Kemp's cabin and shooting the bear that had been about to feast on Haskell himself. Maybe he was dead, or nearly dead, and his half-dead brain was conjuring this craziness in the frenzy of its last sputtering moments.

She reached forward and sandwiched his face in her hands, leaning forward, concern showing in her pretty, flashing eyes with their long, gold lashes. "Bear?" she cried, as though she thought he was on his way out.

"I'll be damned." He placed his hands on her wrists, squeezing the one in his bare right hand. "It is you."

"It's me!"

"Did" — he glanced at the huge, lumpy carcass lying in the snow to his left — "you shoot the bear?"

"Yes." His expression must have mirrored his befuddlement because she added, "I was packing my father's Sharps .56 in the sleigh." She glanced at the rifle leaning against her left thigh. "I was aware of the rogue grizzly that haunts this area even in the winter sometimes. The crazy thing seldom hibernates, for some reason. I guess some are like that. I was heading to town to fetch you and Marshal Gunderson when I heard the shouting and the grizzly's horrible roaring. Oh, Bear, something awful has happened!"

In his addled state, Haskell vaguely wondered if she was referencing the bear, but then he realized she meant something else entirely — whatever had lured her out here into the storm. He blinked up at her dully, skeptically.

"My father is dead!"

"Huh?"

"My father is dead! Murdered! I was heading to town to fetch you and the marshal. It wasn't yet storming when I left the ranch."

"Oh, Jesus," Haskell said. The young woman's pronouncement had been the bracer he'd needed to shake off the bear attack and to clarify his thoughts. "I need to . . . I need to . . ."

"Ahhh . . . oh, mercy!" The cry had risen behind him, on the heels of a cracking sound. There was a dull thud, another cry, and a groan. "Oh, hell . . . ah, hell . . . oh, someone help me . . . !"

Emily gasped. "Who's that?"

Haskell turned to look past the bear. "Knute?"

"Help!"

"Oh, Christ!"

"Help me, Bear!"

Haskell heaved himself to his feet and moved stiffly through the snow, Emily following, holding her skirts above the tops of her fur boots with one hand, her Sharps in the other hand. Knute lay in the snow at the base of the pine he'd climbed, on top of the branch he'd apparently been clinging to before it had broken off. The old man lay on his right side, atop the arm Haskell had plunked a bullet through. He was writhing, kicking his legs in pain.

"You all right, old-timer?"

"Oh. Lordy. Oh, mercy. It's my arm!"

Haskell dropped to a knee beside him. "Which one?"

"The good one, goddamnit!" He glanced at Emily and added, "Uh . . . sorry about that, miss."

"What's wrong with your arm?" Haskell asked. "Did you break it?"

"Oh, lordy. Oh, mercy . . . I think it's separated. Hurts like a catamount, I'll tell you that!"

"Let me take a look."

"Oh, no — don't move me. It hurts somethin' powerful!"

"I have to move you to take a look, you old devil."

"Ohhh!" the old man cried as Haskell shoved him over onto his back. He kicked his legs in the snow. "It hurts like a catamount!"

Haskell removed his second mitten and gently probed the man's left shoulder with his fingers. He could tell by the odd bulge in the man's coat that the bone had slipped out of its socket, all right.

"Take a deep breath, Knute," Haskell said. "I'm gonna give your arm a quick tug, slip that bone back into the socket."

"Don't touch me — it hurts somethin' aw . . . *ohhhhhh, you bastard . . .* that hurt like a motherfucker . . . !" As Haskell released the man's arm, which he'd given a quick tug and watched in satisfaction as the bone had slid back into place, Larson's eyes rolled back in their sockets and he sagged back in the snow, out like a blown candle.

"I'm gonna have to get this old goat back to his sleigh," Bear said, sitting back on his knees, drawing a deep breath.

"It's gone."

Haskell looked at Emily.

She shook her head. "From the south ridge, I saw the mule bolt when the bear started bellowing. It's probably halfway back to town by now."

"Shit!"

"My own sleigh is on the south ridge, just yonder. I tied my horse. I'll fetch the sleigh, and we'll take old Knute to the Circle C." Emily glanced at the snow coming down

479

harder and faster. "It's getting too thick out here to continue to town. I was about to turn back when I heard the bear."

She placed her hand on Haskell's right shoulder and scowled at his bloody, torn coat sleeve. "You're going to need tending, too, Bear. Those cuts look deep."

Haskell glanced at the arm of topic. "Burns like a . . ." He let his voice trail off in chagrin.

"Like a motherfucker?" Emily gave a wry, crooked, smile. It was quickly replaced with a sad scowl, a dark shadow passing behind her eyes, reminding Haskell of the information she'd imparted.

James Carr was dead. Murdered.

Rising, she patted Haskell's bare head. "You'd best get your hat and mittens on before you freeze. I'll fetch the sleigh."

"I'm sorry about your father," Haskell called after her.

She glanced back and shook her head as if to say, *Later* . . .

When she was gone, Haskell left the old man where he lay in the snow, and stumbled off to retrieve his second mitten, his hat, and his rifle and pistol, all of which he found in the rumpled powder. As he returned to old Knute, knotting his scarf beneath his chin, Emily and the red, leather-

480

seated sleigh appeared, moving around the cabin from the far side, where apparently the trail dropped into the ravine. A big, shaggy black gelding kicked the snow high around its withers and shook its head, breath frosting in the steadily darkening air.

Haskell crouched over Knute. "You still with us, old-timer?"

Larson muttered several oaths and fluttered his eyelids, but did not regain full consciousness.

Haskell sighed as he snaked his arms beneath the old man's skinny body. Then he lifted Knute up off the ground and carried him over to the sleigh, where Emily was spreading several blankets over the back, leather-upholstered seat. When Haskell had laid out the old man on the seat, he and Emily climbed onto the front seat. She took up the reins, then turned the gelding around to retrace her runner tracks back past the cabin, along a break in the woods.

She turned south onto the snow-covered trail, the sleigh's runners fairly singing through the fresh powder, the horse's bells jingling festively, its hooves clomping dully.

Ahead the trail climbed steeply through a massive drift showing the tracks of Emily's descent. Bear wasn't sure the gelding would make it, but Emily whipped it up smartly, but without cruelty, with an even hand. After a few back-and-forth slips and some uncertain rocking, horse and sleigh slipped up and over the drift hanging down the crest of the ridge and up onto the tableland.

Haskell was impressed by the girl's driving. But, then, she'd grown up out here. She'd probably been handling sleighs and all manner of wheeled wagons and pulling stock since she was six years old. She was adept at many things, and he couldn't help half-remembering their previous night together. A night worthy of remembering, thanks to good ole, dearly departed Joe . . .

Bear looked at her, the snow swirling between them.

"What happened?" he asked her.

She glanced at him. "He and Melvin were having a drink in the parlor. Afterwards, just as we were about to sit down to lunch, my father started feeling poorly. He seemed nervous, began pacing. Then he ran out the back door and started vomiting."

She gave a shudder as she handled the reins. The horse was trotting smartly through a stretch of trail that the wind had cleared.

Staring straight ahead, she said, "His condition worsened, so we took him upstairs. Upstairs, he got worse. He stumbled around as though mad. He was foaming at the mouth! We had to hold him down or he would have hurt himself, maybe hurled himself out a window. We tied him to the bed with sheets. An hour passed — oh, god, the writhing and screaming!"

She was sobbing now, tears streaming down her cheeks. She took the reins in one mittened hand, closed the other hand over her mouth, and sobbed into it briefly before lowering the mitten, sniffing, and composing herself.

She turned to Bear, her eyes stricken, her face ashen, but the sobs quelled. "He died as I was dressing to fetch the doctor. We have three hired men on through the winter, but they were drunk . . . celebrating Christmas early, it would seem. Our Chinese housekeeper, Kwan, is too frail for this weather. Melvin didn't know the way to Sioux Camp, and, with the storm settling, I knew he'd get lost even with written directions."

She'd said this last with no little tone of accusing disgust.

"After Father died, I decided to fetch you and Gunderson."

"Gunderson's dead."

"Oh, Jesus!"

"It's not what you think," Bear said.

"There was a jailbreak." He let it go at that, seeing no need to explain the Thorson fiasco.

Emily gave the lawman a direct look. "Father was murdered, Bear. Poisoned. I know what strychnine poisoning looks like. My aunt took it when I was only six years old, when she discovered that my uncle was visiting a Chinese parlor house in Bismarck. I was staying with her at the time."

"Jesus."

"Who killed my father?"

"I was about to ask you if you had any ideas."

"They must have poisoned his brandy, because it was after he'd drunk the brandy that he fell ill."

"Melvin didn't have the brandy, I take it?"

"Melvin was drinking his own Scotch. Father preferred Spanish brandy."

"Whoever poisoned your father knew his preference." Haskell thought about that and then turned to Emily again. "The banker died the same way, earlier today."

Emily jerked her head toward him in shock. "Poisoned?"

Haskell fished an Indian Kid out of his shirt pocket. "Strychnine. Wannamaker had seen it before, too." He hunkered low against the wind as he struck a match on the dashboard of the sleigh, and touched the flame to the cheroot. He tossed the match into the snowy wind, drew a long draught of the smoke into his lungs, and blew it out. "Tell me, Emily, did your father know Ole Kemp?"

Emily turned the sleigh off the main trail. Now they were heading through hilly country studded with burr oaks and pockets of brush poking up out of the snow. "Just as everyone knows Kemp — as a lout and a drunk. Is Kemp dead, too?"

"Yeah, but again it's not what you think. The bear got him." Haskell winced and adjusted the position of his injured arm, remembering the fierceness of the bruin's attack. "I'm guessing he's been dead for several days."

"But you thought it might have been him who poisoned Father and the banker?"

"That's why we paid him a visit."

"Now what do you think?"

"How often does your father drink his brandy?"

"Every day. He pours some into his coffee around lunchtime and then indulges in a snifter or two before bed."

"Then it wasn't Kemp. Whoever slipped the poison into the brandy must have done so in the past twenty-four hours. A day ago,

Kemp was lying dead in the brush back there." Haskell sat back in the sleigh as they climbed through the hills. He could see through the haze of falling snow a ranch headquarters taking shape ahead of them, on the facing side of a jog of high buttes. He saw the house, barn, corrals, and several outbuildings as well as a windmill — gray rubble against the snow.

A man lay dead there. The killer had been here.

Who?

Why?

The cold wind wrapped around Haskell. It chewed through the tears in his coat, enflaming those the bruin had inflicted on his arm. He tossed away the Indian Kid and shivered.

Thanks a bunch, Henry.

CHAPTER 15

The Carr ranch house was not unlike most Haskell had seen in the remotest regions of the wild western frontier, being first and foremost solid and functional, a bastion against time and the weather.

The Carrs' place, also like many of its ilk, appeared to be comprised of a series of add-ons from the original crude cabin. Part of its lower story was constructed of weathered gray logs propped on stone pylons and fronted by a broad, timbered front gallery, also propped on stones. The rest of the house was wood frame overlaid with clapboards that were about due for a fresh coat of paint. It was two stories with a shake roof and sashed windows, many concealed by closed shutters likely meant to keep out the cold. Haskell doubted they worked. With the wind blowing the heavy, dry snow against the house — up here on the exposed northern side of this butte — and howling beneath its eaves, it looked like a cold damned place indeed.

As Emily drew the sleigh to a halt before the lodge, the front door opened and a dark-haired little man came shuffling out, wincing against the snow and wind and shrugging into a quilted elk-skin coat. He wore elk-skin moccasins, and at first Haskell thought he was Indian, but then he saw the long, slanted dark eyes and the mustache hanging down over both corners of his thin-lipped mouth.

"Emoo-ee!" the Chinaman yelled above the wind as he walked quickly down the porch steps to grab the black's hackamore. "Why you back so soon? The storm turn you 'round?" His puzzled gaze raked Haskell and Knute, who was sitting up on the back seat now, holding the blankets over his head and around his shoulders. He also held his near-empty bottle in his right hand. His rheumy, pale-blue eyes were loose in their sockets. Pie-eyed.

"The storm and a bear," Emily said, dropping the reins and turning to Haskell. "A couple of them, in fact."

Haskell gave a sardonic snort as he leaped from the sleigh and turned to where Knute sat in the back. "You still kicking, old man?"

Larson turned to him, smiling drunkenly,

and held up the bottle. There was maybe one drink left, sloshing around on the bottom.

"Feeling no pain, I see." Bear held out his hand. "Come on — let's get you inside."

Knute heaved himself up out of his seat, wincing as pain in one or both of his injured arms lashed him. He staggered toward Haskell, then fell out of the sleigh and into the lawman's arms. He gave a deep, ragged, drunken sigh, and dropped his bottle in the snow.

"Follow me." Emily grabbed both her own Sharps .56 and Haskell's Henry repeater from the sleigh before brushing past Haskell and heading for the house as the Chinaman led the horse and sleigh around the house toward the barns and stable behind it.

Hefting old Knute in his arms, wincing at his own bear-inflicted misery, the lawman followed Emily up the porch steps, then across the porch and through the heavy, timbered front door, which she shouldered open. An open stairway rose before her, appearing to split the house right down the middle. She leaned the rifles against the wall beside the door, then removed her fur hat and shook out her thick, blond hair. She stood just beyond the threshold, staring into a room opening to the left of the stairs.

It was a big, airy kitchen, Haskell saw, with several windows and a solid oak, circular eating table at which four men were playing poker. A whiskey bottle and several shot glasses stood on the table among the coins, greenbacks, and playing cards. Cigars or brown paper quirleys smoldered from two ashtrays.

All eyes had turned toward Emily, acquiring a definite sheepish cast. The young woman's beau, Melvin Mueller, was among the men — his white silk sleeves rolled up his pale arms, a green visor angled down over his forehead, and a stogie burning in one corner of his little mouth.

"Emily!" he said, pulling the cigar from his teeth. "What . . . what, uh . . . ?" He slid his chair back clumsily, then heaved himself just as clumsily, obviously drunk, to his feet. "What're you . . . what're you doing back so . . . so . . . ?"

The young woman's tone was crisp, incredulous. "What are these men doing in here?" She canted her head to indicate Melvin's three poker opponents — rough-hewn waddies in need of shaves. One wore a pair of wooly chaps over his wash-worn denims. They were all gaining their feet now, as uncertainly as Melvin, in deference to the lady's unexpected and obviously disappointing reappearance.

Melvin glanced from Bear to the old man in his arms, then returned his gaze to his betrothed and said, "What's he doin' here?" He pointed his cigar at Bear.

"I'll ask the questions, Melvin."

Young Mueller frowned, indignant but also somewhat cowed, and hiked a shoulder as he glanced at his cohorts. "I called 'em up from the bunkhouse. You know . . . for a friendly game of poker . . ."

Emily's tone was biting, and Haskell could see from behind her left shoulder that her cheeks were flushed with anger. "While my father lies dead upstairs . . . still *warm*? You're throwing a *poker party*?"

The drover in the wooly chaps stubbed his quirley out in an ashtray. He smiled tensely with one side of his mouth and said, "Uh . . . we was just leavin', Miss Emily."

"Yeah, I reckon we'll be headin' back to the bunkhouse now," said the man sitting nearest Melvin, sliding coins from the table into his cupped palm. He chuckled, then covered the laugh with a loud clearing of his throat.

Emily turned to Haskell and, with a glance at Knute, said, "Go ahead and make him comfortable upstairs. I'll be along to take a look at his arm. First room on the right."

"First room on the right?" Melvin said, scowling at her while his poker-playing buddies stuffed money into their pockets and shrugged into the cold-weather gear hanging off the backs of their chairs. "That's my room!"

"Not anymore, it's not," Emily said as Haskell, clomping heavily up the stairs, basked in the heat emanating from the comfortably appointed, rustic parlor area to the right of the stairs in which a fire danced invitingly in a large hearth.

Haskell went into the first room at the top of the stairs and on the hall's right side, and laid old Knute on the canopied bed. The room was small, but it had a fireplace in which coals glowed warmly. While the old man groaned fitfully on the bed, passed out from all the busthead he'd consumed to kill his pain, the lawman plucked a couple of split logs from a tin washtub that served as a wood box, and laid them on the grate.

When he'd blown on the coals until flames danced up around the freshly added fuel, he went out, closed the door, and started back down the stairs. He stopped a third of the way down as two of Melvin's poker buddies slipped quickly out the front door, which Emily was holding open for them, the same peevish look as before flushing her pretty face. The third one, the man in the wooly chaps who now wore a dirty, torn canvas coat, held his hat in his hands as he turned to the young woman and said, "Sure, uh . . . sure am sorry to hear about your pa, Miss Emily. My, uh . . . my condolences."

"Thank you, Lon, I appreciate that," Emily said, bowing her head with sincerity.

One of the men behind Lon gave Lon's back a playful punch, and Lon loosed an involuntary howl of garbled laughter. Red-faced and snickering, Lon wheeled and strode quickly after the other two, who were also laughing. Emily stared after them, her shoulders tense with anger. Her chest rose and fell heavily.

She turned to Melvin, still standing by the table and looking indignant. "You, too," she said in a low, hard voice.

"Wait. *What?*"

Emily tossed her head toward the stairs. "Fetch your gear. I want you in the bunk-house with the rest of the drunkards. I never understood why Father kept them on over the winter. They were useless. Now I see they're also vermin. As you are, too, Melvin. Obviously, my father was a poor judge of character."

"Now, you just wait. I — !"

"Gather your gear and head for the bunkhouse, Melvin! As soon as the weather breaks, I want all four of you off the Circle C. You can tell the others to report to me for their time. As for you, Melvin — go back to Montana where you came from. If you step one foot on Circle C land again, I will blow you out of your boots!"

Melvin glanced up at Bear standing a third of the way down the stairs, one hand on the rail. The young man's pale cheeks flushed a deeper red — the crimson of humiliation — as he stepped angrily forward, and said, "If you think I'm gonna leave you alone in here with that big — now, hold on!"

Emily had grabbed her Sharps from where she'd leaned it against the wall by the door. Raising the stout rifle in her hands, she clicked the heavy hammer back to full cock. She raised the rifle and snugged her cheek up against the stock, aiming at her former beau's head.

"Emily!" Melvin cowered back against the kitchen wall, shielding his face with his hands, the cigar protruding from his pudgy right thumb and index finger.

"Are you going to follow orders, Melvin?" the young woman asked coolly.

"Yes!"

"All right, then." Emily lowered the

Sharps and jerked her head at the stairs. "You have three minutes. If you're still here by the end of that time, I'm going to start shooting. I killed a bear not an hour ago. You'll be short work."

She glanced up at Haskell, a conspiratorial smile tugging at one corner of her mouth.

"Goddamn crazy woman!" Melvin raked out as he strode past Emily, who'd kept the Sharps in her hands, barrel half-lowered toward the floor. He stomped up the steps and stopped beside Haskell, glaring up at him, eyes bright with rage behind slitted lids. He let his gaze flick toward the lawman's crotch. "You must be hung like a fucking horse!"

Emily gave a shrill laugh. "Oh, he is, Melvin! He is!"

Melvin glowered down at her, grinding his back teeth, then continued on up the stairs, stumbling near the top and nearly dropping to his knees before righting himself. As he disappeared into the room in which old Knute slumbered, Haskell moved on down the stairs, feeling more than a little awkward and out of place.

Emily appeared quite comfortable with the situation, however. Chuckling devilishly at him, she stopped him with one hand splayed across the front of his coat, and glanced at his bloody arm.

She sucked a sharp breath through her teeth, then started unbuttoning his coat. "Let's get you out of this and see how much damage that bruin did to you, shall we?"

When they got his coat off, Haskell walked to the table and sat in a chair, instinctively putting his back to a corner. Emily stoked the big range against the far wall, then filled an iron pot with water from the well pump. When she'd set the kettle on the range to boil, she pulled a bottle out of a cupboard, brought it over, and set it and two glasses on the table.

"Fresh bottle," she said, wincing as she pried the cork free of the lip. "Never been opened. No danger of strychnine poisoning."

She filled both glasses, then slid one in front of Haskell, her dubious gaze finding his and holding it. Meanwhile, the stomping noises in the second floor stopped, and Melvin started down the stairs, carrying two leather accordion bags, a portmanteau hanging from a lanyard around his neck. He stopped about where Bear had stopped on the steps during the dustup earlier, and cast his indignant gaze toward Haskell and his former betrothed.

"Oh, it's all right if *you* drink with your father still lying warm in his deathbed. If I do it, I get sent to the bunkhouse!"

Emily held up her glass to him. "Salute, Melvin. Have a good life!" She threw back half the glass of brandy and smacked her lips.

Melvin bellowed in frustration, shaking his head, then continued down the stairs, bouncing his luggage off the rails to each side. Emily went over and pulled a thick fur coat off a hook by the door, and tossed it over the bag hanging from the young man's right arm. "Wouldn't want you to freeze to death," she said with an angry smirk.

Melvin cursed again as he stumbled through the door Emily held open for him.

"Good riddance!" She slammed the door behind him, then turned to Bear, smiling victoriously. Her cheeks were beautifully flushed.

Haskell held up his own glass in salute to the girl, and took a drink.

She chuckled, set her glass on the table, splashed more brandy into it, then strode back to the range. When she'd gathered the supplies she needed and had filled a porcelain bowl with hot, steaming water, she dragged a chair over to Haskell's side of the table and went to work on his arm. It bore three stripe-like gashes just above the bicep, spaced a half-inch or so apart. There was one more on his shoulder. He thought they were about a half-inch deep.

As Emily cleaned the cuts, leaning close to him, lowering her head to examine the wounds in the gray winter light pushing through the windows, Haskell took another sip of the brandy and said, "You sure you weren't being a little hasty?"

She shook her head as she continued to clean his arm. "No."

"Your father just passed, Em. I know what that does to a person. You likely don't really know it happened. Not yet. Not deep inside yourself. Later, when you do know it, have felt the full brunt of it, you might think —"

She looked up at him abruptly and placed two fingers over his lips. "I know he's dead. While it makes me sad, I also know he sold me to that man out there. To Melvin and Melvin's father. Until today, after my father died so violently, I don't think I ever realized how much I hated him for that. Because, you see, while I was horrified by what I saw up there . . . by how horribly he died in that room, wailing and bouncing off the walls . . . the torture he went through . . . I also felt gratified. Almost as gratified as I felt just now, sending Melvin Mueller out in the snow, to that stinky bunkhouse housing my father's useless, drunken hired hands."

She continued to hold Haskell's gaze. Then she nodded slowly, pressing her lips into a tight, white line. "I'll make do," she said softly. "I'll make do right here. I'll run this ranch better than my father ever ran it. I'll hire new men. Good men. Maybe I'll even marry the best of them. And I'll make do, Bear. Because that's how I am."

Her eyes glazed slightly. A tear collected in the inside corner of the right one and made its way slowly down her cheek, along the fine, pale line of her resolute nose. Haskell lifted his hand and brushed the tear away with his thumb.

"Okay," he said. "Okay, Miss Em."

She grabbed his hand in hers, kissed it, sobbing, then released it, took another drink, and resumed her work.

CHAPTER 16

Haskell groaned deep in his throat as, trying to hold at bay his nearly exploding desire, he slid back from the silky folds of warm, wet skin between Emily's spread legs.

Propped on his outstretched arms and the tips of his toes, he slid up the girl's long, alabaster body and rested his thundering shaft against her heaving belly.

Her head was turned to one side on her feather pillow, honey-blond hair fanned out across her cheek as she dug her teeth into the knuckles of her clenched right hand. Now she turned to stare up at Bear, eyes showing brightly between the mussed locks of her hair. She clamped her heels more tightly against his butt.

"Oh, you devil!" she cried throatily, chuckling, urging him back inside her. "What did you do that for?"

Haskell squeezed his eyes closed. "One hundred," he said through gritted teeth.

"Ninety-nine. Ninety-eight, ninety-seven . . ."

Emily gave a gleeful little shriek that resounded around her small but tidy and femininely appointed upstairs bedroom — right across the room from where her father lay dead on his own bed, in fact. That grisly detail didn't seem to bother her much. An hour ago, she'd sent her housekeeper, Kwan, back to his little shanty in the woods flanking the house, after she and the Chinaman had tended Knute Larson's dislocated arm and changed the bandage on the wounded one before leaving him with food and another bottle with which to drink himself back into oblivion in Melvin Mueller's old room.

Kwan had left, bowing, glancing at Haskell skeptically and muttering his dismay at leaving the girl and the big stranger alone together in the house in which her father had only a few hours ago met his grisly end. Emily had taken Haskell's hand with almost little-girl shyness, and led him up to her room.

Neither one had said anything. They'd simply undressed in the dim, gray light from the room's two windows, then crawled into the young woman's bed with its embroidered quilts, feather pillows, feather mattress, and its two windows looking out over the backyard toward the stables, barns, and corrals . . . toward the bunkhouse in which her jilted beau was likely stewing over a game of poker with his unwashed cohorts.

Haskell and Emily had entered into a long session of kissing and caressing and nuzzling and stroking before she lay back, brushing her fingers across the swollen head of his extremely sensitive manhood, and smiled up at him. She'd rested her head back against her hooked arm and spread her long, slender legs, the rose at her core blossoming with invitation.

Her father was dead. It was a cold, hard fact. As cold and as hard as it was, however, the fact had also given the independent young woman her much yearned-for freedom. She and Haskell were alive, and they'd been attracted to each other from the start. Why should her dead father, who no longer had a care in the world, come between them on such a cold and stormy night?

"Put it back," she whispered, smiling, eyes blazing up at him. "Put it back inside me, Bear. Finish me, Bear."

Haskell shook his head, keeping his eyes closed. "Eighty-nine, eighty-eight, eighty-seven . . ."

"Oh, you!" Grunting, she pushed up

against him, placing the heels of her hands on his chest.

Haskell laughed and let her roll him onto his back. She straddled him, chuckling, and grabbed his rod angling back over the flatness of his belly. She scuttled down his thighs, lowered her head toward his belly, and, smiling nastily up at him, ran her little pink tongue around on the swollen purple head.

"Oh, you're bad," Haskell groaned. "Oh, you're . . . gonna . . . *kill me!*"

She giggled as she lifted her head, scuttled back up to his belly, and rose to her knees. She pressed her tongue to her lower lip as she positioned herself over him. Haskell sighed when he felt her warm wetness enshroud the head of his cock.

"Ohhh," he said through a long breath.

She kept just the head of his shaft inside her as she leaned forward and placed her hands on each side of his face, caressing his cheeks with her thumbs. She locked her gaze on his, smiling tenderly. Her face was a maze of shadows cast by the two lamps, each on a table to the right and left of the bed, as the light filtered through her long hair. Inside those shadows, the gold flecks in her eyes glistened.

Her lips were parted. Haskell reached up

and traced their fullness with the index finger of his right hand.

"Oh, Bear," she whispered, grabbing his finger with her mouth and sucking it.

"Oh, darlin'," he said. He narrowed his eyes as he felt her sliding slowly down his shaft. Slowly, slowly . . . slowly. She reached bottom and then ground against him, her cunt clutching at him, squeezing him greedily, ravenously.

Keeping her head just above his chest, she lifted her beautiful, heart-shaped butt, sliding her love nest back up to his swollen head, and then lowered it again quickly. She lifted it just as quickly, lowered it again, and repeated the maneuver, with each rise and fall picking up speed until she was hammering against him, laughing, breasts jostling, hair bouncing on her shoulders.

Haskell's blood rose to the boiling point. He lifted his hands to her breasts, cupping them, squeezing as he bucked against her and, with a bruin-like roar vaulting from his wide-open jaws, his jism spewed inside her. He'd thought she might pull off of him at the last second, but she didn't. She rode him all the way home, screaming.

When they'd finished spasming together, groaning and gasping, the bed shuddering beneath them, she lowered her head to his chest and curled up taut against him. They didn't say anything. They just lay there together, relaxing in postcoital splendor.

He could hear the wind blowing outside, the snow gusting against the walls, rattling the windows in their frames. A fire warmed the room from an iron stove in a corner, ticking and sighing, giving a soft thump when wood dropped through the grate.

"You could stay, you know," Emily said quietly, twisting a lock of his cinnamon chest hair around her index finger.

"What's that?"

"You could stay here with me."

He glanced down at her. "You mean, like . . . forever . . . ?"

"Sure, why not? You could be my man. I could be your woman. Together, we could run this ranch better than my father ever did. You could sow your magnificent seed" — she brushed her fingertips across his slack scrotum, tickling him — "right here inside me, and in a few years we'd have a whole passel of bear cubs running around, setting the county on fire, no doubt!"

She laughed.

"Whoa!" Haskell said, laughing incredulously, placing his hands on her shoulders. "I've heard of women moving fast on a fella, but you take the prize, Miss Em!" He laughed again, uncertainly, not sure whether she was being serious or just playing with him. Staring into her dubious eyes, he wasn't sure she knew herself.

She rolled off of him and onto her back beside him. She glanced up and saw his big Schofield hanging from the front bedpost. She reached up, unsnapped the keeper thong from over the hammer, and slid the piece from its holster.

"My, what a nice big gun you have here, Marshal Haskell." She stared at the gun in her hands, smiling admiringly, running her hands across it lovingly, the way she'd caressed his male organ during the time of their foreplay.

"Emily . . ." He reached for the gun, but she pulled it away.

"I'm just playing with it." She looked it over carefully, slowly spinning the cylinder and lifting the gun to her ear, listening to the quiet, definite clicks. "A man must feel almighty powerful, carrying such a weapon around."

"No more powerful than you earlier in the day," Haskell said, feeling a sudden, strange tightness in his throat. "When you brought that grizzly down with your .56."

She hiked a shoulder. "That was an easy shot."

"A big weapon."

"Father taught me to shoot it. He'd used it on buffalo." Emily slowly clicked the Schofield's hammer back, listening intently to each taut click. Her mouth shaped a slow, speculative smile as she slid her shoulders slightly away from Bear and swung the pistol toward him. She stared down the barrel, squinting one eye, and shaped her lips beautifully but with chilling menace as she said, "Pow!"

"Now, you know that's no way to treat a weapon," Haskell said, closing his hand over the pistol, sliding the barrel away from him, and firmly pulling the gun from her hand. "Or the man you just tussled with."

Her eyes grew suddenly hard, and she narrowed them slightly as she said, "You men make all the rules. You have all the authority, all the power."

Haskell depressed the Schofield's hammer and frowned at her, puzzled, apprehensive. "What's that supposed to mean?"

Emily rested her head back on the pillow and stared at the underside of the bed's canopy. There was a cold bitterness in her voice as she said, "It means you can make life what you want it to be. At least, more than we women can. We have to make do with what we've been given. With what men allow us to have."

"I'm still not sure I —"

"Only a few short hours ago, I was destined to marry that rube out there in the bunkhouse. That was my father's decision. He was buying a continued business relationship with Melvin's father, using me as the currency. My father's death has freed me of that obligation, although life will now be harder than it would have been if I'd decided to honor my father's will. Harder in some ways, easier in others.

"Still, I'll never really be free. No more than any woman in my situation. A man could leave here if he wanted to. For me, the Circle C is my only anchor." She turned to Haskell, who stared at her from the pillow beside hers, the Schofield resting on his thigh. "If I wanted to leave . . . and maybe I just do . . . where would I go? What would I do? About my only option would be to work as a whore, in the service of men."

She'd stated this last with pent-up rage, glancing away from him toward the stove in the room's far corner.

She didn't say anything for a time. Raw fury was a cloud engulfing her.

Then, suddenly, she laughed. "Emily, how you do go on!" she remonstrated herself, throwing the covers back and rising.

She walked across the room to the stove, picked up a split log from the box beside it, and squatted to open the door. "If you're not careful," she continued to chastise herself, "the marshal is going to start believing you killed your own father."

She chunked another length of wood into the stove, then closed the door, rose, and strode slowly, wonderfully naked, back to Haskell's side of the bed and sank down on the edge. He turned toward her, resting his head on the heel of his hand.

"Did you?" He had, indeed, begun to wonder. He knew now that Emily Carr was far more complicated than he'd at first thought.

"No."

She wrapped her arms around his neck and folded her long-legged, supple body into the bed beside him, snuggling up taut against him once more. The warm, soft globes of her breasts caressed his belly, the tender nipples softly raking him.

"I loved my father, Bear. I know it doesn't sound like it, but I did. It wasn't easy, though. He was a hard man. A hellion from Texas. My mother settled him. But she died so early, during a second pregnancy, when I was only five. Her death and all that she took with her — the promise of a larger family — broke him. I will miss him, but I won't miss being excused from the life he'd planned for me. The *prison* he'd intended for me."

Haskell ran his fingers through her hair, then slid his hand down the long, curving, delicate line of her spine. He believed her. Emily Carr may have been many things, but she was not a killer. She was a beautiful, lonely young woman destined to live out her life in the remote Dakota Territory. She was young and vital, but with few choices or prospects for a man to enrich her life, and to love, and she felt the years rushing toward her. That would give anyone a case of the fantods.

Haskell placed his hands on her shoulders, staring deep into her eyes. They were warm and soft now, and cast with a faint chagrin, which made her look away from him in shame. He pressed his lips to her forehead.

"I'm sorry," he said, holding her tight.

She wrapped her arms around him, squeezing him just as tight. "What is it about you that made me spill my guts like that?"

"Maybe I'm just the only one here."

He felt her lips press against his chest with deep affection. "I think it's more than that."

He drew her head up to his again, and

gazed into her eyes. "I have to find out who killed him, Em. I have to find the killer of all of them."

"Do you think the killer is the same one who killed the others?"

"If it's not you, Kwan, Melvin, or one of the hired hands, I'd have to assume so." Haskell paused, pondering. "Did you and your father lock the outside doors at night?"

She shook her head. "Never. We're so isolated out here, we never thought it was necessary."

Haskell considered that bit of information, too. Anyone could have walked into the house at any time, probably through a back door, and poured poison into Carr's brandy decanter. "Who all knew about your father's penchant for brandy?"

Emily shrugged a shoulder. "Who didn't? He frequented the saloons — and I'm sure the brothels," she added with a sigh — "in both Oxbow and Sioux Camp. Probably anyone who ever drank with him . . . or shared his bed . . . knew his favorite drink was brandy."

"That doesn't narrow the field much. Do you know of anyone who'd want to see your father dead?"

Emily shook her head. "No one offhand. Of course, he's had to fire men. He should have fired the three out there now! But he hasn't fired anyone in a couple of years — aside from laying men off for the winter, of course."

"I doubt it was anyone who'd worked for him. If it's the same killer who killed Dawson and the other men from town — and it *must* be — it's someone who has a bone to pick with the men of business in these parts. Men with power," he added, considering Carr and the postmaster. "There must be something your father has in common with those other dead men."

"If there is, I don't know what it was."

"Did he have business connections with Dawson and the others?"

"None that I know of. Of course, he bought feed and supplies in town, and I've always shopped at the mercantile in Sioux Camp because it has a larger selection than Butterman's in Oxbow. We have accounts at all those places, but that's the only business connection we've ever had with Sioux Camp. Aside from my father's drinking and whoring, I mean." She gave a caustic grunt.

Emily stared across the room in silence for a time. Then she turned to Haskell again. "I hope you find out who killed my father, Bear. And those other men. Whatever kind of father James Carr was, he was a

512

good man deep down. He didn't deserve to die the way he did. Neither did Dawson or the others. They were all good men."

"How do you know?" It was a serious question. Haskell really wanted to know how well she'd known the dead men, and how good they'd really been.

Emily shook her head, then shrugged. "I guess I don't really. I didn't know any of them very well at all." Her mouth shaped a grim smile. "Not even my own —"

"Shh." Haskell pressed two fingers to her lips, then turned to the door, frowning.

"What is it?" she whispered.

"I thought I heard something." He stared at the door, listening. Then it came again — a soft thumping sound. As though someone were moving around downstairs, furtively.

Having heard the sound, too, Emily turned to Haskell and opened her mouth slightly but did not speak. Her eyes owned a fearful cast in the shifting light of the two lanterns.

Haskell pressed his lips to her cheek, then slid to the other side of the bed and threw the covers back. "Stay here."

Quickly, he slipped into his winter-weight balbriggans and socks. He grabbed the Schofield off the bed and walked to the door. Slowly, he squeezed the doorknob

513

until the latching bolt clicked. He winced against the groaning of the hinges as he drew open the door and poked his head into the hall.

The hall was dark between closed doors. The only sounds now were the wind, occasional stiff gusts making the walls groan nearly as loudly as the hinges just had. Bear stepped into the hall and walked slowly toward the landing, moving almost silently on his socked feet. He held the Schofield straight out before him as the well of the stairs grew ahead of him, lit somewhat by the soft light pushing through the downstairs windows.

He walked past Knute's room and stopped at the top of the stairs. No snores issued from the oldster's room.

Staring down the stairs toward the first story, he said quietly but loudly enough to be heard by anyone near, "Knute, is that you down there?"

The only response was the wind.

Haskell swallowed and tightened his grip on the Schofield's handle as he started down the stairs. He'd taken three steps when a door latch clicked behind him. He turned quickly, bringing the Schofield around, pressing his thumb against the hammer, ready to cock the gun.

He stared at Knute's door. That's where the click had come from.

He walked back up the steps and padded over to the old man's door. He tipped an ear to the top panel, listening. Silence. He tapped the pistol's barrel against the door and said, "Knute?"

Again, only silence.

After a few seconds, a long, raspy snore rose from inside the room. It was followed by another . . . and another.

Haskell stood staring at the door in the darkness for nearly a minute, pondering. Finally, hearing no more sounds coming from the first story, he headed back into Emily's room. She sat on the edge of the bed, holding a quilt around her shoulders. Her long, pale legs were tightly crossed and hooked around each other, her feet set one atop the other on the floor. She looked at Haskell expectantly.

"Knute must've gone downstairs for something. He's back in bed. All's quiet."

"That's a relief. For a few minutes there, I was starting to wonder if we didn't have a killer in the house."

"Yeah," Haskell said, sliding the Schofield back into its holster. "Me, too." He gave a soft chuckle, but it sounded wooden even to his own ears. He was thinking about old

Knute. The graybeard had been mighty quick to point out Ole Kemp as the possible killer. But, then, Knute had free run of the county, as well, and as easy access to strychnine as anyone else.

Did he harbor any grudges against the dead men, including James Carr?

Emily leaned toward the lawman, wrapped her arms around him, and placed her cheek against his crotch. "Come back to bed, Bear," she beseeched, kissing him through the longhandle fly. "It's a long, cold winter's night."

CHAPTER 17

The next morning around dawn and by the light of several lamps bracketed to the kitchen walls, Kwan set a steaming mug of coffee on the table before Haskell.

The Chinaman looked down at the lawman and showed his pointed, white teeth like a snarling cur. Kwan wore a long red stocking cap, and his face was menacingly dark in contrast, the exposed white teeth menacing in contrast to the swarthiness of the heart-shaped face. A large, black mole poked up from the nub of Kwan's right cheek.

He wrinkled his brown nostrils, narrowed his eyes, and growled, "Ver bad." He shook his head and glanced at the ceiling above his head, referencing, Haskell assumed, the rutting that had occurred last night in Emily's room. "Verr, verr bad. Diss-speckfull to ra dead." He shook his head again. "Verr bad!"

"Ah, get the hump out of your neck. I doubt Carr heard a thing." Haskell frowned up at the old Chinaman, remembering the sound of movement he'd heard last night down here in the first story. "Did you come back to the house last night, Kwan? After ten o'clock, say?"

"Too cold for Kwan," the old man said, shuffling back to his range abutting the kitchen's rear wall, the heels of his elk-skin moccasins sliding along the floor's worn puncheons. "I say a pwayer for ra dead, an' sleep." He turned back to Haskell, placing a hand flat against his cheek and canting his head to that side, indicating slumber. "You upstays with Emoo-ee. Kwan know!"

"How do you know?"

"Her light on long time! I see you in window! Verr bad!"

"Oh," Haskell said with chagrin. Emily's window faced the rear of the house, looking out toward the barns and other outbuildings, including the old Chinaman's shack. Kwan must have been keeping an eye on the place, the voyeuristic old devil. Haskell gave a wry chuckle, then blew on his coffee and sipped.

"Damn good mud, Kwan," he said, setting the cup down on the table. "Just what a feller needs on such a cold winter morning. Much obliged."

"Verr bad!" was the old Chinaman's only response as he began breaking eggs into the same skillet in which bacon was frying.

"That's how I was born," Haskell said with a sigh, digging his makings sack out of his shirt pocket and tossing it onto the table. As he built a smoke leisurely at this languid, pre-sunrise hour, the storm had blown itself out, but an even more penetrating cold had settled over the newly snowed-over land beyond the kitchen's frosted windows.

He'd risen only a few minutes ago. While Emily slept, curled in a tight ball beneath the covers, Haskell had quietly splashed frigid water on his face and used same to swab his privates, shrinking them considerably. He dressed and slipped down the hall, noting the snores resounding behind old Knute's room.

Now, while the bacon and eggs sputtered in Kwan's cast-iron skillet and the old Chinaman whipped up a bowl of flapjack batter, grunting with the effort, Haskell touched a match to his quirley and inhaled, savoring that first drag off his first smoke of the day. Loud, raking coughs sounded, and Bear turned to see old Knute coming slowly, stiffly down the stairs, coughing into his upper left arm. Both arms were suspended in flannel slings, the right one thickly bandaged beneath his bloodstained, bullet-torn shirt.

"Mornin', old-timer," Haskell called.

Knute coughed again, even louder, as though he were coughing up one lung and half the other. Gaining the bottom of the stairs, he walked over, kicked out a chair across from Haskell, and sagged into it, his bones creaking along with the chair so that it was hard to distinguish between the two.

"I wish you'd quit remindin' me how old I am," Knute croaked out of a phlegmy throat. He winced and turned toward his injured right shoulder, then, as though that movement caused the dislocated left arm to flare, he turned to that limb in kind. "It ain't as if this old body don't remind me every time I take a step, a breath, or dribble down the privy!"

"How you feelin'?"

Larson scowled over at Haskell, as though the lawman had just asked him the most ridiculous question he'd ever heard. "I hurt like hell, an' my whiskey's gone."

"Oh, that's what you must have been rummaging around for last night."

Knute looked at him, pockets as large as purple plums sagging beneath his eyes, the rims of which looked like raw beef. "What?"

"I heard you rummaging around down

here last night. Around ten or maybe later."

"You're hearin' things," old Knute groused as Kwan set a smoking mug before him. Gingerly using his left hand despite the sling, he pulled the stone creamer and sugar bowl toward him and began shoveling heaping spoonfuls of sugar into the coffee. The old man glanced once, quickly — furtively? — up at Haskell, then gazed down into his coffee as he continued shoveling sweetener into it.

"You sure that wasn't you?" Haskell prodded him, keeping his tone casual, nonthreatening, then lifting his own mug to his mouth.

"Hell, no. Leastways, I don't . . . ." Knute held the creamer over his coffee, and froze, staring off thoughtfully. "Unless I was sleepwalkin' again. I tend to do that. I once woke up and found myself half a mile from my cabin. It was cold out, too. Not cold like this, but it was damn cold, an' I nearly froze before I made it back to my shack. I was just wearing a nightsock an' sleepin' gown, you understand. My feet were bare!"

The old man set the creamer down and sipped his coffee, wincing at the pain the maneuver caused in his left arm. "Yeah, that musta been it. Lucky I didn't find my way outside or I'd be froze up like a stone about now." He glanced up at Haskell and gave a devious little grin. "Where'd you sleep?"

Something told Haskell the old man knew exactly where Bear had slept last night. The question was: had he risen from bed and heard the commotion behind Emily's door, or did he just suspect what would naturally occur between a healthy, relatively young man and young woman on a cold and stormy night, believing themselves alone in a big, drafty ranch house excepting for one old, drunk geezer sound asleep in his own bed?

"No talk such things." Kwan had found a bottle somewhere and shuffled over to splash a hearty measure into Larson's coffee. "Verr bad. Disspect the dead!"

"Ah," Knute grinned at Haskell, understanding. He glanced up at the Chinaman. "Thanks for the thunder juice, Kwan. We old-timers gotta stick together."

"Verr bad," was Kwan's only reply as he set the bottle on the table and glanced once more in anger at Haskell before shuffling back to his range.

The sleigh runners slashed smoothly through the fresh powder under a sky the color of purest cobalt without a cloud to be seen above the rolling prairie in any direction.

While several more inches had fallen, the wind had shunted most of it off the trail back to Sioux Camp, piling it up in ravines and gullies and against the north slopes of buttes. Wisely, the trail had been cut over high ground.

There were a few two- or three-foot drifts here and there, sculpted like spoon-smeared frosting on a wedding cake, but the sleigh slid cleanly through most of it. The only place the big Percheron had any trouble was down in the deep gulley in which Cottonwood Creek and the late Ole Kemp's cabin lay. The snow there was nearly up to the beefy draft horse's withers in places, and it had to lunge and fight and snort its way through, jerking the sleigh violently along behind, the sleigh bells lifting a cacophony in the post-storm silence.

Both Haskell and Knute Larson blew sighs of relief when they finally gained the crest and were on the last leg of their journey back to town.

Haskell had borrowed the sleigh from Emily, who'd assured him she wouldn't need it until he could get it driven back to her by either himself or someone he hired in town. He hadn't left the Circle C until she'd paid off all three of her hired men, wanting to make sure none of them gave her any trouble in their badly hungover and owly states of mind.

Melvin Mueller had made no appearance whatever that morning until Haskell spied him in another Carr sleigh he and the hired men had all piled into and which was hitched to another Percheron. Mueller had sat hunched against the cold in the back seat, beside one of the former hired men, his luggage mounded at his feet and in his lap. As the sleigh cut past the front of the house toward the trail that led to the train station in Oxbow, the dandy glanced once at the lodge, where he'd apparently suspected Haskell and Emily were watching from a window, and lifted a gloved hand in a lewd gesture.

The cowboy beside him threw his head back in laughter.

"Good riddance to you, too, Melvin," Emily had said, glancing wryly at Haskell, then taking a sip from her coffee cup.

Haskell had figured she'd be just fine.

Now, entering Sioux Camp, he pulled up in front of Miss Chance's stately Victorian, whose front porch was at that moment being shoveled off by Jimmy Two Eagles clad in a thick fur coat, stocking cap, and mittens. Haskell stopped the Percheron and turned to old Knute. "You sure this is where you want to go? Maybe you oughta hole up and heal for a couple of days in the quiet comfort of your own cabin."

"You ain't seen my cabin," Larson said, grunting with the effort of heaving himself out of his seat with both hands suspended in slings across his chest, under his heavy coat. When he'd stepped to the ground, he turned carefully back to Haskell, and winked. "Besides, Miss Chance has all the right medicine an' injured old feller like myself needs." He winked lewdly. "She gives me a break on the price, too, on account I supply most of her firewood."

He frowned curiously at Haskell. "Say, where you goin'?"

"I best head over to the jailhouse and see if the liveryman kept the fire going during the storm. Otherwise, my prisoner is likely to be frozen up like a big old dog turd."

"That'd be too good fer him."

"Reckon it's kind of a cold trail, now, ain't it?"

"What is?"

"The killers'. If Ole Kemp didn't kill them fellas, with as big a grudge as he had against 'em, who do you suppose did?" Knute stared at Haskell directly, his own expression oblique. Bear had the strange feeling he was being tested — quizzed about his suspicions by a man who might have a dog in the fight.

"That's the big question, ain't it, old man?"

"Goddamnit," Larson said, hardening his jaws. "What have I told you about remindin' me about my age?"

"Sorry."

Knute grinned and winked before swinging around and shambling off toward the parlor house. "Time to go feel young again . . ."

"Good luck!"

"No need!" Knute chuckled.

Haskell watched the old man climb the freshly shoveled porch steps, suspicions caroming through his brain. Knute looked terribly old and frail. Still, he provided firewood for the folks here in Sioux Camp, so he couldn't be all that frail. But could he be hail enough — not to mention cunning enough — to have killed all those men, including the county sheriff and a deputy U.S. marshal, and to have traipsed out to the Carr place to pour poison into the man's brandy decanter without being seen on the property?

Even if he were capable of all of that, why

would he do it?

What would he have been doing on the Carr's first floor late last night? Sleepwalking? Or maybe trying to cover previous tracks he'd only remembered after returning to the Circle C with Haskell?

Now Larson exchanged a few words with Jimmy Two Eagles, then glanced once more at Haskell, narrowing one skeptical, vaguely befuddled eye before pushing through the parlor house's front door and disappearing inside. Haskell looked at Two Eagles, who stood staring back at him, holding his shovel in both hands across his chest. He, too, looked a little dubious as he exchanged long gazes with the lawman in the Carr sleigh.

Finally, Haskell smiled and nodded at the big Indian, who did not return the gesture but merely continued to stare at him stonily. Haskell shook the reins against the Percheron's back, and the runners began whispering once more through the snow behind the horse's muffled hooves, which tossed clumps of the fresh powder back against the sleigh's front panel.

The sun glared overhead, but it had about as much warmth as hell frozen over. Very few folks were out, and most of those were shopkeepers bundled against the cold, heads wrapped in frosty mufflers, shoveling or sweeping snow from the boardwalks or stoops fronting their businesses.

Gray smoke billowed from chimneys on both sides of the street, drifting nearly straight up in the still, frigid air. Haskell drew the Percheron up to the town marshal's office, whose small front porch was fairly buried in white. There appeared to be faint tracks climbing the steps and moving through the snow mounded before the door — tracks that had been made before the storm had drifted south toward Nebraska. They appeared now as shadowy dimples.

What caught the brunt of Haskell's interest was that no smoke issued from the stone building's chimney pipe. If he found Bradley Thorson frozen to death in his cell, the livery hostler, Louie, was going to get an earful — but only because it would make him, Bear himself, look negligent in the report he'd have to write, explaining the situation to Henry Dade. Thorson would be no real loss to this world.

Haskell wrapped the ribbons over the ring protruding from the whipsocket and climbed out of the sleigh. He waded through the deep snow mantling the steps and stopped on the porch, frowning at the door. It was open about an inch. The hostler was supposed to have made sure the door was

padlocked. The lock was not in its hasp —
in fact, it was nowhere in sight. There was a
bullet hole in the door, beneath the hasp.
Someone had shot off the lock, which was
probably buried in the snow around
Haskell's boots.

The lawman shoved the door open,
stepped inside, and stopped dead in his
tracks.

He stared up in shock. "Christ!"

Bradley Thorson was dead, all right. Not
frozen to death, though. Just like Cable
Gunderson, he'd been hanged.

CHAPTER 18

Haskell glanced beyond Thorson's body hanging from the same beam from which he'd found Gunderson hanging. The kid's cell door was half-open. The key, usually stowed in Gunderson's desk, was in the lock.

Haskell looked up at his prisoner again. Thorson's face was the pale cerulean of the winter sky at dusk. His eyes were wide open and staring down at the floor, the whites stitched with the crimson of burst veins. His mouth was wide open, as though he were expressing the horror and shock of his grisly demise even now in a cold and lonely death. His boots were off. Again, Haskell looked into the cell. The kid's boots stood together near the end of the cot, where he'd no doubt left them when he'd gotten ready for bed. His two blankets were on the floor, as was his pillow. He'd likely scuffled with whomever had come for him.

There were bruises on the kid's cheeks, and both lips were cracked and slightly swollen. His dark-blue wool shirt was torn, several buttons missing.

He'd put up a fight, all right. But to no avail. He'd likely been up against more than one man, or maybe against one man who'd outfought him. Maybe a bigger man, or meaner, more determined.

The killer? If so, what had been his beef with Thorson?

Haskell walked over to the stove and opened the door. He removed his right mitten and shoved his hand into the pale ashes mounded over the grate. They were nearly as cold as the air. The stove had been out for several hours, maybe most of the night.

Haskell cursed again. Stuffing his hand back into his mitten, he strode back past Thorson's hanging body and out the door and through the snow to the sleigh. He climbed aboard, turning the Percheron back the way he'd come. After a block, he swung right, heading north, then pulled up to the Sioux Camp Federated Livery & Feed Barn.

He climbed down off the sleigh and trudged through the snow to the big double doors, which were closed. He managed to get one open after much pulling and heaving on the metal handle, the door plowing up a good foot of snow before Haskell could shove himself through the narrow opening.

"Louie?" he called into the aromatic darkness. He saw Knute Larson's sleigh parked against the wall, amidst several wagons for rent, which confirmed the old man's mule had found its way back to town and was probably in one of the stalls opening off both sides of the barn's broad main alley.

Haskell called for the hostler once more, then headed toward the man's office and sleeping room in a lean-to addition off the barn's east side. He pounded on the plank board door with the back of his mittened hand.

"Louie? Louie, you in there, goddamnit?"

"Go away!" came a man's disgruntled voice, sounding sleep-rumpled. "It's too damn cold for business! Go away!"

"It's Haskell!"

"I don't know no Haskell — now, go away!"

Bear rammed his shoulder against the door. The locking nail and hasp pinged to the floor. Haskell's broad bulk filled the doorway as he stared toward where the stout, old, salt-and-pepper bearded hostler, Louie, lay under several quilts on the cot against the far wall.

Louie wore a black stocking cap and

gloves, and young kittens swarmed all over the old man's broad bulk humped beneath the quilts, meowing. A potbelly stove filled the room with heat as well as with old man odors and the stench of cat piss. Louie lifted his head from his pillow in exasperation.

"I done told you, goddamnit — !" He stopped, blinking up at Haskell, scowling. Oh . . . it's you . . ."

"Yeah, it's me. I just got back to town to find my prisoner dead."

Louie scowled at the floor. "You broke the lock on my door!"

"Did you hear me, you old fool?" Haskell said. "Someone hanged my prisoner!"

"I know — I seen when I went over to stoke the stove. I figured you and old Larson must be kilt. I seen Thorson hangin' there, so I figured there wasn't no point in wastin' wood on him. I came back here and went to bed, and if you wouldn't mind, I like to sleep when it's cold!"

"When did you go over to stoke the stove?"

"Around eleven last night. Fought the titty-high drifts for that no-good kid only to find him hangin' there like a side of frozen beef."

"You got any idea who hanged him?"

"Hell, no. Half the county wanted him

dead, though. I ain't gonna shed no tears. Forget him. I'll send the undertaker over when it warms up." Louie started to roll onto his side, giving Bear his back.

"When was the last time you saw him alive?"

Louie sighed and glanced over his shoulder at the lawman. Two of the kittens were now playing down around the hostler's feet while a third was sitting on the floor beneath the cot, staring skeptically at Haskell and curling its tail. The mother cat and two other kittens were lounging on a thick horse blanket near the stove, the mother just then giving one of the kittens a thorough tongue bath.

"Around five yesterday afternoon was the last I seen that joker still takin' up space," the liveryman said. "I gave the potbelly a good stokin' and endured the little bastard's insults until I was about to let the fire go out and let him freeze. Good riddance to the little snipe, is what I say . . . and good riddance to you!"

Anger rushed through Haskell. Wrinkling his nostrils in frustration, he said, "There's a killer on the loose in this town, Louie. The population is getting culled. Sooner or later, he might just get to you, old son."

Louie rolled back around to face Haskell,

the kittens jostling around at his feet, swatting playfully at the moving covers. "Then I will thank you very much for breaking the lock on my door!"

"A lock won't stop the determined son of a bitch."

Haskell swung around to face the livery barn filled with shadows striped with brassy yellow light angling in through the half-dozen windows. His mind was swirling. He felt as though he were being toyed with. First the banker was poisoned practically under Haskell's nose. Then the killer had ridden out to the Circle C to poison James Carr. While Haskell had been checking that out, his prisoner had been hanged in the jailhouse.

"And apparently, nothing will stop *you* from harassing *me*!" Louie shucked out of his covers and swung his feet to the floor. He wore heavy-weight longhandles and a grimy sweater as well as two pairs of thick wool socks, though his big right toe poked out of holes in both socks. He leaned forward, resting his elbows on his knees, and scrubbed sleep from his eyes with the heels of his hands. One of the kittens climbed up on his shoulder and arched its back.

"You don't really think he'll come after

me, do you?" the liveryman asked behind Haskell.

The lawman glanced back at him. "Why wouldn't he?"

"Why would he? I haven't done nothin' to him. I haven't done nothin' to make nobody mad enough to kill me. Not in years, at least!" Louie glanced around. "And I got all these cats to take care of!"

The old man's words reminded Haskell that before the banker had been killed, Bear had intended to speak with the widow of the murdered grocer, Max Weber, to see if he could find out why anyone would have wanted her husband dead. Since he'd uncovered no other leads in the past twenty-four hours, and he was, in fact, nearing his wits end over this whole deal, he might as well continue on with his original plan.

"You got a Circle C horse and sleigh awaiting your tending outside," Haskell said. "Find someone to take both back to the Carr ranch tomorrow. You can put it on my tab."

"You're just full of orders, aren't you?" Louie groused.

Haskell started toward the big main doors. But something the liveryman had said was snagging in his mind like a fishhook catching on the weedy bottom of a lake. He turned around and filled the open doorway with his bulk again. Louie was yawning and hacking up phlegm.

"Not in years, at least," Haskell said.

Louie looked up at him, red-eyed from drink. Two empty whiskey bottles lay on the floor near the cot, and one of the kittens was now batting one around. "Huh?"

"You said you hadn't done anything to give anyone cause to kill you in years."

"And that's true!"

"What about years ago?"

Louie scowled incredulously at him. "It was just a figure of speech. I didn't mean nothin' " — a look of great discomfort suddenly swept across his meaty, bearded face as he finished his sentence half-heartedly with — "by it."

Haskell studied him closely. "You sure?"

Louie stared at the floor for a time, where the kitten was batting the empty whiskey bottle. Louis stared at neither cat nor bottle. He was just staring, his brows furled with troubled thought. Suddenly composing himself, he looked up angrily and flared his nostrils as he said, "Yes, I'm sure! I didn't have nothin' to do with that. I didn't take part, I'm sayin'. Now, leave me alone, dammit. I ain't a morning person!"

"It's almost two in the afternoon."

"Close enough!"

"What didn't you take part in, Louie?"

Louie hung his head, staring at the floor. "Nothin'." He shook his head, hacking phlegm into a sandbox. He glared up at Haskell, red-faced. "Leave me alone!"

"Christ," Haskell snarled in frustration.

He gave the man another suspicious once-over and then swung around and headed out through the barn's big doors. He gave the Percheron a pat on its left wither and then, bracing himself against the cold, headed over to Weber's Grocery Store, which he'd passed several times in his comings and goings on the town's main street.

He went inside, stomping his boots and ringing the cowbell over the front door, and came out twenty minutes later, no better informed than he'd been when he'd gone in. Both Weber's widow and son were working in the store, both in states of great despair. Their eyes had been dry while Haskell had probed them with questions about Max Weber's past, but their answers were mostly composed of shrugs and head-shakes.

Neither the man's middle-aged widow nor his tall, apron-clad son could imagine anyone harboring a grudge so great against their husband and father that they'd be

538

driven to kill him — aside from the crazy wolfer, Ole Kemp, though they'd had a hard time believing even Kemp would actually follow through with his now-infamous threat against all the businessmen in Sioux Camp. Kemp had threatened many people in the past, but as far as they knew, he'd never fulfilled his promise. Kemp was a drunk and a blowhard, but that was all.

The widow and son's grief was still so palpable, Haskell decided not to press them on the matter.

He walked out of the grocery store, looking around the harshly sunlit street, pensive, feeling as though he were drowning in the lack of leads. Louie had started to tell him something. What had the liveryman been wanting to confess? What was he feeling guilty about?

Haskell began strolling along the boardwalk toward the east with the vague notion that he'd head back to the jailhouse, cut Bradley Thorson down if the undertaker hadn't already done so, and get a fire going in the stove. He'd make his headquarters the jailhouse until he had the trouble here figured out, and the killer or killers run to ground.

He was beginning to think it might be spring before he accomplished his task. The thought made him shiver. He drew his collar up higher against his neck and tightened the knot of the scarf he'd wrapped over his head, beneath his hat.

As he walked past the barbershop, a thick figure stepped out of a break between the barbershop and the next building beyond it, and turned to face Haskell. The man was clad in frosted furs, a thick, frosted scarf concealing the lower portion of his face, and a fur hat pulled low on his forehead. Long, black hair hung down over the collar of the big Indian's coat.

In his gloved hands was a sawed-off, double-barreled shotgun.

Both barrels swung toward Haskell, glinting in the harsh afternoon sunshine.

Haskell threw himself to his right as one of the barn blaster's barrels blossomed smoke and flames, and the crushing report assaulted the lawman's ears. The buckshot screeched past Bear's left shoulder as he plunged through the window of O'Casey's Ladies' Wear, the clatter of breaking glass redefining the din around him as the sawed-off's thunder dwindled.

Haskell hit the floor, glass raining around him. He rolled up off his left hip and shoulder, gaining his heels, heart thudding, knowing Jimmy Two Eagles had another barrel he was no doubt just as determined to unload as he'd been the first, and that Haskell's Schofield was at the moment out of a fast reach beneath his coat.

A girl's screams ripped through the shop lined with shelves of bolted cloth and bristling with woman-shaped fitting dummies displaying dresses and gowns and picture hats of all variations. Haskell saw the girl standing behind the counter only six feet away from him. Clamping her hands over her mouth and nose and staring toward Haskell and the broken window, she stood beside an older woman with silver-gray hair pulled tightly back over her head, eyes flashing with exasperation behind her tiny, round spectacles.

Hearing boots thudding on the boardwalk beyond the broken window, Haskell ran toward the back of the small store, knocking several fitting dummies out of his way, and yelled, "Get down, ladies!"

The "ladies" hadn't faded from his lips before he'd vaulted himself into the air to fly over the counter, arms straight out before him, legs spread. The shotgun roared once more behind him, the double-aught buck tearing into the front of the counter as Haskell slammed into the wall behind it. Unable to cushion the blow with his outstretched arms, his head and left shoulder slammed against it, and his six-and-a-half-foot frame fell in a heap to the floor, his ears ringing and blood-red flowers blossoming behind his eyes.

He lay there for a moment, flat against the floor, left cheek pressed hard against it, breathing hard, brains scrambled. He heard the metallic click of a shotgun being broken open.

The bastard was reloading . . .

The girl and the old woman were hunkered five feet away from Haskell, the old woman looking shocked and enraged, the girl sobbing into her hands. The flowers faded behind Haskell's eyes, turning to gray webs. He lifted his cheek from the floor, and shook his head. Boots thumped on the boardwalk. Glass shattered.

The Indian was stepping through the broken window . . .

The thought braced the lawman, who heaved himself to his knees, ripped off his right mitten with his teeth, tossed it onto the floor, lifted the flap of his coat above his holster, and shucked the Schofield. Beyond the counter, glass crunched beneath Two Eagles's boots. To Haskell's left now, the sobbing girl lifted her head to peer over the top of the counter. She gasped and turned her horror-stricken gaze toward Haskell.

Bear leaned toward the counter, edging a glance up over the top of it.

He pulled his head down as the shotgun's roar filled the store, sounding like the explosion of a dynamite keg in the close confines. Wood slivers were torn from the counter's far top edge to slam against the wall behind it.

Again, the girl screamed.

The old lady howled.

Haskell shifted two feet to his right, swung his Schofield over the counter, cocked it, and drew a hasty bead on Two Eagles's chest. "Hold it, Jimmy!"

Two Eagles wasn't having any of that. As he shifted the shotgun to bear down on Haskell's newly adjusted position behind the counter, the Schofield bucked and roared in Bear's hand.

The .44-caliber bullet ripped through the big Indian's broad chest. Two Eagles groaned and stumbled backward, lowering the shotgun's double barrels, then raising them once more, black eyes bright with rage.

Haskell punched two more rounds into the man's thick torso, the second blast coming fast on the heels of the first. Two Eagles stumbled farther backward, toward the front of the store, triggering his second barrel into the ceiling before falling out the broken front window.

His upper body disappeared but his lower legs stayed in the store, hooked over the window's bottom sill. The booted feet moved a little. Outside, the Indian groaned. Inside, the boots fell still.

CHAPTER 19

Haskell let himself into Miss Chance's sporting house and relieved himself of his coat, hat, scarf, and boots, but kept the Schofield in its holster. He slipped the Blue Jacket into his right back trouser pocket. He saw no reason to leave the prized popper in his boot. Besides, it was handy for inside work.

Not that he was expecting any here today . . .

There was no one to begrudge him the weapons. Not anymore. At least, no one to make him give them up.

No one with a shotgun, anyway.

He was here to find out if Jimmy was the killer of the Sioux Camp businessmen and postmaster, as well as James Carr and a pair of badge-toters. If not, why had he tried to blow a hole through Haskell large enough to drive a Baldwin locomotive through?

The lawman glanced into the gambling

room. Empty.

He peered into the saloon. Two men stood at the bar. They were both in their stocking feet, an image which Haskell didn't think he'd ever get used to — men standing at the bar in their socks. No guns, no boots. He had to smile a little at Miss Chance's authority here amongst the men of Sioux Camp.

The bartender was a little, middle-aged gent with thin, sandy hair and dark, snake-flat befuddled eyes. He was definitely middle-aged, but he didn't look like he could grow a beard. His cheeks were as bald as a frog and nearly as warty.

Standing between the two customers but nearly a head shorter than both, he locked his gaze on Haskell and said, "I thought maybe you was Jimmy." To the other two he said, "I was due to get off an hour ago, but Miss Chance wants me to stay till Jimmy gets back from his errand."

"What was Jimmy's errand?" Haskell said.

The little man just looked at him, narrowing his eyes slightly. The other two looked over their shoulders at the big man in the doorway.

Haskell glanced around the room again, and tried another question: "Miss Chance . . . ?"

"Upstairs." The little man poked a finger at the ceiling. "Occupied."

"Which room is hers?"

"I told ya," the little man said, pinching up his small-boned little face with its mean eyes and undershot chin, "she's occupied!"

One of the men standing at the bar said something to the little man. He said it too quietly for Haskell to hear. Haskell assumed he'd told the bartender who he, Haskell, was; information such as a federal lawman in a town the size of Sioux Camp made the rounds fast.

The little man turned his mean eyes to Haskell, poked his index finger at the ceiling again, and said, "All the way to the end of the hall."

"Obliged."

Haskell turned from the saloon and headed up the steps, his cold-socked feet thumping softly on the carpet, which felt deliciously warm after the cold he'd endured outdoors. Felt good to everything but his toes, that was, because he couldn't feel any of those and likely wouldn't for another hour or so.

Cold damned place. Thanks again, Chief!

He strode down the hall and tapped on the door with the backs of his fingers, which were nearly as cold as his toes. At least, he could feel them. Feel them enough to know that they ached like hell.

"Jimmy?" came Chance's voice from the other side of the door.

"It's Haskell."

"Who's Hask . . . ? Oh." A pause. Haskell grimaced. He must have made quite an impression. "I'm bathing, Marshal. Can't it wait?"

"It's important, Miss Chance, but I'll head downstairs —"

"No, no. If it's so important, come in."

Haskell stared a little curiously at the door, then shrugged, turned the knob, and stepped inside. Warm, humid air pushed against him — a womb opening to accept him. Threading the air was the aroma of warm almonds, though he knew from experience it was not almonds he was smelling, but opium.

The sound of lightly splashing water rose from behind an ornately scrolled room partition standing across the room's far corner, to Haskell's right and near a fire dancing and crackling in a small brick hearth.

The room was comfortably appointed with a large, four-poster bed under a red canopy. The bedspread was printed with a gold-and-red pattern matching the gilt-edged red diamonds printed on the wall-paper.

The room, as large as a sitting room or library, appeared part boudoir and part parlor, sporting a deep brocade sofa and two armchairs positioned in front of the fire, near the room divider behind which emanated the aromas of opium and the soft, leisurely sounds of water splashing.

The colors melded together to give an air of good taste and refinement. Even the oil paintings on the walls, mostly of nature scenes and lush trees and flowers in full bloom, seemed to have been chosen to enhance the room's subtle elegance and to blend with everything else.

Only one piece stood out: A mahogany sculpture of a naked black man, fully aroused, stood at the foot of the bed, resting atop a scrolled pedestal of the same dark wood. It was more than a little startling in its raw eroticism and sexuality. The figure seemed to be taunting the room with its oversized pecker carefully carved with a pale, bulging head.

Haskell half-wondered if the piece was a joke, or was it to be taken as serious art? In the circles he ran in, it would be taken in jest. But, then, Miss Chance didn't run with a bachelor lawman's crowd.

The only light in the room came from the sunlight pushing through deep gold lace curtains and the fire, which touched the air with a fragrant, blue haze. No lanterns were lit. Across the top of the room divider were colored glass squares behind which played the jostling, alluring shadows of the young woman's movements in the bath.

"Pour yourself a drink, Marshal. The cabinet is to your right."

Haskell glanced at the cabinet abutting the wall, beneath a diamond-shaped looking glass. He wanted to get on with what he was here for, but he supposed he could use a drink.

"Pour me one, too, will you? The brandy is in the square decanter, bourbon in the round one."

Haskell turned over a couple of goblets and reached for the brandy decanter. He hesitated, remembering that both the banker and James Carr's brandy had been poisoned. He looked at the room divider from which the sounds of splashing water continued and beyond the glass squares of which he could see the shadow of a long, slender leg bent at the knee.

He shook his head, waving off his sudden apprehension. Who would want to poison Chance? Besides, no one woman had (as yet, anyway) been the killer's target. He poured a couple fingers of brandy into one goblet and the same amount of bourbon into a second goblet.

"I'll be right out," Chance called to him. "Have a seat by the fire."

Haskell walked over to the short sofas angled in front of the hearth, set one of the goblets on the table between the sofa and the chairs, and sank into the deep cushions. He took a sip of the whiskey and then sat back, turning his face to the fire, basking in its warmth.

Despite the muffler he'd worn, his cheeks and nose were still numb, but the fire was working its magic on him — or was it the musky aroma issuing from behind the divider? If he wasn't careful, he thought, he was going to get sleepy.

More water splashed in the tub, and Chance's head appeared above the room divider. She'd pinned her hair into a hastily fashioned bun, leaving many wisps and locks to dangle down around her cheeks and fine, copper-colored neck. Her large, warm brown eyes met his, glinting warmly. She offered a wry half-smile as she reached for a robe. Imagining what the divider was hiding, the splendor of her brown body, he felt the dull ache of lust in his loins.

She stepped out from behind the divider, tying the belt of a thick, velvet robe around her. The top was open far enough to reveal more than a little of the deep valley between her breasts. The robe dropped to just above her knees. Her legs and feet were bare. Haskell felt a thickness in his throat as she sat down beside him, on the opposite end of the sofa. He took another, larger sip of the bourbon to calm the blood quickening in his veins.

"Do you like the firewater?" she asked, leaning forward to pick up her own goblet from the table. As she did, her robe opened, giving him a full view of both breasts sloping out from her chest, the nipples raking the inside of the robe.

The knot in Haskell's throat tightened. A tiny fist of desire squeezed his prostate.

He cleared his throat — or tried to. The words came out somewhat strangled, "Good stuff."

"It's from Tennessee, but I buy it in Bismarck." She sipped from her own glass, swallowed, and set the glass on the table.

When she sat back against the sofa, she glanced at him too quickly for him to avert his eyes from her chest. She followed his gaze to the front of her robe, stitched her brows together, then drew one arm across the full orbs straining against their confines.

"I'm sorry," Haskell said, leaning forward and resting his elbows on his knees, taking the goblet in one hand and squeezing it, careful not to shatter the glass. He was beginning to feel sweat pop out on his forehead and behind his ears. He wasn't sure if it was her or the fire. Maybe a combination of both.

Sitting to his right, she narrowed an eye at him. "You're not going to be trouble — are you, Marshal? I thought I could trust you, of all people — that's why I've opened my boudoir to you."

"You can trust me."

"Good. Now, what brings you here? You said it was important."

He turned his head toward her, frowning, genuinely puzzled. "Where are you from, Chance? I mean, I realize you're a native, but . . ." He shook his head. "I've never known an Indian woman like you."

"Why?" She arched both brows at him. "Because I'm so *civilized*?"

Haskell glanced around the room as though looking for a more appropriate response than the one floundering on his tongue. Unable to find one, he lifted a shoulder. "Yeah . . . I guess you could say that. Or . . . cultivated. *Refined.*"

He smiled wryly, happy to have come up with two more words.

Chance smiled as she leaned deeper into the cushions. She sat facing him from the sofa's far corner, one copper leg folded beneath her bottom, the other leg crossed over her other knee. The bare flesh of both knees and long, perfectly shaped calves was only two feet away. She smelled as fresh as a spring morning.

"I am Yanktonai Dakota, and I was born nearby," she said, retrieving her goblet from the table again and running her index finger around on the rim. "When my family was killed by soldiers one winter in the Black Hills, I was adopted by Lutheran missionaries. When the missionaries moved back to St. Louis, they took me with them, and I was educated there. I attended a finishing school as an adolescent. As a white girl.

"My adoptive parents were fond of the arts and of culture, as well as fine furnishings and manners, and passed that fondness on to me. Unfortunately, they were killed in an outbreak of measles in Arizona while I was attending a teachers' school in St. Louis. Finding myself without a rudder but with a small inheritance, I returned to Dakota. It is my home, after all. I used the inheritance to open a brothel in Bismarck. I guess you could say I never took much stock in my foster parents' religion."

She smiled, one cheek dimpling. "When the spur line came this way, I decided to move up here to Sioux Camp. It's remote, I know, but I was born along Cottonwood Creek, and I and my first family returned here every spring, after following the buffalo herds south for the winter."

She glanced around the room, then returned her gaze to Haskell. "I guess you could say my heart is here. As well as my soul." She smiled down at her glass and ran her finger around its rim again. She set the glass back down on the table, then reached into her robe pocket, from which she pulled a bamboo and jade opium pipe. "Would you like some midnight oil? I get it from a Chinese madam in Mandan. It's really quite wonderful, takes the bite out of the cold."

Haskell felt a little dizzy already, the room turning around him slightly. It must have been the woman and the fire.

He shook his head and then cleared his throat and spat out what he'd come here to tell her: "Jimmy Two Eagles is dead."

CHAPTER 20

Chance jerked her head toward Haskell, frowning.

"He tried to widen my belly button with that gut-shredder of his. Came up on me all of a sudden. I had no choice but to kill him."

Chance stared into his eyes, her mouth opening halfway, then stopping there. Her breasts rose and fell slowly, deeply. "Dear god. No." It almost seemed as though it hadn't been that much of a surprise to her. "I told him . . . I told him no . . ."

"What?" Haskell stared at her in shock. "You knew he might come after me?"

She nodded slightly, staring down at the pipe in her hands. "He's . . ." She stopped, tried again, her eyes meeting Haskell's. "There is an old federal warrant on Jimmy's head. He was raised here, too, in Dakota Territory. I met him in Bismarck. That's where I hired him to work in my brothel. I thought it would be good for him to join me in Sioux Camp. The fewer people . . . the less chance there was that he'd be recognized."

"What's the warrant for?"

"He killed a whiskey drummer. The man was selling poisoned alcohol on the reservation where Jimmy's family had been confined. The whiskey killed his father. Jimmy was a young man — this was nearly ten years ago. Federal marshals came for him, locked him in a jail wagon to take him to the territorial court in Yankton. Jimmy couldn't stand confinement. He broke out of the jail wagon, stabbed one of the marshals, and ran away. He's been deathly afraid of being caught again. As soon as he found out that you were a federal marshal . . ."

Haskell scowled at her, incredulous. "He decided he was going to kill me?"

She looked at him. Tears glazed her eyes. "I begged him not to. I assured him that you wouldn't arrest him. It was such an old warrant. I thought I'd put him at ease, but . . ." She stared off toward a curtained window. "Apparently not."

"Are you sure?"

Chance turned back to him. "Sure about what?"

"That that's the reason he came after me?"

Chance blinked, then tipped her head slightly askew. "Are you wondering if Jimmy was . . ."

"The killer. You bet I am."

Chance set the pipe on the table, then slid closer to Haskell. She placed her hand on his thigh, pressing her fingertips into the heavy corduroy of his trousers. "Let me assure you that Jimmy was not capable of cold-blooded murder. Besides, what motive could he possibly have had for murdering those businessmen, the postmaster, or Carr?"

Haskell frowned at her.

"Knute told me about Carr."

"Oh." Haskell nodded, then looked down at the snifter in his hands. "Right."

"What's the matter, Marshal?" Chance said, leaning closer to him, her voice soft in his ear. "Don't you believe me about Jimmy?"

Haskell shook his head. "It's . . . not that." He looked around. The room was slowly turning. His muscles felt a little stiff. Stiff and hot. Sweat bathed his forehead. He also felt anxious; he was having a hard time sitting still. "It's just . . . damn, it's warm in here. And . . . and I reckon I'm getting right frustrated about this whole mess."

Haskell set his whiskey onto the table and

rose, stumbling a little. He hadn't eaten in a while, and the bourbon had gone to his head. The bourbon and maybe the opium still threading the air. Not to mention the intense heat of the fire that wrapped around him like a hot blanket . . . and the woman.

He walked over to a window, slid the curtain aside with his left hand, and stared out into the side yard, staring back toward the heart of Sioux Camp, all the pitched roofs mantled in snow and billowing pillows of chimney smoke. The sun was nearly down — a pale, yellow-orange disk obscured by the blues of high, thin clouds. Shadows were long.

His mind was spinning with disjointed images, loud and garish with frustration.

He heard her bare feet treading lightly across the rug, felt her warm hand on his back. "Here," she said, raising his whiskey glass. "Finish this. You look like you could use it."

Haskell sighed, then took the goblet from her. "Thanks." He threw it back, swallowing.

He looked down at her. She stared up at him. Her robe was nearly open to her belly, exposing all but the areolas and nipples of her heavy breasts. She was doing nothing to hold it closed. His heavy loins fairly burned with desire.

Try as he might, he could not keep his right hand down by his side. As though of its own accord, it rose toward her, angled back behind her head, and closed gently around the back of her neck. He drew her head toward his, lowering his mouth toward hers.

He was surprised when she didn't pull away from him, as he'd expected her to. He thought she'd push him away and kick him out of her room. He'd *hoped* she would, because then he'd be done with her. He could go back to his hotel and take a long, badly needed nap. But she did nothing to resist him. In fact, she raised her hands to his face and brushed her fingers across his cheeks, bristling with several days' worth of beard stubble.

Her lips were full and warm, and they moved with his, her tongue flicking softly against his own.

He pulled his head away, staring into her eyes. She swept her hands up through his hair, raking her fingers through it, caressing his scalp.

"Such a handsome man," she whispered, her mouth only inches from his. "Such a big, handsome man. I must say, Marshal Haskell, you've taken me quite by surprise.

I thought I'd become inured to men. I believe you might be the rare exception."

A lightning bolt hammered through his crotch when she placed her hand against the swollen fly of his trousers.

"Might?" he asked. He had to have her now. There could be no denying him.

She kissed him, and continued running her fingers through his hair.

"Get undressed," she said, then swung around and walked over to the bed.

Haskell felt heavy and drunk with the bourbon, the warmth of the fire, the heat of his lust. He could no longer think of anything but her. Of bedding her. Mounting her. *Fucking* her. It was the only thing for which he had room in his mind. The killings . . . the hanging of Bradley Thorson . . . Jimmy Two Eagles — all those things were as absent from his mind as they'd been a month before Henry Dade had sent him up here.

He unbuttoned his shirt, missing one button. In his haste to rid himself of the garment, he ripped the button off, and it caromed against a wall. Then he started with his trousers, stumbling, the room pitching around him. He glimpsed Chance removing her robe, tossing it over a bedpost, pulling the covers back, and folding her long, copper body into the bed, heavy breasts jostling.

Keeping the covers down around her waist, she lay on her side, cupping her right breast, kneading it, watching him, her eyes like deep, black wells touched with the reflected light of the fire.

Naked, manhood jutting before him, Haskell stumbled over to the bed. She placed her hands on his thighs, stopping him. He stood before her, breathing hard, staring down at her. She smiled up at him, pumping his long, thick, rigid shaft, running her fist up and down its length, thumb curled over her index finger.

"A man," she whispered, lowering her gaze from his broad chest to his belly. "A fine, fine man . . ." She released him. She slid away from him on the bed, then, as he stooped to climb in beside her, she rolled onto her belly. "Take me."

Haskell rolled toward her. She lay belly down, face turned toward him, smiling dreamily.

"From behind?" he said.

She blinked slowly, nodding.

Haskell climbed on top of her, beneath the covers. She licked her hand, then reached behind her and up, clasping his jutting hard-on and massaging her spittle into

it, lubricating it. She licked her hand two
more times, rubbing the spittle into his
cock, getting it slick, working both it and
his ticker into a lather.

"Now, then," she whispered, slipping his
cock between her buttocks.

Haskell frowned in surprise. "There?"

She closed her eyes again, smiling. "Lady's
preference . . ."

Bear shrugged. In his heated state, he was
game for anything. He'd fucked women in
the bunghole before. Some preferred it —
mostly Southern belles, in his experience.
What the hell?

Chance moved her hand away as Haskell's
mast disappeared slowly into the firm,
heart-shaped mound of her rump, her asshole gripping, her saliva crackling. As
Haskell worked away on top of her, she slid
a pillow down beneath her hips, lifting her
butt for more efficient penetration.

"Yes," she whined, rising up on her forearms and turning her head from one side to
the other. "Oh . . . yesss . . ." Quickly, her
hair shook loose from its bun and spilled in
pretty curlicues across her shoulders and
down her back.

Haskell hadn't entered through the back
door in a long time. He wasn't sure if it was
the novelty of this new method or the girl

herself . . . or the heat or the whiskey . . . or something else entirely . . . but his heart was racing, and sweat was streaming down every inch of his body. His vision was blurry and he felt his muscles tightening up.

It was as though someone were shoving steel rods down his legs, through the bones of his arms. Even his jaws were cramping, like they'd been set in cement.

At the same time, he'd never been so aroused.

While anxiety over his peculiar condition was nearly overwhelming — it was like having detonating dynamite coursing through his veins — he couldn't stop hammering in and out of the intoxicating, supple, dark-skinned woman lying belly down before him, her beautiful ass jutting toward his pelvis, jerking against the pillow with his every assault.

When he came, it was with almost as much violence as the exploding of Jimmy Two Eagles's sawed-off shotgun.

Chance rammed her ass back taut against his belly and screamed into the mattress, grinding her fists into the sheets up near her ears.

When Haskell had finished spewing his seed, he collapsed to one side, rolling onto his back, grunting. His jaws were locked.

He looked down his body. It glistened with sweat. His legs and arms were stiff, fists clenched at his sides.

He quivered as though he'd been struck by lightning.

What the fuck . . . what the fuck is happening . . . ?

Haskell stared up at the canopy. Chance moved beside him. He could feel the bed jerking with his own slow, leisurely movements as well as with his own violent trembling. Her face slid into his field of vision, shrouded by the messy locks of her hair. She smiled down at him, smoothing his hair back behind his left ear.

"You've been poisoned, dear heart," she said.

Haskell blinked, stared at her, remembering the bourbon.

She blinked and nodded once. "Indeed. Strychnine."

Haskell's already racing heart leaped in his chest like a striking diamondback. He glared up at her, trying to speak but unable to form words. He was gritting his teeth, trying to pry his jaws apart. His calves were like clenched fists down in the lower thirds of his legs.

Panic overwhelmed him. Death . . . not like this . . . *Christ!*

Chance chuckled huskily. She disappeared for a time. Haskell could smell the cloying odor of burnt cinnamon. Then he managed to lower his head enough to stare down past his quivering feet to Chance standing at the foot of the bed, drawing on the opium pipe, her hair hanging down across her shoulders and curling around from behind her back, like black vines enshrouding her from behind.

Haskell's gaze dropped lower on the woman's body, and another wave of horror hammered him nearly senseless.

There was no neat, triangular muff of hair between the woman's legs. There was hair, all right. But nothing else you would have expected on a female body. Chance's black muff licked up around a man's dick nodding at half-mast.

Chance drew deep on the opium pipe, throwing her head back.

She followed Haskell's gaze to "her" manhood, and gave a sheepish smile. Blowing the opium smoke out her mouth and nostrils, she lowered her hands to her belly, running her fingers along the scars that had been burned into her flesh, above the swaying cock.

Haskell's stupefied gaze was already tracing the grisly, knotted white scars forming a thick letter "C" in a circle, just above her . . . his . . . its . . . belly button.

CHAPTER 21

"Circle C!" the banker, Dawson, had wheezed out on one of his last breaths.

That had been floating around in the back of Haskell's mind ever since. Now, as he stared in horror at the brand in Chance's belly, above the swaying dick, the question must have been in his eyes.

She set the opium pipe on the table by the bed, then sank onto the bed behind the jerking, quivering Haskell, whose heart was a racehorse in his chest. The sheets beneath him were soaked with cold sweat.

"Pretty, isn't it?" she said, leaning close to Haskell, smoothing his wet hair back from his forehead. "James Carr gave me that. Ten years ago now. Him, Max Weber, Sigurd Abel, Burt Hodges, Cable Gunderson, and George Dawson. There were several others who had a direct hand in it, but they were dead by the time I returned here to Sioux Camp, to exact my revenge."

She frowned into Haskell's horror-racked gaze. "Don't fight it," she said. "I gave you only a small amount. Did you know that only a small amount of strychnine won't actually kill — as long as you're given an antidote within an hour or so . . . ? It's true."

She reached into a drawer in the table beside the bed, and withdrew a flat, brown bottle without a label. "A couple sips of this will save you."

Haskell tried to reach for it, but his body was as stiff as a board. It was as though he'd turned to stone. Terror coursed through him — raw, living panic.

"It's a mixture of potassium bromide and chloral. Around thirty grams. I found the recipe in an old home-remedy book. If I'd given you just a wee bit more strychnine than what I'd laced the bourbon with, you'd probably be dead by now. The dose I gave you would take a good long time to kill you — at least a couple of hours. From the same book I learned that when given in small amounts, the poison acts as an aphrodisiac. Did you know that whores in Paris once used it all the time — and some still do, to arouse themselves as well as their jakes who had a hard time keeping erections?"

She chuckled as she continued smoothing Haskell's hair back from his forehead, resting the bottle on his heaving chest with her other hand. "I keep it in here for Jimmy. When he took it, he was much like you. Wild and insatiable — just like I like it!"

She/he gave a husky, delighted laugh, removing her hand from Haskell's head. She played with her dick with one hand, kneaded a breast with the other hand, squirming around beside the convulsing lawman.

Suddenly, she looked at him sharply.

"But you killed him!" She rose to her knees, slapping Haskell hard across the face.

He was in so much other agony, he hardly noticed anything except a vague sting.

"I sent him to kill you. I sensed you might be close to the truth, or would start getting close, the longer you stayed. I was afraid someone would put it together — what happened years ago to that poor Indian girl here in Sioux Camp when on a drunken Fourth of July she and her father, White Bear, came to town for supplies."

The banker had done just that, Haskell thought, far deep in his racing brain. When he'd spat out "the Circle C," he'd been prompting Haskell to look for the brand on Chance's belly. He hadn't had the energy or time to elaborate.

Chance paused, then licked her lips, remembering. "We lived on Cottonwood

Creek, in that shack Ole Kemp moved into later. My mother and little brother died early in my life, so it was just me and White Bear. My father farmed and hunted game for a living, but he was old even then, and his heart was weak. We came to town that day to buy food at the mercantile. There was a saloon connected to the mercantile at the time, with rooms upstairs. Whores' cribs. Mister Dawson refused White Bear's request for more credit, saying that he was calling his note due. Dawson and Carr and the others were all drunk in the saloon — the way they all got drunk back in those wild days when they were fifteen years younger.

"Dawson was a big, ugly, awful man. A bully. He decided to have some fun with my father. He made White Bear 'dance' in the street, shooting bullets into the ground around his boots. The whole town — there weren't very many here in those days — came out to laugh and applaud and egg Dawson on. Carr and the others joined him, and when they'd beaten my father senseless, and cut off one of his ears, leaving him to die in agony, they turned on me. I was fourteen. But my breasts were ripe. Men looked at me in that way . . . of course not knowing what I really was.

"I'd been trying to fight them away from my father, but two men had grabbed me and were holding me down, pawing me, tearing my blouse. Dawson said he'd let me pay off my father's bill upstairs in a whore's crib. Up there they discovered who . . . or, *what* . . . I was. That enflamed them even more. It burned like a wildfire through the crowd of drunken, lusty men. Each one took me. Savagely. And then Carr, other than Dawson the wildest and drunkest of them all, came up with a branding iron. He got it glowing hot in a cookstove and branded with me with it out of pure, wretched, drunken meanness, saying he was going to add this confused young bull to his herd!"

Haskell just stared up in horror at her — in horror for himself, in horror at the story she'd just told.

Teeth clattering, his back arching involuntarily, Haskell managed to ask a question, albeit haltingly. "Why . . . why Thorson?"

"Thorson?" Chance frowned, puzzled. "Oh, Thorson!" She smiled devilishly. "I sent Jimmy over to do that, because that young fool killed Gunderson, of course. How dare he! And for no good reason besides meanness! I was so close to getting them all. Every man who savaged me that night, who was among the crowd who killed my blood father, who died in the street that day, was in my sights. I didn't want any of them to slip away, besides those who'd died without receiving their comeuppance, before I came.

"I'd taken my time, allowed my surviving abusers to get used to me here in Sioux Camp, not suspecting that I was that poor girl . . . or boy . . . they'd so savagely abused that horrific day fifteen years ago, that boy-girl who'd been biding her time, hoping for the opportunity to get back here and do just that. When my foster parents died and left me an inheritance, I knew my time had come.

"Now, each one of those white savages is dead. Two I had to shoot because I couldn't figure out a way to poison them. But, believe me, they knew who shot them. I told them and showed them everything! I laughed in their faces as they died!"

She smiled again, her lovely face becoming a mask of dark malevolence.

"Jimmy killed the federal man from Bismarck. Jimmy knew my story. He was an outcast, much like me. He loved me, wanted to help me exact my revenge. Jimmy poisoned the banker and Carr after you arrived. I was afraid you'd stop me before I could fulfill my plans, so I quickened my pace. I chose to poison them . . . make them die miserably, just as you're dying now . . . slowly . . . since I couldn't let them know who was killing them and why. I'm satisfied with how they died. Now they'll burn in hell for their sins.

"As for you . . ."

She rose from the bed, walked over to a cabinet, and opened a drawer. Turning back around, she aimed a small-caliber pistol at Haskell, holding it straight out in her right hand.

"As for you, you're going to die. It's not what I wanted, but what choice do I have, dear Bear?" Chance walked slowly toward Haskell, narrowing one eye down the barrel of the pistol. "You got drunk and raped me savagely, you see? There was just something about me you — just like the other men — couldn't resist!"

Haskell's throat tightened as he stared at the dark, round maw of the pistol aimed at his head.

Someone pounded on the door.

"Don't do it, Miss Chance!"

Old Knute's voice.

Chance turned to the door with a gasp. Haskell flung his stiff right arm up and grabbed the Blue Jacket he'd slipped beneath the pillow. As the door opened,

Chance triggered her own pistol. Knute yelped and jerked back in the doorway as Chance's bullet tore into the doorframe.

She swung back around to Haskell, who managed to get his quivering finger through the Blue Jacket's trigger guard . . . managed to click the little popper's hammer back.

"Don't!" he croaked at Chance.

Her pistol popped. The bullet plunked into the bed six inches to the right of Haskell's head. He cursed through gritted teeth as the Blue Jacket leaped in his own right hand.

Chance screamed and flew backward. Haskell heard the thump as she hit the floor.

He lay back on the bed.

Knute stood over him, looking down at him, the old man's eyes round with fear. "What . . . what . . . what . . . ?"

Haskell jerked his head toward the flat bottle on the night table.

"This?" Knute said, pointing at the bottle.

Haskell nodded. "Yes!" he raked out.

Knute popped the cork, helping Haskell sit up on the bed. Then he helped him raise the bottle to his lips.

Haskell spent three torturous days in Chance's bed, recovering.

Several times the doctor came and went

after listening to the lawman's heart and swabbing the sweat from his body. Bear filled at least three slop buckets with bodily fluids, purging the poison from his guts and organs. He slept fitfully, haunted by nightmares. His waking moments were pure agony, his stomach flip-flopping, his muscles cramping, and his heart racing.

Over and over in tormented dreams he saw Chance dying as his bullet tore through her. Sometimes she became Melissa Sue Wiggins, dying in his arms, horror in her eyes. And then he would hear the toneless patter of the player piano in the ghost town of Atlantic City . . .

Finally, he woke and the room was not swirling around him. The animal that had been chewing his guts had gone to sleep. Old Knute, who'd looked in on him periodically, brought him soup and bread. Haskell managed to get a couple of bowls down until, after another day and night had come and gone, he woke feeling halfway human, and called for a hot bath.

After the bath, he dressed and went downstairs to find Old Knute sitting by a window in the saloon, near the ticking woodstove, the remains of a meal and a bottle on the table before him. The sleeves of the old man's wool shirt were rolled up his forearms, revealing the white longhandle sleeves beneath. Neither arm was in a sling anymore. Beneath the table, his feet were clad in thick wool socks.

It must have been midmorning, judging by the light outside the window. Everything seemed new and fresh to Haskell, after the long agony during which he'd surely been close to death more than a few times.

"Well, I'll be damned," Knute said. "Looks like we won't need that wooden overcoat, after all. I put an order in with the undertaker for an extra big one!" The old man cackled a laugh.

Haskell stood in the middle of the room, in his stocking feet, hair still wet from his bath, looking around. The building was silent. Outside, the wind blew snow into glittering swirls. A chunk of wood thudded in the potbelly stove.

Bear frowned at old Knute. "Where is everybody?"

"Home." Knute splashed whiskey into his shot glass. "It's Christmas, Bear. Cheers!" He threw back half the shot. Smacking his lips, he added, "The girls and Rollie, Chance's other bartender, done hopped the train to Bismarck. I don't know if they'll be back. Reckon it depends on what happens to this place. It'll no doubt go to the town.

And the town fathers — what few there are left" — he chuckled at that — "will have to decide what to do with it."

He held the bottle up to Haskell, who was trying to wrap his still-foggy mind around everything that had happened. He wasn't sure if it was the strychnine, but he still felt a deep sense of unreality.

Yet, he felt good. Better than he had in days. Physically, that was. The whole horror with Chance, however, had him feeling dark, indeed, reminding him of Melissa Sue . . .

He sagged into a chair across from Knute, who held up the bottle to him. "Thunder juice?"

Haskell waved it off as his stomach turned. "Too soon."

"Good," Knute snickered, replenishing his own glass. "More for me."

Haskell looked across the table at the older man. "When did you figure out it was her . . . or him . . . ?"

Knute turned the glass in his gnarled, brown fingers. "When we learned about Carr bein' killed the same way as the banker, Dawson. I started to put it together again . . . started to think about who Miss Chance might be. I remembered Dawson's last words."

Haskell studied the old man before him. "You were here then, weren't you? Back when . . . it happened?"

Larson brushed a fist across his nose and sniffed. He stared down at his glass, both arms on the table. "Sure was. Wish I wasn't. But I was." He looked sharply up at Haskell. "I had no part in it. None. I was in another saloon with several others from town."

"With Louie?"

Knute grimaced, nodding. "Louie was there." He threw back half the whiskey in his glass, sniffed again, then stared down at the glass on the table. "I seen what those men were doin' to that old man . . . to the girl. And I didn't do nothin' to stop it. None of us did."

He pursed his lips, then shook his head.

He looked up at Haskell again, his eyes sad, sheepish. "Carr an' Dawson an' the others — they was the high-climbers, the men who settled here first, established businesses for themselves. Carr came from a rich ranching family down in Texas, and he was the lord of the prairie back in them days. A dangerous man. Dangerous drinker. He licked that part of himself since — maybe it was what he an' the others did to the girl — White Antelope was her name — that sobered him. An' what they did to the old man. But they was the wealthy an' powerful in this county even then. I was a bangtail. A drifter just come into the country lookin' to sink a taproot. In my forties already. I couldn't go up against them. I should have. But I didn't."

He threw back the rest of the shot.

"The preacher in town took her in, healed her up, and saw that she got adopted to that good missionary couple in Bismarck. They took her back to St. Louis, schooled her up like a white girl. I heard tell about her later in a saloon in Bismarck. I was glad to see that, at least. Now . . ." Knute sat back in his chair. "Now it's come to this. An' that poor girl . . . or whatever the hell she was . . . is dead. Out there in the icehouse waitin' on the ground to thaw."

Haskell entwined his hands on the table. "I wish I hadn't had to kill her." He winced, shaking his head, remembering Melissa Sue, as well. "I got suspicious about her motivations when I saw she was willin' to entertain me in the ole mattress sack . . . and that I wasn't feeling too good. Only after I'd finished the whiskey did I begin to suspect her. So I slipped the Blue Jacket under the pillow."

Haskell shook his head again. "I sure am sorry I had to use it. I don't blame her for any of what she did."

"It was you or her, Bear."

Haskell gave a wry snort at that. Henry Dade had said the same thing less than a month ago.

Knute continued. "I got me a feelin' she purposely missed that shot she took at you. She knew the jig was up. She couldn't go to jail. Not her. She was ready to die."

Haskell sighed. "I think you might be right, old-timer. Still . . ." He remembered something. "Say, was that you I heard stumblin' around downstairs in the Carr house that night?"

Larson raked a hand over his face, yawning. "I reckon it was."

"What were you . . . ?"

"I couldn't sleep for thinkin' about Chance, remembering how that awful day went. I didn't want you to know it was me down there. I didn't want no questions. Not yet. I didn't want to think it was her . . . him . . . comin' back to do the killin'. I'd wanted to believe she'd found a good life for herself and forgot that whole wretched thing that happened on the street out there."

Knute gave another gloomy wag of his head, then pulled his pipe out of his shirt pocket and began to fill it from his tobacco sack. "What're your plans now, Bear?"

"To get the hell out of here soon as the trains make it this far north again."

"Well, hell, that ain't gonna be till after New Year's. No, sir, the spur line shuts down over the holidays. Too little business, I reckon."

"Shit. You mean I gotta sit here and look at your ugly old mug for over a week?"

Knute laughed as he tamped the tobacco down in his pipe bowl. "I reckon we'd better find us a fresh deck of playin' cards. I probably have one over to . . ."

He frowned out the window.

"What is it?"

Knute canted his head toward the frosty glass. "Lookee there."

Haskell looked out the window. Emily Carr was just then pulling her sleigh up in front of the parlor house. She wore a long buffalo coat and buffalo hat, buckskin mittens on her hands. A red scarf was wrapped around her neck. She ran her inquiring gaze across the building before her.

"I got me a suspicion that girl's lookin' for a big old Bear . . . and not the kind she saved us from, neither. Hah!" Knute slapped his hand atop the table. "I got me another suspicion."

"Oh, what's that?" Haskell said, absently, gazing out the window at the young woman climbing out of her sleigh and starting toward the parlor house, scarf whipping in the chill breeze.

"It's about how you're gonna be occupyin' yourself till the train gets here from Bismarck." Knute struck a match and touched it to the bowl of his pipe, laughing through his teeth.

Haskell turned to him, grinning. "You know what, old-timer? I think you're finally right about somethin'."

Bear headed for the door.

Choking on pipe smoke, Knute yelled behind him, "Don't sass your elders, ya big galoot!"

Suddenly, Bear stopped and turned back. "Say . . . what about you, Knute?"

"Oh, don't worry about me. Me? I got a widder lady over to the boardin' house. She's a former nurse, an' she knows just how to curl this ole boy's toes on a cold Christmas night. Even better'n Miss Chance's percentage gals."

The graybeard winked and puffed his pipe.

Haskell laughed and hurried outside and into the waiting arms of Miss Emily Carr.

ABOUT THE AUTHOR

Western novelist **Peter Brandvold** was born and raised in North Dakota. He has penned over one hundred fast-action westerns under his own name and his penname, **Frank Leslie.** He is the author of the ever-popular .45-Caliber books featuring Cano Massey as well as the Lou Prophet and Yakima Henry novels. The Ben Stillman books are a long-running series with previous volumes available as ebooks. Brandvold/Leslie's novels are also published in hardcover editions as well as large print editions, by Five Star Press/Thorndike. Head honcho at "Mean Pete Publishing," publisher of lightning-fast western ebooks, he has lived all over the American West but currently lives in western Minnesota. Visit his website at www.peterbrandvold.com. Follow his blog at: www.peterbrandvold.blogspot.com.

The employees of Thorndike Press hope you have enjoyed this Large Print book. All our Thorndike, Wheeler, and Kennebec Large Print titles are designed for easy reading, and all our books are made to last. Other Thorndike Press Large Print books are available at your library, through selected bookstores, or directly from us.

For information about titles, please call:
(800) 223-1244

or visit our Web site at:
http://gale.com/thorndike

To share your comments, please write:

Publisher
Thorndike Press
10 Water St., Suite 310
Waterville, ME 04901